What ha[illegible]

Footsteps. Not someone walking by outside. Someone walking around inside.

She was either being pressed into the bed or pulled down by it, cold, heavy, like sinking in deep water. Something between a tickle and a prickle teased the skin of her throat and chest. The footsteps didn't belong to living feet. It sounded as if a ghost were walking through the house, his or her paces slow and ragged, weary, injured, ill. Her nostrils filled with the same scent she'd thought she smelled last night, sweet, rich, faintly smoky.

She pried open her eyelids and peered around the room. The light of a streetlamp leaked through the bars of the blinds, casting a milky glow on bedposts, the chest of drawers, the chair. Through the open door to the living room she saw the front windows similarly glowing, but nothing moved against them.

★

Previously published Worldwide Mystery titles by
LILLIAN STEWART CARL

THE SECRET PORTRAIT
THE MURDER HOLE
THE BURNING GLASS

The CHARM STONE

LILLIAN STEWART CARL

WORLDWIDE®

TORONTO • NEW YORK • LONDON
AMSTERDAM • PARIS • SYDNEY • HAMBURG
STOCKHOLM • ATHENS • TOKYO • MILAN
MADRID • WARSAW • BUDAPEST • AUCKLAND

For the muses—Annette, Deni, Garda, Harriet,
Mary Jo, Terey and Sherry-Anne.

Here's to another ten years together!

THE CHARM STONE

A Worldwide Mystery/June 2013

First published by Five Star Publishing in conjunction with Tekno Books and Ed Gorman.

ISBN-13: 978-0-373-26853-5

Printed in U.S.A.

Acknowledgments

I would like to express my gratitude to the Colonial Williamsburg Foundation in general—my visits to the Historic Area have been entertaining, educational and inspiring—and in particular to the CWF employees who contributed patiently and wisely to this story: Glenn Williams, Don Moore, Kay Wilkinson, James Horn and Lou Powers.

ONE

JEAN FAIRBAIRN ANGLED her toothbrush away from the one already in the glass beside the sink, giving them each some personal space. Although, considering how many body fluids she and Alasdair had swapped over the past couple of months, moving their toothbrushes was no more than symbolic.

She wondered if she would ever get used to Alasdair complicating the life she'd gone to so much effort to simplify. She wondered if he'd ever get used to her complicating a life that had never been simple.

In the bedroom, Alasdair spoke in staccato bursts interspersed with moments of silence as he listened to whoever was on the other end of the telephone line. Or transatlantic satellite transmission, perhaps—the male voice that had asked for him spoke with his own Scottish accent. What was up back home? It was almost midnight there.

"That's not sensible at all," her significant other, her other half, was saying.

She'd pretended not to eavesdrop long enough. With one last glance in the mirror—so she looked a little frayed around the edges, it was just the jet lag—Jean strolled out of the bathroom as nonchalantly as she could wearing a long dress and high heels. Or heels higher than usual, the better to achieve this evening's level of posh.

It would take heels of nosebleed height to boost her to even average stature. But that wasn't the issue. Her forty-year-old feet, attached to her forty-year-old body, were the issue. Tripping over her own shoes would threaten more than her dignity. But the demands of fashion were far down the list of worries that had over the past couple of years evoked silver strands from her crown of auburn hair. At least, in a rare moment of style serendipity, those silver strands tonight coordinated with the metallic threads in her black-and-auburn jacket.

Not that anyone was going to pay attention to her, not with Alasdair wearing his kilt. "All right, then, Ian. I'll see to it," he said, and clicked the receiver into its cradle. His eyes, the blue of cold steel, turned toward Jean. His lips curved in a thin smile that didn't mitigate the cogitational crease between his brows, and his brushed-velvet voice was stroked against the nap. "Here's me, thinking we were due a bit of a busman's holiday, but no, that was my chap Ian from P and S. Soon as my mobile's out of range of headquarters, all hell breaks loose."

Jean restrained herself from grabbing the lapels of his Argyll jacket, dragging him off the edge of the bed, and demanding details. Of course it was a holiday. They'd already tried for a honeymoon, in August. "Satan broke out of the dungeon of Hermitage Castle? Protect and Survive does handle security for Hermitage Castle, doesn't it?"

"Oh aye, that we do, but the only devil's involved now is the one who stole the Dunmore Witch Box from Blair Castle. A copy of the Box, that is. Why go pinching a copy?"

"When the original's here in Williamsburg." This morning the bright lights of the display case had made the tendrils and leering faces carved on the small chest seem pale and wan, drained of the power they had once had in candlelit rooms. Or so Jean hoped. "No, that's not sensi… That doesn't make sense."

"The villains working art and antiquities thefts have no

more class than any other. Like as not this one could not be bothered with the facts."

"Like the fact that any potential buyers will know the Box is on display at the DeWitt Wallace Museum."

"Next the portrait of himself, Lord Dunmore, last British governor of Virginia, dressed for the grand opening of the exhibit." Alasdair's smile went lopsided as he glanced down at his own finery, the white kilt hose or tall socks with their red flashes, the red-and-green Cameron-tartan kilt, the simple leather sporran—not a fur one that looked like a scalp—and the staghorn buttons of the dark jacket. A silver pin in the shape of a basket-hilted sword was affixed to the apron of his kilt, complementing the glint of frost in his short-cropped dark blond hair.

Very tidy, Jean thought. And quite modest, considering the finery the male of the Scottish species could put on, given an excuse.

She almost repeated the mantra she'd uttered several times between Edinburgh and Virginia, "All we have to do is the opening reception, then we can play tourist." But that hadn't been true even then.

For one thing, she still had her part of the holiday bus to drive, an article for *Great Scot* about Lady Dunmore, her fabled family charm stone, her notorious Witch Box and all that implied, the implications including an interview she'd been anticipating with wicked glee ever since her partner at the history and travel magazine had set it up. That the Witch Box was turning out to be trouble was just grist for her creative mill.

She asked, "You vetted Blair Castle last month. How did the thief get the Box out?"

"Thieves, or so it appears. A woman created a diversion by opening a door into a private area and setting off the alarm. Someone else walked away with the Box at just that time, likely by tucking it up beneath his coat. Or her coat. It was protected by no more than a velvet rope, much good that'll do, but these old stately piles, they've go loads of artworks and bittie historical artifacts like the Witch Box."

"Which is all three."

"You can lock them up tight, you can hide them away in dungeons and the like—and we do, during the nights—but come the daylight, and you open the doors, then they're vulnerable."

Jean considered Alasdair's armor-plated face and repeated silently, *vulnerable.* "Was it a spur-of-the-moment theft, then? Or were the two people working together?"

"The woman's saying she opened the door by accident, that she knew nothing of the Witch Box itself. Perthshire Constabulary took her name and address, but could not charge her with more than ignoring a 'private' sign."

"Hardly a hanging offense, not like ownership of the Witch Box might have been," Jean said. "So what does P and S expect you to do about it here? Or was Ian just letting you know?"

"Ian's followed procedures right smartly, informing Scotland Yard, Interpol, the FBI here in the States. The first Williamsburg connection, now, is that the replica Box was made here. The second is that the woman blundering through the door is named Kelly Dingwall. She looks like being the sister of your Timothy Dingwall."

"He's not my Timothy Dingwall." Jean dropped onto the bed, so close to Alasdair she caught the scent of toothpaste on his breath. Only one solitary dust mote, a testament to the hard work of the housekeeper, wafted down from the flowered cloth of the canopy onto her glasses. "So the tendency to rush in where angels wouldn't risk their shoe leather must run in the Dingwall family."

Alasdair's left eyebrow quirked upward. "Your sort of folk, then."

"Not necessarily," she protested. "I only know him and his wife through their reputation, and believe me, we academics don't call them the Dingbats in the belfry for nothing. I can hardly wait to meet them for the interview tomorrow—you know, about the whole occult angle."

"I could do with getting shot of that particular angle. And the people round the bend with it."

"It's what I do, Alasdair."

His right eyebrow curled downward.

"We'll never get away from that angle. Or its true believers." Well, *he* could get away from it, more or less, by getting away from her. But if Jean hadn't made a profession out of questioning true believers, they'd never have met. She reminded him, "We're spooky, you and me. We see dead people."

Alasdair emitted a scorched snicker. "Lately dead and long dead as well, though I've noticed nothing here. Yet."

"Yet." Jean glanced into the living room, like the bedroom furnished in tasteful mock-colonial. The small house that was their temporary home, modestly named the Dinwiddie Kitchen, was an original structure, over two hundred years old—a mere blink of an eye in Scotland—and, compared to a Scottish stone cottage, its frame-and-clapboard construction was no more substantial than the little pig's house of twigs.

The faintest of sweet, smoky scents had tickled Jean's nose in the wee hours of the morning, when she'd awakened momentarily from the opium-dream sleep of the jet-lagged. With even her sixth sense comatose, she hadn't considered whether the scent came from this dimension or another, but had simply slipped back into oblivion, glad to have Alasdair tucked similarly comatose beside her.

Now he pulled himself to his feet and paced toward the

living room. Each heel hit the wide planks of the floor with the snap of a drumstick on a snare drum.

Small as it was, the house was still larger than her flat in Edinburgh. The city itself, with its medieval pends and wynds, had been starting to get a little claustrophobic, never mind her flat, where she and Alasdair and her cat, Dougie, jostled for personal space like colliding and overlapping set-theory circles.

Jean had thought back in June she read Alasdair altogether too well. Now, at the end of October, she couldn't exactly read him like a book, but she could scan his index as though on the spines of a set of encyclopedia: A to Ab, Ab to Ac, Ac to Ad, and on over the horizon and far away.

Yesterday they'd crossed that horizon, flying west from Scotland to Washington, D.C. There she had rented a car and headed south on the right-hand side of the road. Driving on the right was like riding a bicycle, she'd told herself. A body-memory you don't forget. Like making love.

Despite offering his own driver's license to the rental-car people, Alasdair had sensibly allowed her the first foray onto the highways. He'd only twice grabbed for the armrest and winced at the traffic whizzing by on what seemed to him to be the wrong side of the Beltway, not for her occasional "no, the other left" wobble—or so his story went. Her story was delivered in paragraphs as they wended their way down I-95 past trees aflame with crimson and gold, passing places with names to conjure with—Mount Vernon, Gunston Hall, Rappahannock, Fredericksburg, Richmond.

She had conjured, at least. Alasdair, well-read on history as he was, and well-traveled, too, knew but didn't feel the ghosts of the American past. Her past. She'd come back, for the first time in almost a year, not to Texas but to Virginia. The Union Jack flew over the Historic Area, but the Stars and Stripes occupied pride of place before the Williamsburg Inn just behind their little house.

The last time she'd visited Williamsburg, she'd been a history professor attending a conference. She'd been married. Now she owned part of a Scottish travel and history magazine. Now she was living in sin with Alasdair, a former detective with Scotland's CID who was working to establish a good rep as the chief of security at Protect and Survive. Whose allergy to the paranormal was as strong as hers.

Picking up her sequined bag, barely big enough for their invitation to the reception and their tickets, Jean followed Alasdair past the tiny pantry that held a coffee maker, a microwave oven, and assorted amenities. Modern amenities, unlike the antique cooking implements and bits of crockery lining the living-room mantel on either side of a clock.

He stood at a front window, hands clasped behind his back, shoulders set, as though he evaluated the view of the small octagonal building called the Magazine for clues. She evaluated her own view, the tartan pleats still swaying back and forth provocatively. Nope, nothing was worn beneath that kilt. Everything was in good working order.

Everything between his ears was in good working order, too, his intellectual mill grinding even specks of evidence exceedingly fine. She said, "Alasdair, we need to get over to the reception. Miranda's going to meet us there. We can either take the bus or we do a little roaming in the gloaming."

He nodded, and by the time he turned around his forehead was almost smooth again. "Grand idea, a wee dauner will clear the head. You'll be needing a wrap—that jacket's none too thick."

"I don't have anything to wear over it that won't look clunky. It's only a couple of blocks and I'll walk fast—see, sensible shoes."

"That's us away, then, lass, minding that this was meant to be a holiday." With a smile that was anything but thin, Alasdair took Jean's hand.

That's us, she repeated silently, and aloud said, "It will be a holiday." Never mind her little internal skeptic adding, *Yeah, right.*

Hand in hand, they strolled outside into a dusk like blush on bronze. Lights shone from the two big hotels, the Williamsburg Inn and the Williamsburg Lodge across the street, but twilight shrouded the Historic Area. The fire basket burning between the Magazine and the Courthouse glowed such a bright orange, the human shapes gathered around it seemed as insubstantial as the smoke rising ghostlike above it. Harsh smoke, Jean noted with a flare of her nostrils, not the sweetly scented smoke of her dream.

Somewhere close by, a helicopter beat up and down—there it was, just over the trees to the southeast, a black shape against the translucent sky. The beam of a searchlight extended downward from its belly like a transporter from an alien spacecraft. From the eighteenth-century street, it looked like an alien spacecraft.

Alasdair tilted his head in consideration. "Police. Chasing a villain or lighting up an accident, I reckon."

"I bow to your expertise," Jean returned, and pulled him gently away.

Just down Francis Street, the uneven brick sidewalk became a more uneven gravel path. It dipped into a ravine, into the shadow of overhanging trees and a pool of cold, damp air thick with the mud and root scent of an open grave. The slightest of chills touched the back of Jean's neck, like refrigerated cobwebs. "Do you feel that?"

"Oh aye," said Alasdair, his pace faltering and then steadying again. "It's gone now."

"No surprise there'd be a few lingering spirits in a place

like..." Something rustled in the overgrown garden beyond a picket fence and Jean jerked. "A squirrel. A bird. A cat, maybe, in pursuit of the above. I thought I glimpsed one outside the house this afternoon."

Alasdair's warm hand engulfed hers, steadfast as his tread. Up the opposite slope, and they saw the lights of the Public Hospital, its cupola outlined against a sky glowing Prussian blue and pricked by stars. A dozen or so people walked across the lawn and converged on the lamplit entrance. Jean glanced over her shoulder, ready to make the dash across the street and join them. A car was coming, catching her and Alasdair in headlights as bright as searchlights picking out escaped prisoners. The white SUV slowed and a piercing wolf whistle emanated from inside.

They were hardly so old that their holding hands could be considered cute. Jean's best we-are-not-amused glance at the car intercepted Alasdair's iciest version of the same. *Oh. Some local idiot is making fun of his kilt.*

The SUV pulled onto the shoulder and the passenger window slid down, revealing a familiar face, the upturned crescent of a smile beneath brown eyes gently crinkled with intelligent humor and a cap of smooth, brown hair. Rebecca Campbell-Reid said, "We were thinking that was you. There aren't many guys wandering about the town wearing a kilt, at least, not until the re-enactors set up camp in July. Good for you, teaching the natives the meaning of style."

Another familiar face leaned into the pale aura of the dashboard lights, a rectangular grin beneath blue eyes dancing with humorous intelligence and a head of shaggy, light brown hair touched with auburn. Michael Campbell-Reid added, "Most likely the Yanks will go muttering about men wearing skirts, all the while handing you bourbon, not real whiskey, and just when you'll want bracing up for the honor of the Auld Sod."

"Their loss, then." Alasdair's teeth flashed in a smile, even though he couldn't brace his back and shoulders any further. "No worries, I'll mind my manners."

"I'd be careful who you call a Yankee here below the Mason-Dixon Line," Jean told Michael.

Rebecca said, "My brother in Richmond was telling him that this morning, but he thinks he gets a pass, being an outlander."

"You're after driving yourself, are you?" Alasdair asked. "Good man."

"I learned to switch sides of the road whilst I was working in Ohio some years since." Michael nodded at his wife, another benefit of that job in Ohio.

Silver-white headlights flashed as a speeding car almost bottomed out in the ravine, then dodged the SUV idling at the side of the road. Jean's skirt and Alasdair's kilt fluttered in its chill draft and she suppressed a twitch of evil memory. Never mind that they were standing on the sidewalk, such as it was, they were still vulnerable to a careless driver. Or a malicious one.

With a screech of brakes and a flare of taillights, the car rounded the corner onto Nassau Street and then, a block further on, turned right into the parking lot behind the Hospital. "Good grief," said Rebecca. "The invitation to the reception didn't say anything about having to punch a time clock."

"It's just now gone seven." Alasdair raised his wrist and its watch into the light.

Jean asked Rebecca, "You're not coming to the reception after all?"

"We have to get back to my brother's place and rescue Linda. My mom probably hasn't put her down since we left this morning. You think she'd be used to grandchildren by now, but no. Maybe she's checking this one over to make sure she's not growing thistles or something."

"Linda's getting on famously with your folk," said Michael soothingly. "It's high time she made the acquaintance of the American side of the family."

Jean supposed the umbilical cord between the Campbell-Reids and their four-month-old daughter stretched only so far, and the fifty miles to Richmond was its limit. Not that she could offer any advice. She'd never had children, and her nieces and nephews had been presented to her as faits accomplis, enjoyable to entertain and just as enjoyable to give back.

Alasdair had no offspring, and, being an only child, no nieces or nephews. What he had was the wisdom not to comment on matters he knew nothing about. "They'll not have rearranged the exhibition since you approved the installation this morning."

"No, the artifacts from Scotland are the Museum's responsibility now," said Rebecca. "You said then you thought the security arrangements were good."

"Oh aye," Alasdair agreed, and glanced at his watch again.

Jean got the message. *Business now, chat later.* "We'll represent Scotland, then, the Museum, the National Portrait Museum, Protect and… Oh! Alasdair just heard that the copy of the Witch Box at Blair Castle was stolen today."

"Was it now?" asked Rebecca, and Michael asked simultaneously, "They've nicked the villain, have they?"

"No, more's the pity," Alasdair replied, and presented the situation in full outline form, signing off with the name of Kelly Dingwall.

"Another Dingwall, is it?" Michael asked. "You'll have heard about Sharon, then."

"No, what about Sharon?" Jean stepped a bit closer to

Alasdair and crossed her arms over her chest. He'd been right, her jacket wasn't heavy enough for the increasing cold of the evening. But curiosity came before comfort.

He put his arm around her. She wasn't sure which was warmer, the wool of his jacket or the solid flesh of the arm beneath. Two more cars passed at much more suitable speeds, one going on toward the intersection with Henry Street, another also turning on Nassau toward the Hospital. "What of Sharon?" he repeated.

"One of the Museum curators was telling us that Sharon, and, I assume, Timothy, are suing a professor at the college for slander." Rebecca waved in the general direction of the campus. "Or libel—that's the one in print, isn't it, while slander is verbal?"

"It's all defamation of character," said Alasdair.

"You Yanks being right quick off the mark with the lawsuit," Michael said, "though we Brits are catching you up."

"Whoa." Jean's agenda cartwheeled, top to bottom, and then sprawled sideways. "Will Tim and Sharon do the interview tomorrow—well, no, they won't turn down a chance to talk about their theories—but they're probably not supposed to say anything about a pending lawsuit. Unless they want to present their case in the media. The suit I was in a couple of years ago, that was for wrongful termination, and the slander was against me. However, I had a good reputation to fall back on, which the Ding, er, walls don't especially have. Not beyond the *National Enquirer* and the fringes of talk radio, anyway."

"The lawsuit's concerning their theories?" Alasdair's gaze shifted from Jean to Rebecca's and Michael's faces framed in the window. "I'm using the term loosely, mind. Theories can be proven."

"Their fancies?" suggested Michael. "I don't know, we've not heard details."

"Just," Rebecca went on, "that a Professor Evesdottir called Sharon either a witch or a bitch or both, though there's got to be more to it than that. Do you know her? Professor Evesdottir, that is."

"Evesdottir?" Jean repeated. "No, I don't. Sounds Icelandic, except in Iceland it's the father's name followed by 'daughter.' But there are lots of historians jostling for precedence. More than a few of us get pushed off the academic merry-go-round and then go looking for someone to blame."

"You weren't pushed. You jumped." Again Alasdair raised his watch, this time giving it a long, hard look. "Let's be getting on, Jean."

It wasn't that he was on duty—his security chieftainship was only honorary, here—or that he was anticipating a social occasion. It was that he'd agreed to appear, so appear he would.

So was she at his side? Or was he the sidekick of Jean Fairbairn, girl reporter? Hard to say, other than that this evening, this trip, was one more exercise in team-building.

TWO

WITH PROMISES TO share information as well as entertainment—dinners, tours, concerts—Rebecca raised her window and the SUV rolled off toward Henry Street and the highway to Richmond.

Jean's teeth were starting to chatter. She leaned into Alasdair's embrace as they scurried across the street and onto a sidewalk angling toward the Public Hospital building. Clever, she thought, how historical Williamsburg compromised between anachronistic streetlights and letting the customers trip and fall—and probably sue—by hiding downward-focused lights in the branches of the trees. Still the glow of Merchant's Square and the college campus, just two and three blocks away respectively, washed out the stars to the northwest.

Pausing at the foot of the steps leading to the entrance, Jean glanced back toward the darkened Historic Area. Above it, the indigo sky was strewn with stars. "How dark were the nights before Edison and his cronies gave humanity a twenty-four-hour day?" she murmured, half to herself.

Alasdair answered anyway. "Dark enough to be generating witches, vampires, werewolves."

"But we're still generating witches, metaphorically, no matter how bright the lights."

"That's another sort of darkness, lass. A matter of perception."

"Like sensing ghosts?"

That one he didn't answer, and almost succeeded in

concealing his half smile, half frown by pulling open the heavy doors.

Within the Public Hospital's orderly Enlightenment-era, Georgian lines, had once been confined the community lunatics. Or mentally ill, as they'd be called today, unless political correctness had decreed some term even less direct. Reality-challenged, perhaps. Jean could sometimes apply that label to herself.

A door to the left of the well-lit lobby opened onto re-creations of both the eighteenth- and nineteenth-century hospitals, showing the transition from warehousing, and often abusing, the insane to attempting to treat them, if with methods that now seemed little more than abuse. And what, Jean wondered, was being done to sick people today that would make future generations roll their eyes in horror?

"May I see your invitations to the reception, please?" asked the college-age woman behind the desk, and, with a quick look at the thick, creamy paper suitably engraved with Jeffersonian script, waved them toward the elevator. The gleaming metal doors glided open the moment Jean pressed the button. Alasdair bowed her inside, not without a half-glance back at the woman, whose black-lined eyes not only hadn't blinked, they had opened wide enough to reflect a ripple of tartan.

Jean swallowed her grin.

Just as the doors started to close, two women entered the lobby, the younger one flashing an invitation, the older saying not nearly far enough beneath her breath, "Rachel, for the hundredth time, get those damned hearts and flowers out of your head! Love doesn't conquer all. It doesn't conquer anything. It's the woman who's conquered."

Alasdair lunged, arm extended, and the doors bounced open again. The two women stepped into the elevator and stood just inside the doors, vibrating like high-tension wires. They acknowledged their captive companions only by their averted eyes and their tightly closed mouths.

The metal cell slipped downward. Alasdair and Jean exchanged glances, his cautious, hers curious.

The two women looked like a sinner with her clerical escort. Rachel's bolero jacket only partially covered her scarlet minidress, made of something shiny that squeaked as she shifted her weight on spike heels so tall and thin they could stake a vampire. Chin-length curtains of blond hair framed her crimson lips and tip-tilted nose, and set off her earrings and necklace, Celtic-interlace silver wires set with small chunky stones. It was probably her perfume that was permeating the confined space, rich and flowery, with an undertone of bubble gum.

The older woman's long, straight, black coat flapped open over a long, straight, black-and-white dress. The high, square, solid heels of her shoes seemed less appropriate for stabbing than for crushing and grinding. Her face was a lived-in version of Rachel's, shrunken around the wide cheekbones and soured about the dimpled chin, with something grim stuck in the corners of thin, red lips. Her blond hair was wrinkled rather than smooth, a streak of silver rising above her forehead and sweeping around to the side.

Jean's brows tightened into a frown. She knew that face and that streak of silver, like crumpled tinfoil. She knew that astringent voice. She just couldn't think of a name and a provenance.

The elevator doors opened and the two women bolted. "Mom, get out of my face and get a life. We're over twenty-one. We're nobody's business but our own. Hearts and flowers? Yeah, right." Rachel's voice was typical of so many young American women, squeezed through her sinus cavities so that it produced a mosquito-like whine.

She had a point about the hearts and flowers, but what

a shame she'd reached it at her tender age. Shaking her head—ah times, ah attitudes, ah when did she start feeling so, er, mature—Jean stepped in front of Alasdair into the lobby of the DeWitt Wallace Museum of the Decorative Arts, which was concealed beneath and behind the Public Hospital building like a secret government installation in a spy movie.

The mother and daughter tapping briskly across the marble floor didn't stop to look at the gift shop across the lobby, where every article for sale—books, pottery, textiles, high-quality souvenirs—was temptingly illuminated. Neither did they pause by the small but choice exhibits of antiques and period art that lined the corridor to the Museum's central atrium.

Jean had to admire Rachel's skill in maneuvering those shoes. Shoes. That was it. "I know her," she murmured to Alasdair. "Rachel's mom, there, in the sort of clerical outfit."

"Eh?"

"She's Jessica Finch, in Women's Studies at the university at Charlottesville. I'm not surprised she's here. Her specialty is the artifacts of witchcraft, like the Witch Box and the charm stone. I met her at a conference a couple of years ago, when she spoke about finding shoes walled up in old houses to defend against witches, something she traced back to shoes being good luck—you know, how you tie them onto the bride and groom's getaway car."

"Shoes," Alasdair repeated, one corner of his mouth twitching suspiciously.

Fine. Let him laugh. To him, shoes left prints at a crime scene. "Her husband Matthew's a historian at the college here. His field is Scots immigrants, not just the convicts and indentured servants but educators and religious figures. Though he's not really well-known. More of an Indian than a chief."

"Ah. A long-distance relationship," said Alasdair, perhaps remembering the six weeks or so that he had lived in Inverness and she in Edinburgh. What was it about distance fanning a big fire but extinguishing a little one? Could you draw a similar conclusion about proximity?

The Finches, mother and daughter, peeled away from each other. Jessica zigzagged past the groups of people gathered in the atrium and disappeared down a side hallway. Rachel ran up the central staircase beneath the huge Peale portrait of General George Washington. His painted eyes seemed to peer bemusedly over the railing at her dress, an assertive but scanty splash of red against the white marble, the white surrounding columns, the white latticework of the ceiling.

A waiter costumed in stockings, knee breeches, and a long waistcoat offered a silver tray filled with tall flutes. *All right! Champagne!* Alasdair seized two glasses and handed Jean one. She drank, the bubbles tickling her nose and throat, and sized up the scene as several of the attendees sized up Alasdair.

To one side, a quartet of musicians dressed in eighteenth-century clothing played light but elaborate music that Washington would have recognized. On the other side, against a display of guns and swords, stood a linen-draped table stocked with food and drink that, Jean assumed, Washington was intended to have recognized—pastries in decorative stacks, dollops of pink fluff that was probably Virginia ham relish, carved pineapples spilling out-of-season grapes and strawberries, mounds of cheese bits and swirls of toast squares.

At the foot of the staircase, front and center, sat a sign reading: *Lord Dunmore and the End of Empire.* A man in a tuxedo stepped forward to the sign and the music paused. So did the murmur of voices echoing from the giant box of the atrium.

Rodney Lockhart had greeted Jean, Alasdair, and the Campbell-Reids that morning with a gleaming smile. Now his mahogany face wrinkled in an expression that was obviously intended to be another smile, but which was closer to a shocked grimace. His deep voice, like Jehovah's rumble, welcomed all and sundry. Then he spoke briefly of the exhibit and of the Scottish institutions that had lent their precious items, the National Portrait Gallery, the Museum of Scotland, the Duke of Atholl and Blair Castle—here Lockhart nodded toward Alasdair, who nodded graciously back—and thanked several contributors, including Big Oil, Big Pharmaceutical, and *Great Scot* magazine.

Jean looked around for Miranda Capaldi, her full-time partner and part-time boss at *Great Scot,* but didn't see her. She had probably stopped off at either a nail salon or a boardroom and was going to be fashionably late.

Lockhart stopped even pretending to smile. "I'd also like to recognize the contributions of Wesley Hagedorn, who passed away suddenly this afternoon—a tragic accident, or so…"

Or so they say? Who said, the police? Bereaved relatives? Or Lockhart himself, spinning… What? Jean didn't have to look around at Alasdair to sense his police-antennae bristling. He had to be remembering the police helicopter.

Lockhart cleared his throat. "Welcome to Lord Dunmore and the End of Empire." To a smattering of applause, he faded back into the crowd and the musicians glided into Pachelbel's "Canon."

"Who was Hagedorn?" asked Alasdair. "What happened to him? Just this afternoon, was it?"

"I haven't a clue. Miranda will know who he is—was—

though. She's been working to set up a beachhead here for several months. You know, Williamsburg and its Foundation as the first step in her conquest of the Americas."

People drifted up the steps much more sedately than Rachel had run up them. "Shall we? Not that we haven't already seen everything."

"But I'm by way of keeping up appearances, and you're working, more or less." Placing their empty glasses on a tray to one side of the table, he eyed a pile of gelatinous green cubes. "Jelly?"

"I bet it's pickled watermelon rind."

Alasdair's eyes rolled in her direction.

"Look at it as American chutney."

"Right." Alasdair offered her his arm and up the stairs they went, making their entrance, showing Alasdair's tartan colors and probably disconcerting General Washington, who at different times in his life had fought both with and against kilted, red-coated troops.

On the landing, Thomas Jefferson, not in oil paint but in the person of an interpreter-scholar, spoke with a couple in black tie and evening gown. "…Charlotte Murray, Lady Dunmore, is a most charming lady, both in personality and appearance. Hers is the better family, related to the Stewarts of Galloway and through them to the now-extinct royal line, as well as to the present Hanoverians, with whom she has found great favor. Her connections have served her husband's ambitions very well indeed, when late he was His Majesty's Lieutenant, Vice Admiral, and Governor-General of the Colony and Dominion of Virginia."

Very late, as in long-dead, Jean thought. But then, in historic Williamsburg, time bent back on itself like a Möbius strip. Modern-day restorers and interpreters had no fear of living amid spirits, ghosts, whatever you wanted to call them and however you might, or might not, sense them.

At the top of the stairs, galleries opened right and left. Since a crush of warm bodies filled the entrance to the Dunmore exhibit, Jean tugged Alasdair in the opposite direction, past long curving platforms studded with chairs, desks, and chests of drawers like jeweler's windows set with gems. Wood shone like satin and intricate carvings cast even more intricate shadows. Jean caught a faint whiff of linseed oil and another of pesticide.

Alasdair looked around politely, but then, he dealt with antiques like these every day, many of them even older and most of them still in use. When they stopped in front of several marriage chests, wooden sarcophagi painted with flowery designs, he said, "There's a custom lasting several centuries, the bride setting off to her new home with a supply of linens and the like."

"My mom had what she called a hope chest, though by the time I came along it was the place you threw games and puzzles missing half their pieces. It sure wasn't anything as interesting as Charlotte Murray's Witch Box. Which probably wasn't a marriage chest—it's too small for linens."

Jean leaned forward to peer more closely at the band of script running around the top of one box, but it was in German and she could read only *Gott mit uns.* God with us or God help us, which was just the sentiment probably felt by a newly married couple.

Alasdair pulled her back. "Lean too far and I reckon you'll go breaking a laser beam and setting off an alarm."

"Oh. Yeah." Jean glanced up at the metallic tracery of the ceiling—it no doubt concealed cameras as well as virtual trip wires. "I did that at the Smithsonian one time. Scared the heck out of me. But you'd think a criminal would be careful not to do that."

"The alarm at Blair Castle worked a treat for the criminal."

"That took teamwork." Her nostrils caught another scent—Rachel's perfume. Her ears picked up a faint giggle that sounded much too girlish to come from the studiedly sophisticated young woman. But there she was, emerging from behind a temporary partition, her face as red as her dress, her hair rumpled. A young man walked not so much beside her as entwined with her. His long, carrot-red hair tied back with a ribbon, his white neckcloth and high collar tucked beneath his chin, his long tailcoat and embroidered waistcoat above breeches, stockings, and buckled shoes all proclaimed him a member of the landed gentry. Or an interpreter playing one.

His sharp, pointed, fox-like features turned toward Jean and Alasdair. Tightening his grip on Rachel's infinitesimal waist—if she'd been wearing a colonial gown, she wouldn't have needed stays—he made a very contemporary "Ya wanna make something of it?" face, pursed his reddened lips, and guided her away.

Again Jean and Alasdair exchanged glances, this time suffused with laughter. "That must be the unsuitable boyfriend," she said. "I bet Mom would think any man was unsuitable."

"No flowers, but hearts beating as one, if hearts are the relevant organs." Alasdair urged Jean in the opposite direction, back toward the Dunmore exhibit.

Speaking of the family Finch, there was Matthew himself, hurrying his steps to match those of an older woman. She wore silver lamé sneakers below a royal-blue satin sack of a dress, which, with the white hair piled atop her whip-thin body, gave her a passing resemblance to a cotton swab. A tall cotton swab. She was almost Matt's height, and he had to be six feet.

Jean glanced back over her shoulder, but Rachel and Unsuitable had disappeared around a corner. Matthew stopped dead. "Jean Inglis, isn't it?"

"Yes," she replied. "And no. I'm no longer married—I went back to my maiden name, so I'm Jean Fairbairn now. This is Alasdair Cameron, from Scotland."

"You don't say?" asked the woman. Her honey-brown eyes took in the entire scene, from Alasdair's shoes to his collar to his glance at Jean. Her own smile, turning every wrinkle upward, revealed the even, white teeth of a denture commercial. She extended her hand. "And here I thought you were Chinese. Barbara Finch, mother emeritus. My son, Matt."

"How do you do," Alasdair returned, with polite handshakes back and forth. "Mind you, Jean here's a journalist, with a talent for stating the obvious."

Jean laughed, if dryly.

Matt considered her face as if gauging how much she'd changed since they last met, and trying to remember what facade he'd presented then. She considered that the fringe of hair around his scalp, an academic tonsure, and his tidily trimmed goatee, had gone iron-gray. The furrows cut horizontally across his forehead and vertically down his cheeks were now deep enough to plant herbs in, and Jean was willing to bet that those herbs were bitter ones. What had happened to him?

The prototypical Mrs. Finch, Barbara, was saying, "Welcome to the Old Dominion State, Alasdair. You probably have a lot of relatives here you've never even heard of. The Scots, they got around. Look at Rodney Lockhart. Lockhart is an old Scottish name—I bet he's got a Scot or two in the family." And she added to Matt's small noise of objection, "You're the expert on Scots settlers."

"I'm not disputing your facts, just the way…"

"That's the one good thing about getting old," Barbara

concluded, "you can damn well say what needs to be said and do what needs to be done. I gather you've been here before, Jean."

"Yes, more than once, actually. The last time was an archaeology conference a few years ago. I heard Jessica speak about the artifacts of witchcraft."

"Do you want to tell her," Barbara asked Matt, "or shall I?"

The light flashed off Matt's glasses like a warning flare beside a traffic accident. "I'm no longer married, either. And Jessica didn't even go back to her maiden name—she made one up. Evesdottir, daughter of Eve or something like that."

"Clever," said Barbara. "Tips you off right up front that she's a rabid feminist. Although she would have gotten more mileage out of 'Lilithsdottir.' You know, Lilith the demon?"

Matt's wince half-reversed itself into a smile, vinegar-sweet as pickled watermelon rind.

Jean caught Alasdair's nod from the corner of her eye. So it was Jessica who was the target of Sharon Dingwall's lawsuit. Surely Matt and Barbara knew about that. And just as surely it wasn't a good topic for reception chitchat. She ventured, "We saw Jessica and, er, Rachel…"

"Rachel." Matt looked around the atrium, but the scarlet girl wasn't in sight.

"…on the elevator. Is Jessica still at Charlottesville?"

"No, she's at the college here. In my department." His eyebrows tightened and then rose, rejecting further comments or second thoughts. "I've been offered a position with an imagineering company, if you'll excuse the neologism on the company letterhead. A place that designs historical exhibits for an audience that has the attention span of fleas—and therefore believes the sort of pseudo-history that you've always worked to debunk, Jean."

She wouldn't necessarily use the word *debunk*—that implied reality was set in stone instead of in little human gray cells—but it was close enough.

"Ah," said Alasdair. "Those of our properties in Scotland that have the money are after doing the same, setting up videos and the like."

"Do the dog and pony shows make it all more accessible, or is it just one more example of dumbing history down to the lowest common denominator?" Jean asked, having more than once had this same conversation with Miranda about her stable of dogs, ponies, and Loch Ness monsters.

Matt's head made a circular motion, both nodding agreement and shaking in protest. "If I take the job I'll have sold out. I'll have run away."

"Now that I'm working for *Great Scot,* I've been accused of selling out and running away. But I see my work as publishing without worrying about perishing. Not perishing at the hands of a tenure committee, at least." But the terrifying moments of the past few months, thankfully shared with Alasdair, counted as too much information.

"Jessica's just had a book published, *Witches and Wenches in Colonial Virginia,* about witch hunts as a function of gender politics. She's been on a lecture tour. She'll be speaking here tomorrow night, Halloween. She's a fine scholar, better than most." Matt's hands clenched into fists at his sides. "Take my advice. Never marry someone in the same profession as yours."

Jean didn't point out that Michael and Rebecca were in the same profession. The wounds of Matt's divorce were still raw. So were the wounds of Jessica's academic competition, the thick heels of her shoes bruising Matt's shoulders as she climbed past him, not that his shoulders had been supporting much of a reputation to begin with, unfortunately. Did he have anyone to pat him on his baby-bottom-smooth head and reassure him? Jean tried a smile blending rue and sympathy, but his molasses-brown eyes were focused on the far distance. And a bleak distance, too, it appeared.

"You're in the history business, too, Alasdair?" Barbara asked.

"Oh aye. I'm leading up Protect and Survive, providing security to historical sites. You might could say I've sold out as well—I was a police detective 'til August."

"Is that how you met Jean—did you arrest her?"

"I only just avoided arresting her," Alasdair answered blandly.

Barbara grinned. "How romantic!"

That was one way of looking at it. But before Jean could change the subject, the harsh jangle of an alarm ricocheted off the marble walls, blanking out the murmur of music and conversation, and was followed a nanosecond later by a woman's piercing scream.

THREE

JEAN CLAPPED HER right hand to her right ear and hit herself in the left ear with her sequined bag. Spinning around, Barbara got tangled up in her own feet, but in a smooth, athletic move had already steadied herself before Matt clutched her arm.

Alasdair took one step forward, then stopped, poised on the balls of his feet, tartan swirling around his knees. Williamsburg wasn't his patch.

It was the patch of a security guard in a neat blue suit, who strode purposefully but unrushed up the stairs. Another, walkie-talkie in hand, pushed past several rubberneckers into the exhibit.

The alarm stopped, leaving Jean's ears ringing, but not so loudly she didn't hear two voices raised in protest. The man's words and the woman's overlapped and intertwined like the parts played by the different instruments in Pachelbel's "Canon," just not nearly as melodious.

The second guard strolled into the exhibit and a moment later retreated, his expression more cautious than concerned.

"Someone leaned too close to a display," Jean said.

Alasdair nodded. "Someone had himself a wee false alarm. Bit of an epidemic of false alarms, eh?"

"Yeah, but I don't see anyone making off with the original Witch Box."

Alasdair muttered something about lads crying wolf just as a very familiar face and form appeared next to another

End of Empire sign. Miranda Capaldi looked around, homed in on Jean, and beckoned.

"There's my partner. Excuse me, duty calls," Jean said to Barbara. And to Matt, but he had spotted Rachel at the far side of the atrium, standing alone beneath a portrait of a woman hemmed in by the folds, frills, and multiple fabrics of her dress. Rachel was unaware of the contrast between her clothing and that of the portrait—her head was bowed and her hands together, not in prayer but in the throes of texting a message on her cell phone.

Barbara followed Matt's tight-lipped gaze at his daughter and said, "Good heavens, she looks like she's wearing a handbag. The jewelry's lovely, though. She made it. Very talented child. All she needs is opportunity and direction."

Smiling and mumbling excuses, Barbara and Matt headed one way while Jean and Alasdair, muttering pleasantries, went the other. Rachel might not appreciate being directed, but the jewelry was beautifully imagined and made.

Miranda was waiting, one stylish but reasonably heeled pump tapping the floor.

"You made it in one piece, I see," Jean said.

"British Airways being dependable as always," returned Miranda. "First time I've seen you in your glad rags, Alasdair. You've missed out your *sgian dubh*."

Alasdair waggled a sock-clad calf, innocent of the small dagger usually considered part of Highland dress. "The natives might be objecting to a semi-concealed edged weapon."

"No kidding," said Jean.

Most people would have been glassy-eyed and gray-faced with jet lag. But not Miranda. Her flowing garment of ice pink and mauve threaded with gold—colors that would have made Jean's skin look like cheese—flattered her exquisite

Scottish complexion and glistened in eyes as clear as her discreet diamond jewelry. For twenty years now, Jean had accepted Miranda as a force of nature, like a rainbow. And what was there to resent in a rainbow?

With a twitch of her golden-red head and a meaningful arch to her eyebrows, Miranda indicated the two voices in the gallery—sober, oh-so-reasonable voices that Jean now heard were lecturing the guard. "...Hair-trigger mechanisms frightening your visitors...should try for a higher standard..."

"What are they on about?" Alasdair asked.

"Sharon Dingwall leaned over the railing, having herself a closer look at the Witch Box," explained Miranda. "The alarm went, and so did she."

"We heard. I wondered if they'd been invited tonight." Jean gave Miranda a quick abstract of the Blair Castle situation.

Miranda's eyes brightened even further. "Well, well, well."

She also recognized Alasdair's cogitational crease, which had reappeared at the words *Dingwall, alarm,* and *Witch Box*. "All the better to be keeping Mr. and Mrs. Dingwall under surveillance, then."

"Good man, Alasdair. Over the top!" Miranda led the way inside past the hapless guard, who was making tracks out of the exhibit.

The 1765 Joshua Reynolds portrait of John Murray, Lord Dunmore, hung just inside the entrance. The soon-to-be governor of Virginia stood proudly, swathed in a great kilt of brown-toned tartan material, with a red-and-black tartan coat and waistcoat and red-and-white-checkered socks. A diagonal black belt suspended a basket-hilted sword at his side. From beneath an early version of a Balmoral bonnet, he peered off into the middle distance, no doubt at the unlimited horizon of his ambition.

Dunmore's ensemble might have seemed like a cacophony in pattern—to modern eyes, anyway—but it delivered the message. The noble pose, the showy clothing, the unlined face set in the calm confidence conferred by noble birth and an advantageous marriage, all proclaimed the privilege that attracted power.

"He must have found it incomprehensible," Jean mused aloud, "the way events in 1775 slipped through his fingers like sand through an hourglass."

"The American Revolution was all part of the master plan," said the already-familiar male voice several paces away. "Dunmore was no more than a pawn for the genuine movers and shakers, the ones who have been secretly orchestrating our history since time immemorial."

Oh yeah, that was Tim Dingwall. Instead of the great man theory of history, it's the great conspiracy theory of history. Jean turned around to see what appeared at first to be John Paul Jones, a tall, heavyset man encased by a navy-blue-and-white colonial admiral's uniform.

Miranda opened her mouth and inhaled. Before she could speak, the admiral stepped forward. The lights illuminating the portrait glinted off his scalp between the stiffened strands of his comb-over. "You are Jean Fairbairn. Miranda here says you will be conducting the interview tomorrow."

"We read some of your articles on the *Great Scot* website before we agreed. It's okay—you can write." The little woman beside him—and she was little, shorter than Jean—was enveloped in a Martha Washington–style getup, ruffled cap, billowing skirts, and all. Except the first First Lady had no doubt worn a *fichu,* a fine cloth tucked into her bodice, and Sharon Dingwall did not. Her breasts bobbled between the ridges of her collarbones and the rim of her bodice like two bowls full of jelly.

Jean sensed rather than saw Alasdair's eyes cross. "Thank you," she replied to Sharon's comment, swallowing the *I think*.

Smiling her most gracious smile, Miranda tried again. "Mr. and Mrs. Dingwall, may I introduce my friend and partner, Jean Fairbairn? And this is her companion, Alasdair Cameron, head of Protect and Survive in Scotland."

Companion was as good, and as neutral, a description as any, Jean thought as she shook hands. Tim squeezed too hard and Sharon barely squeezed at all, as if afraid she'd catch something from Jean's grasp.

His smile polite but cool, Alasdair gripped Tim's hand back again, drawing the slightest of winces from Tim's plump face.

Tim said, "Protect and Survive. That's the British security agency."

"We handle security for historical properties such as Blair Castle." Alasdair was looming, Jean noted, as much as he could loom when he was only five-eight, not that anything about Alasdair was "only."

Tim's considerable height, on the other hand, was crouched combatively. Whether that was a reaction to Alasdair's mention of Blair or his habitual stance, Jean didn't know. He said, enunciating clearly to the fools who surrounded him, "This museum's security arrangements are in dire need of updating."

His jaw set, Alasdair stepped back, but hardly out of the line of fire.

Two spots of color burned high on Sharon's cheekbones and her eyes glittered—she was angry at the alarm rather than embarrassed at her scream. Her head didn't even come to Tim's shoulder. For just a moment, Jean imagined her seated on his knee like a ventriloquist's dummy. But she was perfectly capable of speaking on her own. "We were just telling Miranda, Jean, what a good thing she's not trying to drive here, on the right side of the road and everything."

Did Sharon mean "right" in the sense of "correct"?

Tim took up the tale. "There's adequate illumination elsewhere in Williamsburg, but here in the Historic Area they're trying much too hard to achieve authenticity. By doing so they've left the place impossible to navigate. The place where Francis Street dips into a ravine, we would not have seen the car stopped in the middle of the road if it had not been white and had its brake lights on. Very dangerous situation."

"Boys from the college cruising for girls," Sharon said. "They'd stopped to talk to a couple of them. We have two sons—we know how boys are, always chasing skirts."

Jean did not look at Alasdair, even when she heard the tiny rumble in his throat. So that had been the Dingwalls who'd passed them and the Campbell-Reids, appropriately enough driving like bats out of hell. No wonder they'd misinterpreted Alasdair's kilt.

Now Tim glanced from the portrait to Alasdair and back. "You're aware, I'm sure, that kilts and tartans and all of that paraphernalia began with Sir Walter Scott around 1820 as part of the development of the Scottish tourist industry."

As one, Jean and Alasdair turned toward the explanatory plaque below the Dunmore portrait. "That was painted in 1765," said Jean.

Sharon's pale eyes, already so large as to be bulbous, grew even larger. "You can't believe everything you hear. Or see."

"You're saying this portrait is, ah, misattributed. Or a forgery," said Alasdair.

"You never know who you can trust," Tim told him with a gentle smile. "Let me suggest that you consider the Witch Box."

This time it was Miranda who rumbled faintly, the purr of a cat scenting prey. As she always said, quoting someone accurately played out sufficient rope for them to hang themselves. And watching people hang themselves made for revenue-garnering entertainment. *Which is where I come in,* Jean told herself.

And she recognized where Alasdair came in, his mouth twisted like hempen rope. Yes, it was time to consider the Witch Box.

A knot of guests drifted away from the railed platform in the center of the room, revealing the object of interest. The object of such desire to someone in Perthshire that he or she had stolen a replica of it.

The cracked and dried oak panels of the double-shoebox-sized chest were darkened with age, but its carvings had been done in relief, so that the raised tendrils and leaves and the initials "F," "S," and "B" had been repeatedly wiped clean of grime and were a dull, deep reddish-brown. Iron hinges and an iron clasp showed little rust, but were still grainy as soot. On its circular dais behind the railing, the small Box seemed to hunker down like a toad.

The explanatory plaque was printed in two paragraphs, the first about how the chest probably dated to the sixteenth century and allegedly had belonged to Charlotte Murray's Stewart relatives. Charlotte brought it with her to Virginia in 1774 and took it when she fled back to Britain in 1775. There it came down through one of her children to a present-day John Murray, the Duke of Atholl, who owned Blair Castle.

Jean noted the qualifiers greasing the first two sentences. So far so good. It was in the second paragraph of the plaque that the modifiers thickened into lard. "The vegetal motifs of the Box are likely no more than decoration and probably have no occult meaning at all, let alone any linked to the supposed Green Man legends. Despite the initials carved on the Box, it is not known whether it ever belonged to Francis Stewart, Lord Bothwell, the supposed witch and nemesis of his cousin, James I of England and VI of Scotland, only that a similar Box, complete with what appears to be a stone inset, appears in the woodcuts accompanying 'Newes from Scotland,' an account of the Berwick witch trials published in England in 1592."

Even though "Newes" was part propaganda, part pornography, it had helped inspire Shakespeare to write "The Scottish Play," *Macbeth,* and was as valid a source for the provenance of the Witch Box and the charm stone as any.

Although, since it was standard practice to ignore that which you couldn't explain, whoever wrote the plaque hadn't pursued the story of the charm stone, the mythical object that had reputedly occupied the smooth spot in the center of the Box where the carved tendrils parted. The three-sided smooth spot was, at least, undeniably there.

"It's Charlotte Murray's marriage chest," Sharon stated.

"A mite small for a marriage chest," said Miranda. "Some here in the Museum are almost large enough to be coffins."

"She was a wealthy woman from a respected and influential family," Tim said. "She had a large collection of boxes, chests, and coffers to hold her linens and other household items. The fact that she carried this one around with her and used it for her special things, like a treasure chest, proves it was important to her."

"Or that it was a convenient size," Jean suggested. "How do you know for sure she had it with her at all, let alone used it for anything more than odds and ends?"

"There's an inventory in the Rockefeller Library," said

Sharon, and pointed at the plaque. "See, it says right there, Charlotte brought the Box to Virginia."

Alasdair inhaled. Jean predicted his next words: *That proves nothing.*

But Miranda spoke first, more interested in dangling bait than in debating. "I'm seeing where a marriage chest or the like would be decorated with leaves and plants and all, as fertility symbols. But what about the wee faces?"

Even in the Museum's carefully calibrated spotlight, the small, rudimentary human visages—like leering happy-faces—hidden among the leaves weren't easy to make out. Sharon had probably broken the laser beam trying to see them better. Now she said, "As if the initials aren't enough, the faces, pagan green men, prove that the Box belonged to Charlotte's ancestor Francis, the witch."

Prove? Jean went after something a little closer to provable. "He was her distant collateral ancestor, maybe. Lots of people have 'F,' 'S,' and 'B' in their names. And the initials are in different corners of the chest, not in any particular order."

Sharon bobbed up and down, causing Alasdair to avert his eyes from her all-too-fleshy chest. "Very observant, Jean! Yes, that 'B' could stand for 'Bacon,' couldn't it?"

"The seventeenth-century scientist," Miranda established with a smile so bright it revealed each well-tended tooth.

Better and better. They'd just crossed the "what if?" boundary into Francis Bacon mythology. Among other feats, the seventeenth-century scientist had supposedly written Shakespeare's plays. What she'd be writing was an entire series. Jean rubbed her brain cells together in glee.

"I'm hearing that the Museum sent their best craftsmen to Blair Castle to study the Box," said Alasdair, offering his own juicy worm, "so's they could make an exact copy for display there whilst the original's here."

"Exact is as exact does," Tim said inscrutably and unhelpfully, and plunged on. "Charlotte Murray, nee Stewart, used her contacts to get her husband appointed governor of Virginia."

"Yes, she did," said Jean.

"She obviously wanted, nay, needed, to get to Virginia and recover the *Clach Giseag,* the *Am Fear Uaine,* her family's missing charm stone. That's clearly why she brought the Box with her."

Miranda acknowledged that statement. "The stone was here, was it?"

"Clearly?" Alasdair picked an easier target than Tim's Gaelic pronunciation. "Obviously?"

Jean tried mental telepathy, thinking in his direction: *Miranda and I are playing good cop, bad cop. They're not going to spill the beans about the theft. They're not going to tell you whether there are any beans to spill. Work with us here.*

Sharon said, "Charlotte was the only governor's wife to make the trip—and it was a difficult trip then."

"Difficult enough to make six or so hours in economy class look like a piece of cake," Jean said.

Tim and Sharon stared at her.

Okay. Jean went on, "All of the eighteenth-century governors except two sent lieutenants to do the job—they didn't come themselves. Most of the lieutenant-governors brought their wives. The only other governor besides Dunmore to come himself was a bachelor."

"Q.E.D.," said Tim, his gentle smile annotated by a roll of his eyes. "Proof that Charlotte had a good reason to travel to the colonies. It was essential for her to recover the stone."

"And did she recover it?" asked Miranda, not just hanging on every word, but making sure Tim saw her hanging on every word.

"Charlotte and her husband were forced to leave the area quickly when the Revolution heated up," Sharon said. "Or did someone intend for them to leave quickly, before she retrieved the stone? Hmmm?"

"The stone being good for what? Why was it essential?" Alasdair stood with his hands folded behind his back, but his pose was hardly casual. He was playing neither good nor bad cop, but straight cop, always after just the facts, ma'am.

"It was—it is—green, like the green men carved on the Box. A green stone in a triangular silver mounting." Tim looked around to see several other guests pressing in closely, taking him to be an interpreter like Thomas Jefferson on the staircase, dispenser of historical wisdom.

With a wise smile, his forefinger tapping the side of his nose meaningfully, Tim lowered his voice to a conspiratorial whisper. "Tomorrow, Jean. We'll let you in on some secrets tomorrow."

FOUR

FUNNY HOW THE air in the room had grown so thin. Sagging, Jean took a deep breath that caught a whiff of mothballs. All shall be revealed. Right. And they probably had a bridge for sale in Brooklyn, too. "Eleven A.M. tomorrow, right? Would you like to meet at one of the colonial taverns? Lunch is on *Great Scot*."

"No," said Sharon. "We'll meet you at the Cheese Shop in Merchant's Square."

"Good idea. It's right next to the theater where Hugh Munro and his band are performing. Have you heard them? Great Scottish folk-rock."

"The Cheese Shop has a patio," Tim said. "We will be able to keep an eye on our surroundings there, and take precautions against eavesdroppers."

"It's a date," Jean replied, fully aware her smile had become as stiff as Alasdair's back, but for a different reason. She was suppressing laughter. He was suppressing irritation.

Even Miranda's smile was starting to glaze over. "I'm sure you'll get on famously, Jean, Sharon, Tim. Me, I'll be attending an antiques seminar."

"Tomorrow's Halloween. Woo-woo for sale to the gullible." Tim's dark gray eyes turned toward the Witch Box and then back to his audience.

"Bread and circuses." Sharon curtsied, skirts lifted and spread so far she exposed bony ankles thrust into low socks and backless shoes. "If you'll excuse us, our son Dylan's wandering around the Museum, probably falling over his shoe buckles."

"These rental clothes," added Tim with a low bow, "are cheaply made, and are cut clumsily so as to fit the greatest number of visitors. When our work is complete, so many more visitors will visit Williamsburg that they will then be able to afford better quality clothing."

Side by side, alike in dignity if not in size, the Dingwalls walked toward the door of the gallery—where they were joined by the same young man with whom Rachel had been making use of a private corner. Like his parents, then, Dylan wasn't an interpreter at all.

Jean had seen families dressed in colonial costume, the little boys in cocked hats, the little girls in long frocks. If she'd been a little girl she'd have asked for knee breeches, on the theory that boys, who were not expected to sit in the corner and sew, had more fun. Which brought her into Jessica Finch—er, Evesdottir's—territory, where the trenches of gender politics made your average World War I battlefield look like a field of daisies.

She caught Alasdair's thoroughly jaundiced eye. "In fair Williamsburg we lay our scene, to paraphrase *Romeo and Juliet*."

"That's why Dylan is unsuitable, then," he returned.

"Eh?" asked Miranda.

"We saw Dylan Dingwall there with Rachel Finch, Jessica Evesdottir's daughter…" Jean stuttered, made a face, moved on. "She's the woman who Sharon Dingwall is suing for calling her a witch or something like that."

"The truth of the matter has likely been distorted by the time it came down to us," Alasdair concluded.

"A wee bit scandal, is it?" Miranda asked. "Conflict? Drama? Though no bodies scattered about the stage in the last act, I'm hoping."

"So are we," said Jean, just as Alasdair said, "Oh aye."

Miranda looked over at the family group, Tim speaking slowly, in words of one syllable, perhaps, to Dylan's attentive face, and Sharon standing on tiptoes between them. "A handsome enough lad, though his eyes are right close together. He's a clever one, I'm thinking, but then, his parents are as well. Just our sort, Jean, nutters with verbal ability."

Alasdair's quiet snort signified agreement.

Tim gestured back toward the exhibit. Dylan's eyes turned toward Alasdair and Jean and widened in dismay, so far that they protruded like his mother's. He was no doubt registering that, yes, the couple standing with Miranda could make something of his own coupling with Rachel. And then, as Tim's moving finger included the Witch Box, Dylan's face broke into an unrepentant, even charming, grin.

"Aye, lad," said Alasdair under his breath, "here's the ladies wanting something from your folk. Your secret's safe for the moment." He turned to face a display case, his hands interlocked behind his back in a policeman's studiedly neutral stance.

Jean watched the three Dingwalls less walk than march around the atrium, like generals on a tour of inspection. On the far balcony they nailed a solitary Matt Finch with two glares and another grin. With a tightly coiled shrug—*move along, nothing to see here*—Matt veered off in another direction.

"I'll be off, then. I'm booked to have dinner at the Trellis with Rodney Lockhart," Miranda told Jean, although her gaze targeted Alasdair's disdainful back. "Good luck to you with the Dingwalls. And with Alasdair."

Miranda, as always, was too perceptive by half. "Thanks," Jean told her, and then, a nerve cell firing in one of her brain's back alleys, "Oh! Speaking of bodies, do you know who Wesley Hagedorn is? Was? Lockhart said he passed away this afternoon in a tragic accident. I doubt he meant tragic in the Greek-drama sense, involving hubris and all, but then, that's why I'm asking."

"Oh aye, there's a real turn-up," Miranda said on a long, considering breath. "He's by way of being—he was—a cabinetmaker and interpreter."

"Anything suspicious about his death?"

"Playing the detective once more, Jean?" Again Miranda glanced at Alasdair. Even she had to notice that his ears were twitching backward like a cat's, listening. "I'm inferring from what the staff's saying amongst themselves—always listen to the staff, eh? They know all, see all, even things they're not meant to know and see."

Jean nodded. "Isn't that the truth?"

"Another cabinetmaker chap went to collect him for the reception and found him dead in a small pond next to his flat."

His flat was probably southeast of the Historic Area, beneath the beam of a searchlight. "Any unattended death is considered suspicious," Jean said, as much for herself as Alasdair, "although it might be perfectly natural."

"The police are setting up a full crime scene investigation, I'm hearing. Though I'm hardly needing to know, am I?" Miranda didn't have to add, *And neither are the pair of you.* Especially since she knew that all three of them wanted to know the details, to heck with the gulf between needing and wanting. "We'll have a wee blether tomorrow, Jean, after you've braved your interview. Cheers, Alasdair."

"Cheers, Miranda," he said over his shoulder.

Exhaling through pursed lips, Jean told herself that Wesley Hagedorn's death the day of the opening was no more than an unfortunate coincidence. Judging by the angle of

Alasdair's head, he was trying to convince himself of the same thing.

As for the details she did need to know, so far Tim and Sharon hadn't told her anything she didn't know already, about their half-baked, soft-boiled view of history, at least. They weren't alone in having a less-than-firm grasp of reality. Manipulating history was a money-making enterprise these days, as Jean—and Alasdair—knew to their cost.

They'd dealt with criminals exploiting the romance of Bonnie Prince Charlie, the pseudo-science of the Loch Ness monster, and the claims made by a bestselling novel about Scotland's Rosslyn Chapel. And now they'd crossed the Atlantic to find the same manipulative impulse here. It was human nature. Or so Jean readily admitted.

Alasdair, though—well, she'd sensitized herself to him well enough to detect his slow simmer of annoyance, even though he appeared merely to be gazing at two almost-identical miniatures of Lord Dunmore in later life. So late, Jean thought as she turned her attention to the labels, he was mere days away from his death in 1809. What a contrast this slumped, balding old man made with the paragon of vigor swathed in tartan! Although the old Dunmore was also swathed in tartan, a feathered Highland bonnet sitting beside him. Here he didn't gaze into the distance, into a bright future. Here he gazed directly out at the viewer, both bewildered and resentful, as if asking, *How has it come to this?* But even with death knocking on his door, Dunmore showed no despair.

Another miniature, this one in watercolor, showed a woman's face in profile, a woman identified by the label as Charlotte Murray, Lady Dunmore. Her patrician features—a long nose, a small chin, and between them a stiff upper lip—supported the elaborate rolls and piles of a powdered wig. The weight of the wig brought her chin up and head back, giving her an air as proud and privileged as her husband's, but also exposing a length of white throat.

The frame of her miniature was decorated like his, with a crown, as befit peers of the realm. "Do you think it was a love match?" Jean asked.

"It was likely one of those aristocratic arranged marriages," answered Alasdair.

"They had something like a dozen children, which proves—nothing, really. Maybe no more than that Dunmore had a strong sex drive. You know, that hot Highland blood and all."

"Right," said Alasdair, but his own stiff upper lip loosened just a bit.

"One of their daughters married a son of George III, to great controversy. I'm not sure why. Maybe it wasn't anything more than that the young people didn't ask the king's permission."

"Nothing doing with Lady Dunmore's family's reputation for witchcraft, was it, never mind the Enlightenment and progressive, rational thinking and all. Though I'm guessing that at the end of the day, the witchcraft story's no more than a fancy of the Dingwalls'."

"Well, Francis, Lord Bothwell, was a very real figure—supposedly Shakespeare based *Macbeth* on the trial of him and his coven. The provenance of the Witch Box does go back to the right place at the right time. And there are a couple of independent references to Bothwell owning a charm stone, although its relationship to Charlotte is only the Dingwalls' theory, based on Charlotte's ownership of the Box. So far as I know, anyway."

Alasdair's nod softened the rigidity of his jaw. There were actual facts associated with the matter. Good.

Jean looked back at the miniature in the display case, a life under glass. The tiny portrait ended just as the ruffles edging the neckline of Charlotte's dress began, but the artist had taken care to include a necklace of fine gold wires woven in leaf and flower shapes and studded with small stones, like a more delicate, fairy-style copy of Rachel's handiwork. "Are those dots of pink, white, and green supposed to be, say, garnets, diamonds, emeralds? Hey, emeralds are green stones. Not that there's any significance to that."

Alasdair repeated, "Right. What's this charm stone, then? One of those so-called healing stones, like the Lee Penny? That's the one in Scott's *Talisman,* is it?"

"Belonging to the Lockharts of Lanark, yes—Barbara's right about Lockhart being an old Scottish name. And the Stewarts of Ardvorlich had a stone, too. Those are bloodstone or crystal amulets mounted in silver."

"Sounds to be the sort of thing used for potting a werewolf."

Jean grinned. "The Lee Penny and the Ardvorlich Stone are healing stones. You swish them around in water and then give the water to a sick animal or even person. The Penny was supposedly brought back to Scotland by a crusader, and emeralds came from Egypt back then, and, well, charm stones weren't exactly Christian relics, but were tolerated. Bothwell's stone would probably have been un-Christian and anti-healing. Bearing in mind that the word *charm* is a synonym for *bewitch* and similar concepts, not just for 'wow, this is appealing,' the way we use it today."

"That empty spot," Alasdair made an about-face and once again confronted the small carved wooden Box. "It might be a slot for a coin of some sort, not a stone at all."

"It sure could, assuming you had a three-sided coin. Or some reason to put a round coin in a triangular setting. Of course, saying that the *Clach Giseag* or *Am Fear Uaine...*"

"The Taboo Stone or the Green Man," Alasdair translated.

"...was in a triangular setting could come from the space on the Box. I don't need to tell you how tangled up this kind of story can get."

"No, no need to be telling me, lass." He didn't quite keep the groan out of his voice.

Jean looked at his profile, backlit by the spotlight shining above the Witch Box as though he, too, was a watercolor painting. Once she'd thought his features were ordinary, but not now, not after she'd plumbed the intelligence that had been shaping those features for over forty years. Now she saw his high forehead, his straight dark eyebrows, the hypotenuse of his nose, neither arched nor flat—now she saw his firm but hardly craggy cheekbones and jaw—now she saw his taut and yet supple lips as her America, her newfound land.

In Shakespeare's day, America was new, but to her, America was been-there done-that, something Alasdair definitely was not.

FIVE

A GROUP OF evening-garbed visitors meandered out of the room and it fell silent, with only a faint echo of music, conversation, and clinking glasses drifting in from the atrium. Even so Alasdair spoke quietly, his voice less velvet than sandpaper. "The Dingwalls are pieces of work, aren't they now? And you and Miranda, leading them on."

"You catch more flies with honey. You've interrogated enough witnesses to know that. And Tim and Sharon aren't witnesses to the theft at Blair, your own leading questions to the contrary."

"Not witnesses, no, but persons of interest, with Kelly Dingwall at the scene."

"Well, they're persons of interest to me, too. I told you, talking to these people, it's what I do. What Miranda and I do. We don't make these stories up, we just report them, analyze them, test them for soundness."

"And yet if you didn't cultivate them, all the better to report them, could be they'd go dying a well-deserved death, eh?" Once again he turned his back on the Witch Box, like a bullfighter on a bull, and stepped over to another display case.

This was just one more paragraph in their dialog on credulity, belief, and motive, Jean told herself. It wasn't indicative of any fundamental flaws in the relationship. Smoothing her hackles, she followed.

This display case was long and low, spread with needlework samplers, yellowed pages filled with ornate sepia writing, and a woodcut of Augusta, the Dunmore daughter who had married a prince. Next to them were photos of Blair Castle and Dunmore's magnificent folly, a stone cottage built in the shape of a pineapple that was now a holiday home. The man, Jean thought with another glance at the Reynolds portrait, must have had a sense of humor.

She knew Alasdair had a sense of humor, dry as Scotch whiskey. She said quietly, as several more people walked into the room and swarmed around the portrait, the Witch Box, the miniatures, "Some day I'll be telling Linda Campbell-Reid stories about Santa Claus and the tooth fairy, and you'll be showing her the presents hidden in the closet and lecturing her on dentistry."

This time his snort was one of laughter—presumably not at the thought of him still being with Jean when Linda was old enough for such stories. "Oh aye, you've got that right."

"We, human beings, need stories like we need food and water."

"Aye, that we do. And we're needing the truth as well. I'm thinking your friend Matt'd be agreeing with me."

"*I'm* agreeing with you. It's just that truth can be relative and facts malleable, and it's worth analyzing why. It's worth digging around behind the stories to see where they came from and why people believe them. Then maybe we can have our stories and our truth, too."

"I'm telling you what the truth is not. Opinion."

She knew what he meant. And she recognized his subtext; that, immersed in her academic and journalistic milieu, he felt every bit as wrong-footed as she did during a criminal investigation. Like any man, he was covering his discomfort with assertiveness. But psychoanalyzing Alasdair Cameron was the next best thing to banging her head against the walls of Edinburgh Castle.

Judging by his sideways glint, he knew the feeling.

She considered the manuscript pages in the display case, trying to puzzle out the elegant handwriting. "There's the word *stone*... Oh. It's just referring to repairing the bathhouse at the Governor's Palace. I'll bet Dunmore needed a bathhouse, Highland blood or no Highland blood. It can get positively tropical here in the summertime, and with those heavy clothes, well, there's a reason ladies carried little nosegays. The slaves and the servants didn't have that luxury. Maybe they learned to close those noses, like gills."

"I've no..." Alasdair stepped back and collided with a woman who was pressing close to the display case. "I beg your pardon," he said.

"No problem," she told him, and made an unabashed inspection of his finery. She herself wore black chiffon, narrow glasses, and a hairdo that owed more to static electricity than to a beauty salon. "I'm Louise Dietz, Literary and Cultural Studies at the college."

"Alasdair Cameron, Protect and Survive, Scotland," he returned.

Louise turned to inspect the example of Dunmore's finery inside the case, a slightly frayed waistcoat embroidered with bands of flowers, leaves, designs.

The stitches were laid down in faded reds, greens, and blues by long-forgotten hands, so delicate that even with her glasses Jean had to squint. "Someone ruined her—and it was probably her—eyes on this sort of work."

"Male tailors did very fine work, too," Louise pointed out. "Or are you a friend of Jessica's?"

Who was friends with whom shouldn't make any difference in historical fact, Jean thought. Neither should your political leanings. "Ah, no, we've met is all—you're quite right, tailors did excellent embroidery—excuse me."

Alasdair was working his way toward the door. Again Jean followed. Normally she didn't mind walking behind him, not when he was wearing a kilt, the hem swaying tantalizingly above the braw Cameron calves. But this was getting to be too much. Trying not to think of leashes, she caught up with him and asked, "Did Rebecca say anything this morning about getting vibes, impressions, off the Box?"

"She'd have been obliged to touch it," he replied.

"Well, yes, but it's like the ghost-allergy thing, sometimes it gets so strong..." She didn't know where she was going with that. Was she assuming that the charm stone—assuming it had ever existed to begin with—had really had paranormal powers? How about the Box? Had it picked up some sort of paranormal vibe from the stone, like a second-degree holy relic?

Now it was Jessica of the mutable last name who stood on the landing of the grand staircase, her attitude that of Caesar at the Forum, holding forth to several youths who were probably her students. "...almost always women who were accused of witchcraft, Francis Stewart being one of the few men. And he was also one of the few who survived to tell the tale, masculinity having its privileges then as now."

Wealth and power having its privileges, too, Jean added silently. She and Alasdair detoured to the opposite side of the steps. He murmured, "A bit of a Glenda, I'm thinking, but then, the granny, she was saying that already."

In-your-face feminist, Jean translated, "Glenda" being a slang term based on outspoken actress and member of Parliament Glenda Jackson—who had once played Elizabeth I to great effect. Elizabeth's successor was the son of her rival Mary Stuart, the James who was obsessed with witchcraft and demonology. "Francis survived because he was King James's cousin. Although she's got a point about women being more likely to be accused as witches."

"Oh aye," returned Alasdair. "I'm not denying there was prejudice enough to go round."

Barbara Finch sat on a padded bench below the steps, Rachel beside her exposing five miles of nylon-clad leg. The older woman stared at the musicians without quite seeing them, lost in her own thoughts. The younger woman's eyes focused well beyond her grandmother's somber face.

Ah, yes. Dylan stood against the far wall, his arms folded across his chest, smiling roguishly across at Rachel. She looked at him, looked down, dimpled, looked up again.

Matt stood to one side, a glass of champagne sloshing in his hand, his gaze roaming from Jessica holding court to Rachel flirting with Dylan. His wince had engraved itself so deeply on his features it was now a grimace of pain. *Not fair,* Jean thought. His womenfolk were piling on.

Sharon Dingwall appeared from the throng at the foot of the staircase. "You realize," she called up to the students, "that all you're getting is establishment propaganda."

The students glanced around. Jessica stepped forward, scowling. Her voice was deeper than Sharon's, and fell into a sudden hush filled only with delicate music. "Since when have women's rights been establishment? Get off that stupid hobbyhorse of yours before you fall off, Sharon. Or are knocked off."

"We'll see who's knocked off of what, Jessica. We'll see."

"What? You want me to say it again, in front of all these people? Fine. Sharon, in colonial days you would have been accused of witchcraft. You're one of those babbling women who slanders and scandalizes her neighbors. And we all know what happened to women accused of witchcraft."

His hair-and-skin-striped head glinting above almost everyone else's, Tim pushed through the crowd, seized Sharon's arm, and pulled her away. "See you in court, Jessica," he called. Sharon managed a flounce of fabric before turning her back. Having too little fabric to flounce, Jessica made a neat about-face and continued lecturing to the suitably scandalized faces of her students.

So that was the basis of the lawsuit? Jean asked herself. Did that cut count as slander?

The clamor of voices in the atrium swelled. The Dingwalls started working the crowd, handing out not tracts but business cards. Rachel contemplated her feet, now in awkward, pigeon-toed repose, and Barbara considered her fists clenched in her lap. Dylan seemed to be quelling a laughing fit. Matt had vanished. Embarrassment or disgust, like his daughter and his mother? Or was his absence just coincidence, a call of nature or a table booked for dinner like Miranda and Lockhart?

Alasdair stood as still as a cat at a mouse hole, looking from Jessica to Tim—since he couldn't see Sharon in the crowd—and back again. "No love lost there, eh?"

"We knew that already."

"Aye, but making threats in a public place, that's a bit over the top."

"You call those remarks threats? They're hardly worth a lawsuit."

He considered a moment, and his stance relaxed, if fractionally. "Not necessarily, no."

"Jessica's already over the top," Jean went on. "So are the Dingwalls. Look at them schmoozing the crowd. Trying to justify their work, however you define *work.* Or however I will in my article, rather." Jean helped herself to a dollop of minced ham from the long table.

Alasdair accepted a grape, and didn't ask her to peel it for him. "No surprise they were in a tearing hurry to get here, then."

"And you're in a tearing hurry to get away, I bet." The ham blob filled her mouth with a rich meaty flavor almost overwhelmed by that of salt.

"You booked the half-past-eight-o'clock seating at the tavern, did you? I reckon we'd best be riding the bus, then. You've got our passes?"

That didn't exactly answer her question, but came close enough. "Yep. Come on then, we saw and we've been seen. We're off duty now." Without waiting for Alasdair to lead the way, Jean headed down the entrance passage—and then stopped when her back-of-the-neck sensors registered he wasn't behind her.

There he was, standing beside the security desk, shaking hands with the uniformed guard who had suffered the Dingwalls' indignant reaction to the alarm. He was offering either advice or commiseration—Jean was too far away to hear.

She drifted back toward the desk just as a woman stepped from a side passage. Her severe dark suit, while of a civilian cut and bearing no insignia, was still as much a uniform as that of the museum guard—except the guard's shoes were polished into mirrors and hers were stained with mud. Her black hair was styled just as severely, so short as to be stark, and her black eyes were innocent of cosmetics, not that those luminous eyes and the smooth olive skin in which they were set needed any. The height and angle of her cheekbones reminded Jean of the famous etching of Pocahontas, the only likeness of the iconic figure actually taken from life.

"Detective Stephanie Venegas, Williamsburg Police," the woman said to Alasdair.

"Alasdair Cameron, security chief at Protect and Survive, Scotland. Though my position here's strictly honorary, mind."

Without saying whether she minded, Venegas looked him down and then up again, inspected his face critically, and only then nodded. They exchanged a handshake, as much a part of the ceremony as the mutual review, two knights taking each other's measures beside the tourney lists.

Alasdair added, "And this is Jean Fairbairn of *Great Scot* magazine."

Jean stepped quickly forward. "Hello." Venegas's hand was small and cold, briskly grasping and then releasing, committing to nothing.

Her dark eyes assessed Jean's face, drew no discernible conclusions, and turned back to Alasdair. "Protect and Survive, the security agency in Edinburgh."

"I've just heard that the replica Witch Box has been stolen. A woman named Kelly Dingwall set off an alarm—accidentally, she's saying—and amidst the clamor, someone else pinched the Box."

"Yeah, we got the bulletin." Venegas turned to watch the crowd, where Tim Dingwall's comb-over bobbed up and down like a dinghy on rough seas. From the side of her mouth she said, "I hope you guys have a good time here in Williamsburg."

Jean was caught between cringing at that "you guys"—the dialect second-person plural "y'all" wasn't nearly as grating—and at their abrupt dismissal. At Alasdair's abrupt dismissal.

Distant lightning flashed in his eyes. He opened his mouth, then obviously thought better of pursuing the issue and said, "Thank you. Jean?"

Again she found herself hurrying along behind him, this time not just scrambling to keep up but positively outpaced.

SIX

SHE CAUGHT UP with him and several other escapees at the elevator. Inside, he stood in the same pose as Jessica and Rachel, his body emitting an irritated buzz that was almost audible. When the doors opened, he bolted across the entrance lobby toward the outside door.

"Slow down," Jean called to him. "These may be sensible shoes, but they're not rocket-propelled."

"Sorry." His large, strong, warm hand guided her way too solicitously down the steps and along the sidewalk to Henry Street, where a bus was just pulling up to the curb. She flashed their passes. He handed her through the doorway and onto a plastic seat about halfway back. Smoothing his kilt behind him, he took up a position on the aisle.

"Hey, mister," said a blue-jeaned and T-shirted woman over the heads of her two staring children. "Are you pretending to be one of the English soldiers?"

"Madame," Alasdair replied with the cool courtesy Jean recognized only too well, "I'm not pretending to be anything."

Two other well-dressed couples from the reception took their places and the bus rumbled off. In the darkness, its windows reflected its interior and Jean saw little more outside than the lights of Merchant's Square, Henry Street, and the Visitor Center, where the other couples exited, leaving her and Alasdair alone. Any other time she'd have suggested leaping off the bus and raiding the excellent bookstore inside the Center, but not now. Now she kept her eyes averted, ostensibly staring through the window, when in reality she was watching his reflection, a half-eroded cameo against the night.

She didn't know whether she was more irritated with Stephanie Venegas—maybe she was protecting her turf, maybe she was one of Jessica's uber-femininst fellow travelers, maybe she thought abrupt was synonymous with professional—or with Alasdair himself.

It wasn't that he was irritated because Venegas was a woman. When it came to the gender wars, he was a conscientious objector. He was irritated because even if he could have told her more about the events at Blair Castle than she already knew from the official bulletin, which he couldn't, this was Williamsburg's patch, and she was on the case. And on the case of Wesley Hagedorn's inauspicious death as well, if the mud on her shoes was any indication—she must have come straight from the crime scene at the pond.

Jean was on her own case. "The woman didn't have to be so abrupt about protecting her territory. And you can't follow up the investigation in Perthshire because you're on holiday here." When he didn't answer, she went on, "Yes, this is similar to what happened in August. We've been there, we've done that. Do we have to go there and do it again?"

"When we first met, last May was it?"

Five years ago, it seemed. Her entire marriage hadn't lasted as long as the past six months. "Yes."

"You were having second thoughts about your new job. Your new life. You were wondering what you'd got ahold of. You thought maybe you'd gone and sold out. You were saying as much to Finch."

Maybe she was past the second thoughts. Maybe she was still checking it all out, plumbing the depths, walking the maze, pounding her head against castle walls. "You haven't sold anything out, Alasdair. Sometimes I think you've gone into debt."

"To you, like as not."

"I can't take either the blame or the credit for your retirement. All I did was use my contacts to find you a new job."

"And I'm grateful." His chuckle was flavored more with vinegar than whiskey, but it was a chuckle. He took her hand and tucked it next to the warm wool pleats of his kilt.

A new driver bounded onto the bus. "How you folks doing this evening?"

"Very well, thank you," said Alasdair. "We've booked a table at Campbell's Tavern."

"We'll be there in two shakes of a lamb's tail," the driver replied, and sure enough, within moments Alasdair and Jean were creaking up the tall wooden steps of the old house and giving their names to the hostess in her mobcap and apron. She led them into the candlelit, food-scented, voice-murmuring gloom inside.

"The tavern belonged to Christiana Campbell, probably not related to Michael at all," Jean said as Alasdair held her chair at their designated table. "Still, it's proof of what Mrs. Finch was saying, that the Scots got around."

"Poverty drives folk from their home ground." He sat down opposite.

"Lots of emigrants indentured themselves, sold themselves into servitude, just to make it over here. I sure hope they weren't expecting streets paved with gold. Or even streets, for that matter. Ah, thank you." Jean accepted a menu from the waiter, a man in knee breeches, long tunic, and white neckcloth whose ancestors had probably been sold to the greedy colonial labor market, too, but not with a contract covering a finite term of work. No matter how brutal the conditions, indentured servants, Scots, English, whatever, had some hope of release.

Their small, rather battered wooden table was tucked into a corner, blocking an empty fireplace that exhaled a cool, sooty breath. If they had some of Harry Potter's Floo powder, Jean thought, she and Alasdair could whisk themselves back to Edinburgh. Only to jostle each other around her flat, cheek by jowl, elbow to elbow, familiarity breeding—not contempt, not at all. The friction of familiarity rubbing a blister, one that would make a tender spot all the more sensitive.

She angled her menu toward the candle that gleamed behind its curvaceous glass cover, and ordered fried chicken and spoon bread while Alasdair ordered crab cakes. Wine? Why sure.

The room filled with other diners, presumably the evening's second shift. A couple took the next table, he in black tie, she in black chiffon—oh, it was Louise Dietz, the woman who'd collided with Alasdair at the exhibit. Everyone nodded in polite but distant recognition and turned back to bread plates and butter pats.

"Please tell me, Denny, that you're not going to waste your time with Jessica's lecture tomorrow night," Louise said to her companion.

The man sucked on his moustache and allowed, "It might be amusing. She says she uncovered a new primary source during her sabbatical."

"Sabbatical? When she moved down from Charlottesville in May, you mean, and started crowding Matt in his own lecture hall. Any sources she found on the way were on a rotating rack at a gas station along I-64."

"I wouldn't be surprised if she's building her whole argument on the equivalent, some seventeenth-century laundry list, smoke, and mirrors."

"No wonder she's gotten herself sued. Yeah, Sharon Dingwall would have been brought up on charges of witchcraft during the colonial era, but no need to risk your reputation getting into it with nutcases like her and her husband."

A new primary source? Jean repeated to herself. *What—an original letter or diary?* She made a mental note to attend Jessica's lecture.

Alasdair's dryly entertained stare crossed hers and she shrugged. Yes, their neighbor's conversation reminded her why she'd left academia. Still she felt a twinge of nostalgia—like taking a cold shower, academic infighting felt so good when it stopped.

Silverware chimed, plates clinked, wonderful odors wafted by, and a fiddler played a couple of Scottish reels that had evolved between the Auld Sod and Appalachia to something edgier, higher-strung, almost off-key. The waiter materialized, opening a bottle. Jean sipped. The wine was fresh and clean, a pale shimmer in her glass, scouring away the bitter tastes of antique poverty and modern ambition both.

With it she ate sweet-potato muffins, hot rich spoon bread like corn pudding, and crispy succulent chicken. She traded a thigh for a bite of crab cake, redolent of spices and the sea. In the dim light, through the soft-focus lens of the wine, the room seemed more dream than reality. The dark pupils of Alasdair's eyes almost swallowed the blue irises, reflecting the candle flame when he looked up at her. Dim light was romantic, wasn't it? Bright-adapted eyes could sometimes see too much.

What she saw now were his features eased and his lips glistening with oil. A holiday. Yes, this was a holiday, never mind assorted Dingwalls and Finches and sordid tales of witchcraft.

"That chap Finch," Alasdair said, holiday or no holiday, "looks to have his back to the wall, trapped by three strong-minded women. They make them strong-minded here, I'm thinking."

I was made here, Jean thought. "Are the Finch women *Macbeth*'s three witches? Maiden, mother, crone, the ancient triple goddess. Who could be pretty nasty. Except I like Barbara, and I don't know either Jessica or Rachel well enough to dislike them, first impressions notwithstanding."

"He was blathering on about his ex, wasn't he now?"

"That's not unusual. Most people say they're not going to talk about her or him anymore and then go right on talking, working it all out."

"I never talk about my ex," Alasdair said.

"It would have been helpful if you'd said *something* about her," replied Jean, a bit too quickly. Damn the wine, loosening her tongue and unlacing her inhibitions. To Alasdair's sharp glance upward she added, "I don't talk about my ex, either, but it took so long to get uncoupled from him I think I exhausted all the possible topics before we met. Before you and I met."

"There you are, then. It's all been said. By us, though not by Finch, or so it seems." Alasdair placed his knife and fork on his empty plate and swirled the last of the wine, his hands that could have easily crushed the glass holding it as lightly as a soap bubble.

Her tongue ran on—but then, why should she mince words with Alasdair, being so strong-minded? "Cut him some slack. The guy's lost his wife and might lose his job. Yes, he can hire on with the media company—it's not like he was fired. But I know how it is—once you burn your bridges with the tenure committee, there's no going back. Which is the meaning of 'burning your bridges.'"

"In another minute you'll be saying, it's an academic thing, I'll not understand."

Police departments had their own tangled politics; she

knew that. But there was nothing like the jungles of Academe, not just your average campus but the national and international jungles, where five-hundred-pound silverbacks picked the fruit from grants and endowments and scratched their bellies, while tiny rodents nipped mouthfuls of the peels and each other, then skittered for cover. "You've been known to imply that it's a police matter and I wouldn't understand."

"You haven't always, have you?"

"Then maybe you should cut me some slack."

He gazed at her—*look who's talking*—until she ducked, directing her attention to her plate and the pile of chicken bones, a savory charnel house. Only then did he say softly, "Maybe we should be minding why we're here. Why we're no longer working as academic or police."

"Yeah," she said. "A second start can be a very good thing."

In their former lives, she and Alasdair had both made impossible decisions in defense of justice, decisions leaving embers that eventually led to burning out, burning bridges. Burning up the not-exactly-marital bed, which had its compensations. Still…

Alasdair sat back in his chair as the waiter cleared away the dishes and asked, "Would you folks like dessert? How about some coffee?"

Jean scanned the smaller menu. The offerings that weren't loaded with sugar were loaded with cream. "Would you like to share a piece of chess pie?"

"Chess pie? Some sort of sweet tart? Aye, if you like. No coffee, though, thank you just the same."

"Me neither," Jean told the waiter, and as he walked away said, "It might keep me awake."

Alasdair smiled, recognizing her words from an earlier

occasion, one freighted with more emotional baggage than this one.

No, freighted with another kind of emotional baggage. Once you'd broken the barrier of physical intimacy, you discovered different kinds of intimate barriers behind it. The flesh was a portal, not an end in itself.

She hadn't wanted another relationship. He hadn't wanted another one. But each—call it heart, and not Jessica's lace-edged ones—had compelled the other in spite of burned fingertips and frayed emotions. This relationship had to work. And yet Alasdair didn't want, didn't deserve, someone clinging to him and bleating about "has to." How much could you invest in a relationship without losing yourself?

The waiter set down a generous yellow wedge topped with whipped cream. "Ah," Alasdair said once the man's back was turned. "I was expecting some sort of chocolate-and-vanilla checkerboard design. Chess. Knights, bishops, pawns."

"And the queen is all-powerful."

Letting that comment pass, he sliced off a small bite of the pie, placed it in his mouth, and chewed. "Lemon curd with texture."

"Some say the derivation is 'cheese pie,' others that it's 'chest pie,' a heavy pie that will keep a long time in a food chest or press. The texture is from cornmeal. Ground-up maize, to you Brits."

"A food coffer?" he suggested. "Like Charlotte Murray's marriage coffer."

The lemon custard melted in her mouth and teased her throat, while the slight grit of the cornmeal mitigated the sugary, creamy richness. "Coffer, chest, box, the Scots kist—the ark of the Covenant, for that matter—they're all containers. So is the human body." That was another effect of the wine, if not the wine alone, that melting feeling in the pit of her stomach, the craving for Alasdair's meticulously sensuous touch.

He pushed the plate toward her, for her to finish. She did, while he rummaged in his sporran to find his wallet and pay the bill. They'd have to settle up once they got back to Edinburgh. Funny how uncomplicated her first relationship seemed now, begun when she and Brad had had neither property nor independence.

The academics at the next table started a second bottle of wine, or perhaps whine. Louise leaned cozily across her empty plate, her glasses riding down her nose. "…speaking of conspiracy theories, here's one. Tell me why the college hired Jessica let's-just-make-up-a-new-name to begin with."

"Smoke and mirrors," Denny said again, refilling her glass. "She has the negatives. Not for us to know the reason why."

"If you ask me, they're hoping for some revelation in that source of hers—Nathaniel Bacon was gay, I don't know. If she doesn't come through, she's sunk."

Did Jessica's new source deal with Bacon's Rebellion? Jean wondered. But that wasn't her field. Had she found a new account of a trial for witchcraft connected to one side or the other of the struggle?

Jean wended her way between the tables and out the front door before she laughed. "How well I remember that sort of circular dialog, counting coup on some hapless colleague every turn around the stadium. The Colosseum. Intellectual gladiatorial combat."

"The blether in the police canteen wasn't so different, though it turned on clues, cases—reality, not hot air."

She glanced sharply at him. He didn't realize he'd just insulted her. But they didn't need to revisit that site, either.

"Shall we walk back to the house?"

"Yes, please." With the interior of the building so dark, she didn't have to wait for her eyes to adjust to the night. Its sudden chill raised gooseflesh on her arms. The steps were steep and her knees a little wobbly. Jean supposed she'd never be able to drink without the alcohol going to her knees. Who needed a Breathalyzer, when you had knees?

Alasdair offered her his arm and gratefully she took it. Safely across the street, they crunched from light-puddle to light-puddle up the path paved with broken oyster shells toward the Capitol. Its blunt cupola rose against the starry sky like the admonitory finger of government. Alasdair asked, "Who was Nathaniel Bacon? A relation of Francis Bacon's?"

"No, although the Dingwalls and their ilk claim that he was. He was a young, brash Virginia landowner who rebelled against Governor Berkeley in 1676. The political situation was murky, but basically a lot of it went back to the Civil War in England, with supporters of the monarchy coming over here and lying low until the Restoration. Speaking of crime scenes, things got brutal for a while. Then Bacon died of a fever."

"Or was he assassinated?"

"There you go, Dingwalling me." Laughing, they strolled around the side of the Capitol, past the regular Georgian arches now filled with shadow. If Jean hadn't known that the building was a reconstruction, she would have imagined the ghosts of Patrick Henry and Thomas Jefferson walking the corridors, the echoes of their voices filling the darkened chambers. Or perhaps their ghosts were there anyway, evoked by place and intent and belief.

Leaning on each other, they started along the sidewalks lining Duke of Gloucester Street, where the bricks were kicked up by the roots of trees and tilted by extremes of heat and frost. Overarching tree branches strewed leaves onto the pavement, to swirl in gusts of cold wind. Shop signs swayed and creaked. The street, lined with the faint verticals and horizontals of buildings, the rectangles of illuminated windows and shuttered doors, like an exercise in perspective dwindled into the lights of Merchant's Square and the college almost a mile away. Even further, a siren wailed and a dog set up a complementary howl.

Jean wondered if Alasdair was thinking the same thing she was, about an ambulance crew trying to revive Wesley Hagedorn's inert body. Or perhaps his colleague's discovery had come too late, and it was the crime scene crew who had carried him away, without benefit of siren. And now he lay in the morgue, waiting for the touch of cold steel, the final violation of an unexplained—even if not malicious—death.

A human shape stepped out of a dark alcove, the bright point of a cigarette indicating a mouth. Oh—it was only a custodian, his cart of cleaning supplies and trash containers camouflaged by shadow.

A group of people strolled up the middle of the pedestrianized street, safe from cars if not from piles of horse droppings. Their guide, a woman in colonial garb holding a lantern, was intoning, "...they say she still walks the night." A shiver ran through the group, cold, dark, fear, a good ghost story—a good shiver, soon to be dispelled by spirits distilled rather than legendary.

From inside Chowning's Tavern came the sound of laughter and music, a mandolin, perhaps, and a woman singing, "Early one morning, just as the sun was rising..."

Alasdair tugged Jean gently to the left, toward the path behind the Magazine and their home away from home. The fire basket they'd seen earlier was now only a dull ember or two and a hint of acrid smoke. Not one human figure moved through the shifting shadows.

"The place really clears out at night, doesn't it?" Jean's own breath created a wraith in front of her face.

Beside her, Alasdair's teeth caught the dim light. "I reckon it's right uncanny come three A.M."

Jean glanced toward the Courthouse, a square dark shape to her right, and stopped dead. Alasdair jerked back toward her. And went full alert beside her.

Between the tavern and the Courthouse stood the stocks, the pillory, and the whipping post. How many modern reconstructions of those traditional instruments of punishment had been used up over the years, the wood worn away by children and adults alike playing in places where people had once suffered public retribution? If there had been a reconstructed ducking stool, intended for "scolds" or overly assertive women, visitors would have played with it, too.

Now the low ankle-trapping board of the stocks lay empty, and the post stood solitary, but the pillory that gripped a miscreant's head and hands, that was occupied by a slumped figure trailing limp arms and legs, head hanging. Either a man or a woman in antique man's clothing, white stockings below bent knees catching the light like an inverted V-for-victory.

Jean squinted through the gloom. A dummy. A demonstration set up for some school group expected tomorrow or as a joke for Halloween.

The imprisoned figure twitched and emitted a low moan. Her heart lurched. Alasdair dropped her arm and ran, his own tall socks flashing. She hurried behind him—okay, so this time behind him was good—he heaved at the upper slab of wood, so that it creaked and groaned.

Jean reached out toward the tall, lanky male body unfolding itself from its entrapped crouch—long coattails, white neckcloth, hair tied at the nape, a long face—he was choking.

No, he was laughing. Dylan Dingwall spun away from Jean's hands. "Thanks. She's the prettiest thing I've ever seen, but her sense of humor isn't. Rache! Very funny, ha ha ha, let's just try it on for fit, sure, no problem. Rache! Where did you go?"

Scarlet glinted in the lights of the St. George Tucker House, a block behind the Courthouse. A female laugh echoed. A lissome shape, like that of a wood nymph, glided into and then out of the dense shadow beneath a tree so large it concealed the intersection of Nicholson Street and the Palace Green.

Dylan galloped off across the deserted stretch of grass. "Hey, Rachel!" And the two shapes vanished into the dark alley that was North England Street.

"Good grief," said Jean on an aggravated breath. "The Dingwalls just love false alarms, don't they? He's bound to catch her. She's either wearing those spike heels or she's barefoot."

"She means for him to catch her up." Alasdair levered the upper block of wood back down again and brushed off his hands. "Bugger. I've got a splinter."

"I'll get it when we get back to the house. Don't bleed on your jacket."

"My ancestors marched through here wearing red jackets that would not show the blood."

And went on to defeat at Yorktown, but Jean didn't mention that. Sharing silent disgruntlement—Jean's magnified by Dylan calling Rachel a "thing"—they started back across the street.

Another group following a leader with a flickering lantern came toward them. Behind them, what had to be car lights quivered in the wavy windows of the Geddy House, looking like a candle flame carried along inside—in a skeletal hand, no doubt. Across Palace Green rose Bruton Parish

Church, going on for three hundred years of hymn, and sermon, and mortal shells laid to rest.

A thin beam of light swept the brick facade and round-headed windows of the church and vanished behind the surrounding wall. "That's not a car's headlamps," said Alasdair. "That's a torch."

"No surprise someone's carrying a flashlight."

"That's a torch," Alasdair repeated, "inside the churchyard. I'm thinking it's likely locked up tight this late, eh?"

"They're sure not holding a concert inside—all the lights would be on." She didn't ask Alasdair if he wanted to go investigate. When he stepped out toward the church she was already heading in that direction.

SEVEN

THEY TRIED TO walk softly, their steps blending with the voices of the ghost-hunting groups, the sigh of the wind in the trees, the hum of automobile traffic and a train whistle from the twenty-first century, and they paused at the end of Palace Green.

The cold wind fluttered Jean's skirt and teased her legs but barely disturbed the wool of Alasdair's kilt. Now it was her turn to shiver—from the cold, she told herself with a critical assessment of her own nervous system. She wasn't shivering from the chill weight of the paranormal on the back of her neck and her shoulders, even if her shoulders were up around her ears, trying to retain the last warmth of the food and wine and its subtle sensuality. "That's a flashlight, all right," she murmured in Alasdair's ear. "Not a ghost."

"Not a bit of it," he agreed, shoulders level, head cocked.

To their right, at the far end of the Green, rose the Palace itself, its tall, stately cupola outlined against the glow of the modern town behind it. Invisible to their left, beside and behind the Lumber House ticket office, a swathe of grass led down to the hollow on Francis Street where Jean had been startled by something going bump in the underbrush.

Ahead, she saw the flashlight beam sweep around the east end of the church and over the graves of two of Martha Custis Washington's children, then draw crimson winks from the leaves lingering on the trees in the churchyard to the north.

"You've got your mobile," Alasdair said. "We should be ringing security."

"You don't happen to know the number off the top of your head, do you? Although the church isn't run by historic Williamsburg, so security would just pass the call on to the town police."

"I've written the telephone numbers of my contacts at security, the hotel, the airlines, and the like, on a wee bittie paper." He opened his sporran, then closed it again. "One I cannot see in the dark."

"We could call 911, but until we hear glass breaking or whatever, the situation's not dire enough to turn out the emergency people. And we'd turn out Stephanie Venegas, too."

"Right." Alasdair's teeth snapped on the "t." "The church itself is likely alarmed. Where's the gate?"

"There's one on this end, see?" Jean pointed past a pool of light cast by a tree-mounted lamp to a gap in the brick wall, closed by a rust-red wooden gate. The flashlight flickered between the vertical boards, moving in slow sweeps, then stopping.

They picked their way across the street edging the Green. Jean peered around one gatepost, the brick gritty beneath her hand but holding a furtive warmth. Alasdair peered around the other.

Several gravestones and tombs punctuated the paved area next to the church. It was separated from the churchyard proper by a low railing that, like the velvet rope "protecting" the artifacts at Blair Castle, was no more than a symbolic boundary. The flashlight beam glowed from the top of a grave monument beyond it. Nothing supernatural about that—the intruder had simply set the flashlight atop the stone.

Intruders, plural. Jean saw two shadow-shapes, one large,

one small, huddled together in the space between two headstones. In the dim light the human figures were less distinct than the stones themselves, which sparkled with points of light like the multiple eyes of tiny insects.

The taller shape, who was wearing what looked like a tricorn hat, lifted a long pole high in the air and brought it down so hard Jean heard the thunk of—metal, she assumed—hitting the ground. Both people then leaned on the pole, pushing. "That's creepy," she whispered. "I'd say they were digging in someone's grave, except that's not a shovel."

"They're not Burke and Hare, are they now? These buried bodies have long gone to dust. Or mud, come to that. They look like taking a core sample."

"Yes, that's it, driving a hollow pipe into the occupation layers. But archaeologists wouldn't be sneaking around after hours, in the dark."

The two figures began pulling. The rod rose up above their heads, glinting damply. Grasping it like a vaulting pole, the taller of the two said in a harsh mutter, "Get the light. Let's make tracks."

The smaller person moved in a dark cloud of fabric. The flashlight beam swung, painting a streak of light across the flank of the church, then pooling around the intruders' own feet. And with a cascade of firing neurons sending a bolt of electricity from top to toe, Jean recognized them both.

Tim Dingwall looked as though he was stuffed inside his own skin, his cheeks smooth and round as sausages, while Sharon was so bony she seemed to be assembled from razor blades. So much for the theory that couples eventually started to resemble each other.

"Them," Alasdair said.

"The Dingbats are out tonight." Jean retreated from the gate, down the fence toward the Wythe House, intending to step into the shadow where the fence angled away from the street. But once again she realized Alasdair wasn't behind her. She looked around to see him standing a few paces outside the gate. The wind tossed the leaves surrounding the nearby tree-lamp, so that light and shadow flowed over him like running water, picking glints from his buttons.

"What are you going to do, make a citizen's arrest?" she hissed. "You're not even a citizen of this country. Call your police contact when we get back to the hotel."

Either he didn't hear her, or like Admiral Nelson putting his telescope to his blind eye, was determined to stand his ground.

Okay, Jean told herself, trying not to remember what had happened to Nelson. Surely the Dingwalls weren't packing weapons. She stopped next to the wall just as Tim boosted Sharon over the gate, her skirts billowing. Then he tipped the pole over and swarmed over himself, landing with a thud and a spatter of gravel.

The beam of the flashlight swung around and caught Alasdair full in its glare. With a squeak of surprise, Sharon switched it off, but he didn't vanish. In fact, he seemed to loom larger in the darkness.

"What are you after there, the pair of you?" Alasdair demanded.

"What the hell are you doing here?" Tim demanded in return.

"Here's me, having a dauner along a public thoroughfare. And here's you, trespassing."

Tim and Sharon looked at each other. Jean couldn't see their faces, but she guessed they were uniting their fronts. Sure enough, they stepped closer together and stood shoulder to chest.

"The church won't let us dig a test trench," Sharon told Alasdair, her voice brittle as broken glass.

"So you're helping yourselves, is that it?"

"Core samples will prove the existence of the secret vault in the churchyard," Tim explained, so patient, so reasonable, that his voice was not just flat but prostrate. "Our work here is for the public benefit. Once the truth is out, the number of visitors to Williamsburg and the church will increase exponentially."

"Will they now," said Alasdair.

Tim held the pole, the bore, the sample tube, horizontally in both hands. He could have swung it around like a quarterstaff, knocking Alasdair off his feet. Resorting to violence would hardly be logical, but then, Jean told herself, logic wasn't the Dingwalls' strong suit.

They didn't know she was behind them. She took a slow step forward. If Tim didn't threaten Alasdair, what was she going to do, hit him with her sequined bag? Alasdair had had self-defense training. Tim might be six inches taller, but she didn't need to intervene unless it was to save Tim himself.

Besides, she thought with a pang of shame, she didn't want to give the Dingwalls an excuse to cancel the interview.

"Once we've explained the situation to your, ah, friend Ms. Fairbairn," said Sharon, "you and she can intervene with the church to let us dig."

"And I do not believe you have been afforded any jurisdiction here, have you?" Tim actually hit a valid point.

Alasdair stepped aside, gesturing toward the main street. "No. But I know who does."

"Tattling, Mr. Cameron?" Sharon wagged her finger in his face.

"Making a report, Mrs. Dingwall."

"Let us be on our way, Sharon. There are none so blind as those who cannot see." Tim started off across the Green. Jean took a hasty step back into denser shadow, but he didn't look around. Stumbling over some hidden obstacle, he dropped the pole with a clang, picked it up, settled his hat on his head, and marched on. Sharon gathered her skirts and trotted along at his side.

Alasdair watched as the Dingwalls crossed the Green, passed the Brush-Everard House, and disappeared into the shadows past the Palace wall. In their antique clothing they looked like eighteenth-century ghosts. *Or not,* Jean thought. Judging by the cut of eighteenth-century garments, people carried themselves differently then, especially women confined by the bars of whalebone stays. Tim and Sharon ambled, perhaps even shambled, in twenty-first-century fashion.

She told herself that even if they stumbled over Rachel and Dylan tucked up in a haystack or the equivalent, it was none of her business. And they might not even care anyway, seeing Dylan as a spy in the enemy's camp. Engaging in an undercover operation, maybe.

Groaning at herself, she made her way across brick, grass, gravel, and asphalt to Alasdair's side.

"Good thinking," he said, "keeping yourself hidden."

"Do you mean that, or are you being sarcastic?"

His eyes flashed in the dim light. "You're after interviewing them, are you? You and Miranda, you're after printing up their havering? Secret vault? What's that in aid of?"

"It must be connected to the whole Francis Bacon thing. Supposedly his secret papers are buried here. You know, the ones proving that he was really Queen Elizabeth's son, or that he was Francis Drake's son—could be both, I guess, just for a really juicy scandal—or that he's the author of Shakespeare's plays, or all of the above."

Alasdair didn't blink.

"I bet the Dingwalls have tied all that into the Witch Box and charm stone stuff." She folded her arms across her chest. Adrenaline drained, alcohol evaporated, chicken fat turned to sludge, she was chilled to the bone.

"Come along." Wrapping her shoulders in his right arm, Alasdair guided her down the street, at his side, not at his heels. Another couple, this time in contemporary clothing, strolled past the church. Someone hidden in the shadows whistled "Over the Hills and Far Away." Lights swelled behind them—a car, allowed onto Duke of Gloucester Street after hours, its headlights casting their attenuated shadows before them. As they turned onto the white broken-shell path running alongside the Magazine, a police car rolled past.

"Now they decide to do a drive-by," Jean said between chattering teeth.

Looking neither right nor left, Alasdair walked her across Francis Street, his free hand digging in his sporran for the key to their house. Which, of course, was dark—they hadn't thought to turn on the porch light or leave a lamp burning. At least the low picket fence surrounding it was white, and caught the lights of the tree-lamp across the street and the Lodge further on.

The gate in the fence slammed shut behind them. Releasing Jean, Alasdair bounded up the steps and applied the key to the door—just as something soft and warm caressed her frozen ankles. With a sharp intake of icy air, she jerked aside. Alasdair hit the light switch inside the door. Yellow light flooded the porch, the path, the grass, each blade suddenly leaping into green. "What is it?"

A black-and-white cat stood at Jean's feet, looking up at her with bright, golden eyes. A second cat, this one white-and-black, sat on the grassy margin and looked up at Alasdair. *And your problem is?* each level gaze asked.

Jean exhaled, her breath congealing into fog. "A welcoming committee. Hi there! Are you interpreting colonial mouse-catchers?" With a cat's usual disdain for whimsy—no wonder she'd always thought Alasdair had feline tendencies—both animals roused themselves and faded into the surrounding darkness. "They ought to be inside on a cold night like this. Shame on the owners, letting them out."

"No one really owns a cat," Alasdair counseled. "Or have you not been paying attention to Dougie?"

"How can you not pay attention to Dougie? I wonder how he's doing?" Jean stepped into the faint potpourri scent of the living room and turned on a table lamp.

Alasdair shut and locked the door, then walked around the room closing the drapes. "Reposing himself on silk cushions and noshing on caviar, judging by the cost of his keep at the cattery."

"And feeling he deserves every bit of it, for being abandoned. A shame Hugh's on tour right now—he loves looking after Dougie. But then, since Hugh's on tour, he'll be here tomorrow, and we can have some good music to clean the taste of paranoia from our mouths. I'm taking a hot shower to warm up a bit. I think I may have left my feet back by the church."

Alasdair had removed his sporran from his belt and was digging through it.

"What have you lost? You have your credit card, don't you?"

"Oh aye, and the receipt from the tavern, but the wee bittie paper with the telephone numbers is not here. It fell out, I reckon. No loss." He started for the bedroom. "There's a telephone directory in the nightstand."

By the time Jean had removed her shoes and clothing and was standing in the shower trying to remember Tolkien's verse about hot water poured down the back, Alasdair had reported the Dingwalls and their impromptu survey in the churchyard to Williamsburg police, Venegas or no Venegas.

By the time she had toweled herself off and huddled into her nightgown—okay, it was flannel printed with little sheep, so she wasn't a steady customer of Victoria's Secret—he was inspecting the palm of his left hand in the light of the bedside lamp.

Equipping herself with a needle from her sewing kit and a pair of tweezers and a bottle of antiseptic from her cosmetics bag, Jean sat Alasdair down and balanced his large hand in her small one. "That's a pretty good splinter, but it doesn't look as though it drew much blood, red coat or no red coat. What did the police dispatcher say?"

"That they've been turfing folk out of the cemetery for years now—the fancies about Francis Bacon's papers have spread like weeds. They cannot do a thing about the Dingwalls on no more than our word, but they'll have a look even so. Have a care, you're not doing heart surgery."

"There! Got it!" The splinter seemed to shrink to a fraction of its former size once it was no longer burrowing into Alasdair's skin. She wiped the blood away with a tissue and applied antiseptic. Of course he hadn't turned a hair during the entire operation, no grimaces, no groans. "You owe me one."

"Is a foot rub by way of being adequate repayment?" he asked, with the lopsided smile she'd come to read very well.

"Oh yeah."

"Well then." He headed for the bathroom, peeling off his jacket and unbuckling his kilt.

Jean switched off the lamp in the living room, double-checked the lock on the door, and peeked out the front window. A human shape strolled down the sidewalk just outside, a guard, perhaps, or someone from the night staff at the nearby hotels—in the darkness the shape was unisex. Oddly enough, this person, too, was whistling "Over the Hills and Far Away."

Jean watched the mysterious human shape until it vanished into the night, then tested the window lock and reclosed the drapes. "Over the Hills and Far Away" was one of the standards of Williamsburg's famed Fifes and Drums, she rationalized. No surprise it would be ear-worming two different people. And even if this whistler was the same person who'd been watching from the shadows as Sharon and Tim escaped the tartaned arm of the law, he or she wasn't necessarily following them.

Jean realized she was standing in the dark. Ironic that she could sense ghosts but was also afraid of the dark. Or perhaps the latter stemmed from the former. She scurried into the bedroom.

The house was chilly. No need to turn on the heat, though. There were other options involving turning-on. Thinking of Tim and Sharon making love, her smothered by his flesh, him chipping a tooth on her collarbone, Jean turned back the comforter atop the bed and lay down. Before she had time to take off her socks Alasdair was back, wearing no more than a T-shirt and pajama bottoms but unfazed by the chill in the room. He'd been born and raised in the Highlands, misty snow-covered mountains, chill lochs, and all. He endured discomfort much better than he endured fools.

His warm hands, large as those of a manual laborer, cultivated as those of an artist—he'd have made a good sculptor—drew off her socks and started prodding the tightness in the balls of first her right foot, then her left.

She eyed his down-turned face, the bones beneath the skin softened by the shadow of his lashes. "Why me?" she asked.

"Eh?" His voice was soft as his touch.

"You're basically a loner. The lawman striding down Main Street, cleaning up the town. Why me?"

He smiled. He had a nice smile when one was drawn from him, a perfect trapezoid between the smooth angles of cheeks and chin. "You're the school mistress taking off her glasses and letting down her hair."

"Not the dance-hall girl with the heart of gold?"

"Heart of something a bit warmer and livelier than gold. But dance-hall girl? No." His fingertips massaged her heel and circled her ankles, drawing gooseflesh from the skin of her legs.

"Is it because we both have a taste for history and an allergy to ghosts?"

"There's a bit of a likeness, aye."

"And you find me as stimulating as you do irritating?"

"Is that not obvious?" His hands moved up her calves and the gooseflesh became a delightful tingle surging up through her abdomen. Wine was nice. Alasdair was better. "Why go asking why?"

Instead of telling him, *I'm scared I'm going to fail again. I want to make sure,* she said simply, "It's a female thing," and fell back against the pillow. He was here, proving his commitment, showing not telling. Why ask why?

Alasdair's hands slipped smoothly up her thighs beneath her nightgown. Following them, his entire body pressed against her. She drew his T-shirt from his shoulders, good sturdy shoulders, not grotesquely muscled, but solid. Beyond them she noted, from a great distance, the patterned cloth of the canopy, blue and white leaves, tendrils, flowers, a bit fussy for her taste, but of the time period. Lord Dunmore's embroidered waistcoat was stitched in similar if more colorful patterns. Had he and Charlotte stared up at fabric like this, secure in the possession of wealth, status, and style?

Secure in the possession of the Witch Box, if not of the charm stone, whether either or both implied anything or not.

"Alasdair—" Jean began, but he stopped her mouth with his and applied his supple lips and subtle tongue to hers. His facade of stern policeman and severe security chief hid some positively baroque interiors, not to mention a medieval hall or two and dungeons haunted by clanking chains and moaning ghosts.

Yes, he had an allergy to the paranormal as strong as hers, and he wasn't any more comfortable with it than she was. Maybe his skepticism verging on impatience with the people he called nutters was his reaction, examining and then rejecting the paranormal, just as she embraced and then examined it.

Embracing and then examining Alasdair himself, she could do that. She had been doing that for a couple of months now. They had resembled each other before they met. No wonder they'd been compelled toward each other, propelled from past to present to a still uncertain…

Surrendering to the moment, she let the future go and held on to Alasdair instead.

EIGHT

JEAN AWOKE, PULLED from the depths of a dream where she wandered the halls of Blair Castle, each room opening onto another, and another beyond that—she wasn't at Blair at all, but in a labyrinth of chambers filled with polished furniture, gravestones, empty fireplaces, chicken bones.

What had waked her? A noise? A car in the street?

Footsteps. Not someone walking by outside. Someone walking around inside.

She was either being pressed into the bed or pulled down by it, cold, heavy, like sinking in deep water. Something between a tickle and a prickle teased the skin of her throat and chest. The footsteps didn't belong to living feet. A ghost was walking through the house, his or her paces slow and ragged, weary, injured, ill. Her nostrils filled with the same scent she'd thought she smelled last night, sweet, rich, faintly smoky.

She pried open her eyelids and peered around the room. The light of a streetlamp leaked through the bars of the blinds, casting a milky glow on bedposts, the chest of drawers, the chair. Through the open door to the living room she saw the front windows similarly glowing, but nothing moved against them.

Slowly she dragged her heavy limbs and heavier torso the few inches to where Alasdair slept, not exactly snoring but breathing in pronounced breaths. His back was warm, rock-steady. She plastered herself against his living flesh and bone, like putting her own back to the wall. He shifted, snorted, reached behind him, rested his arm in the indentation of her waist.

"Do you feel it?" she whispered, but he didn't answer. His breathing resumed its regular pattern and his hand on her flank lay heavy as marble, but not at all cold.

The unearthly steps stopped. Something slid, crockery on wood, perhaps, and then Jean heard a splat like bread dough hitting the kneading board. She caught the sharp odor of yeast, and aroma of baking bread. And then, with what seemed like a sigh of cold wind, all the scents and sounds were gone.

Exhaling, she willed her muscles to relax and her body to shape itself against Alasdair's. The cold, wet supernatural blanket lifted from her shoulders.

The clock, she saw as she turned her head, read 3:30 A.M. Alasdair had said that the Historic Area would be right uncanny at three in the morning. He was right. Of course he slept right through the proof of his statement.

Jean dozed off again, and only regained consciousness when she heard Alasdair's voice. "Mmm?" she asked. "What?"

She was alone in the bed, his pillow squashed and hollowed beside her, the covers tucked well around her—he'd done that when he got up. Sunlight filtered through the bedroom shutters and gleamed brightly in the living room. She smelled coffee. That was promising.

Alasdair was saying, "...Hagedorn, Christian name Wesley. No, I've got no idea, save the date of death was yesterday, October the thirtieth. Aye, ring me when you've traced him. Mind the time difference—it's hours earlier here."

Silence, while Ian, his minion at Protect and Survive, responded. At least, Jean deduced he was talking to his minion at P and S.

"She has, has she? Ah, that's the way of it, is it then? Well then, Ian, cheers."

Yawning, Jean stretched. She didn't have to hit the cold, rainy streets of Edinburgh. She could lie around, have breakfast, read the guidebook.

And hit the cold if sunny streets of Williamsburg for her appointment with the Dingwalls, reminding herself not to mention their escapade in the churchyard last night.

Alasdair looked through the doorway. He was fully dressed in chinos, white shirt, and the green sweater she'd knitted for him, the one giving his eyes the blue-green depths of the sea off the Western Isles. "There you are. Did I wake you?"

"Not really."

"I used the phone here to ring P and S. Add the call to my chit."

"Miranda's picking up the tab for this house. It's all going down on the *Great Scot* expense account, just like her room at the Inn. She's even writing off our passes and event tickets and everything, you know, research. Business expenses. You should have used my cell phone—it's set up to work on both sides of the Atlantic."

"I've got my own expenses with P and S," he said. "I phoned for breakfast as well, and made the coffee." He disappeared from the doorway. His footsteps beat a tattoo across the floor, sounding not even remotely like the ghostly steps she'd heard in the wee hours of the morning.

Breakfast. Hard to believe she could be hungry after the sumptuous meal last night, but then, she'd been rather active afterward. Rousing herself, Jean finished her washing and dressing routine and exited the bathroom just in time for a knock on the front door.

A youth about Dylan's age and height, but with considerably more gravity in his expression and melanin in his skin, carried in a covered tray and set it on a drop-leaf table. "Good morning. My name's Eric. Can I get you folks anything else?"

Alasdair was holding the door open. Just past his hand braced on the knob, Jean glimpsed two black-and-white shapes prowling along the fence. She replied, "You can answer a couple of questions. First of all, who do the cats belong to?"

Eric glanced over his shoulder. "One of the Foundation officials lives next door."

"Do you know their names? The cats, that is, not the official."

"Fine old Virginia names," he replied with a flash of white teeth. "Bushrod's the one with the white neckcloth. The one with the white stockings is Bucktrout."

"Bushrod and Bucktrout?" Alasdair laughed.

"There was a Washington named Bushrod," Jean told him, and asked Eric, "When was this house built? It really was a kitchen, right?"

"Yes, ma'am, it sure was. It was originally on the grounds of the Palace, then got moved over here when they were doing renovations for Governor Dinwiddie in 1752."

"Hence the name, the Dinwiddie Kitchen," offered Alasdair.

"I did get that far," Jean told him, wading in before he pointed out that kitchens were once separated from the main house, the better to isolate heat and the dangers of fire. "So the building was moved in the eighteenth century, then, not during the 1930s reconstruction."

"Yes, ma'am. This little house is old, early 1700s. There's a photo of it all leaning to one side and falling down, but the Foundation and Mr. Rockefeller, they rebuilt it back in the thirties to use as an office, and then fixed it up as a guest house just last year."

"Are there any ghost stories about it?"

This time it was the whites of Eric's eyes that glinted. The black pupils swiveled toward Alasdair. Alasdair shrugged. "She's a journalist. She writes about ghost stories."

Eric looked back at Jean. "Ma'am, there's ghost stories about most every building in Williamsburg. The bookstore at the Visitor Center and the college bookstore, they've got racks of ghost books. Me, I don't have much truck with such as ghosts and witches. The real world, archaeology, architecture, that's enough for me." He sidled toward the door, obviously not wanting to talk any more about the paranormal or else expected to hurry back to the modern kitchen at the Inn—or, most likely, both.

Alasdair really should have offered the lad a high-five for his commendable attitude, Jean thought, and concluded, "I write about archaeology and architecture, too. Thanks for the information."

"Yes, ma'am, any time," Eric said, grin restored. "Call room service when you're finished and I'll collect the dishes. Thank you, sir," he added as Alasdair handed him a couple of green bills. He paused by the gate in the fence to pet the cats and then loped away toward the Inn, his shoe buckles gleaming as brightly as his smile.

Alasdair shut the door on the two bewhiskered faces. "What was that about ghost stories? He didn't properly answer your question, but then, not everyone's picking up ghosts like you and me."

"And you'll notice he said ghosts and witches, even though I only asked about the one," Jean said, pouring coffee and helping herself to a croissant and a muffin. "Speaking of which, or whom, you slept right through the ghost who dropped in about three-thirty this morning. He or she was cooking something. Smelled pretty good—a lot better than that wet-dog moldy smell you get sometimes."

Alasdair sent her his best feline gaze over the rim of his cup. "I was dreaming is all, criminals breaking into the Museum and making off with that portrait of Dunmore."

"You work even in your sleep. And first thing in the morning. Why call the mother ship about Wesley Hagedorn?"

"He was an interpreter-cabinetmaker, Miranda was saying. One of the folk who build replica furniture and the like. Here's me, thinking…"

"…that he made the replica Witch Box. He had to have some hand in that, or Lockhart wouldn't have thanked him last night. Did he go to Blair Castle to study the original?"

"That's what Ian's looking out for me. Who visited Blair, when, how long did he stay in the U.K.? The facts." Alasdair considered a yogurt, fruit, and granola parfait. If he'd had a straw, he could have taken a core sample of it.

Jean smeared strawberry jam on the croissant and gave herself a moment for the warmth and caffeine of the coffee to flow down into her stomach and up into her brain. There were facts, weren't there? It wasn't all history gone to legend and myth gone to conspiracy theory. "We don't know whether there's anything suspicious about Wesley's death."

"Not yet." With a sage nod, Alasdair bent to the parfait. "Ah, you Yanks, having sweets for breakfast."

"At least we have a variety of breakfast foods, not the same greasy stuff day after day."

Ignoring that, he went on, "The sausages we ate yesterday were a bit too spicy."

"Yeah, there wasn't enough sawdust in them to make them proper British sausages."

His response was an earnest look cut with pity that mimicked Sharon's and Tim's habitual expressions.

Jean made a face at him. "You may be straining at a

gnat here, about Wesley, I mean, not breakfast. But it's worth pursuing."

"What's strained is my credulity—it cannot be coincidence that Wesley died and the Box he likely made was stolen."

"Sure it could, but..." *But.* Several months of dabbling in crime solving, side by side with a professional crime solver, and her curious nature was turning into a suspicious one. One that made accurate suppositions.

"Ian was telling me that Kelly Dingwall's left the U.K. and returned here. Here to the U.S., though I'd not be surprised at her turning up here in Williamsburg, with Tim and Sharon at work. Perthshire Constabulary had no reason to be detaining her."

Jean started in on her own parfait. Yes, the granola was a bit too sweet, but the slightly acid taste of the yogurt kept it from cloying too badly. "And they haven't located the Box or the thief."

"No, more's the pity. There's no saying, yet, whether Kelly and the thief were confederates or whether it's coincidence her brother's fixed on the charm stone and all." He grimaced.

"So if you come up with any information, are you going to share it with Detective Venegas?"

His grimace contracted. "What would I be playing at, withholding information that could be assisting her with her case? If she can be bothered to listen to what I've got to say, that is. If either Hagedorn's death or the theft of the Box is her case. Could be she was standing on ceremony at the reception last night, reminding Uncle Tom Cobleigh and all that the police are present and accounted for." He pushed away from the table, picked up a folded paper from the coffee table, and opened it up to reveal a color-coded schedule of events. A moment later, muttering beneath his breath, he darted into the bedroom and returned wearing his reading glasses.

Jean didn't say anything about bifocals. Taking the long view, his vision was right up there with an eagle's.

"The town looks like opening at nine or thereabouts. I'm thinking I'll have me a wee dauner to the cabinetmaker's."

"Why am I not surprised?" Jean told him. "The shop's on Nicholson Street, sort of behind Chowning's. It's in a little valley, partly over a stream—maybe that provides power for the lathes, I don't know. And there are a lot of little paths into the trees there, back to the brickyard and some other sites. Dark hollows, spooky little corners. Rachel and Dylan might have been heading that way last night."

"Ah. Tough customers, kids that age." Alasdair turned the pillowcase-sized sheet of paper over and considered the map, with its colored buildings looking a bit like a Monopoly game.

"One of the original cabinetmakers was named Bucktrout, come to think of it." Jean scraped the last of the brown-flecked yogurt from the bottom of the tall glass and decided if she had anything to eat at the Cheese Shop it would be a cracker. "I take it you're not going to come to the Dingwall interview? It's bound to be, well, *interesting* isn't quite the word."

"They'll not be talking to you with me sitting by, not after last night. I'll leave you to it."

"I hope you glean something from the cabinetmaker's shop. Whoever discovered the body may be too shocked to talk to a passing stranger. Or he may be under orders from the police not to."

"Nothing ventured." Alasdair tipped her a brief salute. "And I'll fetch sawdust for tomorrow's sausages, shall I?"

And he was out the door and away, his lips thinned with determination, the crease between his eyebrows set with resolve. Both shaking her head and laughing, Jean piled the dishes back on the tray and washed out the coffee pot. She had to hand it to him—he might have been given a few lemons the past couple of days—or at least limes, not quite so sour as lemons—but he was determined to make fruit juice anyway.

What she needed to make was a couple of phone calls. And a second check of her notes. And there was the ever-useful Internet. Her computer sat on the desk, humming gently, its nylon case set neatly aside. Alasdair had already been at it, seeing what he could find about Wesley Hagedorn, Williamsburg cabinetmaker.

Jean chose Miranda's name from her cell phone menu and pressed the button. But her colleague hadn't yet switched on her phone. Jean recorded a brief account of last night's events—Jessica and Sharon, Sharon and Tim—and then carried on to Rebecca's number.

She and Rebecca and their transatlantic romances, a foot in each culture, needing more than multi-nation-capable phones to keep their balance.

"Hi, Jean," said Rebecca's voice.

"I hope I didn't wake you or catch you feeding the baby or something."

"Nope, one of my nieces has taken her for a walk and Michael's gone along to supervise. How did the reception go?"

"Long story." Jean walked Rebecca through the events of the previous evening and its cast of characters, the Finch family, Miranda, the Dingwalls and their recurring role.

"Whoa," Rebecca replied when Jean finally ran down. "I knew they were out in left field but I didn't realize they were actually climbing the outfield fence."

Jean would have had to explain that metaphor to Alasdair. "And then there's the interpreter-cabinetmaker who probably made the replica Witch Box and who certainly drowned—well, we don't know that. He certainly died, and was found in a pond."

"Next to a pond. That was on the news last night. His name was West-something?"

"Wesley Hagedorn."

"That's it. The police detective—striking woman, looked like an Aztec—said his death was suspicious."

"Oh yeah. And if he's connected with the Witch Box… Well, it's early days yet."

"Not that early, if there's been time for theft and maybe murder."

"Yeah," Jean said, and, grasping at a straw, "The Witch Box here in the Museum is the real one, isn't it?"

"It sure is. I managed to get close enough while they were setting up yesterday to get a wee vibe from it. It's an old chest, right enough and there's something off about it, something uncanny. I'm not surprised occult stories are attached to it, although I bet the stories give it the oddness, not the other way round. True believers can put out a powerful resonance."

One that set off an allergic reaction in the unlucky few. Like the allergy to ghosts. "What about that empty slot on top? Tim Dingwall says it's for Francis Stewart, Lord Bothwell's, charm stone—an emerald, maybe jade, maybe an agate, set in silver."

"*Am Fear Uaine.* The Green Man. Sounds like the sort of thing that would belong to Bothwell."

"Oh yeah. Green's the fairy color, and not tiny, cute, harmless Disney fairies, either. This charm stone could well be a cursing rather than a healing stone, bearing in mind that the stories about Bothwell and his coven in Berwick are as much paranoia as truth."

"Those carved faces on the Witch Box are green men, and might or might not have been pagan symbols. I get the feeling there was once some kind of mineral matter in that gap, but it was a pretty vague feeling."

And not the sort of thing even Jean would consider as evidence, while Alasdair would dismiss it out of hand. "Thanks for that."

"For what it's worth."

"When are y'all going to be back this way?" asked Jean.

"Tonight. We want to hear Jessica's witch lecture and her take on gender politics. You said she was entertaining, especially when it comes to the notorious Mary Napier."

"Ah, yes, one of the few women who was tried for witchcraft in colonial Virginia." Jean reached over and picked up the schedule. "They've been dramatizing her trial here for years, and since tonight is Halloween they're putting on a special show, 'A Matter of Witchcraft.' We were too late to get tickets, though, so we're going to the concert in the church. Either way, you want to do dinner afterward, even if it's pretty late?"

"Who can resist wandering around the Historic Area after dark on Halloween? It's a date."

"I'll find out where Hugh and his fiddle are moonlighting tonight, no pun intended, and make a reservation. Talk to you later." Switching off the phone, Jean opened the lid of her laptop and checked the queue of search items.

Yes, Alasdair had found articles about Hagedorn's death on the local newspaper's and television station's websites. Rodney Lockhart may have discreetly used the words *tragic accident,* but none of the reporters did. One even quoted Detective Venegas's most recent take on the subject: "This is a homicide investigation."

Jean's heart sank into the pit of her stomach like a barometer before a storm, but she wasn't at all surprised.

NINE

WHAT HAD HAPPENED to Wesley Hagedorn, exactly? Why had it happened? And, perhaps most importantly, who had made it happen?

Jean read on, her stomach grumbling under the weight of breakfast and dread.

Wesley Hagedorn had been forty-three, the same age as Alasdair. Never married, no close relatives remaining, built fine furniture and other replicas, including harpsichords that he also played in the occasional concert. The Foundation's official statement expressed shock and regret and stated that Wesley would be sorely missed.

She scrolled on, and found an article on fine woodworking that Hagedorn himself had written for a magazine. Of the photos, all but two were of his work. Jean ran her gaze appreciatively over the curves and curlicues of a set of chairs and a desk. He had been a fine craftsman. Replicating the rough-and-ready designs of the Witch Box wouldn't have been at all difficult after the delicacy of his other work.

Wesley's right hand—the one with the cunning, according to the Bible—was pictured demonstrating its craft to a black-haired, sallow-faced twenty-ish man identified as Samuel Gould, apprentice. While Gould's fingers looked like hot dogs sprouting strands of dark hair, Wesley's were preternaturally long and delicate, with pearly, sawdust-covered nails. They were applying an engraving tool to a wooden surface and producing coiled shavings fine as Linda Campbell-Reid's reddish-blond curls.

Jean knew very well indeed that the size and shape of a man's hands had nothing to do with the delicacy of their touch. And Gould did have a vague Neanderthal charm. Was he the colleague who had discovered Wesley's body?

Wesley himself occupied the center of the last photo, both those remarkable hands depressing the keys of what Jean assumed was a harpsichord. He wore the usual eighteenth-century waistcoat and shirt over a slender body. His salt-and-pepper hair was pulled back from a long, sensitive face, all forehead and chin and slightly watery—from years of sawdust?—hazel eyes behind wire-rimmed glasses.

Jean had seen photos of drowning victims. Imagining Wesley's face blanched and swollen and those fine instruments of hands reduced to sagging meat made her hope that he hadn't drowned after all. Or been drowned, rather, if he'd been murdered. Death in any form, natural or otherwise, was not kind to the physical shell.

Hurriedly she clicked back to the search queue, then stopped—wait a minute. She returned to the picture and its legend: "Wesley Hagedorn plays the newest product of the cabinetmaker's shop, a harpsichord similar to that played by Governor Dunmore's wife and daughters."

This time Jean considered the person standing partly beyond the edge of the photo, a woman, turned three-quarters away from the camera, wearing a featureless black coat. With little more than the angles of her elbow and shoulder in the frame, she looked like a raven crouching over Wesley's inoffensive—okay, maybe he'd had the vocabulary of a sailor, he *looked* inoffensive—back. But no raven had blond hair with a streak of silver, like crumpled tinsel, flaring down one side.

Jessica Evesdottir.

So what? Jean asked herself. The woman was entitled to walk around the Historic Area just like anyone else. And her study of colonial history gave her impeccable motives for doing so. Just because she was standing behind Wesley didn't mean she even knew him, only that she'd been there when the photo was taken.

However, if he'd been researching and then reproducing the Witch Box, Jessica would have been interested. She might even have been working with him.

However again, Alasdair might come back from his mission with another take on the situation entirely. Or Ian might call from Edinburgh with new information. If so, ex-detective Cameron was honor-bound to share it with the inconsiderate but very much active-duty detective Venegas. Despite the mud on her shoes last night, she wasn't letting the grass grow beneath her feet.

With a thump on her touch pad, Jean closed the photo and tried to settle her slightly queasy gut with some affirmations. Wesley Hagedorn's alleged murderer could have had any number of motives—money, jealousy, blackmail. His work on the Witch Box might not have had anything to do with his death. This particular case was none of her business.

Right. Telling herself something was none of her business was getting to be a less effective exhortation all the time. And it wasn't as though her curiosity had ever killed any cats. What it had almost killed was her.

Wincing a la Matt Finch, Jean glanced across the room at the clock sitting on the mantelpiece between a black iron ladle and a brown ceramic bottle. Ten-fifteen. Almost time to set out for the interview, which was her business. She turned back to the computer and skimmed the file with the notes she'd taken from various writings of the Dingwalls'. Then, bracing herself, she clicked on the link to their website.

This time she didn't duck and cover at the sudden flare

of rotating graphics and portentous music, but she did congratulate herself on talking Miranda out of having "Scotland the Brave," pipes and drums and all, come up with the *Great Scot* website.

Navigating the Dingwalls' site was like piloting the Starship *Enterprise,* alarm klaxons screaming, exclamation points flying like photon torpedoes. *The secret plot to control human destiny! Hidden history! What they don't want you to know!*

There's always a *they,* Jean thought. She closed the window and the music stopped. In the abrupt silence, a chill like a trickle of cold water ran down her back—and it wasn't a trace of froth from the website. She looked around.

The clock and the ladle sat on the mantelpiece. The brown bottle wasn't there.

Okaaay.

Warily, she stood up, but the chill had dissipated before it became that all-too-familiar wet blanket. Still, something or someone had moved the bottle. To where?

She found it in the pantry, next to the chrome and plastic of the coffee maker, looking out into the living room. Literally. On the mantelpiece, the bottle's back had been turned to the room. Now Jean saw the medallion of a bearded face affixed to its neck.

It was a Bellarmine bottle, a type of wine bottle named after a fierce anti-Reformation cardinal whose face had resembled the stylized ones on the jars. Inhabitants of an earlier age had occasionally used such bottles as witch bottles, filling them with iron pins or nails, human hair or even urine, and then hiding them around doorways or beneath the household hearth. The idea was to protect the house and those who lived there from a witch's curse—like the role of the hidden shoes Jessica had once lectured about.

Jean wasn't sure when Bellarmine bottles had been

manufactured, but was under the impression their era bracketed not only Lord and Lady Dunmore's relatively enlightened period, but also Francis Stewart's twilit one, when witches and demons, and the prevention thereof, had been taken seriously and often fatally.

What had been in this bottle? Picking it up, she tried a tentative sniff at its mouth but sensed only a vague, damp, sweet muskiness. Her former husband had worn more assertive colognes.

The bottle's cool dimpled glazing, like a reddish-brown orange, felt innocuous. The ghost whose incorporeal hand had moved it was probably harmless, too. He—she?—was just repeating his normal daily round in life, cooking, pouring wine, protecting himself against witches.

She replaced the bottle next to the clock. Time had leaped forward to ten-thirty-five. Now she was going to have to hustle.

Swiftly, but not so swiftly she fell over her own hands and feet, she turned off the computer, called about the dirty breakfast dishes, dabbed on some make-up, collected her mini-backpack, and made sure she had the tools of her trade and her key to the door.

Outside, Bushrod and Bucktrout were settling down on the sun-warmed sidewalk. She stepped around them just as Eric pushed open the gate. Aha, her ploy to attract the knowledgeable young man had worked in the nick of time. "Hello again," she said. "I have another question."

"Yes, ma'am?" He bent to tickle a feline ear.

"That bottle on the mantelpiece."

"The one with the Dumbledore face embedded into it?"

There was an example of being over-educated. Knowing the face was Bellarmine's, she'd seen it as sinister, not benign like that of Harry Potter's headmaster. "Yes, that one. Do you know if it was found in the house?"

"Yes, ma'am, I do—the restoration people were real nice about showing us around. They found the bottle below a loose stone in the hearth. Funny place for a wine bottle, but maybe the folks back then, they were using it to bury their valuables. There wasn't anything in it except pebbles, a couple of old coins, and nails. Metal nails, not fingernails," he added with a grin. "The wax cap was all dried out and broken."

Tempted as she was to keep on pumping him for information, he and she both had places to go and people to see. All she said was "You know your stuff, Eric. Thanks! Do you need for me to unlock the door?"

"No problem either way, ma'am." Detouring around the reclining cats, Eric pulled a skeleton key from his pocket and applied it to the door.

Jean heard the rumble of an approaching bus. Another nick of time! It was beneath *Great Scot*'s dignity for her to arrive for the interview sweaty, puffing, hair flying and glasses askew, not to mention late. Sprinting across the street to the bus stop in front of the Lodge, she clambered onto her natural-gas-powered chariot and whipped out her notebook—a paper notebook, with a pen or pencil, was a less fussy and demanding accessory than a PDA.

"Bellarmine bottle beneath the hearth," she wrote, her pencil jerking as the bus swung around the corner and past the entrance ramp to the Colonial Parkway. "Must have been hidden after the house moved from the Palace grounds in the 1750s. A bit late to be practicing preventive magic, but..."

But what? she wondered, tucking her notebook and pencil back into her bag. Was the inhabitant of the house an older person clinging to the ways of his youth? Or was he simply someone less sophisticated than Franklin, Jefferson, and other paragons of the Enlightenment? Maybe she could ask Jessica's opinion before or after her lecture.

The bus paused beside the Public Hospital Building and then paused again at the corner of Henry and Duke of Gloucester, where Jean hopped off.

In the sunlight, the red brick, Federal-style buildings at Merchant's Square and the college across the street glowed the same sunset hues as the trees. The air was cool, but not so cool she and Tim and Sharon wouldn't be able to sit outside, all the better to see who was sneaking up on them. Snorting in something between impatience and indulgence, Jean eyed the patio outside the Cheese Shop. A few people sat at the wrought-iron tables, but none of them were Dingwalls.

It was straight up eleven. They weren't even fashionably late yet. Jean strolled on to the Kimball Theater and inspected a poster mounted beside the front door.

November 1! it proclaimed. *Hugh Munro and his band, traditional Celtic music with a contemporary awareness.* The photo showed Hugh, his fiddle poised for action. The fringe of white hair around his head looked like the halo on a cherub, assuming the cherub also had a white beard and an impish smile. Behind him stood the lads—Billy on pipes, Jamie on guitar, Donnie on keyboard—ready to either light your fire or douse it with tears, depending on the mood of music that split the difference between sentiment and rock 'n' roll.

Thank goodness Alasdair had a good ear for music and no problem with hearing Hugh, individually and with his group, through the adjoining wall of Jean's flat. But then, thank goodness she—they, now—didn't live next door to the leader of a heavy metal band.

She stepped across to the far side of the door to see another poster, this one advertising a play. "The Scottish

Play," to be exact—Shakespeare's *Macbeth.* This photo showed an actor presumably portraying the Thane of Cawdor himself, wearing the red coat and tartan kilt and plaid of one of George III's Highland regiments. Beside him his infamous spouse hitched up her billowing dress, lifted her heaving bosom, and held a dagger before him, the hilt to his hand. It was his own dirk, probably, trimmed in silver. They leered at each other, their expressions drawing subtexts that would have intrigued Freud if Shakespeare hadn't gotten there first.

Behind the two actors stood the weird sisters, three modestly gowned and visaged witches—not a hooked nose or wart among them—speaking incantations over a cauldron decorated with a scowling face not unlike that of the Bellarmine bottle.

"Hello there, Jean!"

Jean spun around, shedding bits of imagery like water droplets.

Tim Dingwall stood in the doorway of the Cheese Shop. "We're waiting for you. You said eleven o'clock."

No, they hadn't said they'd actually meet her on the patio; she'd just made an assumption. Not the first time she'd been wrong. With her best ingratiating smile, Jean wove her way among the tables and up the steps into the shop.

Tim held the door open for her. As she brushed past, she caught a whiff of stale sweat from his tweed jacket. It seemed as much a costume as his admiral's outfit, Jabba the Hutt playing the respectable academic. Inside, Sharon was inspecting a rack of chocolates, her long brown skirt, fuzzy brown cardigan, and big brown tote bag blending right in. "Not a bad selection," she stated, turning to Jean. "There's no table service?"

"Afraid not." Jean indicated the *Place order here* sign over a counter at the back of the shop.

Sharon and Tim planted themselves in front of a student-age server and barraged her with questions—were the cheeses made locally? Were they kept properly refrigerated? Were the meats fresh? Were the breads whole-grain or gluten-free? Were the chips fried in transfats and were the cookies made with cane sugar or high-fructose corn syrup? After every answer they paused to reflect, as though the fate of the free world hinged on their decisions.

Jean hovered, increasingly aware of the line starting to snake between the shelves of crackers, teas, and wines. She couldn't pretend she wasn't with them. She tried Alasdair's ploy of holding up her arm and staring at her watch, but neither Dingwall noticed.

At last they placed an order, then transferred their attention to the long, refrigerated case holding chilled beverages. There they read labels and debated the merits of different drinks while the slightly shell-shocked server handed two food baskets across the counter to Jean.

By the time Tim and Sharon finalized their choices, and Jean paid for their lunches and her own bottle of flavored tea—what Alasdair didn't see her drinking wouldn't hurt him—she was ready to buy a cup of ice, too, just to put down Tim's and Sharon's backs. Instead, she joined them at a table tucked into the outer corner of the patio and told herself to just sit back and think of *Great Scot.* This was going to make a fine article.

"You should have something to eat," Tim said. "You must watch out for your blood sugar."

"I had a big breakfast. Besides, I need to take notes." And she was still digesting the word *murder.* Jean opened her notebook to a clean page and inspected her collection of two-and-a-half pencils. Yep, nice and sharp.

Sharon eyed the blank paper. "Can't *Great Scot* afford

a PDA? That was a really expensive dress Miranda was wearing last night."

"Entering my notes on the computer gives me a chance to get started on the article," Jean told her, which was almost the truth and didn't make her sound like a Luddite. "You began as journalists in California, right?"

"We met each other at the *Los Angeles Alternative News*." Tim took a huge bite of his pastrami sandwich and went on, words muffled, "Was in Los Angeles we discovered patterns behind major news stories."

On cue, Sharon presented the official Dingwall platform: "The establishment-controlled media and their obsession with junk news keep the public distracted from the truth about the secret societies whose collusion has shaped religious, economic, and political history and controls our lives today."

"Puppet masters," added Tim, still chewing. "Junk-news opiate of people."

Being media herself, Jean knew that the entities pulling the strings and jerking the chains were marketers, accountants, and stockholders chasing the almighty dollar. Pound. Euro. Yen. Rupee. "'Opiate of the people.' That's Karl Marx, isn't it, writing about religion?"

"Good heavens, we're not communists!" Sharon started dissecting her chicken salad sandwich. "Dark meat. Just doesn't sit well. I bet that's where the growth hormones and other chemicals collect. Agribusiness, you know."

Yes, selling meat, like selling stories, was a time-honored capitalist enterprise.

Tim washed down his cud with a swig from his O'Doul's. Alcohol-free beer. What was the point? Alasdair would have asked.

"Religion is no opiate," said Tim. "Religion is prejudice

fomented by the ruling classes in order to keep the rest of the world's population from uniting against them."

"I see." Nothing like throwing the spiritual baby out with the fanatic bathwater, Jean thought, but then, that was a popular pastime these days. She glanced back at her notes. "Then you lived in Roswell, New Mexico, investigating the UFO phenomenon. Do you believe the media is hiding the truth about UFOs?"

"The truth about UFOs is that they do not exist. All the stories about them, no matter how popular, are merely smoke and mirrors. They provide yet more distraction from the real issues."

Sharon reassembled her sandwich, leaving half its components behind, and took a tiny bite. "There's no such thing as the supernatural. No UFOs. No angels, no devils. No ghosts, no vampires, no witches. The witchcraft craze in the sixteenth and seventeenth centuries was engineered by the ruling societies. Their demagogues, their agitators, stirred up fear in order to keep the ordinary people from asking important questions. People should pay attention to the real world and stop chasing after supernatural chimera."

Well, yes, Jean thought. *And no.* Demagoguery didn't limit itself to supernatural foes—look at the Cold War and the Red Scare not long before her own birth, or the fevered paranoia of the present day. She was all in favor of asking questions. "Francis Stewart, Lord Bothwell, was ruling-class, but he was tried for witchcraft. He got off, of course, unlike some of his associates."

"Exactly as we said. The events of world history are controlled by money and power," Tim said, and chomped down the rest of his sandwich half.

Well, yes, Jean thought again. That she hadn't expected these people to make any sense at all revealed her own prejudices. Even if the Dingwalls' definition of *sense* was one of the issues. "Now you're living in Rosslyn, Virginia."

"Yes." Sharon chewed another tiny bite with her front teeth, like a rabbit. "We're right across the river from D.C., where we can monitor all the clandestine activity. Rosslyn's an appropriate name for a center of undercover power, isn't it?"

Trying to keep the groan from her voice, Jean replied, "You're thinking of Rosslyn Chapel in Scotland."

"Yep. An entire building composed of cryptograms and codes. Of course the-powers-that-be won't let anyone dig there and open up the crypts." Jean noted the unintended pun—cryptogram, crypt, Kryptonite—but Sharon plunged on. "You're dong an article on the hidden history of the Scottish borders, aren't you? The one about Ferniebank that's under 'coming soon' in the latest *Great Scot?*"

Jean couldn't pry her teeth far enough apart to answer. Ferniebank. Rosslyn. Been there, done that, had the disease and built up an immunity. Or so she thought. Tim and Sharon were carrying a mighty big virus. She herded the conversation back to Virginia, more or less. "If you don't believe in the supernatural, paranormal, whatever, then why are you so interested in the Witch Box and the charm stone?"

"As sociological artifacts." Sharon spoke to Jean, but her gaze locked with Tim's. "As evidence. Because of their connection with Francis Bacon."

"Are they connected to Francis Bacon? The letters 'F' and 'B' might be carved on the Box, but with the 'S' they could refer to Bothwell just as well. It was his charm stone, right?"

This time Tim's gaze locked with Sharon's, and for a long moment his jaw stopped moving. Then, with a convulsive gulp, he swallowed.

They were hiding something. Great, Jean told herself, now *she* was suspecting a conspiracy.

As if to punctuate her thought, a tinny, electronic version of the theme from *The X-Files* suddenly filled the air.

TEN

JEAN CHOKED DOWN her laugh as Tim fumbled in his pocket, pulled out his cell phone, and inspected the screen. "It's Kelly," he told Sharon.

"She can wait." Sharon grabbed the phone, wiped off the crumbs with her napkin, and set it on the table next to Tim's plastic-wrapped cookie.

Kelly Dingwall, fresh off a transatlantic flight? Jean wondered. But she wasn't supposed to know who Kelly was. "Last night," she said, "you were connecting the Witch Box to Francis Stewart. You know, Charlotte Stewart Murray was his descendant and maneuvered her way to the colonies to search for the charm stone."

"You were paying attention!" Tim seemed surprised. "Yes, the Box belonged to the Stewarts, members of the ancient ruling class of Europe, the families who work together behind the scenes. It has been said that there were dynasties of the *Rex Deus* families, the Stewarts for example, the ones descended from Jesus Christ, but let's apply some common sense. After two thousand years most of us with European or Middle Eastern roots would be descended from Jesus."

Well, yes, assuming that Jesus had actually had children, a not-inconsiderable leap of anti-faith. Jean wrote *listen* on her notepad—and she'd listened to that particular wheeze before. The so-called bloodline of Christ was a marketable story if ever there was one, and had suckered in more than one reader.

"But the conspiracy that we've uncovered goes back a

lot further than Jesus," Tim concluded, his common sense exploding like an overripe pumpkin.

"Francis Bacon," said Sharon, "the greatest genius of his age, perhaps of any age, worked with the Stewarts and their clandestine intrigues. He had no choice if he was going to pursue his work—they were the only game in town. When the Stewarts followed King James to London in 1603, they brought the Witch Box with them. That's where Bacon discovered it, and saw how to use it to conceal his secrets."

"What secrets?" Jean asked. "How could…"

Tim overrode her interruption. "Then the English Civil War began, causing a momentary upheaval in the class structure. At this time, the charm stone was stolen from the Box and brought to the American colonies."

"You mean," Jean said, writing frantically, "by some of the Royalists who came to the colonies to escape Cromwell and the Puritans?"

"No, no," said Sharon, "it was a maidservant, one of the common people, the little guys, who stole the charm stone and took it with her when she went to the colonies as an indentured servant. She thought it was a healing stone."

"How do you know that?"

"Of course it's neither a healing nor a cursing stone. There is no such thing as the supernatural. Please continue to pay attention." Tim ripped open a bag of potato chips and contemplated the foil-lined interior as though Jean's actual question, not the one he answered, was hiding inside. "The theft of the stone dented the conspiracy of silence surrounding the subterranean cabal of movers and shakers. That set in train events that caused Bacon's Rebellion in 1676. The Rebellion was, very simply, a cover-up."

"Of what?" asked Jean.

"The Stewarts," Sharon said, "and the other ruling families had been secretly trading with the Americas for centuries."

Instead of asking, *Trading what?* Jean again wrote *listen.*

"Nathaniel Bacon was a great-nephew of Francis Bacon. He inherited the old man's papers and tried to put his enlightened theories into practice, bringing about world peace, but was murdered before he succeeded. He barely managed to hide Francis's papers here, in what would in 1699 be named Williamsburg, before the forces of suppression and secrecy caught up with him."

The issue in 1676 had been Indian incursions into the European-settled areas. Besides…Jean hesitated a moment, then thought, *What the heck* and said, "Nathaniel Bacon wasn't related to Francis Bacon. The names are just a coincidence."

Tim snickered, spraying the table with bits of potato chip.

"And it's just coincidence," retorted Sharon, turning her best pitying smile on Jean, "that one of Lord Dunmore's direct descendants was a certain Virginia Bacon, who left her house in Washington, D.C., to an international association of retired diplomats. Just what goes on there, do you think?"

Jean didn't bother to reply, "Cocktail parties?" Instead, she heard herself saying, "It looks like you've really been bringing home the Bacon."

Leaning forward, Tim asked, "Are you making fun of us, Jean?"

"People do that, sometimes." Sharon's smile reversed so that her lower lip protruded. She used her dill-pickle spear to move bits of chicken and celery around her plate.

"Just a lame joke. I'm sorry," Jean said, genuinely contrite. Although part of her job as debunker was to laugh, she preferred laughing with someone than at them.

She looked in appeal at the bronze statue of Thomas Jefferson seated nearby. His eyes, intelligent even in metal, assessed the glittering display in the window of the jewelry store across the street as if formulating theories in metallurgy and geology. He had seen history as a grand progression to enlightenment and progress, and yet he himself had traded in dark human flesh. In an earlier era, he would probably have defended himself against witches.

Tim followed her gaze. "Jefferson knew more than he let on, as did all of his companions in the establishment of the United States. Many of them were Masons, you know. In fact, most of the Founding Fathers of the United States were Freemasons. And—" he lowered his voice and glanced around "—right here in Williamsburg is a Masonic Lodge founded in colonial times!"

"There was an old boys' network," Jean allowed.

"Can't we just hear," Sharon muttered into her bottle of water, "Jessica babbling on about Founding Mothers and an old girls' network?"

Yes, we can. Although Jessica didn't babble. What Jessica said was direct and to the point. Jean opened her mouth to ask about the lawsuit, never mind it being outside *Great Scot*'s brief.

Tim spoke first. "Francis Bacon was a Mason, too. Of course the entire conspiracy ranges far beyond Bacon, Jefferson, and all. The full narrative is revealed in our movie, *Lords of the Lie*." He inhaled the rest of his sandwich and smacked his lips appreciatively.

"You're producing a movie?" Jean asked. "You're not writing a book?"

"The publishing industry is government-controlled, as we stated already. If we approached a publisher, the book would be rejected." Tim's stubby forefingers drew quotes around *rejected.*

"Suppressed," Sharon said, just in case Jean didn't get it. "Besides, who has time to read anymore? It's all film festivals, YouTube, TiVo. And if *Fahrenheit 9/11* or *Fast Food Nation* made waves, *Lords of the Lie* will be a tsunami. Here you go." Opening her tote bag, Sharon retrieved a glossy file folder and passed it across the table.

Its cover was black, with the words *Lords of the Lie: The True Facts of History* printed in garish crimson. *Well, well, well,* Jean thought, anticipating Miranda's response. And adding on her own behalf, *True Facts? Like free gifts?*

With thumb and forefinger, she opened the folder to reveal flyers and postcards in bright colors. The neatly printed press release included excerpts from Tim and Sharon's newspaper, magazine, and web articles, and quotes from other conspiracy mavens. The number of exclamation points scattered across the page made it look like a briar patch.

So far as Jean could tell from a quick glance, *Lords of the Lie* was the Dingwalls' grand unified theory of occult history—occult meaning hidden, not paranormal, as Rebecca had used it. They traced conspiracies that ranged from the secret mathematics used by the builders of the Great Pyramid through the arcane practices of the Vatican, the Knights Templar, the Freemasons, and the Rosicrucians to the manipulations of the modern-day Trilateral Commission and the Bilderbergers, making long pauses at the Illuminati, the Jesuits, the Rothschilds, and the CIA, and garnishing the elaborate construct with anti-Semitic and anti-Catholic asides. Jean supposed if she read further she'd find digs at every other major religion, too, including accusations that the Dalai Lama was masterminding the suppression of Bacon's papers, whatever they contained.

Oh yes. They contained the secret of world peace. *If only,* Jean thought, closed the folder, and looked up.

Sharon's pale eyes and Tim's dark ones were fixed on her, unblinking. Tim wasn't even chewing his chips. They expected her to validate their work. As if she had the power to do so. "Ah, um, QED Productions. That's a new one on me."

"It's our own company," said Sharon. "Named after our sons, our twins, Quentin and Dylan. It's a play on words, Quentin *et,* meaning *and,* Dylan: QED."

"Quod erat demonstrandum," Jean said. "That which is proved."

Sharon's sharp features smoothed with a maternal glow. "Dylan just got his degree in cinematography from UCLA. He had to work nights and weekends to supplement his scholarship. We have to pinch our pennies—much of our work is *pro bono publico,* since we're throwing Latin around. He's a bit clumsy, but he's a good kid."

"He sounds intelligent and dedicated." Even though his taste in girlfriends might be—and certainly was, by Jessica—questionable.

"Quentin paid his own way through school, too." Tim's heavy features lightened with a paternal beam. "He attended the University of Missouri and was awarded a degree in journalism. He's not a hard-core journalist like you, but a real writer. He wrote the material on the website, and the press release, and is writing the narration for the movie in his free time."

Hard-core? Jean could hear Alasdair's laugh. She didn't say anything about real writing and exclamation points but repeated, "Dedicated and intelligent. So when will *Lords of the Lie* be released?"

"It's not quite finished. We—ah—we're arranging financing—a second mortgage..." Tim cut himself off, judging correctly that the delicate state of their bankbook was none of Jean's business.

"We need to finish studying the Witch Box and the charm stone," Sharon said in a rush. "We need to consult Francis Bacon's papers."

"Do you know where they are? Do you know where the charm stone is? You must have some source for the theory, the story, that an indentured servant stole it and brought it here. A name, a place, something."

Sharon's face went as blank as a shuttered window. Tim leaned over his cookie and delicately unfolded its wrapper. Yes, they were keeping something secret. Perhaps they didn't want their campaign to peak too soon. More likely, they didn't know where either papers or charm stone were.

Jean went on, "All you've said was that there was an inventory proving Charlotte brought the Box here to Virginia, and from that you inferred she was looking for the stone."

"Yes, yes, the inventory was written up by a clerk here in Williamsburg named—" Tim paused for effect "—Robert Mason."

They expected her to react. React she did. "There's George Mason of Gunston Hall, who signed the Declaration of Independence. There's the Mason of the Mason-Dixon line…"

"Exactly," said Sharon. "That just proves our point. Q.E.D."

Prove was a word being thrown around altogether too freely, even if she did buy that the inventory proved Lady Dunmore had the Witch Box—the Museum itself cited that fact. "The names are another coincidence. Synchrony, even. That sort of thing happens all the time. The official in charge of the Dunmore exhibit is named Lockhart, like the Scottish family who once owned another charm stone, the Lee Penny. The Lees were an important family in Virginia, with houses here in Williamsburg. Robert E. Lee, the Confederate general, is descended from them. How many people do you encounter on a daily basis whose names are *not* appropriate to…" She stopped without concluding, "…whatever bee you have in your bonnet?" and said instead, "So do you know, or think you know, where the charm stone is?"

Tim's and Sharon's eyes lit up. "Lockhart! Lee! We missed those!" said Sharon.

And Tim said, "Thank you, Jean. It's good to see you're sympathetic to our work."

Damned if she did, damned if she didn't. *Give me strength,* Jean pleaded to her guardian angel, even as her guardian devil murmured about *Great Scot* and circulation figures approaching those of the *Sunburn,* Britain's answer to the *National Enquirer.* Although she'd rather do without the circulation than emulate the *Sunburn.*

Jean glanced at Jefferson again. One of his mentors had been a Scottish minister named James Blair. Synchrony.

Tim finished his cookie, then seized and crunched into Sharon's pickle. His phone warbled again. With a glance at his wife, again he let it go to voice mail. Sharon frowned, probably at the telephone rather than at the pickle, which was just going to waste along with most of her sandwich.

The bits of chicken salad lay on the bread slices like a body on an autopsy table. Like Wesley Hagedorn's drowned body. Bludgeoned body. Strangled, stabbed, shot—if he'd been shot, surely someone would have heard, but then, maybe someone had, which was Venegas's brief.

Jean closed her eyes. When she opened them, she saw Hugh Munro heading into the Kimball Theater with a fiddle case in one hand and a guitar case in the other. Collecting her wits, such as they were, she waved. "You made it! How was the flight from Edinburgh?"

"Why do some folk have children, and others have malignant homunculi? And the adults are worse. But I've survived to tell the tale, in song and story." Grinning, Hugh threw his arms as wide as he could without casting guitar and fiddle to the wind, indicating his delight at being armed with musical instruments.

"Where are you playing tonight?"

"Chowning's Tavern. A chorus or two of 'Allison Gross,' I'm thinking, to accompany Mary Napier's trial at the Courthouse next door."

"Not that Mary Napier was actually a witch," Jean returned, and then stopped with her lips still parted and her teeth still closed on the "ch." This time around, the name "Napier" rang a far and distant bell, signaling more synchrony, no doubt, but darned if she knew where it was jangling.

With another wave, Hugh disappeared into the theater. Jean looked back at Sharon and Tim to see them looking at her like a couple of hyenas considering a carcass. "Who's that?" Tim demanded. "Why was he coming in from Edinburgh?"

"He's Hugh Munro, the musician I was telling you about last night. He lives in Edinburgh. He's my next-door neighbor. He's here this week as a sidebar to the Dunmore exhibit. You should hear his version of 'The Girl I Left Behind Me'—scurrilous rather than patriotic."

Sharon's face puckered with doubt. "Can he be trusted? Odd people, artists and musicians."

Jean opened her mouth, shut it, and looked down at her notebook and her idiosyncratic shorthand. *Listen. Ask questions.* "So if you find the charm stone, then what? And Francis Bacon's papers? How can you consult them when they're, ah, hidden?"

"We shall find them," Tim said, chin set. "We have..."

His phone warbled. Sharon swept it into her bag, where it kept on warbling forlornly for a moment and then fell silent.

Tim smiled shamefacedly at his wife and mumbled, "Her plane was due to arrive in Richmond at eleven-thirty. I have no doubt that she needs transportation from the airport."

"She can rent a car," Sharon muttered back again.

"She's a member of our family," Tim hissed.

Something in Sharon's glare at her spouse reminded Jean of the thin ends of wedges and camel's noses in tents. Was Kelly as much an irritant as an in-law?

And more to the point, what had Tim been about to say? "We have a map"? "An old manuscript"? "Inside information"? But now he was staring at Sharon and she was staring at her plate.

Jean took advantage of the awkward silence to drain the rest of her tea. It was too sweet, too flat, and left a plastic coating on her teeth. She said to Tim's pleading and Sharon's stony faces, "Okay. You find Bacon's papers. Then what? How does proving he wrote Shakespeare's plays bring about world peace?"

Tim straightened. "Proving his authorship of Shakespeare's body of work confirms Bacon's brilliance. It's his other papers that prove the secret underground stream of history, the conspiracies of the ruling class. Once those conspiracies are exposed, the population of the West and hopefully the world will no longer allow themselves to be used as pawns. Knowledge is power. You shall know the truth and the truth will make you free. Freedom is the cornerstone of American civilization. We should never give it up for comfort. Never."

A strand of Tim's comb-over came loose in the breeze and waved like a banner above the dome of his head. A chocolate crumb flecked the corner of his mouth, his thick lips set too firmly to take it in. Sharon huddled in her dun-colored cardigan, obviously chilled, and her dun-colored curls—if they'd ever been red as Dylan's, the color had drained away—stirred only limply in the wind. Still, her huge eyes blazed up at Jean with fierce sincerity, unfazed by discomfort or middle age.

Doggedly, Jean wrote everything down. They were pathetic, weren't they? And yet they were sympathetic, too.

She felt a pang of guilt at exploiting their delusions. Their idealism. And it was idealism, of a sort, even if it was hidden amidst their creative lunacy like Bacon's papers—well, no, Bacon's papers didn't exist. As for the charm stone, the Dingwalls were evading her questions about that, never mind their repeated calls for truth, justice, and the American way.

Franklin had said something about people who gave up freedom for comfort and security deserving neither. Jefferson had written about the blessings of liberty extending to everyone. Tim and Sharon would say those forefathers had both been part of the conspiracy and part of the solution to it. Where did the evasions and delusions end?

Not in the churchyard of Bruton Parish Church, that was for sure.

The chill from the metal of Jean's chair radiated upward, tightening her lower back. It was like and yet unlike that ectoplasmic trickle of chill that all too often tautened her shoulders, her mortal flesh alerting to the presence of the past. Would she be discredited if the Dingwalls knew she saw dead people? Would Alasdair be less of the tough cop in their eyes if they knew he did, too?

Funny, when Alasdair went oppressively rational on her, she slipped toward the intuitive side. But when she was dealing with people to whom rationality resembled a Gordian knot—it might hold together, but more for the quantity of its strands than the quality of their interweaving—she edged back toward Alasdair and his version of Occam's razor, that the simplest explanation was likely the correct one.

Setting down her pencil, she flexed her fingers and glanced at her watch. It was noon. Wave after wave of people flowed through Merchant's Square, intent on lunch. In fact, there was Matt Finch standing at the side entrance of the Cheese Shop, watching the Dingwalls' backs while they watched Jean. The moment she registered his presence, he offered a cramped wave and slipped through the doorway.

Tim looked around. "Your musician friend again?"

"Another acquaintance," Jean said, and picked up her pencil. One hour of Tim's bloviating and Sharon's smug smiles was enough. "I've got all I need for now. Can we schedule another interview tomorrow, after I've had time to, ah, organize my notes?"

"Well," Tim said ponderously, while Sharon said quickly, "It depends."

She needed to close with something innocuous, to lull them into another interview. To pull their strings. "One of your sons is here with you. Dylan?"

"Yes," said Sharon, settling back in her chair with what Jean would swear was relief. "Quentin's in the U.K. He's starting with the *Sunburn* in London this week. Prestige job, as an investigative reporter."

Jean's pencil looped the loop. The *Sunburn* specialized in junk news, not prestige, but a job was a job. "And the Kelly who just got into Richmond?"

"She is my older sister," Tim answered, "She was good enough to take Quentin on a tour of the U.K. as a graduation gift. We brought Dylan to Williamsburg with us for the same reason."

Dylan might think he was getting the short end of the stick, except Jean hated to call Rachel a stick—even if she resembled one.

Sharon sat up again, slowly, eyes flashing. "That's right. You're with the Cameron guy, aren't you? You already know about Blair Castle and the copy of the Witch Box and everything."

"Yes, I do. I'd like to hear your side of the story."

"Police harassment, pure and simple," declared Tim. "Quentin expressed a wish to see the copy, since he would not be able to join us here and see the original. Kelly very kindly conducted him to Blair, but lo and behold, Scotland's finest descend to picking on a Yankee who was merely in the wrong place at the wrong time. Or perhaps I should say Scotland's worst. Cameron is one of them, a real prick, I say without fear of contradiction."

No, she wasn't going to contradict him, but not for the reason he thought. Sputtering faintly, Jean hid her face by leaning over her notebook and drawing more loops.

"He told you about picking on us last night, didn't he?" Without waiting for an answer, Sharon went on, "We needed to get a core sample from the churchyard. The church will let us dig once we prove there's a secret vault holding Bacon's papers."

"People have dug in the churchyard before," Jean pointed out.

"Not in the right place, beside Robert Mason's gravestone."

"Who? Oh, the clerk who did Charlotte Murray's inventory."

"He was employed as a secretary for Governors Gooch, Dinwiddie, Fauquier, Botetourt, and Dunmore," Tim told her. "He spent over thirty years in the service of the Crown, hearing myriad secrets, writing multiple confidential letters, and then he died on the eve of the American Revolution. That's more than a little suspicious."

"He had to have been pretty old when he died, if he'd been working for more than thirty…"

This time it was Sharon who leaned forward intently, her sincerity brightening into fanaticism. "Bacon's relationship with the Stewarts, with the Dunmores, is the keystone of our work. His papers will prove the secret underground stream of history that leads from the Pyramids, through the life and death of Jesus, through King James and Francis Stewart and Francis Bacon and Nathaniel Bacon to the present day."

And they were pulling her strings, too. They needed publicity—just as long as they could control the variety. "So who do you think stole the replica Box? And why steal a replica?"

"Who cares about that?" Tim waved dismissively, almost knocking a canned drink from a passerby's hand. "The replica's not even a very good one. The real Witch Box is here—there's no question of that."

"The real one is here, yes, but..." Everything was related to everything else, through plot and via conspiracy that made the highway interchanges outside D.C. look like Roman straightaways, and yet the theft was inconsequential? "Did you know Wesley Hagedorn, who made the copy?"

Sharon's bag erupted with the *Mission: Impossible* theme. Cursing, she dived into it, throwing manila folders onto the table. One spilled newspaper clippings. From the second peeked photocopies—pictures of the Witch Box, with red marker circling the space where the charm stone had supposedly rested.

With another four-letter word, Sharon grabbed the photocopies and stuffed them back into the folder, leaving Tim to dig into her bag. He found his own cell phone, then came up with Sharon's. She snatched it from his hands and flipped it open. "Kelly, we're busy right now!"

"No, I do not believe we are," Tim said. "Miss Fairbairn here has drawn the interview to a conclusion. For now, at least."

"All right, all right," Sharon snapped to her sister-in-law. "I get the message. You're jet-lagged and don't want to drive. But it'll take us a while to get to Richmond. Work on the cipher or something, okay?"

Jean's ears pricked. Cipher? And Tim had said something, too—what was it?

A digitized female voice emanated from the phone. "...playing the patsy over Hagedorn's Box, just because I've got the bankroll..."

Jean's ears positively twitched. There was a bit of information for Alasdair—if Kelly had told the Perthshire Constabulary that she knew nothing about the Witch Box, then she had lied.

Emphatically, Sharon switched off the phone and gathered up the envelopes. "Sorry about that," she said to Jean, while her glower was directed at Tim.

Tim's ingratiating smile was directed at Jean. "We shall talk again soon, okay?"

"How about some time tomorrow?" she asked.

They were standing up, Sharon shaking out her skirt, Tim picking bits of brown cardigan fuzz from his jacket. He collected the last of the cookie, she her tote bag. "It was nice talking to you, Jean," Sharon said, and they zigzagged between the tables toward the main sidewalk.

"Nice talking to you, too." Jean considered their retreating backs, their casual present-day stride. Casual. Like their brushing off the theft of the Witch Box replica...

That's what Tim had said. "The replica's not even a very good one."

And she asked herself, *How do they know that?*

ELEVEN

JEAN PROPPED HER elbow on the edge of the table and her forehead on her hand. In her mind's eye she saw the photos in Sharon's bag, photos of the replica or the original or both, with a red puddle like a bloodstain indicating the vacant spot.

Where had they gotten those photos? From Wesley Hagedorn? But surely his replica had been exact.

In her mind's ear she heard Tim's words from the night before. "Exact is as exact does."

Does? Did the Box *do* something? The Dingwalls didn't expect it to emit avenging spirits, like Indiana Jones's Ark of the Covenant. Their fantasies were based on historical revisionist puzzles, the sort of puzzles where, if one piece had a protrusion and the other piece had a recess, the fit was close enough to be proof. But they had something on their devious minds. Some reason why they were searching for the charm stone. Some reason to assume it was here in Virginia. Some reason they weren't telling Jean.

As though playing a word-association game, Tim and Sharon had used the words *cornerstone, gravestone, keystone.* One of them had said something about the supposed codes carved into the fabric of Rosslyn Chapel, medieval symbols bewildering the modern mind—like the symbols carved on the Witch Box, their meaning lost as the charm stone was lost.

Tim had told Kelly to work on a cipher. Previous searchers for Bacon's vault had treated the graveyard at Bruton

Parish Church like a giant cipher, making plans of the graves and anagrams of their inscriptions. Maybe that's what Kelly was supposed to be doing, deciphering a secret message recorded on Robert Mason's gravestone.

Yeah, Jean had encountered the whole grave-inscription-as-secret-message ploy before. Believers in clandestine history came in a variety of flavors, but they all left the same taste in her mouth.

She realized a couple was hovering nearby with their sandwiches and drinks, looking for an empty table. She slapped her notebook shut, thrust it and her pencils into her bag, and lunged to her feet. Waving the couple toward the table, she, too, headed for the street, only to find Matt waiting for her beside a planter box.

"Hi," he said, and gestured toward the retreating Dingwalls with a paper bag no doubt holding his lunch. "Get anything coherent out of them?"

"Yes and no. They're all for asking questions, but answering them, not so much."

"Sorry about the scene at the reception last night. You'd think Jessica could keep her mouth shut in front of the local A-list, but no. That's Jessica, never spouting off when you want her to, always spouting off when you don't."

"Is that why Sharon's suing Jessica, because she called her a babbling woman who slanders and scandalizes her neighbors? That seems pretty slight to cause all the trouble and expense of a lawsuit."

"I'm sure there's more to it than that. They've been at each other's throats since just about the time Jessica moved down from Charlottesville and Sharon came to her for help with this whole Francis Bacon thing. There's no honor among thieves."

"Say what?"

"I used to joke that they were thick as thieves, so I was

just playing on words." He raised his free hand in a *stop right there* motion and shook his head so vehemently his whole body shuddered. "Never mind. The Dingwalls turned up here just about the time Jessica and I broke up, so I associate them with, well, you've been there. It's a bad time."

"Yes, it is. It was."

"You're totally, legally divorced, I guess?"

"Yes."

"Well, we're still, you know, working things out. Speaking of trouble and expense."

"I'm sorry," Jean told him, and, both to change the subject and because she wanted to know, "Do you know of any lists of indentured servants who came here in the seventeenth century?"

Nothing like asking about a man's academic specialty. Matt perked up. "Sharon wanted the same lists. I sent her over to the Rockefeller Library. They've got ship's manifests, contracts—a very fine reference collection. Something specific you wanted to know?"

"Yeah. What did Sharon specifically want to know?"

"You're right—she and Tim are better at asking questions than answering them, but I do know she was trying to track down one particular woman who was born on the east coast of Scotland and shipped out from London. Whether she found the one she was looking for, I don't know—there were thousands. She wouldn't even tell me the name. I bet Jessica knows. Not that I'd ask."

Jean nodded understanding, and not just of Matt's reluctance to ask Jessica. Sharon was looking for the woman who had supposedly stolen the charm stone. Speaking of thieves. Speaking of sources, for that matter…

Her train of thought ran off the rails when Matt turned away and said, "Well, I've got to get back to the office. I saw you with the Dingbats and thought I'd just say hello."

And pump her about what they had said? She might as well pump him in return. She grabbed the sleeve of his jacket—tweed, like Tim's—and the wiry arm beneath. "Matt, did you know Wesley Hagedorn?"

"Yeah," he replied quickly. "Oh yeah. I missed Lockhart's 'tragic accident' announcement last night, didn't hear about Wes until Rachel mentioned it—kids, they think it's all a video game—Mom, now, she took it pretty hard."

"I'm sorry." Jean allowed him a moment of silence, then asked, "Wes made the replica Witch Box, didn't he?"

"Oh yeah," Matt said again, more slowly, and turned back around. His dark brows that contrasted with his hair, both cranial and facial, knotted over the bridge of his nose. "He was a good guy. A first-class craftsman. My mother owns a harpsichord he made."

"Is that the one in the picture in the magazine article?"

"With Jessica standing over him like a vulture? Yes. She and Rachel were at the cabinetmaker's shop checking out Mom's harpsichord. Mom never really liked Jessica, and vice versa, but they tried to get along—they still do—for Rachel's sake."

The ties that bind and strangle, Jean thought. "Wesley played the harpsichord, the article said. Your mother does, too?"

"What doesn't she do? Retired academic, musician, aerobics instructor, volunteer in a half-dozen different charities—all of which she's trying to organize to her own standards. She had a minor stroke a couple of years ago, but the only way that affected her was that she gave up smoking. Cold turkey. My father died in Vietnam when I was nine years old. Mom learned to be self-sufficient."

And you learned to do without a father. Jean remembered Alasdair's comment about Matt being trapped by three strong-minded women. No wonder the arm she still held quivered slightly, as though he was wound like a watch spring, ready to break free as soon as the tension was released.

She let him go. “Any speculation as to what happened to Wesley yesterday afternoon?”

“No. Not from me, anyway. You’re the one who’s into crime solving, now, you and your Scot.” His expression wavered between a frown at Wesley’s name, cutting the furrows in his face almost to the bone, and an asymmetrical smile, no doubt intended to let her know he wasn’t criticizing her. “Sorry, Jean, I’ve got to go. I’ve got classes, until the end of this semester, at least. Then it’s decision time—sell out or starve. Why don’t you stop by the office when you get a chance, get back in touch with your academic side?”

“Thanks. I’d like that.” Again she offered him a smile of mingled sympathy and rue.

His smile leveled out in response even as something both hunted and haunted lingered in his eyes. “Thank you,” he said.

“For what?”

“For understanding. You know, the divorce, the job.” With a firm *I’ll be all right* nod, he turned west toward the college. Jean considered his departing back—you could tell he was an academic, his shoulders were comfortably rounded from years spent in the gravitational pull of books and manuscripts—and then turned east toward the Historic Area.

It was time to compare notes with *her* Scot. Heck, it was time to organize her notes and perhaps try some word-association of her own. For one thing, someone other than Tim Dingwall had recently used the phrase “smoke and mirrors.”

She crossed Henry Street and headed up Duke of Gloucester, pulling her phone from her bag. She’d ask Alasdair to meet her at the churchyard for a daylight recce of last night's misdemeanor scene and to see what it actually said on Mason's tombstone. Then they could grab some lunch. Brain work should, by rights, use as many calories as legwork.

Her thumb on the keypad, she remembered that since his phone didn't work on this continent, he'd left it behind. Unlike Rebecca, Miranda, and Jean herself, until now he hadn't had a reason to get the equivalent of a universal translator.

No problem. She was already halfway to the church—a quick look and she'd catch up with him.

Assuming he was back at the house. Surely he'd exhausted the possibilities at the cabinetmaker's shop by now. Maybe he was strolling around the Historic Area, storing up questions to ask her about the history, the architecture, and the ghost stories. He was one of the most self-sufficient people she'd ever met, but self-sufficiency only went so far.

The sky was the color of Alasdair's eyes, ranging from clear blue overhead to hinting of gray cloud on the horizon. Despite the noonday sun, the air was cool, scented with woodsmoke, horses, and baking bread or cookies. Flanked by gleaming red and gold leaves, the long vista of the street narrowed into the distance and came to a point at the tidy, rational facade of the Capitol. Visitors ranged back and forth like single-celled creatures, combining, dividing, drifting away from the group to make solo stands in front of shop windows. An interpreter trotting along on horseback doffed his tricorn to the ladies whether they were wearing long skirts or tight jeans.

Jean skimmed along beside the brick wall separating the churchyard from Duke of Gloucester and into the gate at the side of the church. The Dingwalls hadn't been poking around the table tombs and monuments rising from the terrace outside the western doorway, the one beneath the bell tower. They'd taken their sample from a grass-covered grave protected by trees and shrubs at the far side of the enclosure.

The low railing was meant to discourage casual passersby from wandering off the paving. Still, an elderly man was taking notes at a monument several paces past it. She too, was on a mission. Jean lifted her foot to step over the rail.

From her bag burst "The 1812 Overture," that staple of July Fourth celebrations which had nothing to do with American Independence Day. Lowering her foot, Jean retrieved her phone and checked the screen. "Hey, Miranda."

Nearby, a siren whined and then stopped abruptly, timed just right to blank out Miranda's words. "Sorry, I didn't hear you," Jean said, and strained to look over the eastern wall. The sound had come from that direction, hadn't it?

"How are you getting on, Jean?" said her partner's voice, smooth as single malt.

"So far so good. The Dingwalls are weaving an awfully tangled web, and so far I can't say how much of it is fact and how much imagination. Or even who all is involved. There's Tim's sister Kelly, fresh from taking the rap at Blair Castle, there's Jessica Evesdottir, ex-Finch, who might have been working with Wesley Hagedorn and who was certainly working with Sharon Dingwall."

"Jessica and Sharon exchanged a few words last night, did they? Sorry to miss that, but then, Rodney and I had a lovely blether over a fine meal, if with the ghost of poor dead Wesley Hagedorn occupying a place at the table, like Banquo's ghost in *Macbeth*."

"What's Lockhart's take on the man's murder? And it was a murder."

"That it was. And here's Rodney, thinking there's something doing with the Witch Box, it being Wesley who studied the original at Blair and then made the replica."

"Alasdair already guessed that."

"Well done, Alasdair! I reckon he's not guessed, though, that Jessica was working with Wesley on the Witch Box project, oh aye, and more—they were by way of being a couple, if keeping it under wraps, so to speak, with her still being married and all."

"Oh boy. Speaking of tangled webs." Jean made a face. Did Matt's slow *oh yeah* mean that he knew about Jessica's attachment to Wesley? Who he called "Wes," familiarly. Matt would have found that an embarrassing triangle. Jessica might not. As for Wes, he wasn't going to be offering any opinions, not now.

Had Jessica known he was dead when she was lecturing Rachel about love and conquest? Or had it been a love affair at all, or merely a connection of convenience?

"...mind you," Miranda was saying in Jean's ear, "I was hearing this from the waiter who brought my breakfast this morning. If Rodney's knowing, he's not saying. Don't ask, don't tell."

"Jessica and Wesley got together at the Inn?" Expensive surroundings for a bit of afternoon delight—or an all-nighter, even. But Jean didn't need to tell that to Miranda, who was probably staying in the same suite the Queen of England had occupied for the Jamestown anniversary celebrations.

"That they did," said Miranda. "Eric the waiter, he knew Jessica from a luncheon speech about witchcraft—right interesting, he was saying, if hardly credible—and just now recognized Wesley from the photo in the newspaper. They tipped him very nicely when he delivered a meal to their room a few weeks back, so he was keeping an eye out for them."

Eric, Jean thought. And there she could have been pumping him for all sorts of information.

People were hurrying across Palace Green and down Nicholson Street, lured by the brief wail of the siren. What was going on?

Miranda said, "I've just phoned Rodney, asking him if the investigation's any further forward, but he's Historic Area Duty Officer the day, his folk are telling me, and he's left his office to go putting out some sort of fire."

"I bet I know where the fire is." Jean headed out the back gate of the churchyard, where she and Alasdair had confronted the Dingwalls, and across Palace Green.

"Eh?" asked Miranda.

With eighty-eight original buildings lit by open flames, fire was always a danger. But Jean smelled no smoke. She stopped beside the massive tree whose shadow had concealed Rachel last night. It was an oak, she saw now, its limbs writhing almost to the bare ground below and its canopy a vibrant rusty orange and gold. But she was more interested in the vista past the Tucker House, past the lawn behind the Court House, past the Randolph House.

"Jean?"

There, where the street dipped in front of the cabinetmaker's shop, the way was blocked by a clot of jacket-clad backs and jeans-clad bottoms. Beyond the kibitzers, lights pulsed, harsh against the autumn glow of the trees, as crude beside the period houses as a finger in the eye. "Great. Something's happening at the cabinetmaker's. Call you back."

"Oh aye, you do tha…" Miranda's voice evaporated as Jean thrust her phone into her bag and ran.

TWELVE

OKAY, SHE THOUGHT, the jar of her feet against the pavement shooting rationalizations through her mind, maybe one of the craftsmen had cut himself or dropped a chunk of wood on his foot.

The flashing lights couldn't have anything to do with Alasdair and his questions, could they?

Jean pushed her way through the onlookers, muttering apologies, to see two police cars, one belonging to the city of Williamsburg, the other to the Foundation. Her peripheral vision registered several other vehicles, including a horse and carriage driven by a liveried driver.

The central part of her vision recorded the burly, black-haired man, dressed in eighteenth-century shirt, apron, and breeches, who was climbing into the city squad car. Or rather, was being put into the car by two uniformed officers. He might not have been handcuffed, but he was obviously, in the British euphemism, helping the police with their enquiries. His scowling face was wedged into a thick neck above a broad chest puffed resentfully, indicating that he wasn't volunteering.

Samuel Gould, Wesley Hagedorn's apprentice.

Rodney Lockhart stood with Stephanie Venegas in the doorway of the cabinetmaker's shop, matching black suit for black suit, black gaze for black gaze. He gestured toward Gould, hand open, palm up. *What do you think you're doing?* She folded her arms and raised her chin. *My job. Get over it.*

On the graveled shoulder of the street, between one of the squad cars and the path leading down to the shop—between a hard place and a couple of rocks—stood Alasdair. His chin was tucked and his hands braced on his hips. His eyes no longer gleamed the peaceful blue of the sky, but were as crisp and cold as a glacier calving icebergs into a northern sea.

If Jean could read Lockhart and Venegas by their body language, she was downright telepathic when it came to Alasdair. Venegas had arrived to haul away Hagedorn's colleague. She'd found Alasdair there asking questions. She'd sent him outside and he'd gone quietly—there might not be honor between thieves, but there certainly was between law enforcers.

He had something to say. If necessary, he'd stand there until those icebergs drifted into the shipping lanes, but he was going to say it.

The squad car and its prisoner drove away down Nicholson Street and past the sleepy, spooky hollow where the eighteenth-century jail nestled in the trees. One of the security officers began shooing away the bystanders while the other muttered into a radio and was muttered back at. The stream that ran beneath one end of the shop burbled cheerfully.

Venegas made some conciliatory remark to Lockhart, who made some politic remark in return. With a wary handshake, they parted, him to the interior of the building, her through the gate of the shop and up the slope, her polished black flats grating on the gravel.

Alasdair blocked her path. She'd have better luck pushing through a stone wall, Jean thought. But Venegas didn't try to dodge around him. She had something to say, too. "You forced my hand, barging in here and asking so many questions. What if Gould had made a run for it?"

They would have stood nose-to-nose, except in her low-heeled shoes she was an inch the taller. Unimpressed, Alasdair pointed down the street toward the squad car decorously turning the corner onto Waller Street—the same route once taken by carts carrying the condemned to the gallows. "It does not follow from Gould finding Hagedorn's body that he murdered the man. Someone had to be finding the body."

Deja Déjà vu, thought Jean, inching forward. That's how she and Alasdair had met, when she'd been the someone. Even though there'd been more to it than that.

"There's more to it than a stramash over a missing chisel," Alasdair went on.

"A what?" Venegas demanded. Now it was her arms braced on her hips.

"An argument. I'll credit Gould making threats against Hagedorn three days since, and Hagedorn threatening to sack him, but the other craftsmen, they're saying the two reconciled, filled with brotherly love and all."

"There's more to it than that. Yeah. I get it. What do you know about it, Mr. Protect and Survive?"

"The theft of the replica Witch Box from Blair Castle is tied to Hagedorn's murder."

She did him the courtesy of not saying sarcastically, *Really?*

"Hagedorn visited Blair in May. He made photos and drawings. He returned here and made the replica. A week since, all his measurements, photos, plans, and all, were stolen from his flat."

Really? thought Jean. Coincidence? Or were the Dingwalls up for housebreaking and theft?

The onlookers were drifting away. The horses and carriage clopped by. One of the horses cocked its tail and made a steaming deposit on the asphalt, to the delight of a couple of little boys. Jean had to hand it to Williamsburg for letting the chips, so to speak, fall where they might, providing a lesson in why period domestic decor only included carpets in rooms without heavy foot traffic.

Jean dodged the kids, the pungent pile of authenticity, and one of the crowd-control cops. “Hey!” he called after her.

“I’m with him,” Jean returned, pointing at Alasdair. At his back, which was not as straight as that of a soldier on inspection, but as that of the regimental sergeant major who was making the inspection.

With a shrug, the cop desisted and Jean tiptoed closer.

“Yeah,” Venegas was saying, “Hagedorn reported the break-in. Thing is, there were some valuables taken, too.”

“A diversion.”

“Maybe. Maybe not.”

“Fingerprint evidence?”

“Inconclusive.”

“Things is,” said Alasdair, “whilst Hagedorn was not married, he was seeing someone, but his colleagues don’t know who. And his colleagues are thinking there was a break-up, a bad one, not so long since. Look for the woman, eh?”

Jean took another step forward. “He was seeing Matt Finch’s soon-to-be ex-wife, Jessica Evesdottir.”

Blue eyes and black turned toward her. Alasdair acknowledged Jean’s arrival, not to mention her information, with a quirk of his eyebrow and a crimp of his lip. After a quick but comprehensive glance, as though flipping through a database, Venegas ID’d her and demanded, “How do you know that?”

“Miranda,” Alasdair said.

“Yep,” Jean told him, and explained, “My partner at

Great Scot. A server at the Inn named Eric took a meal up to Wes and Jessica's room several weeks ago."

"Eric, at the Williamsburg Inn." The name inscribed itself in Venegas's mental notebook.

"The last few weeks," Alasdair went on, "Hagedorn was a changed man. Worried, the other craftsmen are saying. Nervy. Looking over his shoulder. The third man, not Gould, he's saying it seemed Hagedorn was under a spell. Or a curse."

"Yeah, right." Venegas's pink lips curled upward, but not in a smile. Her voice would have curdled milk.

There are various ways of being right, thought Jean.

Alasdair inhaled, perhaps to say the same thing, but Venegas cut him off. "Okay, I'll buy that you're investigating the theft of the replica. But by digging around here, you interfered with a murder investigation."

"You've had the post-mortem, then?" he asked, not wasting time refuting her charge.

"Wesley Hagedorn was struck twice at the base of the skull by a sharp-edged instrument about an inch wide. A woodcarving chisel, maybe, one used for roughing out designs. Wesley had a favorite, steel blade, wooden knob, about a foot long. He kept it sharp. He accused Sam Gould of losing it. Or stealing it. That's when they argued. It's still missing, you know."

"I know. The lads inside, they told me."

She glanced back at the shop, where Lockhart was placing a *Closed* sign on the door with one hand and holding his cell phone to his ear with the other. "Then he fell or was pushed into the water. His assailant held him down, probably by kneeling on his shoulders and pressing his face into the mud and water until he drowned. Gould's big enough to do that, easily."

"Were the lads in the shop not showing you Hagedorn's coat hanging behind the door? He was no bigger than—you."

Alasdair could edit his words, Jean told herself, but Venegas had no doubt noticed his modest physical stature. And his mental acuity.

"I've got the M.E.'s measurements, thank you. And yes, before you say it, I realize that once you jab a sharp instrument into someone's neck, size stops being an issue. The assault laid him out, and he was drowned in Dunwich Pond—a few hundred yards behind his apartment complex."

Dunwich? Jean repeated silently. That, too, rang a bell. By now there was a veritable handbell choir clanging away in her memory. One of these days she might find a minute or two to listen to it.

"He wouldn't have walked there with a stranger," Venegas was saying, "not when he was so nervous. And it was Gould who offered to give him a ride to the reception. Which he hadn't yet dressed for, by the way, although his suit and tie were laid out on his bed and his invitation was sitting on his dresser. He died a couple of hours before he was found, probably, about four P.M."

"Were there—?" Alasdair began.

She rode right over him. "No one saw Hagedorn leave his apartment. No one saw him walk down to the pond, with or without a companion. The area's surrounded by trees and underbrush. Site of a seventeenth-century farmyard, the locals say. We found some empty beer cans, but it's not a high-crime spot, no drug deals or that kind of thing. That we know of."

"Just a murder," said Jean, and when the two sets of eyes turned toward her again, asked, "If Gould didn't walk down to the pond with Wesley, how did he know to look for him there?"

"Exactly," Venegas said to Alasdair, not Jean.

He acknowledged that point with a nod. "You've not found the weapon, then, if you're guessing it was Hagedorn's own chisel. Are you dredging the pond for it? Were there footprints in the mud or water plants trodden upon? What about—?"

"Okay, that's it." She made a slashing gesture—three strikes, you're out. "Let me remind you, Cameron, that you don't have one lick of jurisdiction here. You're not even a cop."

Yeah, Jean thought, *slip that one, both of them, between his ribs, why don't you?*

His eyes narrowed and his lips thinned. In a voice as dry and cold as sleet pellets against a frosty window, he said, "I am a cop. I was. I've only just retired from the Northern Constabulary CID with the rank of Detective Chief Inspector."

"Is that so?" Venegas shifted her weight backward.

"I apologize for upsetting your plans by asking questions at the shop. But you were saying yourself, my brief is investigating the theft of the replica Witch Box. I didn't know you'd staked out the man Gould, did I?"

"The theft happened in the U.K.," Venegas protested, but her voice was no longer as sour.

So they'd come back around to that. Time to step on the merry-go-round. "I've got some new information about that," Jean said, not bothering with the ingratiating smile.

"Eh?" asked Alasdair.

"Huh?" Venegas inquired.

Several harried-looking adults herded a group of children dressed in Halloween costumes up the street. Several of the superheroes and more than one Disney princess were carrying plastic muskets almost as tall as they were, "firing" merrily away at squirrels, birds, and imaginary British troops, all with the appropriate sound effects. Alasdair glanced at them, shuddered, then looked back at the two women, pretending he hadn't seen a thing.

"I just came from interviewing Tim and Sharon Dingwall," Jean said. "They..."

"Who?" asked Venegas.

Now that she was the undistracted target of those obsidian eyes, Jean had to stop herself from taking a couple of steps back. She drew herself up to her full height, such as it was, stood her ground the way Alasdair had, and responded first with the abstract. "They're conspiracy theorists, who, among a lot of other theories, believe the charm stone that was once attached to the Witch Box is somehow the key to finding Francis Bacon's mythical papers."

"More Francis Bacon nutcases? Jesus Christ!" Venegas half-turned away.

"Oh aye," said Alasdair. "I caught them digging in the churchyard last night."

"Taking a core sample, they say," Jean added.

"I sent them away with fleas in their ears, or so I'm hoping. No worries, I reported them."

"Ah," said Venegas, turning a quarter back again.

Jean plunged on into the specifics. Jessica and Sharon working together and then falling out. The photos in the envelopes. Tim saying the copy wasn't a good one. Kelly's phone calls and her lie to the Perthshire police, along with her comment about "playing the patsy." "It can mean that Kelly deliberately took the blame," she translated for Alasdair.

"It means 'fall guy.'" By now Venegas was turned fully back around and leaning forward, eagerly rather than aggressively, almost close enough to close the third side of a triangle of personal space.

"Well then, Kelly was involved after all." Alasdair's eyes lit with satisfaction. "Who was by way of being her confederate?"

"I bet it was Quentin Dingwall," Jean said. "Dylan's brother. He's working for the *Sunburn* in London. Can you get Ian to see if he was at Blair at the time of the theft?"

"Perthshire Constabulary is saying the CCTV records from Blair don't show the actual theft, but might be showing if Quentin was there at all. If we had a photo—"

"He and Dylan are twins. So if Dylan has that bright red hair—"

"Then so might Quentin have. I'll phone Ian—"

"Time out!" said Venegas. And, lowering her voice, "You mean these Dingwalls might be connected to Wesley Hagedorn's death?"

"So might the theft of the replica," Alasdair told her, with the merest trace of a smile. "I've got my second in Edinburgh collecting data. I'll be letting you know—"

Jean scrounged in her bag and produced her cell phone. "No time like the present. Use my phone already." She pressed it into his hand.

"Right." Alasdair turned away, his fingertips playing the keypad. "Eh, Ian. Alasdair here. There's been a wee bit of a turn-up..."

Jean looked up the street, Venegas down. A helicopter clattered far overhead, this one military. A chill gust of wind rustled the leaves of the nearby trees and flapped Jean's jacket. The gray clouds were no longer a hint on the horizon, but flocked up the dome of the sky like dirty sheep.

"She did, did she?" Alasdair darted a look at Venegas. She pretended she didn't notice, although tightening her arms across her chest, like a protective cuirass, gave her away.

Jean eyed the detective's sleek black hair, cut high over her ears. Her lobes were pierced, but she wasn't wearing earrings. She wasn't wearing any jewelry at all, not even a wedding ring. If Venegas was Williamsburg's finest, Jean asked herself, then what was she? America's exile?

Two strong-minded women. And yet Alasdair wasn't cornered. He could always find a bolt hole.

"Right." He switched off the phone and thrust it toward Jean without looking at her. She almost fumbled the hand-off and for a moment thought she was going to bat her phone across the street. "Detective Venegas, Ian's saying you rang him asking if I was who I was claiming to be, asking if Protect and Survive was actually here."

"What?" demanded Jean, jamming her phone back into her bag. Alasdair made a subtle *down, girl* gesture. Okay, she got the message—Venegas was a good cop, cut her some slack.

"I needed to make sure I knew who was throwing a monkey wrench into my investigation, and whether the two cases really are connected." Venegas wasn't looking at Jean, either. Jean could almost hear the sizzle, water droplets on hot iron, as blue gaze and black clashed.

"Throwing a monkey wrench?" Alasdair asked.

"A spanner," murmured Jean. "The one in the works."

Alasdair went on, smooth as ice. "Our cases are connected, right enough. Ian's confirmed that Wesley Hagedorn spent almost a week at Blair Castle, studying the Witch Box. And he was not on his own. An American woman named Jessica—fits the description a treat—arrived with him, then went traveling off to the east coast and to London, she was telling the folk at Blair, doing research."

Jean heard bells clanging. The east coast of Scotland, where Sharon's indentured maidservant had supposedly been born. The one who maybe stole the charm stone. No way did Jessica believe all the implications of that story. But she was sure onto something.

Smoke and mirrors. That's what the academics at the tavern last night had called Jessica's new original source. The one that was supposed to increase her stature in the jungles of Academe. Rats, Jean thought, she should have pursued that issue with Matt. What if Jessica's source…?

"Thank you," Venegas was saying. "I see we'll be talking to Ms.—what was her name again?"

"Evesdottir," said Jean, slamming a padded door on the clangor of the bell choir. "She changed it as a feminist statement."

"You're not kidding, are you?"

"Neither is she." Jean acknowledged Venegas's incredulous, almost offended, expression with a slight shrug. A shame she couldn't eavesdrop on Venegas's interview with Jessica. Who would be better able to comment on gender roles than a female police detective?

"I've got Ian onto both Perthshire Constabulary and the *Sunburn,* following up on Quentin. I'll be keeping you informed, eh? I promise not to go teaching your grandmother to suck eggs," Alasdair added, smiling, if thinly as the blade of his *sgian dubh.*

"Say what?"

"I'll not go telling you your own business."

The black eyes flashed. Then Venegas actually laughed, a cool chuckle that softened her mouth just enough to reveal a row of white teeth like ivory beads on a string. "Can the two of you come down to the station? I want to hear about these Dingwalls, Ms. Fairbairn."

"You remember my name?" Jean asked.

"She was asking Ian about you as well," said Alasdair.

Unrepentant, Venegas pulled a couple of business cards from her pocket and handed them over. "Here's where we are. You have a car, right? See you in a few minutes." Without waiting for an answer, she turned like a soldier on parade and strode toward the waiting police car. Another chill wind, perhaps the one blowing no one any good, made dried leaves dance down the street.

Alasdair considered the card, then his new colleague making her exit. They were on the same page now, but Jean wasn't going to accept any kudos as facilitator. Alasdair was simply the Brit who was in the right place at the right time. "So the game is afoot. You think she has the wrong man, don't you?"

"My gut's telling me she does." He pocketed the card, and marched away in the direction of Market Square and the path back to their house. Or to the parking lot, rather. So much for the leisurely lunch, comparison of notes, and confirmation of the evening's activities. "Jessica needs checking out, no doubt about that, and the Dingwalls, and Matt Finch as well," he said, without looking around to make sure Jean was behind him.

She was wearing flats now. She was beside him. "Matt?" she repeated. And with a gaseous wobble of her by now empty stomach, she thought, *The ties that bind and strangle.* Matt and Wesley had known each other. Wesley had an affair, however brief, with Jessica. Many a murder had been committed because of jealousy.

Not Matt, her own gut said. He was a decent guy, if a troubled one. Not that she really knew him.

Once upon a time she'd pegged Alasdair as a decent if troubled guy, but she really hadn't known him, either. And now look where they were. "Yeah," she said to his patient smile, wider than a blade but just as sharp. "Yeah. You have to check out Matt."

"Jessica's choosing men she can dominate, isn't she now? Mind what she was telling Rachel, about love not conquering all, about the woman being conquered? His mates were saying Hagedorn was soft-spoken, aiming to please, save when it came to his work, his designs, his tools, and the like. And then there's Matt."

"An academic like me. An easy conquest." Her words came out more sourly, not to mention surly, than she'd intended.

She felt rather than saw Alasdair's edged glance. "No one's conquering here, lass" was all he replied.

They crossed the grass between the white clapboard of Chowning's Tavern and the worn red brick of the Courthouse, skirted the pillory where Rachel had playfully trapped Dylan, then hurried across Duke of Gloucester Street toward the Magazine.

Surrendering to the inevitable, Jean groped in her bag with her free hand and found her car keys. But her stomach still wobbled with a hint of motion sickness, a touch of indigestion, a lingering sense of unease, all settling down into her abdomen like the upper plank of the pillory settling onto her wrists.

THIRTEEN

JEAN USED HER fork to sweep a few remaining cornbread crumbs around the rimmed pewter plate, mopping up the last of her Brunswick stew. *Delicious.*

"Tastier than stuff out of the vending machine at the police station, right?" asked Rebecca from across the table.

"No kidding. A package of crackers, a bag of cookies, and a can of diet soda hardly count as food. I thought I was trying to digest musket balls."

"And here's me, asking for a cup of tea. Looked like warm piss and probably tasted like it as well. This, though…" Alasdair drained his glass of dark ale and smiled the smile of a man who'd had a productive day. Law enforcement was hungry work. Butting heads with Venegas was, too. He'd consumed his plate of pulled-pork barbecue with excellent appetite.

Michael grinned, not at Alasdair but at the two women. "Americans have not been brewing proper cups of tea since they threw the lot off a ship in Boston Harbor."

"No argument there," Rebecca told him.

Jean leaned back against the wooden bench, the settle, her half of the booth set against the side wall of Chowning's Tavern. Now, after nightfall, Chowning's was as dim as Campbell's had been the night before, lit only by the subtle gleam of candlelight on glass, brass, and pewter. The darkness concealed any slips between plate and lip as well as replicating the feel of a genuine colonial tavern, although a genuine tavern in the colonial era would have smelled of things a lot less pleasant than food duly inspected and passed by various health agencies.

Tonight the next table was occupied not by a couple of waspish academics but by a family, a little girl in a mob-cap and two older boys in tricorn hats, their parents trying to keep them at least quiet if not exactly seated. Jean had once been that little girl, imitating her brothers and trying to differentiate herself from them at the same time. She lifted her glass to the child, wishing her well, and drank.

The mild but fragrant lager filled her mouth, warmed her throat, and committed delightful indiscretions with the food in her stomach. Everything was okay, she told herself. Thanks to her notebook, she'd re-created her interview with the Dingwalls, from the soup of Francis Stewart through the main course of Francis Bacon, down to—well, Tim and Sharon were the nuts themselves, more or less. Venegas had interjected tart remarks and tarter disclaimers, and then had ejected Jean herself to the lobby, the vending machines, and Miranda on the other end of the cell phone, while she and Alasdair questioned Sam Gould.

There had been a murder, yes, but the investigation was well in hand. In Detective Venegas's hands, with Alasdair doing only the light lifting. Jean told herself that her earlier unease had meant as little as the elusive ghostly presence at their house, a simple—okay, a complex—emotional resonance from the past. And yet… "The past hasn't died. It's not even critically ill. Williamsburg being a case in point." *And us.* In the gloom beneath the table, Jean pressed her knee against Alasdair's. With a sideways glint so quick she couldn't tell whether he was amused or bemused, he pressed back.

"And us," said Michael, "cursed with a sixth sense. So the bogles are moving things about your wee house, are they? We've seen that one before." He shared a glance with

Rebecca redolent of old misunderstandings and threadbare fears. How easily the Campbell-Reids interacted after several years of marriage, Jean thought. Not like two carriage horses yoked together but like a dance team, sometimes moving as one, sometimes proceeding separately.

"I've not seen anything moving myself," said Alasdair. "When we ran into the house late this afternoon, the bottle was sitting in its place, never mind it might well have been dancing a Highland fling two minutes earlier. But moving objects is the sort of tale I'm hearing from P and S properties, though like as not most are covering up folk losing objects or even nicking them."

"Speaking of crimes," Rebecca said, "how did Samuel Gould hold up under questioning?"

"Same as when I was talking to him at the cabinetmaker's shop. Resentful and uncomfortable, aye, but no sweating, no squirming, and no contradicting himself. He went looking for Hagedorn at the pond because he and his mates knew Hagedorn liked mooching about the old farmyard, watching the birds and working on small objects. He's agreeing that Hagedorn was worried and nervous, but no one's knowing why."

"He could be saying that to divert suspicion," said Jean.

"Aye, but assuming Hagedorn died at four P.M., as the medical examiner is reckoning, Gould's by way of having an alibi. Mind you, I was hardly in charge of the interview. Detective Venegas, she offered me a seat on the bus, but I was obliged to take one in the back."

"You were expecting anything else?" asked Michael.

"Not a bit of it," Alasdair said, showing little discomfort and less resentment. "A detective's obliged to do what a detective's obliged to do."

Just as Jean was wondering whether he was referring to himself or Venegas, a flash of light caught her in the corner of the eye. She turned toward the window at her side, but saw only her own face reflected dimly between the broad wooden slats of the blind, as though she was in jail.

It was Sam Gould who was in jail, if only overnight, while Venegas and her minions checked out his story. His alibi. By tomorrow morning she'd be agreeing with Alasdair that the case was more complicated than it first appeared, that the issues were greater than a missing chisel. Or even a missing replica. Although Jean was pretty sure Hagedorn hadn't been cursed, at least, not more than metaphorically. But something had happened to threaten him. Surely the break-up with Jessica wasn't it, despite Alasdair's rather smug *Look for the woman.*

Blinking, her eyes resolved the scene outside the window. Leaves and even tree-lamps thrashed in a cold wind, making the shadows gutter as fiercely as the flames in a couple of fire baskets in front of the Magazine. Even the candlelight in the windows of the Courthouse wavered gently, as though to a slow heartbeat.

A tour group walking through Market Square had apparently collided with a tour group walking up Duke of Gloucester Street and were now sorting themselves out. The wind whirled away their shouts and laughs. The lanterns and flashlights wielded by the guides shot beams of light in all directions but failed to illuminate the dark night beneath a sky lidded with cloud.

Jean turned away from the window and its chill aura, back into the room that was cheerful despite its dimness. With her tongue she dug a shred of chicken from between two molars, then, realizing her grimace could be construed as editorial comment on detectives and detection, smoothed her features and changed the subject.

"I was going to ask Jessica about witch bottles tonight. A shame the lecture was canceled. Thanks for calling to tell me, Rebecca. We would have broken our necks getting to the Museum auditorium by five. And I'm not sure we could have waited until after the concert for dinner. We'd have been eating our programs."

"No problem," said Rebecca. "I'm just glad I called to check on the time. They didn't say whether she'd been nicked by the police, just that someone performing in the witch trial tonight had fallen ill, and since Jessica wrote the script she was conscripted…"

Michael snorted. Alasdair grinned.

"…to play a part."

"Which part?" asked Jean. "Not Mary Napier herself?"

"No, one of the people she supposedly cursed."

"Witchcraft is like conspiracy theory," said Jean. "It's a way of explaining why things happen. Of finding a scape-goat. It's not chance, it's not coincidence, it's not even synchrony. It's enemy action."

"And the best defense is offense," Rebecca concluded.

Alasdair provided a coda. "Or making the assumption we've got free will."

"Amen to that," said Michael.

The waiter arrived to clear away their dishes. "Dessert? Another drink?"

Jean had already rejected such exotic concoctions as the Witches' Revenge, a blend of light and dark rums, apricot brandy, and pineapple juice, figuring she'd need a dose of insulin as a chaser. And one lager was enough. If wine went to her knees, then beer went to her cheeks, and right now her face was so hot she was sure she looked like Rudolph's nose—you could even say it glowed.

It didn't seem appropriate to turn up for a concert in the church, let alone meet Miranda there, so obviously under the influence. Miranda was no teetotaler, but she'd never exhibit poor enough taste to get tipsy.

They were refusing further food and drink and requesting their bills when the sound of a guitar came from the front hall of the tavern. “Ah,” said Alasdair. “Hugh’s arrived.”

Sure enough, Hugh made his entrance, dressed in knee breeches and a shirt not just cut voluminously, but voluming out over his Santa Claus belly. Hoisting his guitar, he began to play and sing a contemporary version of “Allison Gross, the Ugliest Witch in the North Country.”

“I’ve always felt sorry for Allison Gross,” said Rebecca. “There she is, trying to seduce a handsome young guy, but he acts like she’s a slime slug.”

“No surprise it ends badly,” Jean added, “when she exercises her prerogative as a woman scorned and turns him into a worm.”

“Not a newt?” asked Michael with a grin.

“Newts have feet. She was wanting a creature that could not escape her clutches.” Alasdair’s wink at Jean conveyed the message *just kidding.*

A shame, Jean thought, he felt he needed to annotate his joke. She didn’t weigh in with the difference between “worm” and “wyrm,” or fire-breathing, maiden-devouring dragon.

By the end of the song Hugh had reached the far side of the room. He bowed to Jean and her cohorts’ enthusiastic applause.

Alasdair asked him, “This is you taking things easy, is it?”

“That it is.” Hugh’s cheeks were polished by the brewmaster’s skills as well, and behind his glasses, his eyes radiated good cheer and keen intelligence. “Who were your friends outside the theater this afternoon, Jean? Like Jack Sprat and his wife, though the other way round.”

“Tim and Sharon Dingwall, conspiracy theorists. They’re

after the charm stone that was on the Witch Box, which will, through a presumably non-magical process, prove that some great conspiracy is the driving force of history. I'm doing an article on them."

"Have a care, then. Tim's spit in the form of a woman was infesting my flight from Edinburgh. Aiming for the Dunmore exhibit as well, like as not."

"That was Tim's sister Kelly," Jean stated, as beside her Alasdair sat to attention. "No wonder he and Sharon asked me who you were and why you were in Edinburgh. You must have gotten an earlier flight from Newark to Richmond than she did."

"Oh aye, I barely caught the plane and worried all the while that my instruments had not."

"You spoke with Kelly?" asked Alasdair.

"No, thanks to all that's merciful. When she was not harassing the air hostess, she was poncing to and fro handing about brochures promoting a film, so far as I could tell with a pillow over my head. Voice like a foghorn, that woman, and not lacking opinions."

"Thanks, Hugh. Funny, Tim and Sharon said the film wasn't finished yet."

"Not according to Kelly. My ears are still ringing. And after playing for some years next to a set of bagpipes in full throat, that's saying something." Hugh turned to the next table, beamed at the children, and started a bouncy ditty about a red yo-yo with a wee yellow string. Which had political implications over and beyond a missing yo-yo, but the children and their parents, blissfully uninformed, simply clapped along.

"Well then," said Alasdair. "Here's hoping Kelly dropped a hint or three as to the whereabouts of the replica. Or why she and Quentin nicked it to begin with."

"Maybe Tim and Sharon wanted to do a compare and contrast," Rebecca offered. "The question is, why?"

"Venegas looked them out at the Woodlands, behind the Visitor Center, but they'd not answered the phone by the time we came away from the police station. Nor had Dylan, come to that. I reckon they all went away to Richmond to collect Kelly. I'll be having a word or two with her." Alasdair's humorless smile gave warning—anyone who lied to the constabulary, any constabulary, was on his hit list.

This time Jean's grimace really was a comment. "Interviewing the Dingwalls was like watching a kaleidoscope, except their perfectly genuine little pieces don't actually make a pattern. They conflate, pick, choose—they don't distinguish between fact and what Alasdair would call opinion and what I would call interpretation flavored with one's own biases."

"Yet they've got real evidence about the charm stone?" Michael asked.

"It's mostly smoke and mirrors, but not all. Once you get past the Bacon bits—" she only realized what she'd said when everyone groaned "—there's provenance for the Witch Box, and some charm stones are still extant, and I assume Robert Mason actually existed, as Francis Stewart and Charlotte Murray certainly did. And, well, speaking of conflating, if Tim and Sharon have an actual source for the story about the servant stealing the charm stone, and Sharon was working with Jessica, and Jessica's claiming to have a new source, what if they're quarreling over the same one? A letter, another inventory, something?"

"Why did they fall out? Over who gets to do the dog and pony show with it?" Rebecca was an old hand at academic infighting.

So was Michael. "There's likely more to it than that, with the lawsuit and all."

"Sure there is. I was talking to Matt—he happened to be at the Cheese Shop, too—but didn't know enough then to ask him about it. I will tomorrow. Plus I want to find out the name of that servant, already." Jean shook her head. The dang handbell choir was still dinging away in her mental back room. Fine. She liked to do research. "I hate to say this, but it looks like Tim, Sharon, and Kelly—and maybe the sons, too—are up to some sort of, well, not cover-up per se. A secret plot or plan."

"A plan to make money," said Alasdair, "never mind the bit about working *pro bono*."

"Well, yes, considering how much time, energy, and money they've invested in their work. But I still think they're basically crusaders. Reformers. Rebels without a clue."

Alasdair, Michael, and Rebecca laughed in agreement just as the waiter appeared at the end of the table with the bills.

A sudden chill breath from the window drew goose-flesh from Jean's arm and shoulder and felt icy against her face. Again she looked out through the bars. Venegas's jail was much nicer than the one where Mary Napier had languished in 1685. That one wasn't even here—it was at Jamestown—the farming settlement called Middle Plantation wasn't formally transformed into Williamsburg, the capital of the colony, until 1699.

Hagedorn's Dunwich Pond had been a seventeenth-century farmyard, Venegas had said. Something about the name, Dunwich—what had Jessica said, way back when, in her lecture about the artifacts of witchcraft? Sociological artifacts. Witch boxes and charm stone. Plays about Mary Napier.

Hugh was joking with a table of young men about the title of the folk song "When She Came Ben She Bobbit," about a maidservant coming into the room and bobbing a curtsey. A servant from eastern Scotland. Francis Stewart's coven in Berwick, in eastern Scotland. A woman named Napier accused of witchcraft…

"Earth to Jean," said Rebecca's voice.

Jean collected her thoughts, pinned them firmly to a backing, labeled them, and closed a glass lid on them. They'd keep. "Coming." She accepted Alasdair's hand to slide off the bench and put on her coat, replying to the quizzical tilt of his head with a shrug.

The shadows were hardly thicker outside the tavern than within, but they were a lot colder. People dressed in the clothing of two different eras huddled around a fire built on the shoulder of the street. The wind whined past the corner of the tavern, adding an eerie undertone to the voices of the people spilling down the steps of the Courthouse toward the post and the pillory.

"They're having the last act of 'A Matter of Witchcraft' out here," Rebecca said. "I read up on it while Linda was napping this morning."

"We've had good timing, then," said Alasdair.

The two couples jockeyed for position behind the ticket-buying customers, ending up on the grassy area between the back of the Courthouse and Chowning's darkened garden. Jean looked over her shoulder at the hulking shapes of the houses and trees along Nicholson Street. A solitary custodian trundled his or her cart past the Randolph House, any sound of footsteps or wheels muffled. The sky was a starless, charcoal gray.

The light, Jean told herself, drove away the shadow. It wasn't that the shadow threatened to engulf the light. Still, she stepped close to Alasdair's side and he wrapped his arm around her. Her hair blew into her face and she scooped it back. The warmth drained from her cheeks.

Several interpreters-cum-actors, wearing the broad collars of the 1680s, started down the steps of the Courthouse. Jean craned her neck but didn't recognize Jessica among the women.

A solidly built man wearing a long coat, a brimmed hat, and a scowl, grasped the arm of a young woman wearing a modest apron around her slender waist and a cap over draggling strands of blond hair. How old had Mary Napier been? Jean wondered. Quite young, if this portrayal was accurate. So much for the perception that only old hags were accused of witchcraft.

From the top of the steps, an official in frock coat and wig began speaking, and the crowd fell silent. "Mary Napier is accused of enchantment, charm, witchcraft, or conjuration to tell where Treasure may be found and to prevent the rightful owners of said Treasure from reclaiming it to their own use by inflicting illness and dearth upon them."

"They're hitting on all cylinders there," whispered Jean to Alasdair—Michael and Rebecca had been absorbed into the crowd of spectators. "She's not only making her victims sick, she's also depriving them of Treasure, however that was defined. Cows? Corn? Coins?"

"After all due testing, questioning, and testimony, it is the opinion of this court that the said Mary is guilty of what is laid to her charge, and it is therefore ordered that the Sheriff take her and carry her to the common pillory, there to reside until such time as she may repent of her misdeeds."

The "sheriff" hustled "Mary" toward the pillory, the crowd parting on either side. She walked with her head bowed, exhausted from her ordeal. Several voices called, "Burn the witch!" and "It's a fair cop!" knowing their Monty Python better than their history—no witches were ever burned in the American colonies and only one was ever hanged in Virginia, and that was without benefit of trial. The colonies had always taken a more practical view of charges of witchcraft than the parent countries in Europe. Even the frenzy in Salem, Massachusetts, had been brief, although knowing that would have brought its victims little consolation.

At the last moment, Mary shied way from the pillory, turned her pale face to the light, and began a quavering speech of repentance. It hardly mattered whether she'd actually committed any crimes, if confessing to them would get her off the hook.

Never mind the antique pronunciation of the words, Mary's voice was a nasal sine wave. Rachel Finch. Jean hadn't recognized her without the cosmetics.

The chill of the grass oozed upward through Jean's shoes. And something else oozed down the back of her neck, just the briefest rill of psychic ice water. But that was enough to draw a shudder rippling through her body.

"Cold?" asked Alasdair in her ear. "Or is it—wait, there's something..."

As one, they turned and took several steps toward Nicholson Street, along the broken-shell path that cut the expanse of grass like a pallid ribbon tying a dark package. Something glinted in an upstairs window of the Randolph House, a candle flame flaring and then dying, perhaps. Or perhaps the light of the fire baskets had been caught by a pair of eyes, eyes that looked quickly out into Market Square and then vanished back into another dimension.

"It's gone," Alasdair said, his words leaving his lips in a wraith of warm breath.

"Yeah." Jean rotated her shoulders, then, having inadvertently shrugged off his arm, crunched several more steps away from him, the crowd, and Mary/Rachel's tearful testimony. Most people, she thought, would walk away from a haunted house, not toward it. But most people let fear—or common sense—conquer curiosity.

The wind, scented with smoke, earth, animals, tossed the leaves of the enormous tree across from the Tucker House. In the darkness beneath its canopy, something glinted. Something quite corporeal, Jean told herself, testing her neck and shoulders for extrasensory data and finding none. As she stepped off the path and across the carpet of grass, a very different kind of unease pricked her shoulder blades.

"Jean?" Alasdair came up beside her. "What… Ah."

A long bundle hung from one of the lower branches of the tree, swinging gently back and forth, dappled in shadow and silence. At its top, a pale splotch like a moon in eclipse waxed and waned as the bundle turned.

Her lips were cold. She could hardly form words. "Someone's hung a dummy from the tree, a joke about the witch trial, a Halloween prank, something."

Alasdair was already striding forward. Jean had to force her suddenly heavy feet to lift, lower, and follow.

He stepped onto the bare earth beneath the heavy branches. His large, capable hands halted the swing of the bundle. The brown, fabric-wrapped bundle.

A backless leather shoe lay on the ground a half-inch below a sock-clad foot and bony white ankle. A glint of orange-tinted light was the metal case of a cell phone, clutched in a hand like a blanched talon. The face below a tumble of dun-colored curls was suffused crimson, contorted into a gargoyle's leer. The huge eyes bulged between half-closed lids, shot with red, filmy, dull, sightless.

Between collarbones sharp as knives and a pointed chin, a rope encircled a scrawny neck mottled red and purple. The rope stretched over a low branch, a taut diagonal leading from shadow into gloom. For a long breathless minute the wind faded, the voices from the Courthouse weakened, and Jean heard only the creak of that rope as the body suspended from it twisted in the wind.

The body. The very dead, past all hope of revival, body.

Then, over the rush of her own blood, she heard Alasdair's hoarse voice. "Your mobile, Jean. Give me your mobile."

Numbly, dumbly, she reached into her bag, pulled out her phone, flipped it open. The sudden flare of light illuminated Alasdair's taut face, thinned lips, bleak eyes.

Jean looked back up at Sharon Dingwall's body, and the only words that coalesced from the careering kaleidoscope of her thoughts were: *I'm sorry.*

FOURTEEN

JEAN STUMBLED AWAY from the tree, the hanging tree, the horror, onto the lawn. It stretched like the dark pall covering a coffin toward the buildings and their lighted windows. No matter how dimly lit, the windows and the rooms within were brighter and warmer than this wilderness. And as unattainable as the surface of the moon.

Bowing her head, Jean covered her face with her hands. She realized her shoulders were shaking, the cold night penetrating to her bones. But even then she wasn't as cold as Sharon.

Or was Sharon cold? She couldn't have been hanging very long—the murderer had hauled her up into the tree—how had he managed to do that without her shrieking—well, someone choking didn't have much breath to shriek.

Through the rushing in her head and the pounding in her ears, Jean heard Alasdair, sharp as an icicle. "...the tree at the corner of Nicholson and the Palace Green, between the Courthouse and the Tucker House. I'm telling you, this is no prank. Aye, I'm certain she'd dead. No, I've not touched anything."

Applause echoed from the Courthouse. A strain of music coiled down the wind. The show was over, and the show was going on.

"Jean? Alasdair?"

She knew that voice. Rebecca.

Behind her the cell phone chirped again. He was making

another call. Stern as stone, he said, "Stephanie? Alasdair. There's been another murder."

Several people strolled laughing and chatting down the path toward Nicholson Street. Two more materialized from the fireshot gloom in front of Jean. "What's that… Oh my God." Rebecca reeled back, her hand over her mouth.

Michael caught her from behind. "Who is it?"

"Sharon Dingwall." Jean hardly recognized the thin tight sound, like the warm-up vocalization of a banshee, as her own voice. The lager that had been so tasty going down now bubbled up in her throat, a foul, frigid acid, and she gulped. The acid drained through her stomach, down her limbs, and out her toes. Nowhere to go, nowhere to hide.

With a jittery, impatient dance step, she turned back toward the tree. Alasdair was standing there all alone. She had somewhere to go, to him.

What she thought was his shadow moved independently, gliding away from the darkness beneath the thick tentacled branches of the tree. A slender figure in pants, either a man or a woman, with something square beneath its arm. "Hey!" Jean croaked, then swallowed and tried again, this time achieving a shrill cry of "Hey, you, stop!" that was imitated and then expanded upon by the distant wail of a siren.

Alasdair whirled around. "Here! What's this?"

But the figure had already broken into a run, long limbs rising and falling like pistons, carrying him/her through the lamplight at the end of Nicholson—red hair flared—and back into darkness, around the corner onto the blacktopped road edging Palace Green.

Dylan Dingwall. It had to be. And he was carrying his mother's tote bag with the plans and the photos of the Witch Box, plans and photos that might have been stolen from Wesley's apartment.

Galvanized, Jean pitched her mini-backpack to Rebecca

and leaped forward. He was a witness, maybe even the killer—matricide happened outside of Greek tragedy. Catching him was something she could do. Feet up, feet down—cold air warming in her chest—her hands clenched at her sides. Move, breathe, move. The soft grass beneath her shoes gave way to graveled asphalt. She skidded, caught herself, pounded on past the intersection.

"Jean!" shouted Alasdair. Another siren blended with the first. Footsteps thumped behind her. A woman screamed—it had only been a matter of time before someone else leaving the Courthouse saw the coda to the play.

Geez, Dylan was fast, or she was slow, or both—where did he—there he was, vaulting the fence in front of the Brush-Everard House. For just a moment the shape was a supple blur against the pale, painted clapboards. Then it vanished into the thick shadow between the house and its outbuildings.

A gate in the fence—Jean fumbled for the latch, found it, opened the gate, and hurled herself through. Behind her the gate swung shut again with a crash. She sensed brick beneath her feet, and walls looming on either side, and darkened windows, her own shape a ghostly movement in the warped old glass.

A scramble ahead of her, a clank, and the crash of another gate shutting. Aha, he'd gone through this one instead of over.

There was the fence, gray pickets in a row, and beyond that billow upon billow of looming blackness like curdled thunderclouds. Jean dredged her memory—she'd been through here on a garden tour—those were massive, ancient boxwoods, shrubs that in the formal garden behind the Governor's Palace were carved, with fingernail scissors, no doubt, into decorative hedges. Here the bushes had run riot, growing into heaping hulks of shadow straining against the fence that surrounded them.

Dylan had gone in there. She heard him pushing along the overgrown path, branches scraping.

Footsteps closed on her from behind and a ragged breath made the skin on her neck crawl. Spinning around, she collided with a tall, lanky body. He'd circled around, he'd trapped her between the house and the fence. She struck out, but her blow was absorbed by a padded coat.

Hands seized her shoulders and a breath scented with ale bathed her face. "It's me, Michael. Alasdair couldna come chasing after you—folks are gathering and he's minding the scene."

"Oh," Jean managed to gasp. "Sorry. Come on, the guy's gone in here."

"Jean…"

"Go back the way you came and catch him on the other side. I think there's a gate behind the house—can't remember the name—the one across from the Randolph House."

"Jean…"

She pushed at him. "Go on!"

"Alasdair'll have my head if I let you go in there on your own!" Michael whispered urgently.

"No one *lets* me do anything. I'm a free agent!" And she opened the gate and plunged through.

"Aye, you and Rebecca both," Michael said just loudly enough for her to hear. He caught the gate as its counterweight pulled it shut and followed.

The path was narrow, spongy underfoot, prickly on the sides, dank, chill, and utterly opaque. Her hands in front of her—cobwebs, there had to be cobwebs, complete with spiders—Jean pushed on. She registered only the lumps and hollows of the shrubs on either side and the faintest luminescence overhead. Unless those quick sparks weren't her own nerves firing, but were the eyes of green men, nature spirits like those carved on the Witch Box. Spirits that could be malevolent, those of nature *au naturel,* not manicured into better homes and gardens.

Away to her right, sirens howled closer and closer and stopped abruptly, leaving a subliminal whine in her ears. Car doors slammed. A low murmur of multiple voices blended with the wind whipping the trees. Was that a step, a twig breaking, straight ahead?

She stopped dead, trying to listen over the pounding of her own heart, hearing Michael's breath but nothing else. She knew what he was thinking, channeling Alasdair: *Are you daft, woman?*

Yeah, I'm nuts. We're all nuts. She pushed on, dodging right and left, wondering if she was following the path or just stumbling through gaps in the brushy wall. Spiders, snakes, goblins, potholes, trapdoors, and a murderer waiting up ahead.

Okay, so the odds were that Dylan wasn't the murderer. And he wouldn't go looking for confrontations, especially if he was trying to get that tote bag out of sight, if hardly out of mind.

Jean stumbled on a sudden slope and fell to her knees. A twig caught her glasses but she grabbed them before they flew off into nothingness. Michael tripped over her, flailed around, fell sideways into a shrub, and, cursing and thrashing, pulled himself to his feet.

Cats had been in here, Jean's nostrils told her. It was one giant alfresco litter box. She brushed off something hovering in front of her face that looked like a white starfish—Michael's hand, she hoped—heaved herself up, and peered into the gloom. They couldn't get lost, the thick tangle of bushes covered only a small area. If they just kept going they'd find the surrounding fence. Which Dylan had probably scaled by now, and hotfooted it down the path to the Woodlands. She needed to get back to Alasdair and set the dogs on the young man's trail.

She should have stayed with Alasdair to begin with, said that snotty little schoolmarm voice in the back of her mind. She'd recognized Dylan, she hadn't had to chase him, Williamsburg's finest could have been waiting for him at the hotel.

Like he'd go back to the hotel, if the police were waiting for him there.

Gritting her teeth, Jean crashed on along whatever path opened before her, Michael either doggedly following or leading when they found themselves in a cul-de-sac. They'd been in here half the night, hadn't they? Surely a rescue squad of Boy Scouts would appear at any moment, carrying flashlights and spooling out thread behind them. And if any of them made Monty Python jokes about shrubbery…

Lights, there were lights, cold red and blue glows pulsing against the clouds overhead like a localized version of the aurora borealis. Follow the lights.

They were in a narrow alleyway between ranks of bushes. Jean broke into a trot. Buildings materialized on either side and she walked into a gate in a fence. The lights beyond it were so bright she flinched and covered her eyes.

Michael, wisely holding his tongue, reached around her, opened the gate, and ushered her through. A few steps brought them to Nicholson Street, which was now clotted with vehicles and thronged with people, anxious faces washed into anonymity by the lights.

Dim figures were raising blue tarpaulins to demarcate the area around the enormous tree. Robin's-egg blue, a color much too cheery for the occasion. Alasdair stood just where the shine of a police car's headlights faded into shadow. He might no longer be serving as a one-man crime scene perimeter, but his expression in the cold, harsh light was still dour, unmoving and unmoved. On the outside, at least.

"Excuse me, pardon me." Jean shoved forward, arriving at Alasdair's side just in time to glimpse what looked like drops of dried blood spattering the ground below the dangling body. Then the tarpaulin shroud covered the site, leaving those rusty splotches burned in Jean's eyes. Fallen leaves, not blood at all. You didn't have to bleed to die.

Alasdair turned on her. "Are you daft? You had no call haring away like that!"

"It was Dylan Dingwall," Jean said, finally getting a full breath into her chest. "He was carrying Sharon's tote bag, with the photos and stuff."

"Was it?" That shape on Alasdair's other side was Stephanie Venegas, voice slicing, eyes flashing. "Alasdair says Dylan Dingwall is standing right over there."

What? Jean peered into the shards of light and dark surrounding the scene. A fog was rising—no, her glasses were smudged, no doubt with her own fingerprints. Focusing, she spied Rachel Finch, her face the same bleached white as her cap and apron, her mouth set in a thin line above a trembling chin.

A couple of long paces away stood a tall, gangly young man with pointed, fox-like features and carrot-red hair cut short and spiked—last night, then, he'd been wearing a wig to match his costume—there was nothing at all roguish about his expression now. It was closed as tightly as a bricked-in vault, only his eyes, huge as his mother's, glinting in the moving headlights, spotlights, flashlights…

Oh. "That's not Dylan," Jean said. "Rachel's just standing there. He's just standing there. If that was Dylan, wouldn't they be hanging on to each other?"

"Ah," said Alasdair.

"Then who—?" Venegas began.

"Quentin," Jean and Alasdair said simultaneously.

"Snap," he added, the sound of a blade falling. "He's come back to the U.S. with his auntie Kelly. I'll have Ian—"

Stephanie pointed out, "I have resources."

"Then you'd best be using them," retorted Alasdair.

And why, Jean asked herself, would he be in a good mood? Why bother to compliment her on her clever deduction about Quentin?

Leaving them to it, she stepped a few paces away, to where Rebecca was picking bits of leaf and twig off Michael's jacket. Jean looked down at herself—yep, splashes of mud, green stuff, brown stuff. She just hoped that no insects were burrowing inward looking for warmth.

"Here's your bag," Rebecca said. "You were gone a good twenty minutes, maybe longer. Alasdair kept pacing over to the road, then back to the tree, then back to the road. Talk about a man between the devil and the deep blue sea."

"Yeah." Jean shouldered her bag and Alasdair's anger as well, although he was as angry with the crime, and his own position in it, as he was with her.

"I wasn't thrilled myself." Rebecca hooked her arm through Michael's. "So that's Quentin over there? It really was Dylan making a getaway with the plans?"

"He was running around in that part of town with Rachel last night. And who knows how long he'd been here with his parents, getting to know the shortcuts and back ways. Of course, he and Quentin both could have been coming here for years—I don't know how long Tim and Sharon have been on the Francis Bacon's papers bandwagon." Jean looked around to see Rachel and Quentin still standing side by side, each in a different time zone. "So where is Tim? Where's Kelly? Where's Jessica, for that matter? She was supposed to have been performing in the play but I didn't see her."

Other voices and other thoughts were catching up with her, falling forward, retreating, falling forward again, like waves encroaching on a beach of that deep blue sea. Her stomach roiled and the manic energy ebbed from her limbs. A brief spray of cold rain slapped her face. She was tired. She couldn't stop now.

Yet another car pulled up and Rodney Lockhart bailed out, his expression considerably darker than his complexion. He was not having a good day, but under the circumstances could hardly complain.

Lockhart joined Alasdair and Venegas—okay, she was Stephanie now—Alasdair had spent more time with her today than he'd spent with Jean.

The tarpaulins flapped in the wind and lights strobed in the interstices between panels while the shadow of Sharon's body swayed back and forth behind them. Jean didn't have to look at Michael's and Rebecca's faces to know that they were thinking the same thing she was. The worst thing about being murdered wasn't necessarily death itself. It was how your mortal shell was robbed of dignity, no longer human, simply an exhibit to be probed, laid open, inspected by strangers who resorted to mordant jokes to keep their sanity in the face of the horror you'd become.

She hoped the occasional pungent whiff that reached her nostrils was that of horse droppings—carriages and wagons stopped here in the shade of the tree.

Someone else appeared on Jean's other side and blearily she looked around. It was Miranda, her shoulders hunched and her hands tucked deep into the pockets of her navy-style wool coat. Her lips were colorless, her eyes dull. "Sharon Dingwall, eh? So the poor woman's DOA?"

"No, she's DRT. Dead Right There. And," Jean added, "I'm not writing an article about the murder."

Miranda raised her hands placatingly, her burnished nails glinting like pearls. "It's murder, then, not suicide?"

Once again Jean saw Sharon's naked foot, dangling only an inch or two above the ground and safety. It might as well have been dangling off the Forth Bridge. "It's murder."

"Damn," Miranda said reverently.

In the distance, organ music swelled and faded. Bach's "Toccata and Fugue," appropriate music for Halloween. For a dramatic scene. "That's right. The concert."

"There's me, waiting for you and—oh, hello there, Rebecca, Michael—in the bittie lobby below the bell tower. Had a lovely blether with the lady you were speaking with at the reception, Barbara Finch. A keen gardener, I reckon, as well as musician. Then we heard the sirens. I'm thinking, no Jean, no Alasdair, sirens. This is no good. Barbara went on into the church—there was seating only in the balconies by then—and I had me a wee lookie toward the tavern, passing a bearer or two of bad news on the way."

"You didn't see Jessica at the church, by any chance?"

"No, nor Matt. Jessica's performing in the play, isn't she now?"

"It ended right when we found the—Sharon. Rachel's over there." Jean pointed, then realized Rachel was being urged away by several other interpreter/actors, including two women in long skirts. Maybe one of them was Jessica. Rachel finally acknowledged Quentin's existence, looking at him long, hard, and futilely, before allowing herself to be walked away.

Quentin didn't seem to notice her. He stood, eyes downcast, swaying slightly, bookended by a Williamsburg cop and a security officer, probably awaiting if not Stephanie's pleasure then at least her spare moment. Whether she was going to admit Alasdair to the impending interview—the impending round of interviews—was beyond Jean's present ken.

Her ken was contracting to a pinpoint. Even wrapping her arms around her own body didn't allay the seeping chill that deadened her muscles but not her nerves. She was trembling. Go figure.

Among her cascading thoughts, two stood up like rocks at high tide. Had the same person killed both Wesley Hagedorn and Sharon Dingwall? If so, were both murders committed for the same reason?

For just a moment, she wished she didn't care, but she did.

FIFTEEN

MIRANDA PRESSED A mug into Jean's hands. They were so cold that the pottery seemed searing hot. Her lips were cold, too, and even her tongue, but the gush of sweet, hot, milky tea past them and down her throat was delicious, as close to soothing as she was likely to get tonight. "That's the best cup of tea I've had since I left home."

So now Edinburgh was home.

"I stood there in the kitchen 'til they made a proper job of it," said Miranda. "The cook, she was after adding lemon after I'd already added milk. 'We're not making curd,' I said."

Stephanie was supplying her own metaphorical lemon, Jean decided. The detective stood at the window of Chowning's small upstairs room, her lips pursed with determination when she wasn't articulating orders both into a cell phone and face-to-face to a variety of underlings. Or sidelings, in the case of the security people. If she'd been a man her golden skin would be shaded with whisker stubble. As it was, it stretched tightly as a drumhead on its bone armature. Her svelte figure was outlined against the spotlights outside, the ones that were driving back the night—for the moment. There were plenty of hours of darkness yet to come.

Rodney Lockhart had gone to consult with those who needed to know, leaving the Foundation's director of security, safety, and transportation at the scene. Michael and Rebecca, having had their fill of the evening's unintended consequences, had gone back to Richmond and the solace of little Linda. Hugh had cleaned Jean's glasses for her, patted her shoulder encouragingly, then bundled up his guitar and headed to the hotel where he and the other members of his band were staying. The usual evening program of games and songs at Chowning's had been canceled and the visitors and interpreters who'd witnessed the ghastly finale to "A Matter of Witchcraft" sent away.

Alasdair sat on the other side of Jean's table, his hands cradling his own mug of tea, the crease between his brows deep as the Mid-Atlantic. "Millions of visitors," he said, half to himself, "acres of property, outhouses, gardens, woods. We'll be using the telephone book as our list of suspects."

Jean didn't point out that *outhouse* meant here in the U.S. what *earth closet* meant in the U.K. What *privy* or *necessary* meant to the interpreters. Nor did she query his "we" and "our." "Did you see anyone hanging around…?" Wincing, she edited her question. "Did you see anyone standing near the tree before we found Sharon?"

"Everyone in the vicinity was watching the play."

"Well, no, there was a custodian…"

"…with a trolley, walking away from the scene. Oh aye. You never quite notice the staff, do you now?"

"Always speak with the staff," Miranda repeated her injunction.

Stephanie called across the room, "We intend to," then turned back to her phone.

Of course she would be an excellent multi-tasker. Jean went on, "Big question. Were both murders committed by the same person? If so, then Kelly's out for the first one and Sam Gould's out for the second. Bigger question—were both murders committed for the same reason? The same motive?"

Alasdair's eyes seemed to be dusted with ash, but they were as direct as always. "Money, jealousy, revenge, protection, a cover-up. There's many motives for murder. And before you go reminding me, most murders are committed by someone knowing the victim, not a random passerby."

"Never mind the telephone book, then." Miranda plucked a few stray leaves from Jean's hair.

"Thanks," Jean told her, feeling like a monkey being groomed for lice. She asked Alasdair, "Do you think Dylan killed his own mother? Or was he just trying to get his parents' incriminating papers away from the scene?"

"I'm thinking he needs careful questioning, soon as may be."

"Soon as we find him." Stephanie paced across the room, inserting her cell phone into her pocket. "We found Tim Dingwall and Kelly at Huzzah, the restaurant at the Woodlands. They'd just ordered dinner, but it hadn't come yet. Table for two."

"They were not expecting Sharon, then. Or Dylan. And they'd just arrived." Miranda set her elbows on the table and steepled her fingers a la Sherlock Holmes.

Stephanie regarded her with her best—or worst—obsidian gaze. "Mrs., ah…"

"Miranda Capaldi. Ms."

"Capaldi's a Scottish name?"

"Aye, that it is."

"Ms. Capaldi, you weren't present when Miss Fairbairn here, Jean, and Alasdair found the body, were you?"

"No. I was likely walking to the church just then."

"From where? You're staying at the Inn, right?"

"Oh aye, but I'd been having myself a coffee and a keek at the bookstore at Merchant's Square. I wasn't near the scene, sorry."

"Then I need for you to leave. Please. We'll talk to you later."

Miranda shot a rueful glance at Jean. Jean summoned a wobbly smile. "Nice try."

"Very well then." With good grace, to say nothing of gracefully, Miranda stood up and headed for the door. "I'll be phoning you the morn, Jean."

"Please do." Jean darted a glance at Stephanie, expecting to be kicked out, too, but apparently she'd earned the seal of approval as body-discoverer, or fount of Dingwalliana, or just as friend-of-Alasdair.

Miranda opened the door, revealing an officer poised to knock. Tim Dingwall hulked behind him. With police murmurs from Miranda, impatient ones from Tim, and silence from the officer, everyone jockeyed around each other.

The whitewashed room with its dormer windows, furnished with a few simple tables and chairs and a stark, empty fireplace, seemed to shrink when Tim entered it. His hands opened and shut powerlessly, his jowls quivered in a tug-of-war between belligerence and despair. His eyes were so bloodshot that the gray irises were almost invisible. They turned to each feature, each face in the room, assessing every one for potential conflict.

His thick lips wavered, parted, flapped. Words burst forth. "She could not have killed herself. She was happy, anticipating the conclusion of our work and the final production of the movie. No, she was not pleased that Quentin resigned from his employment in London so precipitately, but then, he discovered that the *Sunburn* is no refuge for responsible journalists."

"I'll not be fainting in amazement at that," Alasdair murmured.

No kidding, Jean thought. Quentin didn't know the true colors of the *Sunburn?* Come on now, a visit to the paper's website would have told them all they needed to know. In fact, the *Sunburn* would probably be one of the few publishers happy to serialize Tim and Sharon's work, especially now that murder had validated it.

Or had murder validated their work? Did someone take

the Dingwalls' conspiracy theories that seriously? Sharon as the target of a killer seemed as unlikely as Hagedorn, the soft-spoken craftsman, being the target of one.

"Please sit down," said Stephanie. "Do you know…?"

"Yes, we've met," Tim said, and chose a chair at the table furthest away from Jean and Alasdair's.

The door opened again, admitting a young man with blond hair trimmed in a military-style cut and a broad pink face, open and intelligent. He looked no older than one of the Dingwall twins but was probably thirty, in the irritating way that some men were either blessed or cursed, depending, with Peter Pan genes.

Stephanie had already introduced her sergeant, Olson, first name unspecified. Now Olson set a small glass in front of Tim and chose yet another table, where he opened the notebook he'd been using to collect names and addresses, clicked his pen, and looked up expectantly.

Alasdair eyed the young man with approval. A good sergeant was like a good sheepdog, quietly and efficiently herding witnesses into their proper places. A bad sergeant—as Alasdair could testify—would rush barking at the sheep and scatter them all over the hillside, where they'd sulk and refuse to cooperate.

"I'm Detective Venegas," Stephanie said to Tim. "We need to ask you a few questions."

"She did not kill herself," he told the glass, and tossed back the contents—whiskey or brandy, probably, though presumably not Chowning's best brand.

"No, she didn't. There was nothing for her to have stepped off of, to begin with. And the bruises on her throat indicate she was strangled manually before being hanged. This is a homicide case."

Tim stared into the glass, hardly mollified. *And who could blame him?* Jean thought. If she'd just lost her partner—

and she hadn't known Alasdair nearly as long as Tim had known Sharon—not that she and Alasdair had achieved the same level of commitment… Alasdair's gaze was fixed on the witness. She drove that train of thought into a dark tunnel and abandoned it.

"We'll need you to identify the body," Stephanie told Tim.

"I have—already looked at her—it's her. It's Sharon." Tim hid his face in his hand.

"The identification is just a formality." Giving him a moment, Stephanie said to Alasdair, "We've scheduled a press conference for tomorrow morning. Just a quick PowerPoint presentation. Could you say something about the theft in Scotland?"

"No problem." Alasdair no doubt remembered many a news conference in his past.

Tim looked up. "Oh, good, I shall explain our work and its significance. Sharon would have wanted that."

"You won't be involved, Mr. Dingwall," Stephanie stated. "Now. Where were you between, say, six-thirty and seven-thirty this evening?"

"Where was… You don't mean to imply that I'm a suspect?"

"The spouse is always a suspect. For the reason that the spouse is often the killer."

"Listen, I've just lost my wife—how dare you accuse me of…" Tim's language skills devolved to a sputter. He finally managed, "Obviously my poor wife was murdered by a robber."

"Obviously?" muttered Alasdair.

But Stephanie was on top of it, just as she was on top of Tim, standing over him and signaling dominance instead of sitting down and pretending to be his equal. "She still had her cell phone and her wedding ring. A robber would have hit her over the head or even shot her. Going to the effort of hanging her…" The words twisted as Sharon's body had, in the wind.

"It was personal, you mean?" Tim demanded. "Well then, you need to look no further than that two-faced witch, that self-serving bitch Jessica Finch. Evesdottir. Whatever name she is calling herself. She killed Sharon to stop the lawsuit, which we would most assuredly have won. Why question me, not her?"

Jean knew that Jessica was already above Stephanie's event horizon. But all the detective said was "What was behind the lawsuit?"

"Jessica's big mouth. She slandered Sharon at a conference last month. Called her a witch, right out in public."

Well, no, she hadn't, not if what she'd said at the reception was an exact repetition of her original statement.

"We believe Jessica and Sharon were working together on, um, some research," Stephanie went on.

"Jessica shares our interest in some aspects of colonial history, but Sharon would never descend so far as to actually work with her."

Stephanie almost but not quite kept herself from glancing at Jean, acknowledging the contradiction. She asked Tim, "What aspects? The history of the Witch Box?"

Now it was Tim who glanced suspiciously toward Jean. She looked blandly back at him. The Dingwalls had known up front she was going to repeat everything they told her—that was the whole point of the interview. If he was thinking about the photocopies and plans accidentally spilling across the table, and Sharon's speed in shoving them back into the bag—you'd think they had something to hide, wouldn't you?—then he wasn't going to call the detective's attention to them. As for his provocative statement about the replica Box not being exact, did he even remember saying that?

Now Tim said, "The history of the Witch Box is an important part of our research."

"We've gotten that far. Now I'd like to know why you're calling Jessica two-faced and self-serving, if you and Sharon never worked with her."

His eyes focused abruptly on the top of the table and the empty glass. He was stonewalling. Hiding something, then, was more important than pinning the crime on Jessica.

Stephanie shot another glance toward Jean, a direct one she interpreted as *No, I'm not opening the Witch Box can of worms any further right now.* Turning back to Tim, the detective asked, "Did you and Sharon have a problem with Dylan seeing Rachel Finch?"

"Really, Miss, er, Detective, er…" A mottled red flowed into Tim's cheeks and then faded. "Our private family relationships have no bearing on the situation in hand."

Situation in hand? Jean repeated to herself. How about a spouse's murder?

"It was no robber who removed Sharon's tote bag from the crime scene," Stephanie told him. "It was your son Dylan."

So I have some credibility after all, Jean told herself, and looked over at Alasdair. He was sitting back in his chair, indicating approval, rather than leaning forward. In August he'd butted heads with the officer in charge, an old colleague. An old male colleague.

Well, he'd butted heads with Stephanie until she accepted his bona fides.

Olson's pen stopped moving as Tim looked blank, perhaps visualizing the scene beneath the tree. No surprise he hadn't noticed that the bag was gone. At last he said, "I thought she'd left her bag in the room—of course it has many valuable papers, understandable that she would want to keep an eye on it—but Dylan? Someone is imagining things! Or casting aspersions—this is not the first time we've been the target of slander."

"Do you know where Dylan is?" Stephanie asked.

"Well, no, I haven't seen—Sharon went off with him and Quentin about six-thirty or so, to show Quentin the area and have a bite to eat—Quentin was among the first people on the scene—poor, poor lad, finding his mother in such a state."

We found his mother, too, Jean corrected silently. Dylan, now, he'd probably wandered over to the Courthouse looking for Rachel. By how many minutes had he missed saving his mother's life? Was he on the scene quickly enough to have seen the killer? Unless… No. Until she had further evidence, Jean wasn't going to think Dylan was himself the killer.

For a long moment Tim sat shaking his head, his face set in the bleakest of frowns. Then, suddenly, he jerked upright and declaimed, "There's your solution. One of our enemies lynched poor Sharon—that's the word, *lynched*—in order to stop our work and prevent us from releasing our movie and revealing all. The conspirators are trying to suppress the truth. That proves that we're right, doesn't it? It proves that we're closing in on them!"

Alasdair winced. Even Stephanie retreated a step at that. Judging by the movement of Olson's pen, he was drawing a series of question marks across the page. It was his smooth tenor that broke the silence. "If the killer wanted to hinder your work, why didn't he steal the tote bag? Why leave it there beneath the tree for your son to pick up?"

And to run, Jean thought, as though the very hound of hell, not a mild-mannered historian, was on his tail.

"You're working with them," Tim stated, his jowls trembling with self-righteousness. "You're trying to stop us and our sons from proving our conclusions—I should have known, an official government body like the police—if we don't toe the official line then there's no help for us, is there? If only Dylan or Quentin had been there, if only I'd been there, Sharon would be alive now and giving you a piece of her mind."

Stephanie's black arches of eyebrows rose and fell. "If she was alive now, we wouldn't be having this conversation. Where were you between six-thirty and seven-thirty this evening?"

"I was eating dinner with my sister," Tim spat, "who I have not been fortunate enough to speak with on an individual basis for quite some time. We had just ordered our meals when Sergeant Olson here appeared at our table."

"That's where you were at eight. Where were you earlier?"

Even more sullenly, Tim said, "I was doing some work in our room, Sharon's and my room. Kelly was recovering from her difficult journey—really, the people allowed on airplanes these days—in her room, on another floor. Even though we had booked adjoining rooms, the hotel was unable to provide them. The manager will be hearing about that."

So did Kelly have a motive for killing her sister-in-law, Jean wondered, other than general friction? "Why didn't Sharon eat dinner with you?"

Tim blinked at her. "We were hardly joined at the hip."

Well, no, Jean thought, *if only because of Kelly.*

"Sergeant Olson here will escort you back downstairs," Stephanie told Tim. "Tomorrow morning you and your family will be giving us formal statements." And to Olson she said, "Bring Kelly up. And Quentin's there?"

"Yes." Olson stood up.

So did Tim, hauling himself to his feet with ponderous dignity. His features kneaded themselves and Jean wasn't sure whether he was going to start crying or deliver a crushing retort. At last he said thickly, "Sharon died standing up for what she believes in! What we believe in!" and blundered, choking, from the room.

"Standing up for what you believe," Alasdair said to the doorway, "is only a virtue if what you believe is worth standing up for."

Only when the door shut behind Olson did Stephanie release her patented, cool chuckle. "Good one."

Alasdair shook his head, rejecting her compliment. "Believing, that's the issue here. Someone's believing they were justified in committing murder. And stealing the replica, come to that."

Jean slumped over the table, massaging the rubber-band-tight skin of her temples. She didn't need a mirror to know how she looked—pale, eyes wide, hair standing on end, lips clamped and bracketed with pleats from the effort of keeping them shut. Fortunately the acid fermenting in her stomach wasn't also on public display.

"Have you turned Jessica up, then?" asked Alasdair.

"She never replied to the message I left for her this afternoon. She did show up for the play, but her role's only in the first part, so she left before it was over—even Rachel didn't know where she went. However, we tracked her down to the Lodge. There was an academic confab there, and one of the attendees, Louise Dietz—do you know her?"

"Louise Dietz and a guy named Denny were at the reception last night," Jean answered, "then sat next to us at Campbell's. They were dissing Jessica up one side and down the other."

"Well, now Louise says Jessica came into the lounge just before eight and ordered a drink. They schmoozed a few minutes, until someone else came in with the news about Sharon. Then she took off. Do you know the word *schmooze?*" Stephanie asked Alasdair.

"Oh aye, Jean's taught me a wee bit American vocabulary."

Jean added, "So tonight Louise and Jessica are having a cozy little schmooze? That figures."

Stephanie offered no opinions on the social habits of academics.

"Have you found Jessica's husband, Matt, as well?" Alasdair asked.

"Why should they be looking for him?" Jean's mouth demanded before she could stop it.

"Over and beyond him maybe knowing where Jessica's got herself off to," replied Alasdair, one eyebrow cocked just so, "Tim's just contradicted what Matt was telling you about the women working together. Though I reckon it's Matt who's closer to the truth. The mobile phone in Sharon's hand, the last number she rang was Jessica's. Not half an hour before she died."

"Oh." Jean went back to massaging her temples. Breathe in—the lingering cooking odors weren't unpleasant—breathe out—neither the room nor Alasdair was quite cool enough to turn her breath into fog.

"Rachel's gone to her father's house," Stephanie said, which didn't answer Alasdair's question. She walked over to the door and peered at the stairs. "Where the heck is Olson?"

Biting her lip, Jean fixed her aching eyes on Stephanie and tried to be helpful. "Speaking of witnesses, Detect—er, Stephanie. Hugh Munro was on the same flight from Edinburgh as Kelly Dingwall. He said she was walking up and down the aisle handing out promotional material for the Dingwalls' movie. But Sharon and Tim told me the movie isn't finished yet."

"Is that so?" Stephanie looked around. "They must be under some pressure to get it out, then, especially with Kelly—what did you hear her say on the phone? Something about having a bankroll?"

"Yes. Makes you wonder just what sort of return she's expecting to get on her investment," Jean replied, just as footsteps came racing up the stairs.

SIXTEEN

JEAN EXPECTED OLSON to lunge into the room reporting that Tim and Kelly had made a break for it. Not that either of them was guilty of murdering Sharon, but Tim, at least, was manifestly feeling more than a little paranoia in regards to law enforcement.

And why not? You're not paranoid when someone really is out to get you. Or your spouse. Or your friends, for that matter. Of course, defining who your friends were seemed to be one of the issues here.

It wasn't Olson who burst through the doorway. It was either Tim in drag or his sister, all but running over Stephanie, who leaped back against the fireplace with the agility of a gymnast.

Kelly was tall and beefy, like Tim, but unlike Tim, she sported lipstick, a full head of wavy, brown hair, and a bosom cantilevered like the flight deck of an aircraft carrier. Two flight decks—her soft, white blouse revealed more than a hint of cleavage. Her blue pantsuit was less masculine than Stephanie's black one, and Kelly was wearing jewelry, rings both in her ears and on her fingers, as well as a necklace of Italian millefiori beads. While her features weren't nearly as heavy as Tim's, the resemblance was still so strong that Jean suspected Kelly was the older sibling by only a few minutes. Twins did run in families.

"Now listen here," Kelly began. Hugh was right—she had a voice like a foghorn.

Heralded by another scramble of footsteps, Olson catapulted into the room and narrowly prevented himself from crashing into Kelly's back. "Ma'am, there was no need to shove me aside."

"There was no need to insult me," Kelly retorted.

"Insult?" asked Stephanie, taking a wary step forward.

"He said he'd escort me upstairs. What, do I look like I'm not capable of climbing stairs?"

Alasdair muttered "Glenda" from the side of his mouth, toward Jean.

Yep, she thought, *gender was one more area where people went overboard. Like with conspiracy theories and witch hunts, just without lethal consequences. Usually.*

Olson said, with an admirable lack of sarcasm, "I beg your pardon," and sat down with his notebook and a roll of his eyes toward Stephanie.

Who said, her voice not just curdling milk but turning it to cheese, "I'm Detective Venegas. Please sit down, Ms. Dingwall."

"According to her driver's license," murmured Olson, "her last name is Polito."

"Ms. Polito," Stephanie amended.

"No, no, no," said Kelly, fending off the name with raised hands. "It's Dingwall. I've got to get that license fixed."

"Divorced?"

"Yes, I am. Finalized last spring. Biggest mistake of my life, getting married. All he did was get in my way and make trouble for my business. He wanted half my income without doing any of the work, the jerk. I finally had to scrape him off like a barnacle."

"And your business is?"

"Designing and manufacturing clothing for the normal-sized woman. You've probably seen the shops, although you're too thin to have ever been in one. Queen Bee Fashions, they're called. In malls all over the country. Sex appeal for *real* women."

Jean had never been in one of the shops, either, but Kelly's eye didn't assess her size.

Stephanie said only, "Your sister-in-law was very petite. Wasn't she a real woman?"

"I won't speak ill of the dead," Kelly said with a sniff, and in response to Stephanie's gesture toward a chair, "I'm not going to be here long enough to sit down. I just want to tell you…"

"What you're going to tell me is where you were between six-thirty and seven-thirty tonight."

Kelly's dark gray eyes, not at all bloodshot, swiveled toward Jean and Alasdair. "Who are they?"

Alasdair, ever the gentleman, stood up. "Alasdair Cameron, Chief of Security at Protect and Survive, Scotland. And this is Jean Fairbairn of *Great Scot* magazine."

Not his partner, companion, significant other, alter ego, or thorn in the side. "I interviewed Tim and Sharon…" Jean began.

Dismissing her with a glance, Kelly concentrated on Alasdair. "Protect and Survive. Blair Castle. The replica Witch Box. I see overly officious police forces are no respecters of national boundaries. You've gone to a lot of trouble and expense to follow me here, for no reason."

Alasdair sat down again, rather abruptly. He'd be wasting his breath to point out he'd reached the U.S. twenty-four hours before Kelly had played the patsy at Blair.

Jean waited for Stephanie to inform Kelly that it wasn't all about her. Instead she said only, "Where were you…?"

"I was recovering from my difficult journey—you would not believe the people allowed on airplanes these days—in my room. Then my brother and I went to share a meal, as we haven't been able to speak privately for quite some time.

We had barely placed our orders when your sergeant—Oliver, Orson—interrupted us."

Stephanie glanced at Olson, not, Jean estimated, to verify his name, but to see if Kelly had indeed almost exactly repeated Tim's words. With a quick flip of his notebook, Olson nodded an infinitesimal affirmative. Alasdair's nod was less subtle, and was annotated by a humorless smile. *Gotcha.* Even though comparing notes and straightening their stories before their interview didn't necessarily indicate anything sinister, Jean told herself, in a half-hearted effort to be fair.

She had to ask Kelly, too, "Why didn't Sharon eat with you?"

Kelly stiffened. "We had a few words earlier, nothing important, a minor disagreement, but she went off in a huff. It's all about her, of course."

Yeah, well, at the moment it was about Sharon.

Kelly took a step toward the door. "If you're finished, my poor nephew downstairs needs my attention."

"What do you think might have driven Sharon into committing suicide?" Stephanie asked, taking two steps forward.

"It wasn't suicide."

"How do you know that?"

"Any fool can see that!" Kelly's voice warned off ships as far away as the Azores. "She was murdered. She was lynched. Someone was trying to shut her up. Probably that Jessica woman, the traitor."

"Traitor?"

"That's it—that's all. Tim and I are finding a lawyer." Kelly turned and strode toward the door, her low heels reverberating on the pine planks of the floor.

"Fine. Suit yourself," Stephanie called to her retreating back, and said to Olson, "Quentin."

Olson leaped up. His lighter steps trailed Kelly's down the stairs, to be greeted by Tim's bellow.

"Well then," said Alasdair.

"Yeah," Stephanie replied.

Jean knew what that terse exchange meant. *We're just getting started.* Follow-up interviews, timetables, forensics reports—she'd learned a wee bit police vocabulary, too. "It's very rare to see a murder committed by hanging. Alasdair and I were once involved with one where the weapon turned out to be a garrote, but this..."

"...is a genuine hanging." Across the table, Alasdair's eyes reflected a quick image of the past and blinked it away, but not before Jean caught it. He'd sat across a table in a café in Fort William, respecting her enough to share the facts of the case with her. That's when she'd noticed him.

Here she was now, sharing the facts of the case with him and Stephanie.

"Yes," Stephanie said, either oblivious to that subliminal exchange or politely ignoring it. "The rope was already there, and had been there so long the branch beneath it was grooved and rubbed smooth. Sometimes the childhood-play interpreters set up a swing. Sometimes the wagon drivers demonstrate loading techniques while they rest their horses."

Surreptitiously, Jean inspected her soles. Just because she didn't smell anything didn't mean she shouldn't clean her shoes once she got back to the house. If she ever got back to the house.

Downstairs, Tim was still bellowing, now in duet with Kelly. Stephanie didn't seem inclined to rush down and rescue Olson.

Alasdair said, "Sharon could not have weighed more than seven stone."

"Stone?"

"Fourteen pounds," Jean amended. "Sharon didn't weigh more than a hundred."

"Even so, the dirt and leaves beneath the tree were messed about by two pairs of feet," Alasdair went on. "She managed a good struggle."

"And you saw how her muscles were clenched around her phone. Cadaveric spasm, that's called. Her free hand seems to have traces of blood and tissue beneath the nails. There might be defensive marks on her assailant, even though almost anyone would have a longer reach."

"The villain got her round the throat, preventing her from screaming—and she had a screech like a herring gull on helium, we heard her at the Museum—and overpowering her. Then he looped the rope round her neck. In a right crude knot, by the way."

"And he hauled her just far enough off the ground for her to choke to death. No broken neck, not like that. A good thing she was probably almost unconscious by then."

Probably, Jean repeated. *Almost.* But no one dwelled on that point. "It would take some strength to pull her up, wouldn't it, even with the branch being too smooth to snag the rope?"

"Some, yes, but mostly it took brains," said Stephanie.

"The killer made himself a sort of lever, a primitive winch..."

Jean's mind skidded, then realized Alasdair didn't mean wench-with-an-e, like in the title of Jessica's new book.

"...by wrapping a sturdy stick in the rope just where it's tied to the trunk of the tree. Brace the end of the stick against the tree, twist it a bit, and the rope shortens by an inch or two."

"An inch is all it took," Jean said. There was something inexpressibly vulnerable, infinitely pitiable, about the shoe lying on its side below Sharon's foot.

"And probably just a couple of minutes," added Stephanie. "The thing is, it's not just any old stick, it's one turned on a lathe, maybe a spindle or rung from a chair. Or for a chair—looks like it's never been used."

Tim's bawl and Kelly's bleat suddenly stopped. Stephanie looked over her shoulder.

Alasdair lowered his voice. "The spindle's likely from the cabinetmaker's shop. Pity Sam Gould's got the best possible alibi—that might be a clue."

"It still is," Stephanie said. "We'll see what forensics says."

"If the murder was by means of hanging," Jean thought aloud, "while a witch trial was playing out nearby, then the murderer's motive was to make a statement as well as—what? Eliminate a rival? Remove an obstacle? Carrying a big stick to use as a winch, that's hardly a crime of momentary passion. So who had the opportunity? Who made themselves an opportunity?"

Footsteps trudged up the stairs before anyone could answer what were now only rhetorical questions, and Quentin plodded into the room.

Exhaling a breath that she feared was badly in need of mouthwash, toothpaste, or even a mint, Jean settled down in her chair for the next act.

Alasdair, too, took up his position, leaning back with one arm on the table. But his fingers tapped out a pattern on the battered wood, indicating he was anything but a passive audience.

"I'm Detective Venegas," Stephanie began yet again. "Please sit down."

Quentin stared at her dully, then at Jean and Alasdair. When Olson came into the room Quentin stared at him, too. The young man's eyes were a darker gray than his father's, but were even more bloodshot. He didn't sit down, less out of belligerence, Jean supposed, than because he didn't register the invitation.

Olson sat down with a thump. "Tim and Kelly are accusing us of police brutality because we want to talk to Quentin here. I had to insist."

"No problem," said Quentin, his expression contradicting his words.

Stephanie plunged ahead. "Where were you between six-thirty and seven-thirty tonight?"

"Mom and Dylan and…" His voice caught and croaked. With a swallow that made the Adam's apple jump in his long throat, exposed by the open collar of a polo shirt, he mopped the sleeve of his jacket across his face. Its cuff rode up, revealing a bony wrist, its white flesh scored with bruises. "Mom and Dylan and I left Dad and Aunt Kelly at the hotel. We came over here, like, about six-thirty. I haven't been here since I was a kid. We were going to look around and then feed our faces."

Stephanie waited. The room was so silent the scratch of Olson's pen seemed as loud as the grumble of voices downstairs and the whimper of the wind outside.

"I stopped at the ticket office, the one at the end of Palace Green, to see what other shows were on, since it was, like, too late to get tickets to the witchcraft play. Dylan went off to the Courthouse anyway—he was all, 'I'm going to wait for Rachel, then she can eat with us.' Rachel Finch. She was playing Mary, you know, the lead role."

Which might be why Rachel had trapped Dylan in the pillory last night, thought Jean, as a sort of post-modern commentary on all matters of witchcraft.

"Mom missed a call while we were on the bus, so she said she'd meet us outside the Courthouse after she returned it."

"Who was the call from?" asked Stephanie.

Quentin managed to raise his rigid shoulders in a slight shrug. "Some business associate, she said. Someone she was supposed to meet later on tonight."

Alasdair's fingers straightened and flexed again, registering the fact that therefore Sharon was supposed to meet Jessica—as strange bedfellows or what? Jean wondered.

"And then," Stephanie prompted.

"There was a good-looking girl in the ticket office, so I hung around talking to her. When I came out, people were milling around, going, whoa, there's a body hanging from the big tree, a real one, someone's been murdered. I couldn't find Dylan, so I walked over there with Rachel, and, and, it was my mom. Someone lynched my mom. She was there, and then she was, was, wasn't..." His voice breaking, his face contorting, Quentin didn't so much lose the thread of his thought as throw it away.

Stephanie waited until Quentin's face unclenched, if only a bit. "Do you know where Dylan is now?"

"No. I tried to call him, but he's not picking up. I tried Rachel, and she's gone to her dad's place and hasn't seen him, either."

Jean visualized Matt patting Rachel on the shoulder the way Hugh had patted her.

"Were your parents all right with Dylan seeing Rachel?" Stephanie asked.

"You mean with Mom, like, suing Jessica? They've got enough going on without doing the whole Montague and Capulet thing."

"What do they have going on?"

"They've gone out on a limb with their movie. *Lords of the Lie.* It's make-or-break time, you know?"

"And how does your aunt play into that?"

Jean assumed Quentin meant for the abbreviated strands of his hair to stand up on end. It looked as though he'd been tearing at it. His long chin and hollow cheeks gave him a lean and hungry look, as much psychic as literal.

"Kelly," Quentin said. "She's helping them out. She's making sure they, like, know she's helping them out."

"Did your mother and your aunt argue about that tonight?"

"They were always arguing about it."

"Kelly was helping you out as well," said Alasdair, "taking you on a tour of the U.K."

Now Quentin turned toward Alasdair with curiosity, even alarm. "Ah geez, you're the guy from Scotland."

"Did you steal the replica Witch Box from Blair Castle?" Stephanie asked.

"No, no, I didn't—I couldn't—I wasn't even there—that's all a big mistake." He hid his face with his hand. By this time his shoulders were framing his ears.

The tuck at one side of Alasdair's mouth acknowledged Quentin's denial, not just of the theft but of even being present. "Why did you give up your job at the *Sunburn* and come back to the U.S.?"

"I never had a job with the *Sunburn*." Quentin's voice was muffled, directed into his palm, as if passing on some dark secret. "I had an interview, but they didn't want to hire an American. Mom and Dad, the, like, embroider stuff."

Stephanie looked at Jean. Jean looked at Alasdair. Alasdair appealed to the ceiling. *No kidding.*

"I've gotta move back home. Dylan's already moved back home—he's got a job at Starbucks and I need to find something." Quentin looked up and from face to face. "Guys, my mom's been murdered, my brother, he's run off somewhere, my aunt's freaking out, my dad, aw geez, my dad's acting like he's gonna punch someone out."

"Is he prone to violence?" Stephanie asked, and Jean thought, *She saw those bruises, too.*

Quentin stared, obviously realizing what he'd just said. Licking his lips, he answered, "Well, I mean, he kind of pitches things around, you know, when he's mad. Like his fist through the wall when Mom wouldn't..."

"Wouldn't what?"

"I don't know. I wasn't there. It was Dylan who saw it. Really. Don't ask me."

"Where did you get those bruises on your wrist?"

"Huh?" He looked down at his own arms as if they were attached to someone else's body. "Oh. I dunno. Wrestling with Dylan."

Jean remembered her mother telling her brothers they were acting like wolf pups, the way they communicated by wrestling. They still did, with each other and with their own sons.

"All right," Stephanie told Quentin. "Go on back to the hotel. If you hear from Dylan, have him call me. Got that? Tomorrow I'll get formal statements from all of you."

"Yeah. Sure." Quentin backpedaled toward the door, then made his escape down the stairs.

"Don't worry," Stephanie said to Alasdair, "he's not going anywhere."

Instead of pressing his own case—two local murders took precedent over a distant stolen object—Alasdair replied with a firm nod. "We'll bag him yet. And recover the replica as well."

"Did they bring it back here with them?" Jean asked. "It's about the size of a small toaster oven. You could fit it into a large suitcase."

"Where the metal hinges would show up a treat on airport security scans. A shipping company would do very nicely. For enough money, they could have had it here in the States the day it was nicked. And Kelly's got money, or so they're all saying."

"So is the Box sitting on the Dingwalls' doorstep in Rosslyn?" asked Jean.

Alasdair repeated incredulously, "Rosslyn?"

"A suburb of D.C. Yeah, they've already pointed out how apt it is that they live there."

Stephanie opened her mouth, apparently thought better of asking for an explanation, and said only, "We'll keep an eye out for it. Olson?"

"Got it," he said, making a notation on his page.

"Make sure the Dingwalls have police protection tonight. We can't be sure someone's not trying to pick off the whole family."

"And we'll grab Dylan if he shows up. Got that, too." One more time Olson headed for the staircase.

Again voices rose and fell from downstairs. Doors slammed. More voices erupted from beneath the windows, accompanied by flashes of light. Cameras. Newspeople. Not Jean's inoffensive "journalist" but pack-of-wolves style reporters. *Been there,* she thought. *Done that.*

"Someone's lying." Alasdair stated the obvious. "I'd not be surprised if all three were lying, about one thing or another. And they all three used the word *lynch.*"

"*Lynch* is as good a description as any, with the witchcraft implications—Jessica calling Sharon a witch, Tim calling Jessica a witch..." Her voice trailing away into a frustrated growl, Stephanie walked over to the window and gazed down at the media scrum. Car doors slammed. The shouts grew more urgent. An engine started.

"Jessica didn't call Sharon a witch," said Jean, "not at the reception, anyway. She said that Sharon was the sort of woman who was accused of being one, because she babbled and slandered and scandalized her neighbors. Or something like that."

"Jean's after splitting academic hairs with the best of them," said Alasdair.

"I should hope so," Jean told him.

"Whatever," said Stephanie. "It's not sufficient cause for a defamation-of-character suit. Although when you have criminals suing homeowners for defending themselves during a break-in…"

Jean spoke before Alasdair's indignant expression became critical words. "I've been wondering all along if the suit's not just the tip of the iceberg. I suspect they're quarreling over a letter, an inventory, something about the history of the charm stone and where it is now. Jessica's supposedly got a new source that ties in with Bacon's Rebellion, but while that's the right time period, that's not her field. I don't know. My brain hurts."

"Yeah. The old gray matter is taking quite a beating." Stephanie rubbed her hands over her face and through her hair, then stretched like a cat. "Why don't you guys call it quits? For now."

Reminding herself not to let that grating "you guys" set her teeth any further on edge than they already were, Jean hauled herself to her feet. She managed not to groan from the effort of straightening her spine. Her desperation had drained away to a dull stubbornness. This was Stephanie's case. Alasdair could indeed call it quits. For now.

He got to his feet and methodically rotated first his shoulders and then his head. He flicked a quick, distracted smile in Jean's direction, but by the time she returned it, he was on his way to the window to stand beside Stephanie. *Quits? Alasdair?*

The commotion had died away below. No doubt the police and security between them had removed the three Dingwalls to the Woodlands.

"Well done," Alasdair said.

Stephanie's laugh was more of a raspberry. "Yeah, right. Tell me that when I've got Sharon's killer behind bars. And Welsey Hagedorn's, if it turns out to be two different people. And Hagedorn's thief, for that matter."

"And my thief. Four crimes, one motive," said Alasdair. "Or related motives, even if there's more than one villain."

"Yeah. Maybe."

Jean thought of Wes's photos and diagrams, stolen along with some valuables. Right now she would reject gold, silver, actual paper money, in favor of valuables like peace and quiet. And the soothing properties of chocolate on dyspepsia that was more mental than physical. There were packets of cocoa in the pantry at their house. There was hot water in the bathroom. There were crisp sheets on the bed.

Lobbing a loud "Good night" at Stephanie and Alasdair both, Jean sidled toward the door.

SEVENTEEN

RESPONDING, THANK GOODNESS, to his cue, Alasdair also exchanged a good night with Stephanie. By the time he'd joined Jean in her headlong trudge toward a time-out, the American detective was playing another number on her cell phone.

"I've got your mobile," Alasdair told Jean as they started down the stairs. He groped in his pocket and handed it over.

Just when Jean removed her hand from the railing to take the phone, her lead-weighted feet snagged on a step. For a moment she and Alasdair clutched and balanced—and there was a metaphor for a relationship if ever there was one.

"Are you all right, lass?"

"I'm just tired," she replied, opening herself up for a repeat of his "You had no call haring away like that."

He said only, "As am I."

Olson was waiting in the foyer at the foot of the stairs. In the half-light he looked even more like a schoolboy—all he needed was a skateboard under one arm. "This way," he said, and led them to the back of the building and through the kitchen.

Jean squinted at the abrupt transition from dim light to bright, from eighteenth-century wood and pewter to twenty-first-century stainless steel that was getting yet another polish from the cleaning staff. Then she was blinking at the sudden darkness outside, and at the frigid air, like the gust from an open freezer, while Alasdair made sure Olson locked the back door behind them. "All secure?" he called softly. "There's a good lad."

Yeah, so far Williamsburg's finest were pretty darn fine indeed. Intelligent. Free of chips on shoulders. Compatible, even.

Something in the back of her mind, behind lead shielding thicker and heavier than the cold lead weighting her steps, whispered about honey catching more flies than vinegar.

Together, they picked their way between the tables and over the uneven paving of Chowning's garden eating area. A thin mist filtered through the overhead arbor and onto Jean's glasses, so that every light seemed to smear and run. From the gate that opened onto the Courthouse lawn, she looked over at the tree, the hanging tree, to see the tarpaulin-screen had been replaced by yellow police tape. Not the sort of yellow ribbon that indicated a happy homecoming.

A couple of flashlights were witch-lights below the rust-flecked canopy, ghosts unable to rest, demanding if not vengeance, at least justice. She could hear them wailing… No, that was just the wind in the branches surging overhead.

Alasdair held the gate open for her, on automatic pilot, she estimated—his gaze was fixed in the middle distance. She could almost see the smoke from his intellectual mills wafting from his ears.

Side by side they walked quietly across Duke of Gloucester Street, away from the camera- and microphone-equipped figures camped in the aureole of light at the tavern's front door. The church was now dark and the street vacant, although a distant shout or two echoed from the light-filled oasis of Merchant's Square half a mile distant—college kids, probably, taking advantage of Halloween falling on a Saturday night.

Halloween. All Hallows' Eve. Samhain, the old Celtic

quarter day, the end of the old year, when the gates of the otherworld opened and dark forces walked abroad.

Dark and yet very human forces were walking here, concealed against the dark silhouettes of buildings and trees. Jean peered into the night, but the tiny nebulae of treelamps threw out no more light than your average firefly. She increased her pace along the milky way of the crushed shell path, Alasdair crunching a rhythm beside her until they stopped at Francis Street. The dim shape of their own house, sanctuary, stood just beyond the crosswalk. Looking right and left along the ribbon of licorice that was the street, they stepped off the curb.

And something heavier than lead settled on Jean's shoulders, so that her knees almost buckled. The hair on the back of her neck rose like antennae. Beside her, Alasdair gasped as though he'd been punched in the stomach. As one, they turned toward the ravine where the street fell and rose again, the leaf and branch-clogged hollow where, last night, they'd walked through a pool of dank air scented like an open grave.

In the blackness beneath the trees, something, someone, moved. She wasn't glowing—despite cartoons and movies, ghosts didn't glow—but her white apron, her white collar, her white face below a white cap, reflected just enough of the lights radiating from the Inn and the Lodge to define themselves against the gloom.

She was a substantial woman, her jowls, her broad shoulders, the hillock of her chest all drooping toward a protuberant belly. The furrows in her face counted out her years, too many of them for her to be pregnant—she was merely well-fed.

Her eyes were dark holes ripped in the mask of her face, staring unfocused into another world. She held something in her hands, something round, with a tall neck.

The Bellarmine bottle.

Walking slowly and painfully, old or sick or both, she crossed from the north side of the road to the south and disappeared into the underbrush. A gust of wind spattered rain across the pavement, and across Jean's face, and filled her nose with a thick rich scent—cooking meat, baking bread, spices, sweetness drifting down the air like an angelic chorus—no, the scent was of raw meat, swiftly turning rancid.

The smell vanished just as surely as the ghost. Jean sniffed, sensing nothing but rain on vegetation with an afterglow of exhaust fume.

She only realized Alasdair's hand was wrapped around her upper arm when it clenched and let go. The quick pain broke through the weight and trickling chill of another dimension. She looked up at his face, ashen in the tentative light. "Did you…?" She gulped what felt like glue and tried again. "Did you smell the food cooking? And rotting?"

"Oh aye. If our wee house was once a kitchen, then I'm thinking we've just met the cook."

"She was carrying the bottle from the mantelpiece."

"The witch bottle, to match the Witch Box, eh?"

"But a witch bottle protects against witches, and the Box seems to have been the tool of…"

The headlights of a car sent their shadows leaping toward the ravine. They lunged for the opposite curb, and stood watching the lights glare down into the ravine and then up again, illuminating nothing except damp leaves squashed onto the asphalt.

"A tool of the sort of tale-telling and foolishness that leads to murder," concluded Alasdair. He opened the gate while Jean dug out the key, too tired to argue yet again about the complexities of seeing-as-believing and believing-as-seeing.

The living-room lamp they'd left on glowed a welcome through the curtains even if it didn't light the keyhole. Jean sniffed again, detecting a hint of smoke. Not the sweetish smoke she'd sensed in the house twice now, but the acrid reek of a cigarette. And there was the cigarette itself, a wrinkled filter tip lying on the cement step. "We had a visitor."

"I don't see a note."

"I've known ghosts who'll open and shut locked doors." Wiping her shoes on the mat, Jean stepped inside, Alasdair wiping and stepping just behind.

Two black-and-white whiskered faces looked up at them from the rag rug.

"Well then," Alasdair said, "I've never known a cat opening a locked door."

"They must have slipped inside when the housekeeper came to turn down the bed. Hi, Bushrod, hey, Bucktrout—sorry I don't remember which of you is which…"

"I think I'd better let you know that you're not alone," said a woman's voice behind them.

Jean's heart careened into her throat, knocking her wits from her head. She tried to seize them, but they ran through her mind like sand through her fingers. *What the...*

In slow motion, Alasdair spun around. In even slower motion he seized Jessica Evesdottir by the wrist and hauled her forward onto the rug.

The cats seized the opportunity and made a break for the great outdoors.

Oh, Jean thought. Jessica. She wasn't a fugitive after all.

Her hair was scooped clumsily back from her face and its silver streak was matted with spray or gel—no doubt she'd been wearing a cap for the play. Her mascara had smeared beneath her eyes, making the slack skin there look like the black sheep's bags of wool. Her flamingo-pink T-shirt, reading, "Well-behaved women never make history," her windbreaker, designer jeans, and high-heeled boots all signaled that the show was over and she was off the interpreter's clock, free to wear something considerably more assertive than a seventeenth-century goodwife's garb. And her eyes were hardly downcast and demure. They targeted Alasdair. She wrenched her wrist from his hand. "Great reflexes you've got there."

"How'd you get yourself in here?" he asked, every word a pellet of hail.

"I'm friends with a manager at the Inn. No, I'm not going to give you a name. I don't want to get anyone into trouble."

"Then why come here?"

Settling her heart in its usual place and taking a deep breath, Jean forced her feet to carry her over to the door, which she shut against the darkness and rain. When she flipped the nearby switch, the ceiling light filled the room with blessed illumination. Candlelight might be romantic. So might the glow of the small table lamp. Right now romance was the last thing on anyone's mind.

"I don't know who I'm less eager to see, the Dingwalls or the media," Jessica explained. "So I thought I'd hole up here until they all went away and as a public-spirited citizen I could turn myself in to Detective What's-her-face. Yes, I got her messages. Typical woman in a traditionally male profession, she has to out-tough the tough guys."

If she was trying to be tough, Jean thought, wouldn't she call herself "Steve"?

Alasdair frowned, but Stephanie didn't need him—or Jean—to defend her. "Why come here?"

"I saw you two talking to Matt last night, and outside the cabinetmaker's shop this afternoon talking to—that was Stephanie Venegas, right?"

"Right."

"Typical police, can't do a thing about the break-in at Wes's place, then bark up the wrong tree with Sam Gould.

His bark is pretty loud, but he has no bite at all, if you'll excuse the play on words."

Alasdair's face showed not the least trace of amusement.

Jean responded to a grumble from her stomach by sending a longing look toward the pantry and the packets of cocoa. Delayed gratification, she told herself. "Sit down, Jessica. Would you like a cup of tea?"

"Thanks." Jessica plumped down into one of the wingback chairs by the hearth, where, judging by the wrinkled throw pillow, she'd already been sitting, her purse and a garment bag close by. She nodded at the cup and saucer on the coffee table. "I fixed myself tea, sorry, but I was here for a couple of hours, and the cats didn't offer to run over to the Lodge and get me another gin and tonic."

Jean chose the desk chair, not without a suspicious glance toward her computer—the lid was shut, the power off. Beside it sat the witch bottle. Had Jessica moved the bottle or had it moved on its own? But Cardinal Bellarmine's ceramic face revealed nothing.

With a surreptitious sniff—she didn't smell horse shit on anyone's shoes, not that her nose was a finely tuned forensic instrument—Jean slid her notebook and a couple of pencils out of her bag and prepared to play Sergeant Olson's role. Her movement didn't escape Jessica's notice. With an exaggerated roll of her eyes the woman settled back, all but groping for a seat belt.

On the couch, Alasdair assumed full interrogatory mode, elbows on knees, hands clasped, snow gathering on his brow. "Why us? How'd you know where we're staying?"

"I called Matt this afternoon and asked who you were. He filled me in, especially since he'd already looked you up on the 'net. You might be head of a security agency now, but you used to be a cop. And you and Jean are getting a pretty good track record solving crimes."

Hence Matt's remark about crime solvers. Jean didn't have to glance at *her* Scot to know he was thinking about reputations and two-edged swords. What she was thinking was that she hadn't told Matt they were staying at the Dinwiddie Kitchen. But it wasn't as though they were in hiding.

"Well," Jessica went on, "there's been a crime and I'm suspected of committing it. And I bet Detective Venegas would love to finger me for poor old Wes's murder yesterday. I could use some respectable allies."

"Then you'd best be telling us the truth."

"Yeah." Jessica looked at Jean. "I didn't recognize you last night. I was distracted by Rachel. Silly girl, Dylan might be good for a few laughs, but not for the long run. She should hardly be worrying about the long run. Marriage is a crock, you know. Men and women should just live next door to each other and get together for happy hour."

There was something to be said for that, Jean thought. Alasdair didn't respond.

"You're Jean Inglis. Fairbairn now, Matt says."

"I got divorced and went back to my maiden name."

"Your maiden name is still your father's name, evidence of a patriarchal society. But gender nomenclature isn't our topic for tonight, is it?"

"Ms. Evesdottir," said Alasdair, reclaiming her attention.

"Dr.," Jessica corrected. "Let's get this over with. No, I'm not a big fan of Sharon Dingwall's, but she at least has some intelligence, unlike that oaf of a husband. She's—she was—the brains of the operation. The problem is, it's Tim's sister who's the money. I'm shocked, appalled, fill in the appropriate verb, that someone killed her. It wasn't me. I didn't do it. I'd check out that brute of a husband, if I were you. Thumbscrews might get his attention."

"Where were you between six-thirty and seven-thirty this evening?"

"Getting ready for the play, then saying my lines at the beginning."

"Why not stay for the entire program, especially with your daughter playing the lead role?"

"I wrote it. I know how it ends. And Rachel plays Mary like a victim."

"Wasn't Mary a victim of gender prejudice and paranoia," asked Jean, "you know, society using accusations of witchcraft to keep women submissive?"

"Sure. But I'd rather think of Mary as defiant. Her story is longer and more complex than I knew when I wrote *Witches and Wenches,* damn it, but then, this way there'll be a second edition."

"And yet you're avoiding the media?" Jean couldn't help but ask.

Jessica laughed. "*Touché.* Let's just say that to every press conference there is a season. Anyway, I did my bit in the play and headed over to the Lodge for a drink."

"You didn't get there until almost eight," Alasdair reminded her.

"I stopped to change my clothes in a restroom at the Lodge. No one saw me, I'm sorry to say, but at the time, I didn't know I was going to need an alibi." Jessica rooted around in her purse and produced a pack of cigarettes. "May I?"

"No," said Alasdair. "You've already left a fag end on the porch."

"A cigarette," Jean translated quickly.

"I know that one. I've traveled in the U.K." With a shrug and a crinkle of cellophane, Jessica stowed the pack away. "I know I should stop smoking, get me a nicotine patch, but I've already got an estrogen patch. You know what they say, once you're past fifty it's patch, patch, patch."

That one sailed right by Alasdair, Jean estimated. He

didn't bother grabbing for it, but went on, "Sharon rang you from her mobile just before she was killed, replying to you phoning her."

"Yeah, we were playing cell phone tag. She wanted to meet me after the play. I called her, she didn't pick up, so I left a message. By the time she got back to me I'd turned off my phone and was hoping everyone in the audience had, too."

Jean remembered Tim and Sharon and their respective calls from Kelly, at a time they'd been cautious about who could overhear. Sharon, at least, learned quickly.

"I told her to wait for me beside the Courthouse, but I didn't pick up her message saying okay until I got to the Lodge. Little did I realize it was a message from beyond the grave." Jessica shrank into the chair, leaning her head on her hand. "I called her back, to tell her to come up to the Lodge instead, but again, voice mail. If I'd only looked for her behind the Courthouse…"

She might still be alive, Jean concluded, and swallowed the acid welling in her throat. Had Sharon's phone been playing the *Mission: Impossible* theme while she died?

Alasdair was doing his best great stone face impression. "And why was Sharon after meeting with you the night? With the both of you being on such good terms and all."

"Business." Jessica made the word an acid hiss. "Nothing to do with the murder."

"It's for the police to be saying what's doing with what."

A faint ding-dong resonated in Jean's gut, first one note, then two, then an entire peal of bells. Great, it all came back to her now, when she was so tired. She put down her pencil and wriggled her fingers. "Your business with Sharon was the new material for *Witches and Wenches.* It's the new original source Alasdair and I heard Louise Dietz and her friend Denny talking about."

"Louise." The name was another hiss. "She descended on me tonight like a wolf on a lamb. All right, on a sheep, on mutton dressed as lamb—no one gets less respect than a woman of a certain age."

Alasdair's expression was blank as driven snow.

"She was all sweetness and light and dig, dig, dig. All because I asked her to help with a literary reference. Second-rate scholar that she is, living on borrowed glory."

Standard academic procedure. Jean picked up her pencil. "I heard her say something about Nathaniel Bacon, so I've been thinking your source had to do with his rebellion. What—did you say something about the Dingwalls and 'Bacon' and she extrapolated, logically enough, from there? But Nathaniel Bacon isn't your field. You helped Sharon track down the name of the indentured servant who supposedly brought the charm stone to the colonies in the 1660s. Mary Napier."

"Eh?" asked Alasdair.

Jessica stared at Jean, her expression shifting swiftly from astonishment to anger.

"You went to eastern Scotland and to London—the British Library, maybe—while Wes was studying the Witch Box at Blair. Berwick is in eastern Scotland. Francis Stewart, the Earl of Bothwell, and his supposed coven of witches were tried in Berwick—when? 1590?"

Jessica's mouth set itself in a stubborn line.

The snow gathered on Alasdair's stony face, forming the sort of overhanging cornice that could collapse into an avalanche and carry away anyone in its path, the guilty and the innocent alike. "I'd be answering the question, if I was you."

"I'm not trying to trump you academically," Jean insisted. "I—we—are trying to help solve a murder. Two murders, counting Wesley's."

Closing her eyes, Jessica rubbed her lids. She probably

hoped to see something different when she opened them. Water dripped outside. A bus drove by and somewhere someone was whistling “Over the Hills and Far Away.”

No, just as Jean recognized the tune, the whistle stopped. Maybe all she was hearing was the air leaking from her brain.

Several splats resounded from the window above the desk and she leaped out of the chair.

EIGHTEEN

JESSICA HALF-ROSE, then fell back as Alasdair dematerialized from the couch and rematerialized at the door. Throwing it open, he hurtled onto the porch. Great reflexes, indeed.

Dropping the pencil, Jean raced across the room and switched on the porch light, then a fraction later switched it off again—no need to make him a target.

The sound of laughter and running feet came from the street, and she caught a glimpse of several people—young people, judging by body shape and gait—loping away. A couple were wrapped in sheets, another wore plastic armor and helmet over a sweatshirt, a fourth boasted a wide-brimmed and plumed pirate's hat. "Happy Halloween!" called a young woman's voice, and they were gone, absorbed into shadows.

"The pranksters are out tricking," Jessica said. "Only little kids actually ask for treats. Rachel has a vampire costume to wear at a party, but she's gone to Matt's house. He's a better mother at times like this than I am."

Again Jean gulped her heart back down to her chest. With an aggravated sigh, Alasdair disappeared around the side of the house and a few seconds later returned. "They've chucked eggs against the window. Like moths, attracted by the light. The rain'll wash most of it away. And send the rascals inside—it's a dreich night and they'll get drookit, right enough." He wiped his feet, slammed the door, and locked it. Water droplets glistened on his hair and the shoulders of his sweater like diamond dust.

Hoping the cats were safely tucked away at their home, Jean went back to her chair and angled it a bit further away from the window. This would have been a good night for a fire in the little fireplace and a cozy conversation, drinks, cuddles. But right now she felt as cuddly as a cactus, and she'd rather grasp a nettle than Alasdair. She took up her back-up pencil and waited, lips sealed.

Alasdair sat back down. "You were saying, Dr. Evesdottir?"

"I wasn't," Jessica said with a laugh. Rueful, sardonic, but it was a laugh. "I asked for the third degree, didn't I? Yeah, Wesley was murdered, too. I'm even more shocked about that, since he was considerably lower on the obnoxious scale than Sharon. I had a very brief affair with him, seemed like the thing to do since we traveled to the U.K. together. I broke up with him a couple of weeks ago, all very nice and civilized—much more civilized than the break-up with Matt, if the truth be told. Although Matt and me and that, that arrogant dictator-mother of his made a pact to spare Rachel the worst of it."

"Good of you," said Alasdair, with only a trace of sarcasm. He didn't point out that Wesley's mates thought the break-up had been traumatic for him. "Civilized" could simply mean that she hadn't slashed the tires on his car.

"And no, I didn't kill Wes, either. He was getting threatening calls, he wouldn't tell me from whom. Since he did say 'he,' I think they were from Tim, the animal."

"Not Matt?" Alasdair asked. "Was he not jealous?"

"He liked Wes. He didn't know about Wes and me. We were discreet."

Discretion being in the eye of the beholder, Jean told herself, and shifted uncomfortably on the hard chair.

"Why would Tim be threatening Wes, then?" Alasdair asked.

"Wanting Wes's information about the Witch Box. He finally just stole it."

"Possibly." Alasdair leaned back, ceding the floor to Jean.

"The Berwick witch trials were in 1590?" she asked.

"Yes."

"One of Francis Stewart's coven of witches—so-called coven, although he was undoubtedly up to something."

"Playing games, hocus-pocus, woo-woo," Jessica said. "Witchcraft was about social issues, about who holds power, about definitions of right and wrong and justice, not the supernatural."

"Some people see supernatural," Jean told her. "Some people see conspiracy or witchcraft, others..."

"See ghosts?" Jessica asked with a smirk.

She'd heard them talking as they came in. Alasdair's cornice of snow thickened. Jean plunged on. "One of Francis Stewart's associates was named Barbara Napier. Like Francis, and unlike their other associates, she got off, supposedly because of her social status."

"Rumor has it she was the widow of Earl Archibald of Angus or the wife of an Edinburgh burgess. In reality she was neither. She was reprieved because she was pregnant. The witch-killers were perfectly happy killing children, or orphaning them, but this time the victim got off."

"Maybe she was protected by Francis Stewart's family," Jean suggested.

"Probably she worked for them. Barbara—same name as my mother-in-law, which doesn't tell you a thing but probably should, interfering, bossy… Well, Barbara Napier may or may not have been servant-class, but her great-granddaughter Mary Napier certainly was. Mary was born in Berwick in 1660 and followed the Stewarts back to London after Cromwell and the Puritans lost power—she shows up on a palace payroll as a scullery maid, then is listed on the manifest of a ship leaving London in 1675. She was indentured to a John Armstrong of Middle Plantation as a cook."

Jean's spine tingled. She felt rather than saw Alasdair draw himself up and cast a glance at the bottle sitting at her elbow—of course he'd noticed it wasn't where it belonged. But life expectancy was against Mary living in this little house in the 1750s.

Jessica went on, "As a skilled laborer, Mary's indenture was probably for no more than five years. But the only further record of her is in 1685, at her trial for witchcraft in James City County. After she'd been ducked or swum here at Middle Plantation, she confessed to casting spells and charming her neighbors—I used the exact words from the trial transcripts for the play. People will confess to anything under torture, even woo-woo."

"Francis Stewart." Alasdair pronounced the surname as only a Scot could, pressing it through a pinhole until it exploded out the other side. "Women named Napier accused of witchcraft. Is there a legitimate connection with the Witch Box, or is that a fancy of the Dingwalls?"

"Sharon came to Matt asking about immigration and witchcraft. Since he'd helped me find material on Mary Napier for my books, he sent her to me. Oh, I knew Sharon had some unorthodox ideas, but she was so knowledgeable I blamed that all on Tim and worked with her. Big mistake."

"You'd already written about Mary's life here in the colonies," Jean said. "It was only when Sharon asked about Mary's ancestry that you traced her back to the Berwick witches. That's why you went with Wesley to Blair, to use resources in the U.K."

"Imagine my amazement, and my gratification, when Sharon's hunch actually paid off. At the time, I thought Mary's ancestry would be an interesting sidebar to the story of the Witch Box, like the story of the charm stone. I kept on working with Sharon so I could nail down the facts, get enough for a second edition." Jessica let her head fall back against the chair. "And now I'm in deep shit."

"Oh aye," said Alasdair, and waited.

When Jessica didn't speak, Jean asked, "So why did you fall out with Sharon?"

"Why has she been going around calling me two-faced and self-serving, and why did I respond that she was slandering and scandalizing—well, she started it, dropping hints that *Witches and Wenches* was plagiarized from her and Tim's unpublished, or unfilmed, to be accurate, work. Yeah, right." Jessica lifted her head wearily, as though it was too heavy for her neck, and turned her face toward Jean. "Matt says you blew the whistle on a plagiarist and it cost you your career."

"Matt looks like being quite well-informed," murmured Alasdair.

No kidding. Not that Alasdair needed to point it out with such relish. "It gave me an excuse to give up my career is all. You didn't answer the question. Why did you and Sharon fall out?"

"I found documentation I hadn't expected. I wanted to publish it academically, with proper referencing, in my own book and in refereed journals. But Sharon wants, wanted, to use it in that movie. Which turned out to be more fantasy-paranoid than I'd thought. Hoped. Feared." Jessica snorted. "Yeah, I sure pulled the wool over my own eyes."

Jean didn't miss the subtext, the pressure to publish, and

publish well, or perish. You didn't have to be ambitious to want, to need, a good rep. "So what is it?"

"Is what?"

"The documentation," Alasdair enunciated.

"Imagine a trumpet fanfare here," Jessica said with a pinched, pained smile. "I have a note from Charlotte Murray, Lady Dunmore—which was her husband's title, of course—at any rate, she wrote the note shortly after she returned home from Virginia in 1775, about the history of the charm stone, with a sketch of the Box."

"Whoa!" Jean's pencil hit the page with a thunk. "Where did you find that?"

Jessica looked suddenly down at her lap, at her hands and their red nails kneading her denim-clad thighs like a cat's paws.

The curve of Alasdair's eyebrows indicated conjecture. Jean saw his conjecture and raised it with a surmise or two. *Listen,* she told herself.

Outside, the wind whined and water dripped off the roof. A bus rumbled by, its tires whooshing along the wet pavement. Inside, the clock ticked and something creaked in the bedroom.

"What do you know about the Witch Box replica? Is it an exact copy?" Alasdair tried leading questions.

Jessica inhaled, then blew the breath out between lips hard as the iron hinges on the Witch Box. "Damn straight it is," she said to her lap. "Wes spent days measuring and making sketches. He didn't do sloppy work."

"And he turned over the archives at Blair searching for documentation."

She looked up sharply, her gaze glancing off each face. "You never met Wes. You've got to realize that he was, well, not the classic absent-minded professor. An absent-minded artisan. Just last week he misplaced a chisel and thought Sam Gould took it, and actually lost his temper. But that was Sam's fault. He couldn't just let it all slide off his back—he had to get defensive."

Jessica didn't know—or shouldn't know—that Wesley had been jabbed with a chisel. "Did he find it?" Jean asked.

"Yeah. He'd taken it home with some other tools."

Where, as the flicker in Alasdair's eyes registered, his killer had probably picked it up. A killer who he'd known well enough to admit to his apartment—or to meet by the pond. "And Hagedorn just happened to bring the paper with the note and the sketch home as well? That paper's the property of the Duke of Atholl."

"Can he prove he ever had such a paper? I don't think so. A secretary showed us into a room stacked with books and files, pointed to the right time period, and took off. Wes figured the odds of finding something useful were slim to none, so he concentrated on the Box itself."

"It was you striking lucky, then," said Alasdair.

"Maybe I got lucky at a street market in London. Maybe that sketch has nothing to do with Blair." She smiled sweetly.

Alasdair scowled.

"Does the sketch show the charm stone?" Jean asked. "What does Charlotte's note say about that?"

"The Box looked in her day like it does now. There's a space that Charlotte says used to hold Francis Stewart's charm stone, but that the stone was stolen by a maid and taken to the colonies. No mention of the servant's name, but I've settled that."

"So did Charlotte find the stone here in Virginia?"

"She doesn't say. She was an educated aristocrat living during the Enlightenment, remember? The laws against witchcraft had been repealed in 1736, even though people still believed in it—Switzerland killed a witch as late as

1782. Hell, people still believe it—look at all that hoo-hah about Harry Potter." Jessica rolled her eyes. "But to Charlotte, a charm stone was only a curiosity."

"Does she say why a non-aristocrat stole the stone during a more superstitious era?" Jean asked.

"Charlotte thought the servant had heard how settlers dropped like flies here in the colonies, so wanted to use the stone's healing properties. Me, I think she thought it would empower her. A pretty bold move, emigrating."

"Sharon thought if the stone belonged to Francis Stewart then it was more likely a cursing stone."

"Like there's any such thing as either a healing or a cursing stone."

Jean couldn't resist playing devil's advocate. "The Berwick witches met horrible deaths. Francis Stewart was permanently disgraced. Mary was tortured. Wesley's dead. Sharon's dead."

The minute movement of Jessica's shoulders was either a shrug or a twitch.

"And now the sketch has been stolen again, has it?" Alasdair asked, taking his usual position on the side of the angels. "Along with Hagedorn's plans and photos."

The plans and photos in Sharon's tote bag, Jean told herself. The ones Dylan wanted to keep from falling into the hands of the police. If the Dingwalls, singly or collectively, were capable of stealing the replica Witch Box, then they were capable of stealing Wesley's plans.

"A savage like Tim is good for a little breaking and entering," Jessica said. "But while he got the photos and scale drawings and Wes's annotations, he didn't get Charlotte's note."

"Aye?" Alasdair prodded.

Jessica's brow puckered. Looking at neither Jean nor Alasdair but at a framed Tasha Tudor print across the room, she said, "I can't tell you where it is. It's safe, okay? It's being authenticated—everything with the Dingwalls' fingerprints on it is suspect and I don't want there to be any question about this. There's too much at stake."

Again Jean and Alasdair exchanged a glance—Jessica might have told the truth, but it wasn't the whole truth.

"That's why you've come to us, then," Alasdair said. "Let alone being a person of interest in Sharon's murder, you've committed a crime in the U.K. Or you're covering up a crime committed in the U.K. I'll own it was Wes who actually took the document. Sharon knew that as well, did she? And Tim?"

Jessica's features might as well have been carved of wood, although by a finer hand than the one that had originally made the Witch Box with its primitive tendrils and small, atavistic faces.

Thick as thieves, Matt had said. *No honor among thieves.* Yes, Matt was rather too well-informed. That didn't mean he was guilty of any more than snooping.

And Tim had said, *Exact is as exact does.* Jean wondered again just what he and Sharon thought the Witch Box was supposed to do. Either Witch Box. Had they stolen the replica from Blair knowing how difficult it would be to steal the original from the DeWitt Wallace Museum? And yet Tim had said Wesley's copy wasn't exact.

Well, no—the copy had never included the charm stone, had it?

Jean's temples ached—when she hadn't been clenching her teeth she'd been frowning in concentration or dismay. Her mind was still echoing, but not necessarily with bells, just like a bell, the thoughts dinging back and forth inside her skull.

She watched Alasdair watching Jessica. How much

more were they going to get out of her before turning her over to…?

The room burst not with Jessica's trumpet fanfare but with an electronic version of "The 1812 Overture," the cannon accompaniment provided by Jean's feet hitting the floor, ready to fight or flee.

Oh. Her cell phone.

She scrambled for her bag, then for the phone. She didn't recognize the number on the screen. "Hello?"

"This is Stephanie Venegas," said the by now familiar voice, tart as citrus. "I'm sorry—I realize it's late. Is Alasdair there?"

"Yeah" was all Jean could force past the drumming of her heart in her throat. One more surprise and it would burst from her chest and flap around at her feet like a fish out of water. She gave Alasdair the phone, saying, "It's Stephanie, your new best friend."

And she realized what she'd said when Alasdair's eyes lit with both anger and dismay, like northern lights flaring over a snowy tundra. Turning away, he put the phone to his ear. "Alasdair Cameron. Oh aye, press conference at nine A.M. No need sending a car—I'll drive myself—I've registered for the hire care as well."

By pushing on the arms of the chair, Jessica managed to thrust herself into a standing position. She reached for her purse and the garment bag.

Alasdair's large, exceedingly capable hand fell on her arm. Into the phone, he said, "I've got Jessica Evesdottir here. I'll walk her over to the tavern, shall I? Ah, well then. Cheers."

"You bastard," Jessica stated, with more weariness than malice.

"I'm taking you at your word, the one about public-spirited citizen." Closing the phone, Alasdair handed it to Jean without looking at her.

She tucked the phone back into her bag, wishing she could creep in there with it. Where was her pencil? Oh. On the floor. She tucked it into the bag, too, and closed her notebook.

"Sergeant Olson's coming round to collect you," Alasdair told Jessica.

"Yeah. Fine. I knew I should have called my lawyer while I was sitting here waiting for you, but it's a Saturday night. And he's a divorce lawyer. He has colleagues who know how to deal with this sort of situation."

"What sort of situation is this, then?"

"Murky," Jessica said. "Real murky."

A fusillade of thunks hit the clapboard siding of the house—not the squashy splat of eggs but the more sharply defined impacts of what were probably rocks. If one of those hit the window…

"Bugger!" Releasing Jessica's arm, Alasdair headed for the door, Jean at his heels, if not leaping like a gazelle at least not lumbering like a hippo. She was already hyperventilating from the sudden blare of "1812"—and from the words that had escaped her lips. *Your new best friend.*

Alasdair wrenched open the door and stepped onto the porch. Just as Jean lurched out beside him, that cold, wet blanket of perception landed on her shoulders, leaking ice water down her back.

The wet sidewalks, the damp streets, were empty. The lights of the Inn and the Lodge were smudged by the drifting rain, distant galaxies. From an even greater distance, to say nothing of through the corridors of time, came the faint cries of derision and the impact of more rocks, and a trace of that rotting-meat smell, too, all percolating up from her own senses, not in via the sound and light waves of ordinary physics.

Extrasensory perception. Extraphysical transmission. Woo-woo.

"Our ghost was not the most popular person in town," whispered Alasdair, more to himself than to Jean.

"Kids teasing, throwing rocks—I wonder why?"

Without answering, let alone looking at her, Alasdair stepped back into the house. Again she followed. Tagged along. Played second banana. Or maybe third.

Jessica was staring at them as though they'd suddenly started dancing a springle-ring. "What the hell is wrong with you two?"

She hadn't heard or otherwise sensed a thing, had she? Jean rolled her shoulders, ridding herself of the weight of one sort of consciousness, even though the weight of another still sat on her chest like a demon dismounted from his nightmare.

A car pulled up outside and Alasdair turned back to the still-open door. "Olson's arrived."

"That's my exit line." Jessica hoisted her garment bag and her purse. "Oh, I was looking around while I was waiting for you—and no, I didn't go through your dresser drawers—I'm glad to see that Bellarmine bottle is still here."

"You've seen it before?" Jean asked.

"I brought Rachel and a couple of her friends here last year, when the archaeologists had a sort of open house, with a display of the artifacts they'd turned up. Bits of pottery, food bones, stuff like that, nothing interesting except the bottle. They found that buried beneath the hearth, obviously with apotropaic significance. Meant to turn away evil."

"I know what *apotropaic* means," Jean told her, while Alasdair said nothing.

"Nails, scrap metal, pebbles—the contents weren't typical of a witch bottle, but then, that's the point, how people attribute magical properties to just about anything, rabbit's feet, four-leaf clovers."

"One of my brothers," said Jean, "would wear the same pair of socks all through basketball season. I'd chase him around the house with a spray can of deodorant."

Olson appeared in the doorway. Alasdair said, "Here she is, Sergeant."

"I hope you're going to offer him a signed receipt," Jessica said to Olson. "No? Okay then—excuse me if I don't say thanks for the hospitality."

Olson, however, did call "Thanks" over his shoulder as Jessica led the way down the steps.

Alasdair shut the door behind them, locked it, and for what seemed like an hour but was more likely a minute stood with his back against the panels and his face turned toward the far wall, his features not dull but as blunt as the sort of instrument that had not been used on Sharon.

And every second of that minute Jean watched him and waited for him to speak.

NINETEEN

HIS EYES WERE more gray than blue, arctic ice during a long autumn twilight. The crease between his brows deepened and dragged down the crevices beside his eyes and at the corners of his mouth.

Last night he'd been angry at Stephanie's abrupt dismissal. Tonight, Jessica had made a valid point—while women in general were more likely to tend and befriend, women in traditionally male professions often defaulted to male-pattern bully-ness. However, once the territorial issues had been suitably defined for Stephanie, she was perfectly happy to add another member to her team.

So how many people made a team, anyway?

Jean dropped down into the desk chair, trying to make herself look small, unthreatening, not that Alasdair would ever find her threatening, not that she ever wanted to threaten him.

He turned toward her. She could almost hear the tension humming in his muscles. She did hear it in his voice. "Here's me, including you in the investigation as best I can, but no, you're still resenting my work. It's because she's a woman, is it? Don't be daft, Jean—she's got a partner, a significant other. His photo's on her desk. He's one of their forensics boffins."

"You asked her whether she was unattached? Why does that even matter?"

"I didn't ask her—we were having a blether is all. Are you that jealous, then?"

"Jealous?" she retorted. But what other word was there? *Why?* she'd asked him last night. And now this. She was acting like the sort of needy, grabby woman she despised. The sort of woman she'd never been before.

Alasdair had a lot to answer for.

"Don't be daft," she told him. "I don't think you're going to dump me for her. I'm sorry I made a snide remark. I'm sorry I implied your work is secondary to mine. Although..."

"Although I've implied your work is secondary to mine?"

"Stephanie and her whatever are both in the same profession. Matt said never to hook up with someone in the same profession. Either way, it's like two one-man bands meeting on a tightrope." And she added to herself, the word Matt used was *marry.*

"Ah. Matt. Maybe I should be returning the favor and muttering about your—well, no, you've known him a wee while."

"We're not talking about gender issues."

"What are we talking about, then?"

"The totality of our lives. The baggage we're carrying. The albatrosses around our necks. What did you say last night, about remembering why we made second starts? Or are you having second thoughts about changing jobs?"

That wasn't what she was asking, and he knew it. The real question—*are you having second thoughts about me?*—swayed between them like a hanged body, swollen and silent.

"Ah, Jean," he said at last, his voice rasping over the rough edges of doubt, disappointment, dignity. And perhaps a hint of fear deeper than his already-cavernous natural reserve.

He walked away into the bedroom.

The thoughts no longer pealed through her mind or

dinged against her skull. They fell like the thuds of a hammer on an anvil, each one reverberating in bone and tissue and heart.

We're tired. You say stupid things when you're tired.

Sometimes the truth comes out when you're tired. Maybe it was just a matter of time until they'd realized their lives were too complicated to ever mesh.

She knew he was too smart to cut off his nose to spite his face, and sure enough he made no move toward the couch but readied himself for bed and lay down on his half of it. No need for her to trim her own profile, either. Groaning aloud, she jammed her notebook into her bag, only then remembering she'd never offered her notes to Olson. No problem. He and Stephanie would be creating their own.

She switched off the lights, passed the pantry without a glance at the cocoa—her stomach was now clenched into a ball the size of her fist—and went through her bedtime rituals. The soap, lotion, toothpaste seemed odorless and tasteless. When she slid between the cold sheets she gazed not at Alasdair but up at the canopy. In the blurred stripes of light and shadow cast by the streetlight outside the window, it seemed more like a smothering lid than a cozy cover. Last night a cot would have been big enough for them both. Tonight she wished the bed were king-sized instead of queen-sized. Personal space. Maybe that was the real issue.

"The wee bottle's moved again," Alasdair mumbled.

Say what... Oh. There, on the dresser, barely discernible in the darkness, sat the Bellarmine bottle. Its ceramic face was turned toward them, judge, jury, executioner. But the sheets were just starting to warm up. She wasn't going to take the itinerant artifact back to the living room.

Light drove away the shadow. Shadow engulfed the light. The rain slowed to the occasional plunk. Alasdair's breathing evened out but never fell into the deep rhythms of sleep. Still he lay immobile as a gravestone.

The red numbers of the bedside clock rearranged themselves to read 12:00. Midnight. The witching hour. Dozing, she found herself strolling through the cemetery at Bruton Parish Church, the stones engraved with the names of both the quick and the dead. Waking, she remembered she'd never checked out Robert Mason's grave.

Again she dozed, and heard rocks hitting the side of the house and window glass tinkling down onto the bed.

She woke with a gasp, but couldn't move. Smothered beneath a prickling cold pall, she listened to the slow footsteps from the other room, smelled yet again that rich, sweet, smoky scent. Maybe she should drag herself out of the bed and ask the ghost to bring her that cup of cocoa. But ghosts were only memories made perceptible.

A pallid shape walked by the living-room door, white cap, white apron over a big belly, white face bland and blank. Yes, it was the same apparition they'd seen in the street.

Even though Alasdair was lying two feet away from her, Jean sensed his rigidity and the chill radiating from his flesh. He was awake. He was feeling the ghost, too. That was something they had in common, a sixth sense. And less than a year of intense mutual experience, including some knock-down, drag-out fights.

They could just as well have had another of those this evening. But no. *By all means,* she thought, *let's be civilized.* Ice wasn't as dramatic as fire, but it could be just as final.

The tactile cold, the elusive odors, ebbed, and the house slipped into silence. The Bellarmine bottle sat on the dresser, unmoving if not immovable—the small face was now turned away from the bed.

Alasdair exhaled, long and slow. Jean closed her eyes

again and started counting sheep, and big-footed rabbits wearing dirty socks…

She woke up with a start at a brisk knock on the door. After a fuzzy moment she realized it was morning, if a dim one. She was lying alone in the bed, stretched out flat as a grave effigy an inch from her own edge. The rest of the covers were so smooth she wondered if she'd imagined Alasdair sleeping there at all.

"Thank you kindly," said his voice from the living room.

Eric's voice replied, "You're welcome."

"You've spoken with Detective Venegas, have you?"

"With Sergeant Olson. Not much I could tell him, just that I'd delivered breakfast to Mr. Hagedorn and Miz Evesdottir. I only recognized her at the time, not him. A real shame about Mr. Hagedorn and then Miz Dingwall last night."

"Oh aye. A right shame."

"Thank you, sir," Eric said, presumably for another tip—Alasdair was nothing if not punctilious about observing foreign customs—and the door shut.

Breakfast, Jean thought, her stomach no longer clenched but flaccid. Breakfast signaled a new day, even if it began burdened with the old.

By the time she dressed, the ambrosial aroma of coffee filled the house. Like one of Pavlov's dogs salivating at the dinner bell, all she had to do was anticipate caffeine and the lint clinging to her brain began to dissolve.

She found Alasdair seated at the table, a plate of bacon and eggs and a newspaper before him. He looked up at her over his reading glasses. "I organized an omelet for you."

"Thank you." She sat down, poured herself a cup of coffee, doctored it with milk, and drank. After a few bites of her everything-but-the-kitchen-sink omelet, she felt strong enough to try some talk so small it was infinitesimal. "American cooks put tomatoes and mushrooms in an omelet, but not on a plate with eggs and sausage."

"No accounting for tastes." He turned the page of the paper. Reading upside-down, Jean saw a story about the sudden rash of murders, footnoted with soothing quotes from Foundation officials. She, civilian, hanger-on, whatever, knew more than any of them.

"You know," she said, "a few historians would be interested in a message written and sketch drawn by Charlotte Murray, but there's nothing in particular at stake. I don't see why that document's a motive for murder. If it is."

"Jessica's hiding the truth." Alasdair smeared jelly over a piece of toast.

"I noticed. Do you think she killed Sharon? Or Wesley, for that matter?"

"If Jessica was trying to keep first Wesley and then Sharon from grabbing the document and the glory as well, then…"

"But she came to us."

Crunching the toast, Alasdair said thickly, "She's got neck, Jessica."

Nerve. Yeah. And ambition. "The Dingwalls claim that Charlotte manipulated her husband's posting to Virginia, so she could come here and search for the charm stone. I'm sure Tim will extrapolate her mentioning it at all into proof Francis Bacon's papers are hidden here, original Shakespeare manuscripts, plans to split the atom, whatever. You know, Mary Napier stole them from inside the Witch Box and brought them to Nathaniel Bacon."

"There's a house of cards, and no mistake."

"More of a palace of cards."

That drew a hint of a smile from his lips, even as dark circles cradled the ice blue of his eyes beneath his glasses. His skin was even fairer than usual, the white of bog cotton or sea foam, indicating that his blood supply had been diverted to his brain. Motive. Opportunity. Suspects. Alibis. Now more than ever he had to prove his competence.

So did she, damn it.

He paralleled his knife and fork across his empty plate and pushed back from the table. "I'll be ringing Ian, then, Sunday or no Sunday, with the latest developments. And then I'll be driving myself to the press conference. Fancy joining me?"

There was a rather bedraggled olive branch. A shame she didn't have one of her own. "No, thank you, I have to do some research in the Historic Area."

"Very good then." He paced into the bedroom. She heard him using the bedside telephone to make his call, when her phone was… Probably still on. Carrying a second cup of coffee to the desk, she found the phone in her bag and checked it over. It was still juiced despite its busy day yesterday, which was more than she could say of herself.

She booted up her computer and listened to Alasdair's voice outline the facts of the case. Then it was Ian's turn. Jean, pretty good at extrapolation herself, filled in the news from P and S.

The CCTV system at Blair didn't have a camera focused on the corner where the replica Witch Box had been sitting—Ian might should have a word with Blair about that—but the tapes showed that Quentin had most certainly been there. Notch up one lie to Quentin's account.

Kelly had had herself a right good look-around before opening the alarmed door, nothing casual about it. Notch up suspicious behavior to Kelly's.

Since the replica hadn't turned up on the British antiquities market, or on a rubbish tip, for that matter, come Monday Ian was hereby delegated to make inquiries of the different shipping companies. And whilst he was chatting with Blair, ask after an eighteenth-century document missing from the muniments room. Just now Alasdair had better be getting himself to Williamsburg Police headquarters.

Desultorily, Jean checked her e-mail—nothing interesting—and indulged herself by scanning the message boards at The One Ring.net.

Unlike the Dingwalls' fantasies, Tolkien's were good and solid. They were fantasies to live by, ones to explore, ones that didn't melt away like cotton candy and leave a bad taste in your mouth. Tolkien had given one of his heroes, Elessar, the high king, a green stone set in a silver brooch, a charm stone in a way, intended to bless and heal.

Last May, when they had first met, it was when Alasdair had made a Tolkien reference that she'd noticed him again. Now she noticed him bustling through the bedroom and across the living room, clad in a sports jacket and Celtic-interlace tie, professional and personable at once. "Well then, I'm away."

She held out the car keys. "Here you go."

He plucked them from her hand.

"Alasdair," she said, at the exact instant he said, "Jean, I'm not so sure…"

What? Not so sure about the relationship? Or not so sure about driving, or Jessica's testimony, or whether Wesley's and Sharon's deaths were related—well, no, he couldn't be wondering about that.

He'd better not be reading pathetic neediness in her expression. But then, she could read no more in his than the firm mouth of duty and the steady gaze of first-things-first. This was a man who'd made opacity an art form.

Don't ask, don't tell.

"See you later" was all she said, with the best smile she could summon, touched as it was with rue.

And he was gone. The car was parked in the lot next to

the Inn. She waited long enough for him to reach it, and longer, but she heard no squealing tires or crumpling metal. It was only a few blocks to the police station, after all. If he was versatile enough to change jobs and take on an outlander, he was versatile enough to drive on the right.

She no longer felt a hammer thudding on an anvil inside her head. Now she was hearing a sound like the drone of bagpipes, a low reverberation that was both discordant and harmonic, underlying every lilt and lift of thought, of speech, of movement. *Alasdair...*

Duty called. First things first. Jean opened the website for Bruton Parish Church. Aha. The first church on the site, when the area had been Middle Plantation, had been built in 1674, just about the time Mary Napier was deciding to try her luck in the colonies—perhaps because her luck had run out at home, where officials took a fatal view of thievery.

The present church dated from 1715, the year of one of the Jacobite Rebellions in Scotland that had failed miserably to put the Stewarts back on the throne. No matter how precarious life had been on what was then a frontier, life wasn't any more secure back in the Auld Sod.

She read for a few more moments, then switched off the computer and tucked it away in its nylon carrying case. With a mutter of "Sit, stay," she replaced the Bellarmine bottle on the mantelpiece, and marched off into the cold, hazy, cat-free morning. Bare tree limbs made black cuneiform against a moist, matte sky. The reds of bricks and leaves were softened by the uncertain light and the voices of visitors and interpreters were hushed.

Averting her eyes from the tree behind the Courthouse, Jean made it as far as the Greenhow Store before realizing she could have stayed at the house and watched the press conference. But her investigations on behalf of *Great Scot* would help solve the murders.

That was her favorite excuse and she was sticking to it.

Cars were ranged outside the church. Not only was it Sunday, it was All Saints' Day, the calm after the Halloween frenzy, when the ghosts and goblins had been swept back under the carpet. She strolled in through the side gate and across the wet-leaf-strewn brick pavement, considering the monuments and tombs beyond the low barricade. The buried citizens of Williamsburg had no doubt worn as many shades of gray, ranging from unblemished saintliness to villainy of the darkest dye, as the people of any locality.

Tim and Sharon hadn't been using their primitive corer inside the footings of the 1674 church, to the northwest of the present-day structure, even though those foundations had been uncovered by some of their Baconista ancestors in 1938 and disturbed again by their Baconista cousins in 1991. No, the Dingwalls must have felt that particular mine was played out.

They'd have as much luck locating Shangri-La or Middle Earth, as a secret vault in Bruton Parish's much-studied cemetery.

From the church came the voices of a choir, practicing for the nine-o'clock service, no doubt. They were not singing "When the Saints Go Marching In" but something slower and sweeter, about gold crowns and white robes, alleluia.

She stepped over the railing onto the wet grass and sodden leaves. Robert Mason, Robert Mason, come out, come out, wherever you are… She would have avoided walking on graves, except the churchyard was filled with them, mostly unmarked, the turf no more than a skin atop a jumble of bones and coffin fittings. And yet she felt not one prickle, nary a shudder, only the sad certainty of mortality.

There. Mason's monument was a modest stoop-shouldered slab, stained and eroded by time, wind, and rain. The tidy eighteenth-century printing incised on its face read: *Here lies, in hope of a joyful Resurrection, all that was Robert Mason, late of this city. 1706-1775. I cannot sigh and say farewell, where thou dwellest, I will dwell. Frances his wife 1710-1781. Stewart his son 1734-1737. Betty his daughter 1731-1753 and her husband William Hathaway 1731-1776.*

A winged skull, symbolizing the flight of the soul, and a simple garland decorated the rounded top of the stone. Both were carved in folk-art style—clumsy but appealing.

Poor Frances Mason, Jean thought, surviving not just her husband but her children. Scant comfort that she'd seen her daughter, Betty, married—and respectably, otherwise why would Hathaway be included on the monument? Frances could have used a healing stone. Or some antibiotics.

Tim had told Kelly to work on the cipher. Technically a cipher was a key to a code. But he might not have been using the word in its exact definition, never mind that exact is as exact does.

"William Hathaway," Jean muttered. If William Shakespeare had taken his wife's last name instead of vice versa, he would have been William Hathaway. Despite William being a very common name—look at the name of the town, for heaven's sakes—Tim and Sharon probably thought that was significant.

Jean craned back and forth, but saw no cracks or chips that suggested alternate meanings. And there were no alternate spellings to the words and names, either, unless you counted "Frances" with an "E," for a woman's name, as distinct from "Francis" with an "I," for the man's name. "Stewart" wasn't a common man's name of the time period, not like Robert or William. Perhaps the Masons had latent Jacobite tendencies—the poor little boy had arrived and then departed during a period of considerable Jacobite plotting, as the Dingwalls no doubt found significant.

Pulling her notebook from her bag, Jean copied the

inscription and made a drawing of the flying skull. Its broad forehead and pointed chin made it look like one of Roswell's aliens with their almost-triangular faces, and the wings might just as well be leaves…

Maybe they were leaves. Leaves surrounding a triangular space, like the slot for the charm stone on the Witch Box. Mason had included the Witch Box on the inventory he did for Lord and Lady Dunmore—perhaps this image was intended to evoke that one.

She tried one of the conspiracy theorist's favorite games, an anagram. "Robert Mason" deconstructed into "treat no mobs," which at least summed up Dunmore's policy toward the people he perceived as rebels, the people who perceived themselves as freedom fighters.

But Alasdair was right, the simplest explanation was the best. The letters "F," "B," and "S" were carved on the Witch Box. It was the names Frances and Stewart, with Betty to provide the "B"—and William Hathaway and Mason for lagniappe—that had drawn the Dingwalls' attention to this stone. The names and the evocative frame of the flying skull. Part coincidence, part Mason's associations, whatever, the combination would be proof to a dyed-in-the-wool conspiracist.

Just "B" and "S" summed up Jean's opinion of conspiracy theory, but then, she was feeling particularly cynical this morning. Go figure.

Stuffing her notebook back in her bag, she turned toward the church and almost tripped over a small stone at the foot of the Mason family plot. She glanced at it, then stopped and took a good hard look. The weathered letters read: *Thos Napier 1775.*

Thomas Napier? Mary's son? If she'd had an illegitimate child, he would have her name, not his father's. So when had he been born? Even if Mary had given birth at age forty or so, around 1700, he would have been relatively long-lived.

The wind sighed through the branches overhead and sprinkled Jean's head with cold rain, an ad-libbed baptism. With a sigh and a command to her already-frayed nervous system to start processing the data, she picked her way back to the low railing and the pavement.

TWENTY

PEOPLE WERE GATHERING at the tower door as overhead the bell pealed a summons.

She might as well attend the service, too. The glorious language of the Book of Common Prayer both soothed and uplifted. A prayer to ease Sharon's spirit, and Wesley's, too, wouldn't hurt—the souls of murder victims were as uneasy as those of their murderers. And while she hopefully had the ear of the Almighty, she could ask forgiveness for all her snide remarks about Sharon, whether vocalized or not, and request a free pass for continued snide remarks about Tim and now Kelly, ditto.

She tried to scrape the mud and grass from her shoes as she walked toward the door—and then stopped on the threshold, spotting a familiar tuft of white hair just beyond the churchyard wall. A person of interest, Alasdair would say. Someone who'd been in the vicinity last night.

Dodging upstream, Jean walked out the southern gate to find Barbara Finch distributing vases of flowers to two other women from the back of a monstrous black SUV, an old hunk of Detroit iron that would squash a Japanese vehicle like a Japanese beetle. Today she was wearing a lime green double-knit pantsuit, a size too large, over brown shoes that looked like cut-down hiking boots.

"Good morning," said Jean, trying to look more casual than inquisitive.

"Well hello there," Barbara returned. And, to one of her minions, "Sorry I'm late—take these right up to the altar."

"Those are beautiful." The bronze and yellow flowers burst exuberantly from their greenery, symbolizing rebirth as surely as a spring bunny bearing eggs. "These are chrysanthemums, right?"

"I have no idea. You'd have to ask the florist. Here." Barbara thrust the last vase into Jean's hands and slammed the hatch with a thud that resounded off Jean's eardrums.

"I'll take them in for you. They're heavy." Jean tightened her grip of the vase.

Barbara whisked it away, every wrinkle of her face set. "I may be old, but I'm not weak. There are few epithets as bad as 'old woman,' you know. That implies not just weakness, but incompetence and even invisibility."

Barbara and Jessica, Jean reflected, were matched better than either would admit. "I'm sorry I missed the concert here last night. Bach, wasn't it?"

"Yes, it was. Come to the free concert at the Palace. Seven tonight. I get to dress up in period clothing like an interpreter and play one of Wesley Hagedorn's harpsichords, in memoriam. May his killer rot in..." She stopped, her thin pink lips snapping shut on a word Jean guessed was not *peace*.

"I'd enjoy hearing you play," Jean replied.

Barbara peered at Jean past the yellow and bronze petals, her eyes bright as a wood nymph's. "You and the kilt, you're helping the police chase down Wesley's murderer."

"And Sharon Dingwall's. That's why we weren't at the concert last night." Jean made a feeble gesture toward the tree. The crime scene. The murder site.

"I didn't see you at the play, either."

"No. We couldn't get tickets. I hope to read Jessica's new book about Mary Napier, though."

"Her book's about all the witches, not just Mary. All the witches who weren't suffered to live as they pleased, to misquote the Bible. She sees witchcraft as a social issue, prejudice against women, trendy ideas about gender equality that would never have occurred to someone in that era." Beneath the slight quaver of age in Barbara's voice, steel clanged.

"Do you think there was something to the charges of witchcraft, then?"

"You want me to reference Shakespeare? There being more in heaven and earth than are dreamed in your philosophy, Horatio."

Jean nodded in unspecified agreement. This time her gesture was sideways, lofting over the roof of the church. "I was just looking at Robert Mason's gravestone. Tim Dingwall thinks the inscription holds some sort of clue to the whole Bacon's-vault theory. Me, I'm wondering if Mason meant the design to refer to the Witch Box."

"Tim Dingwall's not nearly as smart as he thinks he is." The face behind the chrysanthemums puckered with a canny smile. "Mason, now, Mason was a curious man, like Jefferson but in his own way. If he'd lived in Massachusetts in 1692, he'd have been strung up, and nothing about being a victim of gender issues… Yes, I'm coming!" Her comrade was gesturing frantically from the gate. With an "I'll look for you tonight" Barbara bustled away.

Curious. Inquisitive and/or peculiar. There was a lot of that going around.

Jean, too, started for the gate, but had taken only two steps when her phone emitted its jaunty, even defiant, tune. Stopping dead, she found it right at the top of her bag, amazingly, and glanced at the screen. "Hey, Rebecca. How are y'all doing this morning?"

"No nightmares last night, thank goodness. And you?"

"I'm fine," Jean lied. She heard little Linda babbling and Michael's voice babbling back. What kind of accent was the baby developing? Would she be able to sort her biscuits from her cookies?

"Are you watching Alasdair's press conference?"

"Stephanie Venegas's press conference, you mean, with Alasdair allowed in the back door?" Jean slumped against the icy metal of Barbara's car, glad he hadn't heard that remark. She tried to retrieve it. "Well, he's part of the team, he's contributing information from P and S. And no, I'm not watching the show."

"It's been short and sweet so far. Alasdair talked about the theft of the Witch Box, but the reporters were more interested in how he found Sharon's body. And yes, he was with someone else at the time, but wild horses couldn't drag the name from him—not that he said that in so many words, but you can tell from his expression."

"I can just see his expression," Jean said, and she could, his face so tightly closed a chisel couldn't pry it open.

"Now Stephanie's saying they've released their original suspect in Hagedorn's murder and arrested Jessica Evesdottir."

"I'm not surprised." Jean filled Rebecca in on the latest events, concluding, "I wonder what Barbara will say when she finds out Jessica's been arrested. As for whether Jessica is guilty, I don't—I just don't feel that she is."

"Have you got any better candidates?"

"Maybe Tim killed Sharon himself, to make it look as if those secret societies wanted to shut them up." The choir, Jean saw, was gathering outside the door of the church, music books in hand. "By the way, there's going to be a free concert in honor of Wesley Hagedorn at the Palace tonight at seven..." Her call-waiting signal beeped just as Linda set up a wail.

"Feeding time," Rebecca said. "Enjoy the concert—

we've got a set of great-grandparents arriving tonight for a baby-showing, so we have to stick close to home."

"We'll miss you!" Jean hit her keypad. "Hello?"

"Good morning, Jean," said Miranda. "How are you getting on?"

"I'm checking out a lead at the church," Jean answered, which was less a "how" than a "where," but it gave her a chance to make her report. "You're up early."

"I was after watching Alasdair's press conference."

He'd be pleased at how both Rebecca and Miranda put him in the driver's seat. "Yeah, I was just talking to Rebecca about that. Alasdair took the reporter's bullets for me, I'm afraid, though mostly I'm grateful."

"Good man, Alasdair."

Yes, he was. And he would never have the poor taste to point that out to her.

"Now Tim Dingwall's staging a show outside the police station—I'm assuming he and his ilk were there making statements, and he's taking advantage of the audience."

"Oh yeah. I'm sure Stephanie's thrilled." The processional hymn resounded from the church and the choir, singing of gold crowns, et al., processed inside. Okay, so she wasn't going to attend the morning service.

Rousing herself from her slump against Barbara's car, Jean strolled around the corner onto Palace Green. Ahead of her rose the Palace itself, the tall main building embraced by two one-story outbuildings, called "dependencies," in the symmetrical elegance of the time period. The tall cupola beckoned, the gold crown on the weathervane glinting.

"Tim's introduced his sister Kelly," Miranda said. "She's been promoted to chief sidekick, I'm thinking. And the red-haired lad behind, that's never Dylan—one of the reporters just asked if he's been found yet. Must be Quentin."

"Dylan's still missing."

"Oh aye, that he is. Left town, I reckon. I doubt Jessica's wishing she'd left town as well. You're saying she and Wesley pinched a document from Blair?"

"She hasn't admitted to that. Yet. If she's charged with Sharon's murder, to say nothing of Wesley's, she might decide pocketing an eighteenth-century memorandum is the least of her problems."

"Oh aye," Miranda said, and continued her play-by-play. "Tim sounds to be a wee bit desperate. His face is all twisted round, like one of those television evangelists you lot have here. He's got news for us. It's essential we listen. Everything we believe about history and government is false, the proof's in his wife's murder, and we've been duped by the perfidious media, which, mind you, he's using to great effect just now."

"He does see himself as an evangelist. Besides, push has come to shove financially. Now or never. Bacon or bust." Jean allowed herself a look at the huge tree, at its branches heavy behind the orange and gold confetti of leaves. Would other ghost-allergic souls soon be picking up frissons from it? But it wasn't the tree's fault that some human had used it to—what? Scrape off an inconvenient colleague or relative like a barnacle?

She started down the street toward the Palace, stretching her legs, inhaling the chill, smoke-flavored air. "Is that all?"

"He's saying the results of the core sample from the graveyard are 'inconclusive.' Lowering expectations, eh? And that's all, aye… No. Kelly's pushing forward, going on about *Lords of the Lie,* and Tim looks to have swallowed a frog."

"He doesn't yet have his keystone or capstone, Francis Bacon's papers. And he thinks he needs the charm stone to find them. Maybe he's planning to insert it into the slot on Robert Mason's grave, and that will open up a secret stairway to the vault." With a jump and a skip, she dodged a puddle on the pitted blacktop. "That's it! That's exactly what Tim expects to happen! He and Sharon were looking for a shortcut with their core sample, because they can't find the stone."

"That's no more daft than their other fancies," Miranda said with a laugh. "Ah, Tim and Kelly are handing out brochures and saying they'll be conducting tours of the Historic Area the afternoon. Quentin's pretending he's never before seen the lot of them. Poor lad."

"Poor lad indeed. Eventually he's going to have to admit to Alasdair that he helped Kelly steal the replica Witch Box."

Miranda clucked her tongue over that. "I've done my share of promotion over the years..."

Jean grinned. "Really?"

"And I'm guessing that Kelly's moved too soon, flogging the film. It's no good promoting the product if it's not available, or available within the attention span of the average reporter—present company excepted."

"I'm a journalist, not a reporter."

"Aye, that you are. Kelly was chatting up folk on the airplane, you were saying?"

"Hugh was saying, yes. I bet you're right, she's plunged on ahead, and Tim's not ready. He thought they knew where the charm stone was, but they didn't. He and Sharon were under a lot of pressure, and things start breaking under pressure. People start dying." Jean reached the brick wall surrounding the Palace, and looked through the open gate on the left toward the cluster of small brick buildings that were the domestic offices—smokehouse, bathhouse, kitchen.

Kitchen. Mary Napier had been a kitchen-worker. The Dinwiddie Kitchen had been moved from the Palace during renovations in 1751. Mary would have been ninety-one then, if she'd still been alive—and that wasn't likely. But what about her son, Thomas? Maybe the ghost was his wife.

"My breakfast's just arrived," said Miranda in Jean's ear. "I'll be saying cheery-bye."

"Have a good—oh! There's going to be a concert at the Palace tonight, with Barbara Finch playing one of Wesley's harpsichords. Can you join—us?" No reason Alasdair would turn down a concert.

"Sorry to be missing out," Miranda said, "but this is the evening I'm away to D.C. to join Duncan, for the embassy reception the night and the seminar on the Monday."

"That's right. No surprise I'd forgotten. Safe journey, and I'll keep you in the loop."

"I'm expecting that, right enough. Cheery-bye."

Jean visualized Miranda and her silver-haired companion and lover—Duncan had the polish of Count Dracula without the appetite—holding forth to the British ambassador about dealing with crazed Americans, even though she knew darn well the seminar's topic was marketing Britain to America.

She switched off the phone, stowed it away, and started toward the kitchen, only to be caught up in a group being ushered into the Palace itself. Okay. No problem. It had been a long time since she'd been there, and now she had a different perspective.

Instead of comparing contemporary tastes in fabric and wallpaper to those of the Dunmores, she compared the intricate arrangements of pistols, muskets, and swords in the entrance hall to those at Blair Castle and other British historical sites, displays intended to send a message to the peasantry. She eyed the secretary's office, imagining Robert Mason doing the usual paperwork, all in the finest script. *Hearing the secrets, writing the confidential letters,* Tim had said.

Although Mason was much more likely writing confidential letters about disgruntled colonists than about mythical charms and delusory witch hunts, he had manifestly been intrigued by the story of Charlotte, Lady Dunmore's, charm stone.

Perhaps the Witch Box had been stored in the pantry. Perhaps it had been stored in the governor's dressing room, or sat next to Lady Dunmore's dressing table in an upstairs reception room. Did it even then seem to squat like a toad? Or was its almost-medieval appearance and reputation no more than a jarring note in the beautifully appointed—for the colonies—chamber, where tall windows, not arrow slits, looked out over Palace Green toward the church?

Had Charlotte come to Virginia looking for the charm stone? If she'd found it, where was it now? Lying anonymously in a corner at Blair? Or maybe she hadn't found it, because Mary Napier, realizing it was bringing her bad luck, not good, had chucked it into the nearest ditch or buried it in the woods.

Jean strolled through the ballroom and the supper room and exited into the formal gardens, the tidy beds bright with seasonal flowers. A hard left took her back to the little courtyard and on into the kitchen.

She stopped dead on the doorstep. A delectable scent filled the two rooms of the whitewashed cottage, a sweet, rich, smoky scent. The same nose- and mouth-filling scent she'd sensed in the Dinwiddie Kitchen, wafted through time if not through space.

A copper pot filled with amber liquid simmered on the vast hearth. Beside it stood a bearded interpreter dressed in simple striped vest, white shirt, and breeches, talking to a group of visitors. "…small beer was the everyday beverage in Virginia. People knew plain water would make them sick but they didn't know why—it was polluted by sewage from the town. We know today that boiling the water is what made the beer safe. You soak barley or wheat bran, then boil the liquid with hops and sometimes molasses, then add yeast. Sometimes the brewers would add a cock, a rooster, to the beer, but we're not doing that."

The visitors giggled, if a bit uncomfortably. Jean thought, *That's not a recipe, that's magic.*

Stepping forward to a table filled with attractively presented dishes of food, he went on, "The kitchen staff would work all morning cooking the governor's dinner. Roast pigeon and other meats, fried ox-tongue, ragout of cucumbers, mince pies. Vegetables, seafood. Jellies, syllabubs, cakes and cookies. We don't know nearly as much about the food of people further down the social scale. The governors would bring their own cooks from Europe, but the kitchen staff, like the other Palace staff, tended to stay through different administrations."

Like Robert Mason, Jean thought. She asked, "Did Mary Napier ever work here?"

"The witch?" asked another visitor.

The interpreter blinked behind his wire-rimmed glasses. "Why yes, to both questions. Mary worked in the earlier kitchen, before Governor Dinwiddie's renovations in 1751-52. That building was moved and is now a guest house."

I know, Jean said silently. "And what about Mary's son?"

"Son?"

"There's a gravestone marked 'Thomas Napier.'"

The interpreter crossed his arms and hooked a hip on the side of the table. "That would be Thomasina, not Thomas. She was—he was—well, the child was a hermaphrodite."

The other visitors leaned forward, leading with their eyebrows. Jean's bag slipped down her shoulder and almost landed on a stuffed cabbage, but she caught it in time.

"The poor child was seen as God's visitation on Mary.

Thomasina tried dressing as a man and doing male work, but was forced into women's clothing and women's work. Not that cooking was necessarily women's work—everyone had to know how to cook, it was a matter of survival."

If Jessica were here, Jean thought, she'd make a statement about social identity as a function of gender. Jean herself was chalking up another—well, not curse. Bad things happened. Like noting synchronicity in names, the human mind noted synchronicity in events.

"Thomasina worked with Mary, and then after Mary's death worked on here. Dinwiddie took pity on her and let her live in the old kitchen after it was moved. She baked bread and brewed beer, well into old age—no social security then. She was found dead not far from her cottage."

In the ravine that crossed Francis Street, Jean concluded. And children would throw stones and tease the poor old—person—who threatened assumptions about men's and women's roles.

"There's a book just out that tells the story. *Witches and Wenches in Colonial Virginia.* It must be selling well, there were some folks asking about Mary and Thomasina just a couple of days ago, what sort of valuables they might have had, that sort of thing."

"A big guy," Jean asked, "like a roast pig without the apple in its mouth, and a tiny woman?"

"Yes. Friends of yours?"

He obviously had not been watching television this morning. Jean was saved from another lie by her phone ringing. "Thank you," she told the interpreter, and retired to the doorway, her hand in her bag. The phone registered another anonymous caller. "Hello?"

"Jean, it's Matt."

Behind her back, one of the visitors asked, "Is all this food made out of wax?"

"Hi, Matt," said Jean. "How'd you get this number?"

"I saw Alasdair at the press conference and thought you must be with him, so called the police station. They put him on the phone and he gave me your number. Sounded like he was in a hurry."

Jean could hear Alasdair's voice, courtesy as brisk and cold as a blizzard. *Thanks, Matt.*

"No," the interpreter was saying, "the food is real, but for demonstration purposes only. The mouse that was eating the cookies we didn't refrigerate last night was flouting health department rules. I'm going to have to borrow an eighteenth-century mousetrap from one of our archaeologists."

"I'm doing some work at the office," Matt was saying. "You said you'd like to visit."

Jean faded out of the kitchen into the courtyard, quelling any impulse to keep right on fading over the hills and far away. Her curiosity would just turn her around and send her back again.

Curiosity. Thomasina had been a curiosity.

"Sure," Jean told Matt. "I'd love to drop in for a visit. Where are you, exactly?"

TWENTY-ONE

JEAN WALKED AS fast as she could without breaking into a trot, following the cadence in her own mind, the drone that was Alasdair's presence beneath the complex melody of her thoughts processing, evaluating, compiling.

The church was silent—perhaps the congregation was hearing a sermon about love and forgiveness. Just beyond it stood the one nineteenth-century house on Duke of Gloucester. Not thinking of sore thumbs—the structure was interesting in its own right—Jean passed it by as well as various modest clapboard buildings and gardens not yet withered for the fall. At Merchant's Square, she darted into the Barnes & Noble that was also the college bookstore.

She did a double take at a stack of children's novels that prominently featured Alice Walker's *Finding the Green Stone,* then spent a moment scanning the titles of a rack of ghost stories. She'd take Eric's word that there were none about the Dinwiddie Kitchen. She and Alasdair must simply be on the right wavelength—not that she had a clue how ghosts actually transmitted.

There, several copies of *Witches and Wenches* reposed on an end cap. Jean hoisted one of the heavy trade paperbacks and eyed the cover. It was designed around a caricaturish period print in the style of Hogarth, of two wasp-waisted women in voluminous skirts and hats the circumference of serving trays, neither one of whom could be considered wench or witch.

Nor could Jessica. Her photo on the back was a glamour

shot, sculpted hair, thickly applied make-up transforming her face into a mask, scarf artfully deployed to conceal her sagging throat.

There she'd sat in the Dinwiddie Kitchen, for at least an hour and a half, while Thomasina brushed invisibly by her, brewing, baking, fending off witches with a Bellarmine bottle, clinging to the customs of her youth. Although if the bottle was indeed Thomasina's, she might have been fending off her own ancestry.

Thomasina had worked at the Palace during Mason's tenure. He had to have known her, and about her gender ambiguity, in a day when gender ambiguity was highly suspect. After seeing Lady Dunmore's Box with its empty space, he could well have presented the elderly androgyne to her as both a curiosity and as the daughter of one of Charlotte's family's retainers. Oh to have been one of no doubt many flies on the wall!

A quick application of her credit card, and Jean now owned a copy of Jessica's book.

The green plastic sack and its contents banged at her side as she scurried down the sidewalk and across the street to the campus. Skirting the original Georgian buildings—more red brick, cupolas, dormers, symmetrical windows, round-headed doors, the model of Enlightenment architecture—she spared a thought for roads not taken.

Matt waited at the front door of a structure considerably later and heavier than Georgian, wearing a college-logo sweatshirt and loose cotton pants. With no more than a "Hi," he conducted Jean to the sanctuary of his office.

She collapsed into a straight-backed chair, catching her breath and relishing the scent of academic incense—books, coffee, a pinch of mildew, a soupçon of hair gel—and gazed around her with, if not lust in her heart, then an itch in her memory.

With its overstuffed shelves, student papers, stained coffee cups, computer peripherals, the room reminded her of her old office. Matt's was personalized with a CD player even now tinkling with harpsichord music. Atop the changer sat several intricate bits of metal that Jean at first thought were modern mousetraps, but then realized were puzzles. That's right. Rachel was a skilled metalworker.

Photos tracing the young woman's growth from toddler to siren ended with one of her in cap and gown, Matt on her right, Barbara on her left, Jessica half hidden beneath the picture frame. "What's Rachel doing now?" Jean asked.

"Working as an interpreter at the Palace. Hoping to turn her art degree into an apprenticeship at the silversmith's shop." Matt sat down in the leather chair behind his desk and leaned his head against the back. The crown of skin rising above his gray hair reflected damply in the light from the window. Maybe he'd been out jogging. Maybe he was sweating out some intricate bit of campus politics. Maybe he knew a little too much about the double murder investigation.

"I just saw your mother at the church," Jean said, nodding toward a photo of a youngish couple that had to be Barbara and Matt's father. He looked like Matt on steroids—more hair, thicker neck, squarer shoulders. And a much sterner expression. Right now Matt looked like an armadillo stranded in the middle of a four-lane freeway. "You said she was a former academic. What's her field? Music theory?"

"No, religious studies. She may be retired, but she's still on the go, traveling overseas, even. I'm surprised she can find her way back to her apartment. No pets, no potted plants, she doesn't have time to deal with them."

"Yeah, it can be complicated caring for a pet. Where does she travel?"

"Places like Sedona, Glastonbury, Lourdes, Sri Lanka,

analyzing healing traditions. She's thinking of updating her work on how the witchcraft craze was caused when the rising male medical-scientific profession tried to eliminate village healers."

"Healers using healing traditions like charm stones?"

He shrugged tightly, his hands flexing on the arms of the chair.

No, he hadn't asked her here to see his office. Jean kept on rolling the conversational boulder uphill. "I was checking out Robert Mason's gravestone, because the Dingwalls think it's the key to Bacon's vault, and Barbara implied he was dabbling in the occult or something."

"No, that's what you inferred. He was just interested in the history of witchcraft, which was an iffy hobby in his day. Unlike Walter Scott with his *Letters on Demonology and Witchcraft* a generation later. And back home in Scotland."

Accepting his correction without quibble, Jean asked, "Mason was a Scot, too?"

"From Glasgow, like Governor Dinwiddie."

"He named his son 'Stewart.' A nod to the Jacobites?"

"Probably. But the poor little guy was gone by the time Dinwiddie and then Dunmore arrived."

"And by then Mason knew what side his bread was buttered on," she said with a smile. "His Hanoverian, Georgian bread."

If he got the joke, meager as it was, he ignored it. He took off his glasses, rubbed them with the hem of his shirt, and peered myopically around the office as though everything looked better in soft-focus. Amid the pile of papers and magazines on his desk lay a catalog of the Dunmore exhibit, open to a photo of the Witch Box—artifact, artwork, historical flypaper.

"So all the names on Mason's gravestone are legitimate

names of living, well, of people who once lived. There's no secret code—now there's a redundancy, a code by definition is secret."

"No, there's no code. The Dingwalls are the worst kind of idiots, smart ones."

She knew what he meant, people whose intellectual gyroscopes couldn't tell which way was up. Pointing sideways, toward the catalog, she went on, "What about that carving at the top of the stone, that looks like the slot for the charm stone on the Witch Box? The initials may be coincidence, but that's not. I'm guessing Mason had it carved there for no other reason than social climbing, reminding passersby of his position poking around the cupboards of power."

"That's what Jessica thinks. That's what Mom thinks, too. That's what they both told Sharon, but no, she and Tim kept pumping hot air into the subject."

"Have you written about Mason? What about Jessica and your mom, have they?"

He replaced his glasses and turned toward her. "Why are you asking all these questions about Mason? Do I detect a bit of detecting?" His chuckle came a moment late, and was distinctly hollow.

"Well, yeah. And I'm writing about the Dingwalls for *Great Scot*."

"Are you making any progress in solving Sharon's murder? What about Wes's? The news conference this morning…" He leaned against the headrest, eyes closed, lips so tight his goatee pleated.

We come to the bottom line. She said, "They've arrested Jessica."

"Yes."

"I'm assuming you don't think she killed anyone."

"No!" he exclaimed. "She and Wes, well, I know there

was something. They went off to the U.K. together, for God's sakes, but she's a free agent."

"Were *you* friends with Wes?"

"I wasn't his enemy, if that's what you mean. I wasn't jealous."

Jealous, Jean thought. There are lots of ways of being jealous, as she'd discovered for herself.

Slapping his hands on the leather armrests, making a double report, Matt stood up and paced over to the window. From below came the shouts of an impromptu football game. "Jessica and I met Wes through my mom, who knew him because of the music and the harpsichord. Jessica got her hooks into him when he was commissioned to copy the Witch Box, and then the Dingwalls—mostly Sharon, she's the brains of the operation—turned up and I tried to help her with her research, and so did Jessica and Mom, too. And here we are. No good deed goes unpunished. Mom already found that out, helping Jessica with her book and then getting no credit."

Jean glanced down at the sack resting against the leg of her chair. So Jessica had—not necessarily plagiarized, that was a strong word and a stronger accusation—Barbara's work. But it was Sharon who'd accused Jessica of plagiarization, out of revenge and spite after Jessica refused to share the as-yet-mysterious Charlotte document.

Jessica, Barbara, Sharon, like the three witches, the weird sisters in *Macbeth,* all stirring the cauldron of the Witch Box. Eye of newt, toe of frog, pen of ink and stone of charm.

"You know, I envy you your plagiarization suit," Matt said over his shoulder. "At least something happened in your academic career, something to make you stand out from the herd."

"It wasn't a plagiarization suit, the plagiarized dissertation was just the beginning..." There was another area in which her reputation preceded her. Doing the right thing never went unpunished, either.

"And the Dingwalls. Those crazed theories of theirs, not a logical construct among them, get taken seriously by way too many people, when I've carefully researched and footnoted and now I'm going to be reduced to imagineering, for God's sakes. Betraying everything I've worked for."

"Look at it as using everything you've worked for in a new and different way."

He leaned on the windowsill. "You'd think the damn Dingwalls had cast some sort of spell on our family. Jessica, Sharon, Dylan was probably with Rachel last night—they said he ran away from the scene—she's at that age, swimming with estrogen and not a lick of sense."

Jean suppressed her smile of agreement, even though Matt wasn't looking at her... *Wait a minute. Jessica said Rachel went to Matt's house last night. Had Matt not been there himself?* "Um, surely Rachel was pretty upset with the, er, Sharon's death. And Jessica wasn't at home, she was, ah, being questioned—you'd think Rachel would come to a parent for comfort."

Matt didn't take the bait. The harpsichord music stopped and the CD changer whirred. The notes of Tchaikovsky's "Pathetique" filled the room, the lush romantic-era orchestra in stark contrast to the rippling intricacies of the harpsichord. Jean glanced over at the stack of CDs by the changer and adrenaline shot like drain cleaner through her body.

Matt had an album by Williamsburg's Fifes and Drums. She couldn't see the track listings from where she sat, but she didn't need to. "Over the Hills and Far Away" poured through her mind, drowning out Tchaikovsky. Three times now she'd heard a shadowy something whistling that. Surely

Matt wasn't… What he was, as Alasdair had pointed out, was well-informed.

Hardly aware of what she was doing, she looked over her shoulder to make sure she had a clear path out of the room. And she saw not only the sturdy paneled door but also Matt's wastebasket, looking like her office rubbish bin, teeming with torn envelopes, wadded papers, canceled notes. Except on top of his pile of dead-tree debris rested a small piece of paper with three words printed across the top. *Protect and Survive.*

Shielded by the music and the sounds of sporting revelry outside, Jean slipped out of the chair and reached into the basket. Yes, the list of phone numbers was in Alasdair's handwriting. It was the bittie paper he'd lost Friday night.

Bracing herself, she took a stab in the dusk. "You know, you'll never make a good spy if you go around whistling 'Over the Hills and Far Away.'"

His already-tight shoulders spasmed, drawing his hands into fists and his body into a defensive crouch. His head fell forward. Maybe he was tempted to bang it against the window in frustration.

Okay then, Jean thought. *Guilty as charged.*

Her mouth was dry. She managed to find enough spit to swallow and then speak again. "You went for a stroll around the Historic Area after the reception Friday. Were you thinking about Wesley's untimely death? Were you following Rachel? Or were you following Alasdair and me?"

Slowly Matt straightened to his full height, a head taller than Jean. Slowly he turned around. He saw the paper in her hand, and the quizzical expression was wiped from his face. One blank moment, and then his lips twisted, his eyes flashed, and his skin all the way to his scalp flushed an ugly, angry red. "Yeah. To all the above—Wes was dead, and I was hoping it was an accident, but had a bad feeling…"

"How is sticking someone with a sharp instrument and holding them under water an accident?"

"I didn't know that then."

That he showed no surprise at it now was discomforting, but then, Jean didn't know how many details of Wesley's murder Stephanie had released. Still, she eased herself down and picked up the book in its sack, heavy as a blackjack. With her other hand she thrust Alasdair's note into the outer pocket of her mini-backpack, then gathered it up. It wasn't light, either, and if necessary she could swing it by its straps. And there were pens and pencils on Matt's desk, speaking of sharp instruments.

But Matt made no move toward her. "Rachel's much too good for one of the Dingwall boys, especially Dylan, I'd like to, to…"

"What?" Jean asked, thinking of Tim punching a hole in the wall.

"You and Alasdair should have left him in the pillory. You should have called the police on the Dingwalls in the churchyard. When you didn't, I thought you were working with them."

"What, you were too far away to hear what we were saying?"

"Yes, and he's got a pretty thick accent, too."

No, he didn't. At least she didn't have to squint with her ears to understand him.

"I saw the scrap of paper fall out of his sporran. I picked it up. The phone numbers written on it, the police ad security. And you and he are on the 'net, the Scottish newspapers… He's who he says he is."

"Oh yeah, he sure is." As Alasdair had told the woman on the bus, *Madame, I'm not pretending to be anything.* Transparent the man was not, but he never claimed to be anyone else.

Jean heard her voice sharpening. "You followed us back to the Dinwiddie Kitchen. You were watching me with the Dingwalls at the Cheese Shop. You were wandering around last night keeping an eye on Jessica. Not Rachel, Jessica..."

Had he been wandering around behind the Courthouse, keeping an eye on Sharon, a spindle from Wes's shop beneath his arm? Waiting and watching until he could get her alone?

Jean smiled, hoping he couldn't read the tension in her clenched teeth, stretched mouth, dry lips. "What do you want from me, Matt?"

His return smile was a rictus grin. His molasses-brown eyes softened, and again she saw in them something both haunted and hunted. Maybe he did think Jessica had killed Sharon, and Wes as well. Maybe he was trying to take the blame.

The ties that bind and strangle.

"What do you want?" she asked again, with a long step back toward the door.

"You've got to get Jessica off," he said, in his distress unaware of the sexual double meaning. "It's not fair, arresting her, she's just doing her thing. She can't help being abrasive, getting into problems with people like Wes and Sharon, any more than a black widow can help eating its mate."

"That's not for you to decide. Or me. Alasdair and I will do all we can, but if it turns out Jessica killed Sharon and/or Wes, then..."

His eyes began melting, gathering moisture. His shoulders drooped. The color drained from his face and scalp, so that his gray hair and beard seemed to be absorbed into his ashen skin. Shrinking to a fraction of his height, he sank into his chair, buried his face in his hands, and rocked back and forth, moaning. The chair creaked in rhythm.

Jean considered several parting salvos and settled on a

simple "I'm sorry, Matt." She walked into the corridor and shut the door behind her. The sound of the "Pathetique" followed her down the hall and out of the otherwise silent building.

Yes, she felt pity for Matt. Hell, she felt pity for all the Finches and the Dingwalls. Like Lord Dunmore in 1775, events were slipping through their fingers like sand through an hourglass. And yet, surely, it was one of them who'd overturned that hourglass to begin with.

She dodged the young men playing football, carelessly risking their fresh faces and taut, agile bodies, and crossed the street wondering how much she'd just risked.

Matt had attempted to harm her. It was a stretch to think that he'd had murder on his mind when he summoned her. He'd have a hard time disposing of her body, for one thing, but then, murderers weren't known for logical thought.

Matt was a sneak, not a murderer.

Still, she'd gone to his office without letting anyone know where she was going. She awarded herself a demerit for that, and two more for having cut Matt so much slack over the past couple of days.

Alasdair was probably with Steph—er, at the police station. Pausing by Jefferson's statue, Jean found Stephanie's number in her phone's memory and punched the button. Her mouth was still dry. She practiced saying "Hello."

"Stephanie Venegas."

"Hello, it's Jean Fairbairn."

"Do you want to talk to Alasdair? He's right here."

Of course he was. "No, thank you, I just wanted to draw your attention to Matthew Finch, Jessica Evesdottir's not-quite-ex-husband. I just talked to him in his office, and he, well, you need to talk to him."

"Sooner rather than later, you mean? Thanks for the tip."

Okay, Jean thought as she popped the phone back into

her bag, she'd done her duty as a public-spirited citizen. Although going straight to Stephanie without passing go and collecting Alasdair's two hundred—pounds—might not help the events that were running through her own fingers.

The sound of bagpipes filtered faintly into Merchant's Square.

TWENTY-TWO

AT FIRST JEAN thought she was hearing the music backgrounding the tumble of her own thoughts. Then she decided there must be a program in progress.

Well, yes, there was, sort of. Hugh's band was rehearsing inside the Kimball Theater. She'd recognize those rhythms anywhere, just as she'd recognize the brushed velvet of Alasdair's voice.

She darted into the Cheese Shop, bought a bottle of orange juice, and went back to the theater. The front door was unlocked. She tiptoed into the main auditorium and sat down beneath the glowing chandelier, whose light gleamed on chaste white walls and red velvet curtains alike.

Hugh's colleague Billy stopped playing his pipes, adjusted his drones, changed the reed in his chanter, started again. Jamie plinked a few experimental notes on his guitar and joined in. Donnie swayed back and forth behind his keyboard, hands moving like a priest's performing a blessing. None of them was young—combined with Hugh, they had the experience of more than two centuries. No wonder the music resonated with such feeling it brought a lump to Jean's throat.

And they were playing "Lochaber No More," a song Robert Mason would have known. Lochaber, in western Scotland, land of craggy mountains, deep lochs, lush green fields, whose beauty could catch at your heart and whose harshness could stop it. Lochaber, where she and Alasdair had first met. *Thanks, guys.*

Hugh stepped out of the wings, fiddle in hand. But he didn't tuck it under his chin. Instead, he began to sing, his clear voice filling the hall. "Farewell to Lochaber, farewell to my Jean…" A heartsick young soldier dutifully leaves his girlfriend to go to war, for without honor he would be unworthy of her, but if he returns home, then his heart will be filled with love.

Honor cut both ways. Jean gulped her juice, the thoughts pinging back and forth through her head like the ball in a pinball game, hitting bells, lighting up lights, disappearing into black holes.

If Matt was an example of a sensitive contemporary guy, then she liked the strong silent type. Whether the strong silent type was good for the long run, as Jessica had put it, well… She might as well grab one of Barbara's chrysanthemums and pluck off its petals to the litany of *he loves me, he loves me not* like a schoolgirl. Although, as an adult, her litany was more likely *I love him, I love him not.*

Neither she nor Alasdair had ever used the word *love,* not that she could remember. Which proved only that they'd been heart-burned. He was right—why ask why, show don't tell…

The song over, Billy went back to fussing with his pipes. They emitted the indignant squawk of a man encountering a proctologist. Hugh waved at Jean, and turned around to confer with the lads and a disembodied loudspoken voice recommending sound levels and tone balance.

One song they wouldn't be singing was the one about love and marriage going together like a horse and carriage, including the steaming piles of authenticity. A second marriage, Jean had once told Alasdair, back when the conversation became personal, was a victory of hope over experience. Which summed up the Dingwalls' approach to history. Not a good recommendation, there.

Hugh stepped down off the stage and strolled up the aisle toward her. Once again Jean packed away her behind-the-scenes concerns and turned her face outward, to duty, honor, and the war against crime.

Sitting down, Hugh asked, "How's the investigation getting on? Jamie was saying the polis have made an arrest. Not Kelly Dingwall."

"No, but she's still a person of interest, as Alasdair would say."

Hugh didn't ask where Alasdair was. He'd known Jean before she knew Alasdair, and was under no illusions about them being joined at the hip. "I'm booked for a chat with the polis this afternoon. Now I'm after minding just what Kelly was on about in mid-Atlantic airspace. If I'd known what she'd been getting up to at Blair, and what would be happening to her sister-in-law, I'd not have been so quick to cover my ears with a pillow."

Had I but known, Jean thought. The motto beneath the coat of arms of the human race. "Can you think of anything at all that would help? Other than Kelly promoting the movie as a finished product while Tim's still searching for Francis Bacon's mythical papers."

"And the best of British luck to him," said Hugh. "One thing—the Dingwalls have themselves a copy of the Witch Box, do they?"

"No, there's only the one copy, the one Kelly and Quentin—ahem—allegedly stole from Blair."

Hugh's genial yet acerbic face rumpled in a frown. "Kelly was going on about the Box being a centerpiece of the film, with actors playing both the Francis, Stewart and Bacon, doing scenes with it. She was naming names, although I'm not minding them. Not A-list actors, in any event."

"This only a few hours after swearing to the Perthshire police she'd never heard of the Box, let alone stolen it?"

"Oh aye."

"They've actually signed actors? That suggests they'd been planning to steal the replica for quite some time, and assumed they'd succeed..." One of Jean's tiny light bulbs flickered into life. "Or maybe they'd planned to have Wes make them one, too. If they fell out with him the same time they fell out with Jessica—heck, if Jessica asked him not to work with them—then they might have been motivated first to steal the plans from Wes's apartment, then to steal the replica itself."

Hugh's bright blue eyes glinted. "I've got no idea what you're thinking there, but it's always right amusing watching the steam puffing from your ears. Better you go driving that train of thought past Alasdair. Or the American detectives."

"Preferably both."

"Me, I'd best be earning a living." Hugh stood up. "Concert's at half past seven the night."

"I'm afraid you've been bumped from my schedule. There's a concert at the Palace in honor of Wesley Hagedorn. Sorry. Maybe we can make the show tomorrow."

"No problem, you're hearing us most every day," he replied. "Oh, I was meaning to say, have you spoken with Agnes, your other neighbor?"

"Not recently, no. Her side of my flat has been the quiet one since she got hearing aids and stopped turning the TV set up to supersonic levels."

"Well then, I was having a blether with her son whilst I waited for the taxi yesterday morning, and he's telling me Agnes is away to a care home come the new year. He's after gutting and renovating her flat and then selling up."

"Really? I'll miss those gorgeous flowerpots on the stoop, although I won't miss her accusing Dougie of using them as litter boxes."

"A fine discreet cat, Dougie. Right!" Hugh called to Donnie's beckoning finger, and with an encouraging thumbs-up at Jean, went to rejoin the lads.

A bell dinged in Jean's belfry—someone had said something, somewhere—but with the clamor of bells and whistles on the main floor, she couldn't begin to single out one particular note.

She tilted the rest of the cold, sweet juice into her mouth, then pulled her notebook from her bag. Quickly she jotted a rough transcription of her conversation with Hugh. Maybe if Stephanie plied him with copies of *People* or *Us Weekly* he'd key on the names of the actors. No matter. Each of the Dingwalls was making his or her cameo appearance in the interview room's hot seat.

To the inspiring strains of "Johnny Cope," commemorating one of the few battles Bonnie Prince Charlie had won, Jean returned her notebook to her bag—and knocked the green plastic sack from the bookstore onto the floor. She glanced guiltily toward the stage, but the band in full cry would cover the sound of a falling anvil.

Extracting *Witches and Wenches* from the bag—no damage done—she flipped it open to the index. As Barbara had said, Jessica analyzed not just Mary Napier's story but those of other Virginia witches, or women accused of being witches: Katherine Grady, Elizabeth Dunkin, Grace Sherwood—whoa, there was a man's name, William Harding. *Not quite William Hathaway,* Jean thought, although she wouldn't put it past the Dingwalls to find some relationship.

A quick flip through the text revealed passages on immigration from Scotland and healing practices, material that Jessica might, or might not, have cribbed from Matt's and Barbara's work… Innocent until proved guilty, Jean reminded herself, applied to Jessica and Matt both.

Since Thomasina Napier had never been accused of

witchcraft, she rated only a footnote. She'd dressed herself as a man and worked as a sailor until the other sailors saw that her male apparatus was vestigial at best. The authorities had then forced her into women's clothes. Whether she had female apparatus at all was unrecorded—the feminine pronoun was applied from the outside in, not from the inside out.

So much for the land of the free and the home of the bravely unconventional.

Jean turned several pages back to the account of Mary Napier's trial. She was swum in a pond at Middle Plantation that for years afterward was called Duckwitch Pond, but, said another, much shorter, footnote, was renamed in the nineteenth century and was now known by the fine old English name of…

Dunwich Pond, Jean repeated silently. Where Wesley Hagedorn died. That's what Jessica had said in her lecture about the artifacts of witchcraft, the lecture Jean had heard two years ago. That Mary Napier had been tortured at Duckwitch or Dunwich Pond.

A waspish voice said in her ear, "Don't waste your time with that. Recycled material, a silk purse from a sow's ear."

Jean jumped, told herself she really needed to moderate that startle reflex, and looked around to see Louise Dietz. Her smug smile reminded Jean of Sharon Dingwall. Her live-wire hair did not.

"Sorry," Louise said, "I didn't mean to sneak up on you. I should have realized you couldn't hear me over the music."

Hugh was now playing the soulful "MacPherson's Lament," Jamie and Donnie noodling around the edges. When Billy chimed in, the wave of sound set the chandelier to tinkling.

"No problem," Jean told Louise, and took a deep breath—*see, I'm still functioning*—which filled her nostrils with a faint mustiness and a not-so-faint aroma of musky perfume. She assumed the former was generated by the theater, not Louise's bulky, probably homemade, sweater. She turned sideways in her seat, the better to tackle this new quarry.

"I hear they arrested Jessica," Louise said. "I'm no fan of hers—she's gone a long way on dubious references—but I never thought she was capable of murder. If it's any help, she was her usual obstructive self when I was talking to her in the lounge at the Lodge last night, then went white as a ghost when someone walked in and said Sharon Dingwall had been murdered."

Not correcting Louise's misapprehension about the color of ghosts—some of them appeared in living color, "living" being relative—Jean said, "You may be the best alibi she's got."

"Great." Louise rolled her eyes.

Jean had beat around enough bushes the night before. "Jessica's no fan of yours, either. She said you were trying to get information from her about that new source of hers."

"No kidding. She's spent enough time trying to get information out of me. Tit for tat, I told her. Tell me what this miraculous new source is. Show me yours and I'll show you mine." The pile of papers, folders, and booklets in her lap slipped sideways and Louise grabbed for them. "Okay, to be fair, the reason I'm here helping stage *Macbeth* is because Jessica went off to Berwick in Scotland last spring... Whoa, I'm not supposed to say the name of the play, am I? Bad luck."

The bad luck, Jean thought, was that she herself knew more about Jessica's source than Louise did. Still, witnesses, even casual ones, tended to know things they didn't know they knew. "'The Scottish Play' is based, sort of, on the trial of the Berwick witches, right?"

"Oh yes. When Jessica came back she asked me a lot of

questions about the play and its history. I was looking for a student project, so here I am. Nothing like blood, thunder, and sex to get the kids' attention. Plus some toilet humor on the side."

"When I was teaching history, I learned early on to present it as gossip—what *were* they thinking?" Jean grinned, then asked, "Who do you think wrote Shakespeare?"

"A guy named William Shakespeare from Stratford-upon-Avon. There's no evidence that he didn't. Bacon, Marlowe, Oxford, whoever—that's all just as much wishful thinking and creative extrapolation as the Dingwalls' vault in the churchyard."

"One, two, three, four!" shouted Hugh, and the band launched into "Mairi's Wedding."

Jean's feet tapped, even as she raised her voice. "You're doing an eighteenth-century version of the play?"

"Who's to say what an eighteenth-century version is? Shakespeare wasn't a sacred text then. Heck, he wasn't a sacred text in his own day. The folios that were printed right after his death were typeset from prompt books, transcriptions, notes, who knows what all."

"With typos and other mistakes."

"Oh yeah. No wonder that by the eighteenth century they had no qualms about not just cutting scenes but re-writing the plays, giving *Romeo and Juliet* a happy ending, for example. Even people you'd think would know better, like Alexander Pope, the poet, bowdlerized the text."

Jean nodded, knowing full well how creativity colored historical as well as literary transmission—the story would be so much better if only… Like the trial of the Berwick witches, which Shakespeare conflated with the blood-soaked ambitions of a king from another time period and presented to a patron who had a supernatural bee in his bonnet almost as big as the Dingwalls' conspiracy hornet, no thanks to his cousin, Francis Stewart.

Louise went on, "Then there were the people who forged texts, or cut up original documents for souvenirs. Dodd, Malone, Collier—I'll tell you, some of the eighteenth-century Shakespeare scholars were pretty shady characters."

"But they get students to sit up and pay attention," Jean said, even as she wondered what a shady—or at least dappled—character like Jessica Evesdottir had found in Charlotte Murray's note. A mention of the role her ancestor's trial had in inspiring *Macbeth?* The Dingwalls would—well, Sharon had sold her soul to get her hands on something relating Francis Stewart to Shakespeare and thence, however discursively, to Francis Bacon.

A young man appeared from the back of the theater. "Ms. Dietz? Justin's car broke down and he'll be late, but I saw Mandy heading this way."

"I'm coming," Louise told him, and, still juggling her papers, stood up. "Well, good luck with the investigation and everything."

"Thanks," Jean told her.

Louise escorted the young man into the lobby, where they were greeted by the helium-inflected voice of one of the ladies or one of the witches.

Jean imagined a contemporary re-write: "Is this, like, a dagger which I see before me, dude, its handle, you know, toward my hand?" Muffling a groan, she once again pulled out her notebook and pencil and in her own peculiar shorthand transcribed her conversation.

Hugh segued from playing his fiddle to singing a lusty protest song. *Right on,* Jean thought. Never give up, never surrender!

And yet compromise was what made relationships, from public to personal, work.

Packing everything away, she let the wake-the-dead cadences rouse her weary body from the theater and move it down the sidewalk to the Cheese Shop, where she bought a sandwich. She caught the bus at the corner and, trying not to think, turned her face not up to heaven but toward the smooth ceiling of cloud. The overcast was breaking up, revealing hints of blue sky behind the swags and drags of gray.

Bucktrout and Bushrod sat on the brick sidewalk outside the Dinwiddie Kitchen, poised to capture the first ray of sun. She petted each cat, then went inside to discover that the beds were made and the dirty dishes gone. Everything was in its place, including the Bellarmine bottle on the mantelpiece.

She picked it up and set it back down without sensing any resonance of Thomasina. You could call all the ghosts you wanted, but they appeared on their own schedules.

Just as she sat down with her sandwich and a cup of tea, her bag began to play "The 1812 Overture." She was going to have to change the ring tone to something less assertive, although "Lochaber No More" was not on her short list.

The number was Stephanie's. "Hello?"

"Jean." The voice was Alasdair's at its most polite. "I'm having a look at Dunwich Pond. I'll drive by and collect you, shall I?"

"Yes, please. Have you eaten?"

"I had elevenses of sorts, a doughnut. If that's what American police departments are depending upon for nourishment…" He let that sentence taper away diplomatically.

Diplomacy didn't stop Jean from saying, "And you count that Scottish delicacy, the deep-fried Mars bar, as health food?"

"Don't be daft," Alasdair said. "Ten minutes, then."

Daft is what I do, Jean thought. *Take it or leave it.* And she thought, his first wife was certifiably daft, and they'd left each other.

She set aside half the sandwich for him, and heated water for another cup of tea. It was boiling when he walked in the door, good as his word. "Ah, thank you kindly," he said, and laid a manila folder on the table as he sat down. "You stopped by Matt's office, did you?"

His voice was still polite, if not casual. She saw no lipstick on his collar, not that she expected to. His tie was still knotted precisely against his throat and the frost in his eyes indicated, if not iron in his soul, then armor encasing his psyche.

"Yes," she answered, sitting on her hands to keep from reaching for the folder. "He wants us to make sure Jessica isn't charged with murder. Either murder."

"There's a case to be made for charging her with Sharon's—a public threat, no alibi, and a motive, if not as strong a one as we'd like, control of the Charlotte document. Jessica's not helping herself refusing to give details of it. What else is she hiding, eh?" He bit off a piece of the sandwich half and chewed meticulously.

"Good question. She's still saying she bought the document in London?"

"Oh aye. There's only us that heard her playing silly beggars with it, and blaming absent-minded Wesley, come to that. All she's saying is that it's being authenticated in D.C. Stephanie..." He stopped, perhaps considering whether it would be safer to say "Detective Venegas," then giving up that thought as unworthy. "She's making inquiries at the National Archives and the Smithsonian. Time's closing in on her, Jessica needs to be charged or released soon as may be."

"Tell Stephanie to try the Folger Library."

He looked up, meeting Jean's eyes for the first time since he walked into the house. "Who?"

She met his eyes back again, as cautiously as touching her tongue to a frozen flagpole, and detailed her conversation with Louise. "The Folger Library in D.C. specialized in Shakespeare. If Charlotte said something about *Macbeth,* they'd be interested. And they're quite capable of dealing with paper, ink, handwriting—all the literary forensic stuff."

"Well done, Jean," he said gravely. Lowering his gaze, he ate the rest of the sandwich half and picked up the steaming cup of tea.

"Maybe. Here's your list of phone numbers." She reached into her bag and shoved the wee bittie paper across the table. "Matt had it. He saw us with the Dingwalls Friday night and thought we were working with them, so he followed us here. And then he checked us out."

Alasdair shot a glance in the direction of the college that would have pulverized the stones of Matt's building. When he looked back at Jean his eyes were no longer frosted.

She intercepted his question, running through Matt's testimony and concluding, "He's very frustrated, both personally and academically. Whether that's enough to make him a killer on top of a sneak—and whether he's enough of a sneak that he actually *wants* to pin the murders on Jessica…I don't know. I've been fooled before."

"No matter. You'll not be seeing him on your own again."

She chose to interpret that statement as professional concern, not personal possessiveness. "I don't intend to. Just one thing—I'm not sure Matt was with Rachel last night after all."

"Rachel's claiming to know next to nothing about her mum and Sharon. And I'm not thinking she does. We didn't know to ask her about her dad." Alasdair's forehead crimped. "Dylan now, she knows a thing or two about Dylan. But she's not saying. No more than either Kelly or

Quentin's saying anything about the theft from Blair. Mind you, Kelly admitted last night she'd had words with Sharon at the hotel, and Quentin confirmed it. Now Olson's turned up a housekeeper who heard the women screaming insults at each other, and found a broken glass in Sharon's room as well."

"It was more than Kelly's 'mild disagreement,' then," Jean said. "I wondered if Kelly had a motive to kill Sharon."

"She's claiming not to know about the insurance policy Tim had on his wife. If Tim's as desperate for money as Quentin was saying, well then."

"Well then," repeated Jean. Oh yes, money was a time-honored motive if ever there was one. "And there's something else. You remember that Hugh was on the plane with Kelly? He says she said they had a Witch Box for their movie, they'd hired actors to re-enact scenes with it and everything. Maybe they anticipated getting Blair's replica. Or maybe they asked Wesley to make them one, but either he refused to cooperate or Jessica asked him not to."

"Hmmm. Good thought, that." Alasdair drained his cup. "Hugh's speaking to Stephanie, is he?"

"Oh yes." Jean freshened her own cup of tea. Here they were, a team, just like old times. You could be a team without personal feelings for your teammates. "What else has Stephanie—have you and Stephanie—found out since last night?"

He didn't object to her teaming him with Stephanie. Why would he? "The chair spindle was taken from a stack outside the cabinetmaker's shop. Unless a visitor, a child, perhaps, pinched it and left it beside the tree, its use argues premeditation. Just as you were saying last night."

Thank you. "And that points to someone who knew where Sharon was going to be. Someone with no alibi.

Jessica, Tim, Kelly. Matt." She hurried on. "Are there fingerprints on the wood?"

"A few smudged ones, likely belonging to the craftsmen. The killer might have worn gloves. The problem with fingerprints—or the hair caught in Sharon's mobile, come to that—is having a sample for comparison."

"There was a hair caught in her cell phone? She might have struck at the murderer with it." Jean imagined the scene, then drew a curtain over it.

"They're testing to see if it's Jessica's or Sharon's own, but that's taking time and might could end proving nothing. And Tim's saying he knows nothing about burgling Wes's flat. So far we've got no evidence to make a case against him, not 'til we turn up Dylan and the carrier bag."

"Well, yeah, but when it comes to the murder cases, you've got the evidence of Tim's temper as well as the insurance policy."

The faintest trace of wry amusement loosened a corner of Alasdair's mouth. "You mind what Quentin was saying, Tim punching the wall when Sharon would not do something? Well, he's now allowing that what Sharon would not do is stop hitting him. She was the violent one, he's saying."

"Oh my." There was another image, more sad than comical. Jean remembered Tim's shamefaced glance at Sharon when Kelly's phone calls kept interrupting the interview. "There's a bit of reverse sexism on Jessica's part, calling Tim the brute and a savage. Or size-ism, perhaps."

Alasdair pushed back from the table and collected the folder. "When you're considering domestic abuse, size doesn't matter."

Jean's mind didn't send up any cheap jokes, only an image of Sharon's body gutted like her chicken sandwich on a cold, sterile, metal table.

"Come along, lass, let's be getting ourselves to the scene of the crime. The first crime."

She grabbed her bag and made it to the door as he opened it. He held it for her as politely and as impersonally as he'd help an old lady across the street. Despite the affectionate "lass" he'd let slip, she didn't want to talk about it right now, either. "You want me to drive?"

"I'm the one's been shown where we're going."

By Stephanie, in the office with a map, Jean thought.

As she walked out the door she saw from the corner of her eye that the Bellarmine bottle was now sitting on the other end of the mantel. And neither of them had noticed it move.

TWENTY-THREE

DRIVING ON THE right turned out to be another of Alasdair's unsuspected skills. Without turning a hair, blond or gray, he pulled out of the Inn parking lot onto South England Street and zigzagged southeast.

Jean seized the opportunity to tell him about Robert Mason's gravestone and her encounter with Barbara Finch—he raised his left eyebrow—and Mary's daughter Thomasina, who was surely the household ghost—he raised his right eyebrow—and how their destination had once been Duckwitch Pond, named after the unfortunate moment in 1685 when Mary Napier was accused of following the family tradition.

"Why Dunwich, then?" He parked the car in the parking lot of a well-tended but elderly apartment complex, probably not a pit stop on Williamsburg's singles circuit. A sign out front read, *Dunwich Grove. 756 Columbia Road.*

"It's a respectable name from the old country canceling out the embarrassing memories. And there's a great legend about Dunwich, England. The town was swallowed by the sea and you can still hear drowned church bells." She didn't add anything about the number of bells she'd been hearing recently, drowned, stabbed, or belfried.

"Right." Alasdair climbed out of the car.

Opening her own door, Jean got to her feet and looked toward the building, a double tier of doors, windows, and either patios or balconies ranged in front of what looked like forest primeval but was more likely abandoned farmland reclaimed by trees and brush.

"Hagedorn's flat was round the back, ground floor, overlooking the trees. Easy enough for the thief to cut through a window screen and force open the casement. Here's the list of objects stolen, and the ones dredged from the pond this morning. It's just this way." Alasdair handed over the folder, then started off along a path curving around the end of the building. His feet swished through the fallen leaves, his eyes focused not ahead but casting a chilly look at the inoffensive windows of the apartments. "No one saw anyone walking down by the pond with Wesley the afternoon he died, more's the pity."

Jean shuffled along, trying to manipulate folder and lists without tripping over any rough places on the path. Rays of sun broke through the clouds, vanished, broke through again, brightening and then dimming the fall colors. Sun or no sun, the wind was cold, and colder still in the shadow of the trees. The traffic noise faded away, replaced by the rustle of leaves and twigs, the harsh cry of birds, and Alasdair's steady footfall.

"Did Stephanie's crew search Wesley's flat? What about the Dingwalls' hotel rooms?"

"Aye to the former—the man was uncommonly tidy, she's saying, everything organized just so, making the burglars' work easy. For the Dingwalls' rooms, now, she was obliged to get a warrant, and that meant howking out a judge late on a Saturday night."

"Giving Tim and everyone time to get rid of anything incriminating."

"They're being watched, no worries there."

Who, me? Worry? Jean looked down at the lists. "They found a chisel in the pond. The murder weapon, right? Well, along with the weight of the murderer's own body."

"Oh aye, it matches the mark on Hagedorn's neck a treat. Any fingerprints are all a blur, like on the spindle. The technicians are doing their best, but…"

"Forensics only goes so far." Jean raised the papers again. "Aha, the list of things dredged from the pond matches the list of things stolen. A silver pitcher and platter, a commemorative gold coin, a silver picture frame, a turquoise tie clasp—you were right, the thief stole some valuables to cover up what he really wanted."

The path ran out of the dank, still shadow of the trees and she stopped dead. Duckwitch or Dunwich Pond lay before them, its pewter-colored surface pierced around the rim by tall reeds. Wind sighed in the branches overhead, the water rippled, and the reeds bowed and straightened. Here, too, Jean wouldn't have been surprised to glimpse the faces of green men, perhaps not malicious, but certainly not indifferent.

To one side lay a row of bricks overgrown by what could just as well have been poison ivy as honeysuckle, all that remained of one of Middle Plantation's seventeenth-century farmsteads. Most of the farm buildings had been built of wood or wattle and were long gone, along with the fields its owners and their workers had cleared with sweat, blood, and tears, all reclaimed by nature.

A gleam of sunlight burnished the slow swell of water, then faded. Leaves glided down onto it but didn't break the surface tension. Jean imagined the tower of Bruton Parish Church sunk below that surface. She imagined Tolkien's Watcher in the Water reaching through it to snake a tentacle around her ankle. Or Alasdair's ankle, since he stood closer to the edge of the pond, where the bare dirt of the path ran down to a muddy bank.

"Is this where Mary Napier's tormentors launched their boat? Where they tied her up, hand to foot, put a rope around her waist, and threw her in?" Her own voice seemed unusually loud.

"If she sinks, then she's innocent, but good luck not drowning. If she floats, she's guilty. Mary floated, didn't she?"

"Oh yes. So she went to trial. Jessica's script to the contrary, despite her confession Mary was whipped and pilloried, but that's too graphic for the tourists, I guess. The true story's in the book. Having paid her debt to society, such as it was, Mary survived until 1729—that was the year her will was probated. She had a bit of property to leave Thomasina, some linens, household items. The little house—our little house—belonged to the governor."

"No mention of the charm stone, then."

"Not in that version of the book, no. I can see why Jessica wants to include it in a new one." Another beam of light bathed the surface of the pond, and for a minute the reds and yellows of the surrounding trees reflected as though in a mirror. "I wonder if this place would seem so melancholy if we didn't know what happened here, to Mary and to Wes both."

"Right." Alasdair was inspecting the squashed reeds and rectangular marks in the mud that indicated a temporary plank boardwalk, all encircled by yellow police tape. Of course Stephanie's people were much too skilled to turn a crime scene into a hippopotamus wallow. Taking a wary step closer, Jean made out footprints overlaid indecipherably by more footprints, smears, blotches, and scrapes, and deep parallel gouges perhaps caused by Wesley's feet in their death throes.

Quelling her imagination, she looked back at the lists, comparing the things stolen to the things found—the pitcher, the coin… "Wait a minute. Some polished agates and small pieces of silver plate were stolen, too, but they didn't turn up with the other valuables. Even if some of them were too small to be caught in the net, you'd expect to find a few."

"Significant, are you thinking?" Alasdair strolled fifty yards or so back toward the eave of the grove and eyed the wide, knee-high stump of a tree and some tumbled chunks of wood.

"Hell, yes. Wesley was going to replicate the charm stone, too, maybe send it to Blair, maybe use it on the Dingwall replica, the one for their movie. Assuming there really was going to be a second replica." She frowned, trying to visualize the photos she'd glimpsed so briefly on the tabletop before Sharon swept them back into her bag. Whether the photo was of the original or the replica Witch Box didn't matter. Sharon or Tim had circled the slot for the charm stone in red ink.

The pond mirrored the trees, and the sky, and several black birds flying overhead. Assuming the charm stone still existed, Jean thought, and assuming it existed somewhere it could be found by someone who knew what it was—two big assumptions, there, but ones the Dingwalls had obviously made—then its silver setting wouldn't reflect anything. It would be blackened with tarnish. As for the stone itself, was it an agate or an emerald or something else green? Even the word *green* itself covered a lot of territory, from olive drab to lime.

"I bet Robert Mason showed Thomasina off to Charlotte, for a curtsey and a nod of noblesse oblige, although if I were Charlotte, I'd have asked questions. What if the Dingwalls think Thomasina gave the stone back to Charlotte, and she took it home and tucked it away with the note? Or with the Witch Box, for that matter. Like Jessica did, Charlotte didn't think it was anything more than a family curiosity, like great-grandpa's moustache cup or the equivalent."

"Who's to say Charlotte didn't have it, oh aye." Alasdair crouched over the stump, ran his fingers across its truncated top, then bent sideways to sight across it.

"Sharon knew about Wes bringing home that document, and I bet she knew it was from Blair, not a London street market. What if she and Tim thought he'd found the actual charm stone, too? They'd be frantic to get their hands on it."

Alasdair picked up something from the ground and rolled it between his fingers. "That's not so much of a leap as some of theirs, when they're holding Olympic long-jump records."

Jean sent a smile toward him, but he didn't notice. She said, "Sam Gould and the other man at the cabinetmaker's shop said Wes was looking over his shoulder. Worried. Jessica said he was getting threatening calls. I bet the Dingwalls were nagging him to make the replica, hand over the stone, cooperate somehow."

"No matter him telling them he didn't have the stone, they'd not credit anything they didn't want to hear." Alasdair stood up and glanced around, eyes bright as the sky overhead and the sky, reflected, at Jean's feet. "When he would not cooperate, they burgled his flat for the plans and all, thinking of finding themselves another craftsman. But Kelly had other ideas."

"They kept the agates and silver pieces—probably not thirty pieces, like Judas—and tried them on Robert Mason's headstone, but nothing happened. So then they finally believed Wes didn't have the stone and they started poking around with that probe of theirs. The question is, did one of them kill Wes out of spite? For revenge? Or did they think he was holding out on them? Were they trying to question him here, and the situation got out of hand?"

Alasdair indicated the muddy area next to the pond. "The forensic boffins are having a right headache working through that lot. Looks to be the killer tried obliterating his own prints."

"No surprise there. But what if the killer's a her? Sharon?"

"We've got no evidence against Sharon," Alasdair said.

"Well, no, just that she could get violent." Jean looked across the pond, around the encircling trees, at the forlorn brick wall. All were witnesses to the crime, and none of them could testify. No help there.

Think, she ordered her brain, even though it already felt like a punching bag. "Maybe what the housekeeper overheard was Sharon giving Kelly a piece of her mind for calling just when she did, so I got a look at the photos and heard the bits about playing the patsy and working on the cipher. And Sharon couldn't have been happy that Kelly was pushing the movie prematurely. She did slander and scandalize, like Jessica said. She was a scold. Not that she deserved…" Jean let the sentence float away like yet another leaf wafting down on the pond.

Alasdair picked up a flat piece of wood leaning against the stump. "They ducked scolds as well. There's still the odd ducking stool in village museums in the U.K."

"Yeah." The sun faded again, and the water dulled. "Even if Tim didn't kill Sharon himself—even if Kelly didn't kill her, eliminating an annoyance—they've lucked out that someone did. They've got 'proof' that somebody took their theories seriously enough to try and shut them up. And Tim's got the insurance money. I bet he sees Sharon as the sacrifice bunt for the good of the team."

"Eh?" Alasdair asked.

"Baseball analogy. Never mind. What are you looking at?" Jean walked with the occasional squish to where Alasdair was standing.

The broad stump was surrounded by bits and pieces of

wood, some of them splintered and covered with bark, some weathered, others fresh and smooth. A sprinkle of wood shavings and sawdust atop the stump, along with grooves cut across its rings, indicated it had been used as a cutting surface and makeshift worktable. "This is what I was after seeing for myself," Alasdair said. "Most of the photos are focusing on the body. Hagedorn died where he was found, half in, half out of the water. That's clear enough."

"This must be the place where he liked to sit and work on small projects, then. Like Hugh and his friends will play music just for fun, because it calls to them. The shavings are wet from the rain but they're still pretty fresh, considering."

"The photo of this is none too clear. I'm seeing now just what it is." Alasdair picked up the flat piece of wood and held it out to her.

Rudimentary carvings of leaves, tendrils, and the small leering faces of green men were roughed into its pale, mud-flecked surface. The initials were not "F" or "B," but "J" and "E." "The designs from the Witch Box," Jean said. "You'd think that was on Wes's mind, wouldn't you?"

"Oh aye." Alasdair's forefinger touched an empty, three-sided slot. "Here's a place for a stone."

Jean went on, "This Box looks smaller than the actual Witch Box. Maybe he intended it to be a jewelry box, a peace offering for Jessica. Maybe he was just playing, and she was on his mind, too."

Alasdair crouched again, drawing Jean down beside him. "See the footprints? Big shoes, the tread worn down. Wesley's, I'm guessing. They've shifted back and forth as he moved about the stump, as he sat down on it and stood up again."

"And what about those?" Jean waved her hand over another set of prints, small shoes, smooth soles edged with a rim of stitching. They skewed first to one side and then the other, and beside them… "Oh my. You do have evidence against Sharon. You do have a sample for comparison."

"The prints of those shoes?"

"She was wearing mules, clogs—shoes without heels, Miranda would know the right name for them. Sharon had them on Friday night at the reception. And last night—one of them fell off her foot when she, ah, went up into the tree. Those rounded, cup-shaped marks beside the prints of the shoes are where her heels came out of them. Mud is slippery, and so is leather when it's wet. She was having trouble keeping her balance."

Alasdair nodded, not so much following every word as developing the scenario simultaneously.

"I bet it was a spur-of-the-moment killing. She was horribly frustrated—no charm stone, someone she needed as an ally making gifts for the enemy, her annoying sister-in-law pushing events too fast. Maybe she went into a tirade and Wes argued with her. Was it Jessica who said when it came to his work Wesley could show some temper?"

"Something of the sort, aye."

"As for how Sharon got him to the edge of the pond, she could have confessed to breaking into his apartment and pointed out where they threw his valuables. He left the chisel lying on the stump when he went to look and she picked it up. Maybe she even told him one of his agates or something was lying just at the water's edge, to get him to squat down. And she stepped out of her shoes, planted her feet, braced both hands on the chisel and…"

Jean seemed to hear the sound of the blows echoing across the surface of the pond, and a gasp or two, and the squelch of mud and bubble of water, until all was still except a woman's heavy breath. With a sigh she concluded, "He wouldn't have seen her as a physical threat even if she'd been larger."

"As Stephanie was saying, jabbing a chisel into someone's neck eliminates the size issue, particularly since Hagedorn was not such a big bruiser to begin." Standing up, Alasdair offered Jean his hand. It was chill, hard. He pulled her to her feet, released her, and looked over at the crime scene. "I'm thinking some of the same prints are showing up there."

"Her feet got muddy. So did her socks. There'd be mud inside her shoes as well as outside, even if she tried to clean them off."

"Likely her socks are in her room. The M.E.'s got her shoes." Alasdair held out his hand.

Like a surgeon's assistant, Jean dug out her cell phone and placed it in his palm. She strolled a few steps away, toward the ruined wall, listening to Alasdair make his report—the carvings, the sawdust, the shoes. The scenario.

But why, murmured that logic-circuit in Jean's mind, *why would Sharon kill Wes, when the Dingwalls needed him...*

They didn't need him, not anymore. Kelly and Quentin had provided another Witch Box. If the irritatingly not-with-the-program Wes was gone, he couldn't tell any nosy authorities that he'd made only one replica and the one in the movie was the one stolen from Blair. In fact, with the craftsman who made the replica dying a mysterious death, Tim and Sharon would have yet another marketing ploy, proof that enemies were after them.

And yet—and yet, they still had no charm stone. What? Had Sharon returned to Tim, admitting what she'd done? That would explain why her cheeks had been red and her eyes glittering at the reception that night, and why Tim had been so insufferably smug. Bold action had been taken. A problem had been solved.

And then Kelly had pushed them even further into a corner already crowded by the charm stone and Francis Bacon.

"Very good then," Alasdair said into the phone, switched it off, and handed it back.

"So now we're pretty sure we have two murderers," Jean told him. "Fine, but if Sharon killed Wesley, who killed her? Back to Tim and Kelly, not just eliminating an annoying gadfly but disposing of a loose cannon. Although having Sharon up on a murder charge would have gotten them lots of sensational publicity."

"Or was someone who felt guilty about putting Wes into his predicament after getting herself a bit of revenge?"

"Jessica. Though you could make a case for Matt being the killer. Or go out on a limb and say it was… No, not Rachel, she was at the play, not Barbara, she was at the church concert, not Louise Dietz, she was in a meeting, not Sam Gould, he was in jail, not Rodney Lockhart, he was, well, maybe he was disguised as that custodian who almost saw the murder. Maybe the custodian was the murderer." Crawling back along that metaphorical limb, Jean reminded herself that motivation was as important as opportunity.

Alasdair turned his gaze from the stump to her, a slip of a smile playing at the corners of his mouth.

"Yeah, I know, there's steam coming out of my ears. In another minute I'll be suggesting one of the twins found out about the insurance policy so did the deed to stave off unemployment. But no, Quentin was chatting up a girl in the ticket office. I'm sure Olson's checked on that."

"Just now we're analyzing data, not reaching conclusions."

"Not yet. But soon. I hope." Jean looked down at the derelict panel of wood and its initials "J" and "E," and said silently, once again, *I'm sorry, Matt.*

TWENTY-FOUR

ALASDAIR GUIDED THE car onto Francis Street, heading back to their historic house in the Historic Area as Jean finished expounding her theory of motivation: Wesley became a liability to be eradicated rather than an asset to be wooed or intimidated, depending.

"I reckon you've got the truth of the matter," he replied. "As much as anyone has, that is."

Nothing tarnished as easily as truth, she thought. And there was living proof. In front of Williamsburg's Masonic Lodge stood Tim and Kelly Dingwall, haranguing a dozen people armed with cameras and notebooks, while Quentin lurked half a block away intently studying fallen leaves.

Tim stood with his hand thrust into his coat, looking less like Napoleon than Hermann Goering with an ulcer. Beside him Kelly gestured expansively. All she needed was a laser pointer, casting red dots like those of a rifle scope onto the facade of the handsome little Georgian building.

It had been constructed in 1773 for the local branch of the loyal and ancient society of free Masons. By that time the Dinwiddie Kitchen—the car turned the corner beneath Jean and Alasdair's own bedroom window—had been occupying its plot of ground on the next block for over twenty years.

Did Washington or Peyton Randolph or James Monroe, the old boys' club, celebrate the Lodge's grand opening with a keglet of Thomasina's beer? Jean could buy that image a lot more readily than concepts of cloaked figures in smoke-filled rooms plotting the destiny of the world on charts and chessboards, with or without suitably secret handshakes and passwords.

Alasdair parked the car, locked its doors, and, flipping the keys into the air and catching them, offered them to Jean.

"You might as well keep them," she said.

"Very good then." He tucked them into his pocket.

The sun's appearances were lasting longer and longer, and the clouds were looking less like used laundry detergent than fresh whipped cream. The brick sidewalk had warmed up enough that the two black-and-white catmometers were sprawled across it. Bucktrout—or was it Bushrod?—looked up as the humans skirted around them, then lay back down again.

"We should take relaxation lessons," said Jean as she opened the door.

"Oh aye," Alasdair said, but tension still whetted his voice. "When's the concert, then?"

"Seven."

He looked at the clock on the mantel, several artifacts down from the Bellarmine bottle. "It's just gone two."

"I gucss I'll transcribe my notes, see if any patterns occur to me."

Alasdair stood facing the fireplace, jingling the keys in his pocket. The back of his head revealed nothing.

He'd still be there to deal with later, afterward, whichever came last. Jean sat down at the desk.

As soon as she touched the nylon case of her computer she realized it was empty. Ripping open the zipper and peering foolishly inside was only a formality. She bounded back to her feet with a heartfelt "Oh, crap."

"What's wrong?"

"My computer's been stolen."

Instantly at her side, Alasdair seized the case and shook

it out as though the computer had shrunk to a matchbox and was still inside. "You were working with it when I came away this morning. Was it here when you came in at noon?"

"I have no idea. The case was sitting on the desk is all." With a snort of exasperation, she plopped down on the desk chair. "Someone's taken my computer for the same reason Kelly stole the replica Witch Box instead of the real one. My notes were easier to get at than anything from the police department. Like anything I'd have wouldn't be small beer compared to theirs."

"What notes have you got?"

"My interview with the Dingwalls, what Jessica told us, what Matt and Hugh and Louise said today. And…" She vented a hollow laugh. "…not one word of it's transcribed on my computer!"

Alasdair brightened. "Well then." And darkened again. "Still, someone's thinking you've got more information, more power, than you do. Matt?"

"I must have spent a good forty-five minutes in the theater after I left his office. And I had to wait in line to buy the sandwich. If he came straight here, he—had to get in. Oh! The beds were made and the dishes taken away. What if he got here while the housekeeper was in the bathroom or vacuuming the bedroom? The running water, the vacuum cleaner, would cover any other noise."

"A moment in the door and out again. Matt. The…" Leaving the epithet unexpressed, Alasdair reached for the telephone on the desk and punched in a number, one, Jean noted, that he'd memorized. "Stephanie," he said, "Jean's computer's been stolen. I doubt it has something doing with the case. No, it does have something doing with the case."

In spite of herself, Jean smiled. That Scotspeak "I doubt," meaning "I suspect," had fooled her more than once.

"Very good then." He batted at the cradle, saying to

Jean, "She's sending Olson to take a report." He punched another number. "I'd appreciate your asking Eric, the lad with the food trays, to stop in. Aye, that's all right—when he's free."

He hung up and stalked off across the room, to stop, brooding, at the front window. Jean made a quick reconnaissance of the bedroom and bathroom. No, nothing else had disappeared, go figure.

Back in the living room, Alasdair hadn't moved. "Everything's accounted for save the laptop?"

"Yep." She might as well keep on keeping on, she told herself, and reached for the Dingwalls' press release.

It didn't tell her anything she didn't already know, but the glossy photos of the Witch Box, each carved leaf cut with shadow, the gap for the charm stone brightly illuminated, made great illustrations of grand delusion. Of the subjectivity of perception.

The Dingwalls must have bought one of Blair Castle's studio photos—this wasn't the same photo that was in the Dunmore exhibit catalog lying open on Matt's desk. Poor Matt, like the Dingwalls perceiving himself as powerless. Even more than the Dingwalls—at least they were fighting back, if in their own eccentric fashion.

Alasdair's shadow fell on the page. "Have they got any facts at all in their omnium-gatherum?"

"Oh yes, they've got a fact or two by the tail. And like the farmer's wife, they cut them off with a carving knife." She angled one of the chronologies toward him. "Conspiracy theory is the natural, even scientific cause for events—there's proof of everything."

"Proof?"

"Sure. Evidence against the theory is evidence for it,

because the absence of evidence means someone is trying to suppress what really happened and what's behind it."

"And contrary evidence is manipulated by the conspirators, meaning to mislead."

"Like astrology, if you accept the premise, everything follows."

"But what premise are you accepting?" His words were sharp and cold.

Even as she told herself not to take his tone personally, Jean raised her hands and said, "Don't blame me for these people's choices, even if I do write about them. I enjoy the free range speculation. I enjoy the synthesis of history and legend—I do that, too."

"Oh aye, that you do." This time his voice rasped across something deeper than doubt.

Was it regret? What did that mean? She looked up at him, wondering whether his mood was heading toward global warming or another Ice Age, but read nothing in his sober face.

A series of raps rattled the front door. Alasdair plunged toward it—saved by the knock. Jean pitched the press release onto the desk. "Olson? That was fast."

Alasdair opened the door to reveal not Olson's blond, boyish figure but an even more boyish redhead. Too much to hope it was Dylan—it had to be Quentin.

With a glance over his shoulder, a fox hearing the hounds behind him, the young man pushed into the house. "My dad and my aunt are showing people around the churchyard. I said I was going back to the hotel. But I saw you guys come in here, and…"

Alasdair shut the door and stood in front of it, arms crossed. "And?"

Quentin's famished expression whetted itself into cunning. "Mr., uh, Scottish guy. Is there a reward for the Witch Box replica?"

"My name is Alasdair Cameron," he said, going very still. "Have you got the replica?"

"Well, not really, I sort of know where it is." Quentin looked over at Jean. "Hi."

"Hi." Jean stepped back, away from any ricochets and closer to the desk, where she picked up a hotel-logo pen and paper and put them to work.

"You and your aunt stole the replica, did you then?" Alasdair demanded.

"Well, maybe. About that reward."

"We've got you on the CCTV tapes," said Alasdair. "When you were saying you were not at Blair, you were lying. Not being banged up, lad, that's your reward."

Quentin ducked and covered.

"Not being thrown in jail is your reward," Jean translated, while Alasdair vented an irritated sigh.

Was Quentin really trying to use his family's—more than capers, crimes—to make a few bucks? Or was he growing more and more disgusted by them, and preparing to bail out? Either way would work.

He looked down at the rug, the guile leaching from his face. "Oh. Oh, okay, yeah, Aunt Kelly worked it all out on the way to Blair, she'd trip an alarm, I'd grab the Box. It all went just fine, you know, except for trying to get the thing up under my coat. Sharp edges, and I was, like, in a hurry." He held out his arms, not for the handcuff but to show the bruises on his wrists.

"Where's the replica now?" Alasdair demanded, looming while Quentin shrunk.

"Aunt Kelly took it after we got back to Edinburgh. I think she mailed it somewhere. She was complaining about—it wasn't FedEx, it was somebody else—about their prices."

Aha, Jean thought at Alasdair's stony face. *We got that right.*

If he picked up her message, he didn't show it. "Have you heard from your brother?"

"No." Quentin tore at his hair, leaving the red ends standing on end like a cartoon character registering fear. "I dunno where he is. I dunno what the, the heck is going on here. Me, I was glad to get rid of that Box. It was ugly as sin, gave me the creeps, I don't care it was just a copy. But my mom and dad, they were freaking out about it."

"Freaking out?" Alasdair repeated.

Jean didn't rephrase that—he knew what it meant.

"Your parents and your aunt, they needed the replica for their movie." Alasdair's voice was quiet as a sword slipping from its scabbard. "They thought they'd organized a second replica, but the craftsman reneged on the bargain. Your father threatened him. Your mother and your brother burgled his flat for the plans. Your aunt had you steal the first and only replica. Problem solved, eh?"

"How the—how do you know all that?"

Alasdair's half smile indicated dour satisfaction. Quentin didn't need to know he'd been making an informed guess. "There's a team working against you, lad. And if the car doors slamming outside are any indication, you'll be telling your tale to the rest of them right soon now."

Quentin uttered a four-letter word that wasn't *crap.* He looked desperately around the room, not like Tim assessing the potential for conflict, but like a rat trapped on a sinking ship. His knees started to buckle. Alasdair's strong right arm held him up as his left hand opened the door.

Olson was framed in the opening. "Mr. Cameron. Ms. Fairbairn, what's…"

In a few concise words, Alasdair explained the situation, while Quentin stood swooning beside him. Jean ripped her notes off the pad and handed them over. "Thanks," Olson replied, folding the papers into his pocket.

She met Alasdair's part-indulgent, part-skeptical glance. No, the notes weren't admissible evidence. She was less on the ball than behind the eight-ball.

Saying nothing, Alasdair helped Olson bundle Quentin out the door, past the cocked whiskers of Bushrod and Bucktrout, to the police car waiting at the curb. There a uniformed officer did apply handcuffs, and folded the young man into the back seat, there to await, if not Olson's, then certainly Stephanie's pleasure.

The word's going to get out, Jean thought, *that coming to us*—or maybe to Alasdair, whatever—*just rammed you further down on the hook.* But then, if the word hadn't already spread that they were semi-professional crime solvers, no one would be coming to begin with. Or stealing her computer.

Alasdair led first Jean, then Olson, back into the house, his satisfaction edging into irritation, or so Jean deduced when his gesture at the empty laptop case was a spear-thrust jab of his forefinger. "And now we've been burgled."

Olson inspected the desk and jotted down the answers to the relevant questions, but a vanishing computer was only on his list of priorities at all because it was Jean's, and the odds of a full crime scene team showing up were next to nil. He said at last, "I'll tell Stephanie and write up a report. In the meantime—" he dug into another pocket, produced a folded paper, and handed it to Jean "—Stephanie thought you'd like to have this."

Jean unfolded the paper to reveal a photocopy of what had to be the Charlotte document, eighteenth-century handwriting, sketch of the Witch Box, and all. "All right! Thanks!"

Alasdair craned to look. "Well then," he said, which was better than "I told you so." Jean already knew Stephanie was not trying to compete with her. Saying something apologetic now would just make it all worse.

She half-turned away, smoothing the paper carefully onto the desk but not seeing it, not yet.

"There was a copy of that at Dr. Evesdottir's house and another at her office," Olson explained. "Oh, and Stephanie says thanks for the tips about Mrs. Dingwall's shoes. She'd got forensics working on it. And, let's see, we've found the custodian who was walking along Nicholson Street at the time of the murder, but he didn't see a thing. He'd come around the corner of North England Street, past the Randolph House, not past the tree. He had his back turned to it the entire time. In the dark," he added unnecessarily. Jean could remember the scene just fine.

She asked, "Did he hear anything?"

"No, he was listening to his iPod, with the earbuds, you know. He didn't even hear all the excitement after y'all found the body. We've got no reason to implicate him in the murder, but we'll keep an eye on him."

Alasdair shrugged, almost imperceptibly. So close and yet so far. "Let's be getting the Dingwall lad to the station, then, Sergeant."

Let's? Well, of course. The theft of the replica was Alasdair's case, first and foremost. Of course he'd be the one conducting the witness to the interview room.

"Yes, sir." Tucking away his notebook, Olson threw open the door.

The cats had moved to dead center of the top step. Eric was advancing up the sidewalk under the chill eye of the police officer waiting by the car. And presumably under Quentin's blurry eyes, but Jean couldn't see anything more past the tinted windows of the police car than a lanky shadow.

"Is there a problem, sir?" Eric asked over the two black-and-white backs, even as his dark eyes registered the police incursion and answered his own question.

"And you are?" Olson asked, stepping over the cats and descending the steps.

"Eric Mason," the young man responded.

Jean quelled a groan. He couldn't be named Smith or Jones, could he?

Unfazed, Alasdair homed in on his potential witness. "We've had a computer stolen. We're thinking someone walked in the door while the char…"

"The housekeeper," Jean murmured.

"…was scrubbing the bath or hoovering the bedroom."

"Vacuuming," murmured Jean.

Alasdair darted her a quick blue gleam. He was communicating just fine, thank you.

Eric's amiable face crumpled into a frown. "Oh no. I'm so sorry, sir."

"We're not blaming the housekeeping staff," Jean told him.

Olson added, "We just want to know if anyone saw anything."

"It's a busy intersection," Eric replied. "People are coming and going all the time. I didn't notice anything when I picked up the dishes. I'll ask housekeeping…" He paused, his gaze turning inward as he apparently reconstructed some scene. "There was a man on the sidewalk throwing pebbles for the cats to play with. He had to step aside for the housekeeper's buggy. Bald head with a fringe of gray hair, gray beard, college sweatshirt."

Alasdair's narrowed lips and flared nostrils named a name, but Jean spoke first. "Matthew Finch."

"Him?" Olson asked. "We're already trying to locate

him. I sent a uniform to his office and then to his home, but he's not there."

"Try his wife's house," suggested Alasdair.

Jean said, "And his mother's."

"We're on it." Olson handed Eric a business card. "If you find out anything, let us know."

"I sure will, sir." Eric's gaze moved worriedly from face to face to face.

He and Olson looked like opposing pawns on a chessboard, Jean thought, except they were on the same side. "Thank you, Eric."

"I'm just sorry it happened, ma'am." He backpedaled down the walk and past the policeman.

Alasdair snugged the knot of his tie against his throat, not that it had slipped a millimeter since he tightened it up this morning. You would never suspect he was capable of unbuttoning himself. Jean was beginning to think they'd cycled back around to their first few meetings, when she'd thought ice water ran in his veins.

"Are you all right on your own, then?" he asked her.

She ran through possible replies, from Kelly's "You don't have to insult me," to "I don't feel personally threatened—yet," and defaulted to "Sure. I've got the document to keep me occupied."

"I'll be back in good time for tea. Dinner. Supper. Whatever you folk are calling it." This time his all-business expression didn't even get as far as the ambiguous *Jean, I'm not so sure.* Stepping carefully over the feline double doormat, he strode past Olson toward the parking lot.

Jean stood in the doorway until the police car disappeared around the corner, followed by their own rental car. Then she looked down at Bucktrout—or was it Bushrod?—and asked, "He did mean to include me on the team he mentioned to Quentin, didn't he? He's not deliberately marginalizing me any more than I'm deliberately marginalizing him. We've got our own spheres of influence, that's all. Our own areas of expertise. And if you think of any other trendy catchphrases I can use, just meow."

The cats stretched, strolled through the open door, and settled down on the rug for a grooming session.

With a sigh, Jean followed, locking the door behind her. Then she fell greedily on the Charlotte document.

TWENTY-FIVE

BEING A PHOTOCOPY, the paper was standard 8 1/2 by 11, leaving Jean no evidence for the size of the original document, other than that it wasn't much bigger than 8 1/2 by 11. The writing was perfectly legible—Jessica hadn't reduced its size to make her copy.

Charlotte had written her message in the fine "Italian hand" considered appropriate for a lady. The long-tailed s's that looked like lower-case f's tended to make the unwary reader interpret documents of the period with a sort of lisp, but Jean knew better. Still she mouthed the words as she read them.

Herewith a rendering of ye notorious Witch Box, a valu'd artifact of ye Lord Bothwell of late Memory in my Father's Family. Ye barren Space amongst the carv'd leaves did once hold ye Am Fear Uaine, Clach Giseag, *known to Countryfolk as ye Green Man, a Forest Spirit, ye Forbidden Stone. Ye Stone of green Hue, set in age'd Silver, stolen a Century since by a Maid bound for Virginia, meaning to protect herself from ye many Sicknesses there found.*

Ye Colonie of Virginia today a more salubrious Lieu, I and my Children have returned thence, my poor Husband still laboring to recall the Citizens thereof to their Duty to Crown and Empire. There I spoke with the Maid's unfortunate Child, Thomasina, who apprais'd me of her Mother's Taint of Witchery, as Folk foolishly believ'd.

Absurd Beliefs do however digressively provide us with Pleasance, as Bothwell's Trial inspir'd a Play of Master

Shakespeare's, this Intelligence reaching me from Mr. Malone, who request'd a viewing of ye Witch Box and who gift'd me this Paper as a Gentleman and a Scholar. Charlotte, Lady Dunmore, Blair, North Britain, ye 2nd July, 1776.

Well, Jean thought. Jessica had told the truth about the contents of the document, if not about its origins. And yes, the drawing of the Witch Box did show it unchanged from Charlotte's day to this, even making allowances for the stylized nature of her sketch. She'd used straight lines to denote the sides of the Box and filled them with curving ones representing the plants, the faces, the hinges, all more suggested than detailed. But the spot for the missing charm stone was obviously, evocatively, bare.

Even though Bothwell had died over a hundred years before Charlotte was born, his reputation must have left a tendril of uneasiness curling through later generations. But she acknowledged the relationship right up front—no academic waffle-words for her. And she hadn't found the Witch Box unsettling, either, not if she brought it to the colonies with her.

What she had done was use the politically correct "North Britain." Scotland, in other words, at the nadir of its eternal quest for independence.

Ironic, Jean thought, that on the exact day Charlotte signed her note and filed it away, back in the colonies the rebellious citizens were signing a document of their own—the Declaration of Independence, with its long-tailed s's like lower-case f's. There even Jefferson's rational, scientific soul had flirted with conspiracy theory by blaming George III for a laundry list of villainies—some of them internal American problems—in order to prove George was a despot. And George and his cronies, including Charlotte's friends and relations, returned the favor by saying the rebellion was guided by "turbulent and seditious persons" working to delude the colonists.

Jean spent a long moment admiring the drawing and the shape of the letters while Philadelphia's Liberty Bell clanged in the back of her mind… Wait a minute. That clangor was less celebratory than cautionary. She heard the echo of her own words. *A few historians would be interested in a message written and sketch drawn by Charlotte Murray, but there's nothing in particular at stake. And the Folger Library in D.C. specializes in Shakespeare. If Charlotte said something about* Macbeth, *they'd be interested.*

Well, okay, Charlotte did say something about *Macbeth,* and probably Jessica had indeed sent the original document to the Folger, not that anyone had necessarily asked them yet, between all the other investigations underway and it being Sunday to boot. But Jean's every instinct jostled forward insisting there was more to it than that.

Mr. Malone. A gentleman and a scholar who'd asked Charlotte to show him the Witch Box, and who'd given her the piece of paper. Since when was a piece of writing paper an appropriate hostess gift? And where had Jean heard that name recently?

Behind her, feline tongues slurping through fur sounded like the drip of rain. Outside the window, the sun shone. Her mental search engine dredged up an answer—she'd heard the name from Louise Dietz, at the theater. Something about Malone being a Shakespeare scholar who was a pretty shady character.

Jean reached toward the empty computer case, then thumped the desk in frustration. *Rats!* She'd have to revert to actually asking another human being.

Where was her bag? Ah, on the end of the couch. Dodging around the cats, she dug out her cell phone and punched

Hugh's number. One ring, two, three… Surely rehearsal was long over.

"Hullo, Jean."

"Hugh, are you still at the theater?"

"No, a collection of students turfed us out. They're doing *Mac,* er, 'The Scottish Play,' their instructor was saying."

"I need to talk to their instructor. Louise Dietz. Where are you now? Can you run back to the theater and get her to call me?"

"No worries, we're just finishing our lunch at the café not a block behind the stage door. If they're still there, I'll pass on the message and your number as well."

"Thanks. I really appreciate it." Jean snapped the phone shut and blessed the whims of Edinburgh real estate that had landed her next door to Hugh.

She looked back at the document, this time considering the contractions and the antique phrasing. Tim and Sharon could well have thought there was a cipher hidden in the message or in the drawing. Their fertile brains had no doubt made a leap of not faith but fantasy, deciding that Charlotte came to Virginia looking for the charm stone because she wanted to keep some peasant from finding it and using it to reveal Francis Bacon's papers. And yet there was no need to conjure a conspiracy theory to establish that Charlotte and her families both biological and by marriage wanted to keep themselves members of the ruling class.

Jean stood up. The bottle was sitting on the mantel, its tiny face impassive. The cats were arranged artistically on the rug. She dawdled off to the pantry and made herself that cup of cocoa, thinking, *Preserve us from a disorder chocolate cannot cure*—to paraphrase something Alasdair had once said about whiskey.

A wee dram of whiskey was on her agenda for later, however *later* was defined.

She'd just sat back down and lifted the steaming cup to her lips, when her phone struck up its electronic band. Thumping the cocoa down on the desk and then cringing, afraid she'd splashed the document, photocopy or no photocopy, she grabbed the phone. "Hello?"

"This is Louise Dietz," said the by now familiar, waspish voice. "Your friend Hugh says you want to talk to me."

"Yes, I do, if you've got a minute." And, without waiting for a yes or a no, "When we were talking earlier, you mentioned a Shakespeare scholar named Malone."

"Edmond Malone, yes."

"Is there any way he could have known Charlotte Murray, Lady Dunmore?"

"Sure. He lived in London during the same time she did and hung out with various movers and shakers like Samuel Johnson. Why? Something about the, ah, Scottish play and Charlotte's ancestry?"

"Yes, sort of. You said he was a shady character. Why?"

"He did some very good work at Stratford, correcting the details of Shakespeare's life, and for a while was so trusted people gave him original records, copies of the plays, and so forth. But then he wouldn't give them back, or worse, he gave them back with bits cut out of them, and his reputation collapsed. You say he knew Charlotte Murray?"

"There's a note from Charlotte mentioning Malone. And *Macbeth* and the Witch Box."

Louise's gasp of enlightenment sounded like the preliminary gust of a hurricane. "Is that Jessica's original source? What does that have to do with Bacon's Rebellion?"

"What? Oh, it doesn't have anything to do with Nathaniel Bacon, it doesn't even have anything to do with Francis Bacon, although that name probably came up when Jessica was talking about it." Jean couldn't reveal all—not that she knew all—to Louise or anyone else with the investigations still underway. "Thanks, Louise. I appreciate your calling me. I owe you one."

"But, but…"

Making an apologetic face, Jean hit "end." What she owed Louise was a full explanation. Eventually. Whenever the Charlotte document made its public debut.

Jean turned on the desk lamp, the better to inspect the white paper with its charcoal gray markings. It was creased into four quarters, perhaps by Olson, perhaps by Jessica. A brown dot of cocoa adorned one corner. A couple of thin horizontal smudges were not, say, a streak of pencil eraser applied by Jessica, but had been copied from the original.

What, Jean wondered, was on the back of Charlotte's note? Lines of type that had bled through the paper? Why would the note have been run through a printing press… She jerked upright with a gasp of her own. That was it! Charlotte's note *was* the back!

As for the front, Malone wouldn't have thanked Lady Dunmore for his look at the Witch Box and for the story of her notorious ancestor by giving her a blank piece of ordinary paper. He'd have presented her with a gift. What if he'd given her one of his borrowed—or stolen—bits of Shakespeare ephemera? A playbill for *Macbeth?* That would be valuable, yes. A page from an early printing of the play itself? That would be virtually priceless. Today.

Charlotte, though, a citizen in good standing of the eighteenth century, had not been so impressed with her gift that she hadn't written her note and drawn her sketch on the back. Where better to expand on the topic, after all? And then she'd tucked the page away, just another curiosity in the curiosity-laden halls of the aristocracy.

"All right! Cool!" Jean said aloud, with a fist-pump that caused the cats to look up, ears pricked watchfully.

An electric tingle ran from the crown of her head down

to her toes, making them curl with glee. And with trepidation. Jessica was right. There was a lot at stake here. More than a note from Lady Dunmore, historical figure that she was. More than a sketch of the Witch Box, interesting artifact that it was. At stake was an original Shakespeare document.

Was that enough to motivate murder? Maybe so. Factoring in the Dingwalls' Bacon mania, probably so. Factoring in ambition, jealousy…

The tingle contracted into a wintry prickle. Frost formed on the back of her neck, thickening, weighing her down so that she seemed to be pressed into the chair. The sound she for a fraction thought was sleet against a window was the hiss of the cats. Forcing her stiff, frozen, heavy muscles to respond, she turned toward the fireplace.

The Bellarmine bottle glided through the air, slowly, gracefully, from the mantel to the coffee table. Perhaps Jean caught a shimmer in the air around it, pale hands, pale garments, pale face, nuance reflected on nothingness. Perhaps she merely imagined that human shape, knowing that in some dimension it was there.

Bushrod and Bucktrout backed toward the door, heads down, fur bristling. Jean stared at the bottle that now sat on the table next to the Historic Area schedule of events and Alasdair's newspaper. The chill slowly flowed down her limbs and away, her shoulders lifted and her head tilted. A car passed in the street. The clock ticked. With a gentle thump the heating system came on and its draft lifted one corner of the newspaper and released it again.

Jean shuddered, throwing off the last of the chill. *Now what, Thomasina?* She picked up her cup of cocoa and gulped. It was so cold a wave of pain splashed against her eye sockets and obliterated the faint clink of something that might have been a bell, or might have been a couple of exhausted brain cells falling from their perches. *Thanks.*

After a moment's recovery, she folded the paper and slipped it into her notebook. She got up, opened the door, let the still-agitated cats escape into the free air. Then she picked up her phone—Alasdair was raking Quentin over a pile of peat-fired coals, Michael and Rebecca were playing happy families instead of sleuths, Miranda, though, was…

"…not available just now," said the dulcet voice. "Please leave a message."

As comprehensively and yet as tersely as she could without a word-processing program at her fingertips, Jean backtracked to Thomasina in the Palace kitchen, then gave Miranda a guided tour of Matt's office, the theater, Dunwich Pond, the missing computer, and, last but a far cry from least, the Charlotte document.

"And if there's anyone from the Folger Library at the reception tonight or the seminar tomorrow," she concluded, "please ask them to contact Stephanie Venegas and fax her a copy of the back, er, front, er, non-Charlotte side of that paper!"

She flipped the phone shut. Only then did it occur to her that Stephanie might already have located the document elsewhere in D.C., assuming she would use her resources on something that was peripheral to her investigation. Well, nothing ventured. It wasn't that she wanted to steal a march on the official and quasi-official investigation, oh no.

Jean made herself another cup of cocoa and, sipping the sweet warmth that was both soothing and invigorating, she sat down in the wingback chair and read through her notes. No patterns that she hadn't already noticed leaped out at her. Instead of wasting her own resources creating some out of wishful thinking and whole cloth, she fished *Witches and Wenches* out of its sack.

At first she couldn't help but edit Jessica's prose as she read, and wonder again how much Jessica owed to her husband and her mother-in-law. However, each was properly referenced in the back even if Sharon Dingwall was not.

What had Matt said? *You'd think the damn Dingwalls had cast some sort of spell on our family.* Like Wesley's workmates saying he seemed to be under a curse. Like the charm stone, healing, cursing, whatever.

Offensive witchcraft bad, Jean thought. *Defensive witchcraft good, even if it was still witchcraft.* Not that the sides were as evenly divided as those on a football team.

The human thought process hadn't changed all that much over the years. Something's gone wrong, so let's find someone to blame. The other side started it, it was their fault, we're just fighting fire with fire, we're giving the bad guys a taste of their own medicine. There were any number of ways of saying that *their* end never justified their means, and then turning around and justifying *your* means with your end. And "all's well that ends well" didn't excuse a thing.

That was Alasdair's manifesto as well. She'd have to talk to him about it. Later.

Jean turned back to *Witches and Wenches* and this time let herself be transported to colonial Virginia. When she looked at the clock again, it was almost five.

She'd changed her clothes and was applying lipstick when the front door opened. She peered around the corner to see Alasdair closing it behind him. "Hi. How'd it go?"

Once again he indulged in a grimly satisfied smile. "No one's turned up either Matthew Finch or Dylan Dingwall, but Quentin's turned Queen's evidence."

"Quentin's turned state's evidence," Jean corrected.

"Ah, but the state after dealing with the theft of the replica is the U.K. Stephanie's had Kelly in, but she's saying Quentin's winding her up and Hugh's after making trouble because she's a, how'd she say it, independent womanist entrepreneur."

"Quentin wouldn't have gotten himself into such bad trouble just to tease her. And how could Hugh have known anything about her?"

"Q.E.D." Alasdair started toward the bedroom door, loosening his tie. "The replica Witch Box is not at the Dingwalls' house in Rosslyn—I reckon it's sitting in a warehouse waiting for the Monday. 'Til we turn it up, we've got no real case against Kelly. Nor Quentin. But they're being watched. Stephanie knows to see through a brick wall in time."

That last was Tolkien, not Scots. Jean had to smile, if thinly.

"Stephanie's after making inquiries at the Folger Library also come the Monday, and thank you kindly for the suggestion. I doubt there's a rule that everything's happening on the weekend when staff's not available."

"Like getting sick on a Friday." But Jean wasn't feeling sick. Bouncing on the balls of her feet, she diverted Alasdair toward the desk. "I've got Miranda maybe raising someone from the Folger this evening. Look at this." Like a magician popping a rabbit out of a hat, she presented the document, Louise's testimony, and her own theories.

No need to explain the ramifications to Alasdair. His eyebrows rose. His eyes widened. He exhaled with a whistle. "Shakespeare, eh? Well now, there's a motive for you."

"No kidding. Except you'd think Sharon would have murdered Jessica to get control of something so valuable, not the other way around. If Jessica did murder Sharon. But if Sharon murdered Wes, maybe she didn't just want to keep him from testifying about the provenance of the replica, maybe she also wanted to keep him from testifying about the provenance of this document."

Alasdair held the paper up to the light, inspected it, then

handed it back. "Jessica's not said anything more about this or anything else, come to that. But perhaps we've outflanked her. Well done, Jean."

"Thanks." Her own smile having more than a little grim satisfaction, Jean tucked the paper into her notebook and the notebook back into her bag.

"Half a tick, I'm needing a wash and brush-up." Again he started for the bedroom, then stopped beside the coffee table and cast his cold stare at the bottle.

"No," Jean told him. "I didn't move it. This time Thomasina made sure I knew she was doing it. Everyone else wants something from us, why not her, too?"

"There's a comforting thought, that the ghost's sensing us the way we're sensing her." With a flash of his eyes, light glinting off cold steel, Alasdair went on into the bedroom.

Jean forced her taut shoulders into a shrug. On her extensive list of things making her uncomfortable right now, you'd think a ghost reaching toward her across infinity would occupy a slot near the bottom. And yet it didn't.

Her satisfaction ebbed into uncertainty, leaving only the grim.

TWENTY-SIX

DARKNESS HAD FALLEN across the Historic Area like a curtain across a stage. *And what was waiting in the wings tonight?* Jean asked herself, turning her gaze from the shadowy houses and trees to the lanterns lining the front walk of Governor's Palace. The tiny flames shivered, making the stone eyes of the lion and the unicorn on either side of the gate appear to wink smug assurances of empire. A faint scent of smoke hung delectably on the still, cold air.

She and Alasdair stood well back in the line of people waiting to get in, having opted for a meal before the concert instead of after. Now Jean's sandwich, laden with too many rich dressings, hunkered sullenly beneath her ribs. She choked down a garlicky burp and tried to re-direct part of her blood supply from her brain to her stomach.

Alasdair faced the darkness beyond Robert Carter House, using his own particular version of X-ray vision to see through it or else not seeing anything at all, just contemplating his own digestive processes, or the interlocking criminal cases, or the case of Jean Fairbairn, his significant other, who might turn out to be of questionable significance in the greater scheme of his life.

If she'd stumbled on the uneven brick sidewalks, he'd have offered her his arm. She hadn't. He was almost too adept at leaving her personal space, personal space being so important to him. But just as affection could become intrusion, courtesy could become a cold shoulder.

Her shoulders were cold beneath her coat, with the temperature, not with the paranormal. Her hands were cold. Her nose was cold.

Alasdair hadn't touched her since he'd grasped her arm while they watched Thomasina Napier revisit the site of her lonely death. Or had Thomasina in life thought of herself as solitary rather than lonely? There was something to be said for solitude. There was something to be said for freedom.

Jean's unfocused gaze suddenly sharpened. Was that a human shape slipping along behind the wooden gate now closing off the Palace's kitchen yard? A living, breathing human being, not a ghost, moving so furtively he—or a she not wearing period costume—might just as well have a neon sign proclaiming, *I'm up to no good!*

"Look!" The word left her lips as fog. She grasped Alasdair's arm, like granite beneath the cold fabric of his coat. "Over there!"

He glanced around, eyes sparking in his shadowed face. "Eh?"

"There, behind the gate… Rats. They're gone."

"A rat?"

"No, no, I saw someone sneaking through the kitchen yard."

Alasdair scanned the gate and the wall, but now the only movement was a swirl of dead leaves across the gravel threshold. "An interpreter, like as not. One of the cooks clearing away."

"One of the cooks…" Just as she groped after an elusive tinkle of the mental bell choir, a couple of long-skirted interpreters opened the front gate. The customers pressed through, across the small garden between the two one-story dependencies, and up the steps. Alasdair and Jean brought up the rear. "Moo," she whispered, and beneath her hand his arm twitched as he chuckled.

Candles in glass sconces cast tortuous patterns of light

and shadow across the weapons interlaced on the walls and fanned on the ceiling of the entrance hall. More candles flickered feebly along the paneled walls of the narrow passage beyond, struggling to drive back the darkness.

While the Palace, like the Capitol, was a replica built on the original site, Jean knew she wasn't the only visitor who eyed the shadow-clogged doorways and alcoves cautiously. Conventional wisdom said that nothing was concealed by the darkness that wasn't there in the daylight. But she knew better. Darkness, enclosed spaces, idiots—her phobias were a fairly dull collection, considering.

Alasdair pressed her hand against his rock-ribbed, iron-bound side. Yes, he was there if she asked. She pressed back. *Thanks.*

Footsteps echoing, interpreters herded the visitors toward the ballroom. Rachel Finch stood just inside the wide double doors, handing out programs. Her eighteenth-century garments were displayed to good effect by her erect posture, and her face beneath her ruffled cap was pristine—so much so that even in the dim light, Jean could see how pale the girl was, and how much stronger a resemblance she had to her mother tonight than forty-eight hours ago.

Rachel's eyes, the pupils huge in the gloom, showed no sign of recognition as Jean and Alasdair collected their programs. No, this wasn't a good time to ask about Matt, Jessica, Dylan—any of the actors in the ongoing drama, one which was proceeding to a final curtain. Some sort of final curtain. Any sort of final curtain, releasing the players to deal with that greater scheme.

Alasdair and Jean found seats in the last row of heavy wooden chairs, backed against the tall windows now concealed by shutters. Voices murmured. Chairs scraped. Electronic trills and chirps signaled the hibernation of various cell phones. Jean joined in the chorus.

At night, the Palace was transformed from museum to stage set. The blue walls of the ballroom that seemed startling during the day now seemed bright and cheerful. Against those walls hung huge portraits, James II and Queen Catherine, George III and Queen Charlotte, draped with lush fabrics and jewels that almost overwhelmed their human features, imperious as they were.

Alasdair exchanged stare for stare with the painted faces that now commanded nothing more than a room in a lovingly restored capital. Had his ancestors, free agents, fought for or against theirs?

Candles blazed in the chandelier, their light scattered by its dangling crystals. Candles blazed in sconces and on the three music stands arranged with chairs around the harpsichord. Wesley Hagedorn's harpsichord, Jean assumed, its wood shimmering like silk.

Perhaps there was a slight smear of smoke in the air. Perhaps her eyes were adapting to what was still a very dim light. Romantic, she thought. Sensual. Your eyes no longer dominant, your other senses kicked in—a slight draft at her back, the people next to her talking about ghosts, the scents of aftershave and mildew. Holding up her program, she could actually make out the printed letters listing Handel, Corelli, Rameau, composers of the period and earlier.

Right on time, the doors of the supper room, at the far end of the ballroom, opened. Barbara Finch stepped through. She was consumed by a froth of a dress, pleats, folds, layers of fabric, sleeves dripping lace. Her white wig was the same color as, if heavier and longer than, her real hair. Jean couldn't tell where the wig ended and Barbara's forehead began. If Rachel was pale, her grandmother was almost transparent. The necklace glinting at her throat hung awkwardly over the knobs of her collarbones.

Following her came three men in knee breeches, long

coats, lace cuffs, and curled white wigs. One carried a thick-bottomed viola, the others long wooden wind instruments that Jean guessed were flutes. They sat down while Barbara stood to attention beside the harpsichord.

"Good evening," she said, her voice projected from her throat rather than her chest, so that it sounded slightly strangled. "Welcome to this special concert in honor of our late friend, Wesley Hagedorn. This harpsichord—" her hand, covered by a white glove that ran all the way up her forearm and disappeared beneath the lace, stroked the wood lovingly "—was Wes's masterpiece, patterned after the harpsichord played by Governor..."

Alasdair stiffened. For a moment Jean thought he was going to run for it—*Hey,* she thought at him, *it's not opera.* Then his elbow hit her in her ribs and his chin pointed toward the supper-room door.

Which was slitted open. Through the narrow gap eased Matt Finch. His body contracted into a furtive huddle, he soundlessly closed the door and sat down on the closest chair.

A flurry of skirts by the main door was Rachel slipping out into the entrance hall. She must be intending to go out the front, around the side of the building through the garden, and in the back door, so as to sit with Matt.

Jean caught Alasdair's eye. *It's a family reunion, all we need is Jessica.*

If Barbara saw her son's arrival or her granddaughter's exit, she showed no sign. "...a true gentleman, Wesley Hagedorn." She sat down, removed her gloves, and laid them aside. She sent a directorial nod toward the other musicians, and with perfect timing they began to play.

The delicate, intricate music was as richly embroidered as their clothing. One flute was played vertically, Jean saw, and the other horizontally. She couldn't see Barbara's hands, just her back and elbows swaying gently, a willow in the stream of melody. The viola player leaned forward over his instrument, his wig coming perilously close to the candles flaming on either side of his sheet music. Would a violin player have to avoid running his bow through a candlestick?

Alasdair shifted, looking from Matt to his watch to the front door. The minute this piece of music was over, he'd ask for the phone, tiptoe out, and call Stephanie. Who was no doubt still working, trying either to assemble a case against Jessica or demolish one before the charge-by deadline ran out.

Jean glared at Matt's tense expression, eyes front. *Where's my computer?*

Where was Rachel, for that matter? Unless she hadn't seen her father come in after all, and had disappeared on some other errand. She needed to be in the ballroom, shushing whoever was talking, low and urgent, making an annoying hum below the music.

Alasdair's hand appeared in Jean's peripheral vision. Patience didn't necessarily go with cool. She should have insisted he buy his own phone the minute they landed in the U.S. of A. She reached for her bag, and one of the bells in the back of her mind ding-donged.

She'd almost dropped her bag on a stuffed cabbage in the Palace kitchen, when the cook interpreter had been talking about Thomasina. Then Matt had called, and while she was talking to him one of the visitors asked if the food displayed on the table was real.

She scooped up the bag, pulled out the phone, and laid it in Alasdair's hand. He scooted forward in his chair, ready to make a break for the door the moment the music stopped.

Who was still talking? Jean looked around but saw only silent faces glowing in the candlelight, enrapt by the elegant harmonies. Even Matt's features eased a bit, his gaze not wavering from his mother and the harpsichord.

The voices, Jean realized, were coming through the window behind her. Rachel's mosquito-whine interlocked with a male voice that also sounded familiar, like a variation on a theme… And the bells in Jean's mind pealed in perfect synchrony with music.

The interpreter had said something about a mouse breaking health regulations by eating the food left out overnight.

Seizing Alasdair's arm so firmly she jerked him back in his chair, she leaned over to within a millimeter of his ear. Her nose and throat filled with the scent of his hair, better than that of cookies baking or beer brewing. "When I was here earlier today, the cook said a mouse was eating their demonstration food. We just saw a man sneaking toward the kitchen, not a mouse."

He turned his head, the better to send her a quizzical look.

"Can you hear the voices outside the window?"

"Aye, it's Rachel… Oh! She's hiding Dylan here at the Palace!"

Cat-like, Alasdair slid from his chair and moved swiftly and soundlessly toward the door. Jean followed, taking tiny, tiptoeing steps, and avoided ramming into any chairs or tripping over someone's foot. The interpreter womanning the main door turned in a swirl of skirts to fling it open. She didn't speak, but her stern look rebuked them for leaving while the musicians played.

"Sorry," Jean hissed from the corner of her mouth as she hurried by.

In the entrance hall, the light from the phone cast a green glow on the planes of Alasdair's face, making him look queasy. He didn't quite manage to get outside before the phone's *reporting for duty* trill sounded loud as Jessica's trumpet fanfare.

Cringing, Jean glanced back. And through the gap of the rapidly closing door she caught Matt Finch's gaze, his dark eyes lit with such a sudden, fierce anger that they stayed imprinted on her retina even after the door clicked shut.

She stood alone in the dark passageway, the music muffled, a staircase running upward into shadow at her right hand. Nothing was there that wasn't there… She double-timed it toward the front door and out into the cold night, another garlic burp taking her unawares.

Alasdair stood outside the gate, the phone to his head, speaking too quickly for the listening American ear—Stephanie, Olson, someone—to follow. Every time he stopped and repeated himself his voice grew rougher, each rolled "R" a tiny explosion. She couldn't make out his exact words, but she didn't need to. Rachel's been hiding Dylan at the Palace, he's been eating the food made up by the cooks, they're just outside the east wall of the ballroom, aye, right smartish now.

Pocketing the phone, he slipped along the wall toward the gate into the stable yard. Jean caught up with him, whispering hoarsely, "Wait for me!" just as he looked back and said in a hoarser whisper, "Come along, let's keep them in sight 'til we've got reinforcements."

She nodded, and stepped carefully over the gravel to the aperture in the wall. No, the gate wasn't shut, the restrooms were located around this way. But no one was pursuing a call of nature. The stable yard lay deserted beneath the chill light of the stars, and the surrounding sheds were closed and dark.

Side by side, Jean and Alasdair glided—well, Alasdair glided, Jean winced at every pebble that rolled beneath her feet—between the block of the restrooms and the wall of the eastern dependency, and on into the gardens.

The ballroom windows were tall rectangles of warm light. But soft, Jean thought, since it had been a Shakespearean day anyway, what light through yonder window, er, leaks? She squinted toward the barely illuminated lumps and bumps of flower beds and manicured shrubs. And were young Mr. Montague and Miss Capulet still standing there?

"There," Alasdair said, his voice no more than a skein of mist dissipating in the darkness.

Yes, a white blob bobbed up and down, a humongous flower, a hovering duck, or Rachel's mobcap. The high pitch of her voice carried it over the faint strains of harpsichord, viola, and flutes. "…turn yourself in, Dylan, please. You're gonna make yourself sick…"

A muffled sneeze and ghastly sniff were her only reply.

A siren sounded close by, one squawk and then silence. But that was enough to send a lanky shape leaping away from the side of the building and toward the impenetrable gloom of the main garden. The dark shape beside Jean that was Alasdair leaped in turn, down the faint glow of the white path, oyster shells scattering beneath his feet.

She stumbled along behind—she now owed Dylan for two blunders through the darkness, except this time it was Alasdair who'd gone haring off—and yes, he had a goal in sight…

Applause inside the palace sounded like the pitter-patter of footsteps. Light gleamed across the shrubs and flower beds behind the ballroom and winked out as a door slammed. A tall humanoid shape ran around the corner and the humanoid shape that was Dylan charged straight into it.

"It's you," Matt's voice spat. "I saw Rachel leaving, I saw Jean leaving, I knew it was you. You and your family, it's your fault, it's all your fault!"

"I didn't do anything," said Dylan's congested voice. "Come on, man, lemme go!"

The white cap bobbed forward, converging with the double-male blotch that now heaved back and forth, grunting and crunching. Rachel's voice rose both to a higher pitch and a louder volume. "Oh my God, oh my God, Dylan, Dad, stop it!"

Jean was close enough to make out the three faces, each one contorted in its own way—Matt angry, Dylan desperate, Rachel frightened—when Alasdair shoved past Rachel and forced Dylan and Matt apart. So what if they were each taller than he was, he was the expert. And no matter if he didn't quite have the authority to take control of the situation, no one was going to argue.

"Dingwall," he said, crisp, brisk. "Finch. Stop just there." One of his large, strong hands grasped each shirt front. He braced himself, but neither man seemed capable of more than a perfunctory wriggle.

Jean got in close enough to set a restraining hand on Rachel's cold wrist, its bones fine as balsa wood. Ignoring the sidekick, Rachel leaned toward Alasdair. "He didn't do anything wrong."

"He removed evidence from a crime scene," Alasdair informed her.

"What were you thinking?" Jean asked Dylan. "How did you think you could keep that tote bag hidden? How long did you think you could hide out back here? What were you doing, playing hide-and-seek with security, lurking in the trees behind the pond or something?"

Dylan stared, probably groping through a few too many memories of the past few days to place where he'd seen her before.

She felt Alasdair's gaze sweep across her face like a searchlight. Of course she wasn't going to diss Foundation security, sheesh. What she was going to do was vent all the frustration of the past day. "You came out last night and grabbed some cookies from the kitchen. And Rachel was bringing you food, too—it wasn't as though her mom was home to ask questions."

Rachel jerked her arm away from Jean's hand. "And who put my mom in jail, huh?"

"The Dingwalls," said Matt. "They pretended to be her friends and then they betrayed her."

"Yeah, right, Jessica thought she could use them, they thought they could use Jessica, there's a recipe for harmony." Jean rounded on him. "And what about you? You pretended to be my friend, but no, you steal my laptop!"

Matt's glasses glinted. "What laptop?"

Dylan drooped and swayed. Rachel tucked herself up against his side, dislodging a dank, musty odor from his clothing.

"Give me a break, Matt! You were seen outside our house!"

"Well, yeah, I was going to talk to you but you weren't there."

Alasdair adjusted his grip on Dylan's sweatshirt. "We saw the lad's folk there as well."

A faint steam rose from them all, an elusive ghostly sparkle at the rim of light. Then headlights flared beyond the low roofs and the front wall, and flashlights needled the darkness, and footsteps stampeded forward. Jean stepped back, out of the limelight, but it was too late for the cold air to cool her overheated cheeks.

Inside the ballroom, harpsichord, viola, and flutes began another lace-like melody, muted by darkness and doubt.

TWENTY-SEVEN

STEPHANIE VENEGAS STOOD at the front of the room, arms crossed, eyes black as jet and malleable as adamant, in her charcoal-gray pantsuit looking like a teacher deciding who was naughty and who was nice.

It had taken only a few moments for her and her minions from the city, as well as the ever-efficient security people, to get everyone sorted into the two meeting rooms in the western dependency, between the kitchen yard and the small front garden.

Alasdair, teacher's pet, sat in the front row beside a cold candelabrum. Olson, teacher's assistant, sat just behind him. Jean, superfluous, sat at the back of the room in front of a colder fireplace.

That morning she'd sat there with a group of visitors, listening to their interpreter-guide relate the history of the Palace. The old wooden chairs, the huge map of the British colonies in America, the print of Lord Dunmore's kilted portrait—none of them had changed. What had changed was the quality of the light. Instead of sunshine glinting through the shutters, giving the room an air of shabby gentility, now it seemed as dim and dull as an anxiety nightmare of a classroom, complete with a uniformed cop standing in front of the exit.

Here we go again, she thought.

Damp and dilapidated, his pointed jaw shadowed with auburn stubble, Dylan sat front and center beneath Stephanie's uncompromising gaze. "I wanted to see Rachel at the

Courthouse, but her grandmother and her mom were giving me dirty looks, so I chilled in front of the tavern for a while, listening to the music. Then I wondered where my mom had gone. I found her." He gulped and choked. "I found her beneath the tree. I didn't know what to do."

"Call the police?" suggested Olson.

"But they, you, you'd do forensic stuff to all her stuff and she was carrying important stuff in her tote bag..." He puzzled a moment over his triple repetition, then went on, "You weren't supposed to see her stuff. I had to, like, do something. So I took it and ran. And Rache had shown me the Palace gardens, lots of little hidey-holes and everything."

Was that where they'd gone Friday night? Jean wondered. Tough customers, kids that age, Alasdair had said. Now his head moved left and right, perhaps, like her, thinking how middle-aged lovers defaulted to warm rooms and soft surfaces.

"So I hid, took some cookies from the kitchen, slept on a bench down by the pond, sort of. Rachel didn't help me," he added quickly.

That was a blatant lie already disproved by the fast-food containers and a couple of blankets Stephanie's people had found stashed in a shed. Still, Jean awarded Dylan a point for chivalry.

"It's no business of yours what my mom had in her tote bag. She was murdered. You oughtta be solving her murder."

"We are," Stephanie said. "And it is our business. Where's the bag?"

Dylan didn't answer.

Jean inched away from the chill ash-flavored breath of the fireplace, wondering if the sarcophagus-like stone had soaked in macabre tales from the evening ghosts and legend tours, the way the Witch Box had absorbed the unhealthy narratives of its original owner.

"Where's the bag?" Stephanie repeated.

"I wanna see my dad."

"We've sent for him. Where's the bag?"

Dylan sniffed yet again, loudly, and mopped his nose with his grubby fingertips.

Stephanie's face puckered in disgust. Even Alasdair quailed. Jean fished a fresh tissue out of her mini-backpack, got up, handed it over, and sat down again, this time on the third row from the front. While she was at it, she found an antacid for herself.

Dylan eyed the tissue, then wadded it into a pocket without using it.

Alasdair leaned into Dylan's line of sight. "Do you not realize, lad, that the photos and all in the bag, they'll have gone damp, they'll be sticking together. And the silver bits, they'll tarnish all the faster."

"The silver bits?" Dylan swiveled toward Alasdair.

"Wesley had the charm stone, didn't he? He was playing silly beggars..." Sending an ice-blue look toward Jean, Alasdair amended, "He was teasing you with it."

"Oh yeah, he kept saying he hadn't picked it up in Scotland, it was all just legend, but he had a pile of stones on his kitchen table. But we tried all of them and the pieces of silver were the wrong shape, so maybe he was telling the truth... Aw, shit." Dylan sank down in his chair, realizing he'd been had.

Alasdair looked at Stephanie. Stephanie looked at Alasdair. Olson scribbled in his notebook. The chalky, minty flavor of the antacid clogged Jean's throat.

"You and your mum," Alasdair said to Dylan, almost purring now, "you burgled Wesley's flat. It was your mum, was it, your dad being a wee bit over large for climbing in windows and the like."

Dylan stared down at the dusty plank floor. "It was Jessica's fault," he said, very faintly.

"Speak up," Olson ordered him. "What was Jessica's fault?"

"We had a deal with her. We had a deal with Wesley. Then Jessica was all, 'I want the document myself,' and Wesley sided with her, saying he wouldn't make another Box. He gave Aunt Kelly back her deposit and everything."

"And your mother was mad?" Stephanie asked.

"Yeah. And she could get really mad."

Mad-crazy, Jean thought, as well as mad-angry.

"So you broke into Wesley Hagedorn's flat to get the plans and photos for yourself."

"Yeah." Dylan's sigh sounded like a tire depressurizing. "My mom had a great idea, let's pick up some stuff and throw it in the pond, to make it look like a real robbery. She'd read that in a Sherlock Holmes story, she said."

Well, yes, that bit of business was in a Holmes story, Jean thought, not that her steel sieve of a brain could remember which one.

"A burglary, not a robbery," Stephanie corrected. "And why wasn't it a real one?"

"Well, I mean…" Dylan stammered. "The plans and stuff, they were, like, ours."

"I don't think so."

From outside the window came the sound of footsteps and voices. The concert was over. From closer at hand came the sound of "The 1812 Overture." Alasdair jumped, patted himself down, produced Jean's phone and shut it off. With an apologetic glance in her direction, he mouthed, *Miranda.*

She'd leave a message, Jean assured herself, even as

her palm itched for her phone. Right now these interviews took priority.

"Dylan," said Stephanie. "Your family's already in bad trouble. You don't get a pass on a burglary here and a theft in the U.K. just because your mother was murdered."

Dylan sniffled, a resonant gurgle that sounded like a kitchen sink after the application of drain cleaner. "The bag's in the ice house. I reached in through the bars and propped it up against the side."

Olson jabbed a finger toward the cop, who slipped out the door.

Jean couldn't help but glance over her shoulder, even though what she was looking at wasn't actually there. The ice house was a tunnel driven into an artificial hill at the far back edge of the garden, where ice was stored every winter so that the governor could have his sherbets and other cool desserts in the summer. A time or two she'd peered through the iron bars closing the entrance, eyeing the dark, cramped passageway inside with the same slightly pleasurable, slightly off-putting frisson that the audience at a ghost story would have.

She thought of Dylan collecting Sharon's tote bag virtually from her dead hands, running through the darkness with it, clambering over the fence or finding an open gate to the Palace grounds, wandering around the dark, misty, deserted passages of the gardens, and finally tucking the bag through those cold, wet bars.

She'd have been afraid something would grab her and pull her inside. She looked at the back of Dylan's head with more respect. Not that she wasn't still irritated with him for running away to begin with.

It wasn't so much that Alasdair was spared Jean's imagination as that he didn't let it get to him. "You've not exactly been playing happy families, have you, lad?" was all he said.

And Stephanie said, "Dylan, go sit in the other room for a few minutes, while I talk to your dad. I'm sending you back to the hotel with him. Clean up. Rest. Don't even think of going anywhere, not you, not your brother, not your father, not your aunt. You'll make a formal statement tomorrow morning."

Wiping his nose on the back of his hand, Dylan stood up. "You're gonna find out who killed my mom? You're gonna find out it wasn't, it wasn't..."

"It wasn't Rachel's mother?" Stephanie asked. "No promises."

Olson stood up so stiffly, Jean could almost hear his limbs creak. Like Rachel, he'd aged in the past hours, his features glazed with weariness and pasty-pale. He might actually be able to buy alcohol without trotting out his ID, now.

Olson stepped forward and escorted the youth from the room. Alasdair stood up and stretched. Stephanie sat down in the closest chair, for just a moment, so brief Jean thought she'd imagined it, going boneless. But she hadn't imagined the arch of Stephanie's nose sharpening in the past two days, and her smooth olive skin roughening and taking on a flat gray hue.

Jean asked, "Detec, er, Steph, have you had any rest at all since Friday afternoon?"

"Rest? What makes you think I've had any rest?" There was humor in her voice, but of the bleakest sort.

"I've been involved in investigating murder cases before," Jean said.

Stephanie looked from Alasdair to Jean and back again. "You mean you two are a team? I'd never have guessed."

Compressing her lips, Jean hid her expression by digging

through her bag again. She hadn't meant anything by that. Neither had Stephanie.

From the corner of her eye Jean saw Alasdair gazing up at Dunmore's portrait, utterly expressionless.

"Solving Sharon's murder," Stephanie said quietly, not speaking to anyone in particular. "We've gone through the messages on both Sharon's and Jessica's phones, and yes, Jessica did leave a message asking Sharon to meet her at the Lodge instead of behind the Courthouse."

"That's by way of being meaningless," Alasdair told Dunmore's portrait. "Unless Jessica was lying when she said she didn't know she'd be needing an alibi."

Jean opened her mouth, closed it, went ahead and spoke. "If she'd known, if she'd killed Sharon, wouldn't she have set one up?"

"We're testing the hair caught in Sharon's cell phone," Stephanie went on, without either reprimanding or encouraging Jean's comment. "It's the same color as Jessica's hair. We're testing the traces of skin caught beneath Sharon's fingernails, where she scratched her assailant, to see if they're Jessica's. Plus there was a thread caught in Sharon's broken nail. If we don't get a match with something, though, we're up the creek without a paddle."

DNA testing taking a long time, Jean replied silently, *and the results only being helpful if you have something to compare them to, and you can't hold Jessica much longer without charging her.*

Stephanie massaged her eyebrows. "As for solving Wesley Hagedorn's murder, I think we have, yes. Preliminary tests match Sharon's feet and shoes to the prints by the pond, and there's a small wood shaving in the stitching of one shoe. Her socks and her other clothes have been washed, but maybe not well enough. We'll see what forensics can do to find mud and bloodstains. And we'll test Wesley's clothing as well—there's a good chance Sharon shed a thread or a hair onto his back while she was kneeling on him."

"But you cannot charge a dead person," said Alasdair.

"Tell me about it," Stephanie said, and, at the sound of footsteps in the hallway outside and a hand on the door knob, stood up.

Olson threw the door open and leaped back against the jamb. Tim Dingwall barged past him and into the room, head down, jowls quivering, face a mottled crimson. "What do you have against my family? First I have to get my sister and Quentin out of your clutches and now you're harassing Dylan!"

Olson shut the door and leaned against the wall, notebook unholstered, pen cocked.

Stephanie's black eyes darted a quick message to him, to Alasdair, and back to Jean. *Don't mention Wesley's murder, not now, not yet.* To Tim she said, "Sit down please, Mr. Dingwall."

"Not this time. I know your ploy—I sit down, you stand up, endeavoring to display dominance."

"Whatever." Crossing her arms again, Stephanie faced Tim squarely and said, "Mr. Cameron here has a case against both Kelly and Quentin for stealing the replica Witch Box. If you can tell us where it is, he might—that's might—try for mitigating circumstances."

"How can I tell you where it is when I've had nothing to do with it?" Tim obviously meant his glare at Alasdair to be a look that killed, but Alasdair deflected it with a quick tilt of his chin.

"Have it your way," Stephanie said. "I'll be charging Dylan with removing evidence, the tote bag, from the scene of a crime."

"She was his mother! Have you no compassion for a motherless child?"

"Since he's told us where he hid the bag, we'll try for mitigation. Still, he helped Sharon burgle Wesley Hagedorn's apartment."

"Lies. Harassment," Tim gobbled. He tried to loom, but only succeeded in puffing himself up like a blowfish. "Miss Detective, I demand…"

The door flew open and crashed back against the wall, missing Olson by an inch. He flinched to the side and collided with Alasdair.

Kelly Dingwall stood in the opening, her expression almost identical to Tim's. A uniformed officer danced from side-to-side behind the fur-trimmed collar of her coat. "Ma'am, you can't—"

"Don't you lay a finger on me," Kelly said to him. And to Stephanie, "You're picking on Dylan this time, I see. And Tim again. Fine, our lawyer's on retainer for the entire family."

"Then he or she," Stephanie enunciated, "will be earning his or her money."

Oblivious to Stephanie's sarcasm, Kelly shut the door in the officer's face and plumped down in a chair. "Go on. I'm listening. And I hope Orson here is taking notes."

Olson exchanged an exasperated look with Alasdair that, Jean thought, Kelly deserved.

"Tell me this, Ms. Dingwall," demanded Stephanie. "Why didn't you just go ahead and use Lady Dunmore's note and drawing as publicity for the movie? Why get into the tug-of-war with Jessica?"

"Jessica Evesdottir," Kelly huffed, "used Tim and Sharon's research for her own purposes and plagiarized them to boot. Stop persecuting us and start prosecuting her."

Nice play on words, Jean thought in spite of herself.

"You, both of you, lose the attitude." Stephanie's voice sharpened rather than rose. "You and your family are in deep shit here, you got that? Your whole conspiracy shtick, the catfight with Jessica over some damned piece of paper and that Box in the Museum and a rock, already, it's caused crimes up to and including murder. Two murders that you've had good motive to commit."

Tim looked aghast. "You don't mean to imply—my own wife..."

"The sooner you start to cooperate, the better."

"I am cooperating." Tim's lower lip protruded.

"Like hell you are. Answer the question."

"And while you're about it," Alasdair put in, "Miss Dingwall, Mrs. Polito, can be telling us where she's sent the replica Witch Box."

"You're still trying to pin that on me?" asked Kelly. "What a waste of police resources."

Stephanie's glare ricocheted from Tim and Kelly to Alasdair and back. "Answer the..."

"Sharon," Kelly explained with exaggerated patience, and amended, "*we* were waiting for the note to be authenticated and the movie to be ready for its premiere. We can't have our publicity campaign peak too soon. But the movie's running behind."

Authentication never stopped you before, Jean thought to the back of Kelly's dead-animal-adorned collar. And then she thought, *Whoa.* Stephanie didn't know the full story of the Charlotte document. Did Tim? Did Kelly? Jean was beginning to suspect that Jessica was right—Sharon was the brains of the Dingwall operation. And Barbara had said that Tim wasn't as smart as he thought he was.

Proving Barbara's point, Tim blurted, "We're moving as fast as we can on the movie, I told you that, it's just that we haven't found, I mean, we need..." He looked around at all the ears twitching toward him and gulped down the rest of his sentence.

But Jean finished for him. “The keystone, the capstone, the cornerstone. The charm stone.”

TWENTY-EIGHT

STEPHANIE GLANCED AROUND, serving notice she was not amused. A suspicious ripple of Alasdair's lips signaled a suppressed smile. Olson stared blankly over the rim of his notebook. Tim looked at Kelly, waiting for a cue, perhaps, and Kelly shot a haughty glance back at Jean.

Jean shrugged at them all. *It's not just what I do, it's who I am.*

The door opened again, and the officer almost bowed in deference as Barbara Finch swept past him and into the room. Gown, gloves, wig—she looked for all the spirit world like the ghost of Charlotte Murray in later life. They knew how to dress to impress in Charlotte's day. How to signal social status. No one who had to do any actual work would be dressed so impractically.

"Mrs. Finch," said Olson, "if you'll wait in the other room…"

"I've come for my granddaughter." Barbara's shoulders were straight, her head up, and her face blazed brighter than one of the candles in the ballroom. She brushed not only Olson and Alasdair but also Tim aside, turned her back on Kelly, and confronted Stephanie from her inch or so of superior height. "Where is she?"

"Across the hall," said Stephanie. "We need to talk to her."

Tim thrust himself forward, into Barbara's face. "It's all your fault—you and Jessica promised to help Sharon develop her theories about the charm stone and the Witch Box and then you stabbed her in the back."

"I believe she was hanged," Barbara told him. And back to Stephanie, "My son's here, too, isn't he?"

"Yes, and we need to question him as well."

"All right, then. I'll sit down here." With a swish and swirl of silk, Barbara sat down beneath the portrait of Lord Dunmore. Alasdair's gaze met Jean's over the older lady's head. She didn't know what he was thinking, but she was thinking of the Monty Python episode about Hell's Grannies.

What Kelly thought was obvious. Her lip curled with contempt and she stood up, flicking the hem of her coat away from Barbara's proximity.

Stephanie glared at Barbara. Barbara looked straight ahead. Tim sidled toward the door, moving surprisingly quietly for a man of his bulk. Kelly strode, each stacked heel thumping the floor.

With the tightest of shrugs, Stephanie gestured at Olson—Tim, Kelly, Dylan, hotel. Custody. Rachel.

Olson made it through the door and into the hall without being trampled by Tim and Kelly. His voice rose and fell in concert with another. A second door opened. One set of footsteps shuffled, another tapped lightly. More voices, the slam of a third door, and a mighty sniff receded into the night. Olson returned with Rachel in tow.

"Can't I go with Dylan?" she asked Stephanie. "He needs me."

"You've done enough for him."

"But I've already talked to you," the girl pouted, less than effectively with her pale lips.

"Miss Finch, I can either charge you with aiding and abetting a fugitive or you can sit down."

Rachel tried a flounce, but even with her long skirts it

came out more of a flop. She sat down next to her grandmother and Barbara took her hand. "That's the apron you wore for the play last night. It's the wrong time period for Dunmore's Palace, dear."

"It's the one I grabbed," Rachel said. "Most of these people won't know the difference."

"We have to be true to ourselves."

Well, yes, Jean thought, and stifled yet another acidic garlicky burp. More cocoa. That's what she needed.

Judging by Alasdair's drawn features, what he needed was a wee dram.

Stephanie stepped forward to stand over grandmother and granddaughter together. "To recap, Rachel. Last night you and your mother got dressed for the play in the back room of the Courthouse."

"I was there as well," said Barbara.

"Your mother left the Courthouse after she played her part. You were in the play to the end. You heard the commotion surrounding the discovery of Mrs. Dingwall's body and joined Quentin by the tree."

"Yes," said Rachel, eyes downcast not demurely but truculently.

"A friend, another actor in the play, took you to your car and you drove to your father's house, even though you live with your mother."

Barbara patted Rachel's hand. "Her father's more traditionally maternal than her mother is, in some ways. Perhaps more than I am. I had to be both mother and father when Matt was a boy, though Matthew senior was never far from me."

Jean caught Alasdair's silent and less than charitable remark, even though it wasn't directed at her. *Fine,* she transmitted back at him. *Be that way.* But he didn't notice.

"Let Rachel answer for herself." Stephanie's voice sharpened even further—like a samurai blade, it could cut a man—or a woman—in half.

"Yes, I went to my dad's house. I called my mom and she said she'd probably end up at the police station—and she did, too. Gran was at the church, so I couldn't go to her."

"I'm so sorry." Barbara kept patting, her white glove only a bit brighter than Rachel's hands coiled in her apron.

"Dad wasn't there. He came in later, wet from the rain, said he'd been walking around thinking about Mom and Wesley—she thought she was being discreet, yeah, right—I think he was following Mom around, you know? He knew all about Mrs. Dingwall being murdered and everything, he was there in the crowd."

This time Alasdair's crimped mouth and cocked eyebrow were directed at Jean. *Yes, I know,* she returned.

Stephanie pressed on. "When did Dylan get in touch with you?"

"He texted me about ten-thirty, said he was in the Palace garden. So I told Dad I was going home, and I did, but I stopped on the way and got some food and I took a couple of blankets and gave them to Dylan, too. I said I'd stay with him, but he's..." Rachel turned to Barbara. "He's a totally nice guy. I don't care who his family is. He's okay. He was all, take care of yourself."

Barbara stopped patting and nodded indulgently, although her indulgence had a brittle edge—*let's humor the poor little thing.*

"I kept checking on him the next day, today, he said he'd found a window unlocked in the kitchen and taken some cookies, and he kept walking around pretending to be a visitor, going the other way every time he spotted security. He's, like, exhausted." She looked up at Stephanie, rearranging her expression from truculent Xena to pleading Bambi.

Unimpressed, Stephanie asked, "How much did you

know about the Dingwalls' movie? About the plans and photos stolen from Wesley Hagedorn's apartment?"

"He told me about the movie, and the charm stone opening up the grave, and, I mean, it's all just fantasy, you know? Like a video game. It doesn't hurt anything."

Jean couldn't tell who scoffed more loudly, Stephanie, Barbara, or Alasdair. Even Olson shook his head, before asking, "Do you know about the burglary at Wesley Hagedorn's apartment? Do you know why Dylan was hiding his mother's tote bag?"

Rachel made an impatient gesticulation. "Yeah, yeah, he told me all about it. You're overreacting, all of you."

"I don't..." Stephanie bit off her sentence.

Before the detective could come around on another strafing run, Jean braced herself on the back of the chair in front of her and asked, "And what do either of you know about the Charlotte document? The note and the drawing of the Witch Box that Jessica brought back from the U.K.?"

"Just the sort of thing my mom would go to the mat for," Rachel answered. "But it was Dylan's mom who got her onto it to begin with. Mom said she'd give Sharon a credit in her book but Sharon said no way, the note was hers."

Barbara said, "It's an interesting document, but hardly worth the fuss the Dingwalls were making over it."

"Have you seen the original?" Jean asked, trying not to lead her witnesses.

"I glanced at it," said Rachel. "The bit about the charm stone is cool. Wes was going to duplicate it, you know, but, well, everything fell apart."

"Jessica made me a copy," Barbara said, "thinking it might assist me in my studies."

"And were you assisting Sharon Dingwall with her research," Jean asked, "like Jessica was? Robert Mason, the charm stone, Francis Bacon, all that?"

"The Dingwalls' studies were not entirely without merit, not that I would go so far as to say where there's smoke there's fire. However, their scholarship was sloppy in the extreme. I did what I could to dissuade Jessica from getting involved with Sharon, but she insisted on going ahead. Now she realizes that her association with the Dingwalls could damage her academic reputation." Barbara smoothed her skirts with her free hand as though cleaning that hand of responsibility. *I told her so.*

Jean felt the pressure of Stephanie's gaze and desisted, but she didn't lean back. So had neither Barbara nor Rachel seen the other side of the document? Had Rachel seen it but not its significance? Were they lying to protect Jessica? Or, in Barbara's case, was she lying to protect Rachel through Jessica?

"Go home, Rachel," Stephanie said. "Stay there. I'll see you at the station tomorrow morning. And Mrs. Finch, she can come alone."

"What about my son?" Barbara asked.

"We can question him without your help, too."

"As you wish," said Barbara, her cool rivaling Alasdair's. Together she and Rachel got first to their feet, then to the door, which Olson opened for them.

Stephanie walked across the room, parted the blinds, peered out into the night as though considering how to make her own getaway.

Instead of matching her gaze with Alasdair's yet again, Jean laid her forehead on her arms, still braced on the chair in front. It wasn't that her mental bell choir was clamoring. It was that it had fallen silent, with nary a dong from the biggest bell or a tinkle from the smallest. And yet she knew there was a melody lurking in the still, silent clappers, if only she could start them ringing again.

"Are you all right, lass?" asked Alasdair's voice in her ear.

She raised her head. "I'm no more tired than anyone else. And probably less than Stephanie and Olson—what is his first name, anyway?"

"Danny. Danny Olson." Alasdair sat down beside her.

"Not Jimmy, the cub reporter in *Superman?*"

Alasdair looked at her, amused caution shading the harsh edges of his features.

"Never mind."

Through the doorway cub detective Olson ushered Matt Finch, who shambled along with all the desperate dignity of a condemned felon on his way to the scaffold. His bleary eyes focused on Jean and one corner of his mouth lifted slightly. Then his gaze shifted to Alasdair and the smile died before fruition.

That's why Alasdair had sat down beside her, Jean thought, to signal not ownership or even a controlling interest, but a partnership. No, he wasn't jealous, he was just establishing facts.

Olson found a chair. Waving Matt into another one, Stephanie resumed her position at the head of the room and asked, "What do you have to say for yourself?"

"The Dingwalls," Matt stated, his profile turned earnestly up to Stephanie, "have been harassing me and my family ever since Jessica refused to let Sharon squander the Charlotte document. That lawsuit, completely frivolous, just spite."

"And have you seen the Charlotte document for yourself?" One of Stephanie's smoothly arched eyebrows lifted toward Jean.

"Briefly. Jessica can use it in her work. So can my mother, in passing. But there's nothing there strong enough to warrant Sharon and Tim making so much trouble over it. To warrant thievery and murder and God only knows what mayhem."

Very gently, Alasdair's elbow bumped Jean's ribs. So Matt hadn't seen the other side of the paper. *Okay.*

Having disposed of that issue, Stephanie went on, "You've been following Miss Fairbairn and Mr. Cameron and loitering outside their house."

"Yeah. I thought maybe they were working with the Dingwalls."

"And even after you knew they weren't?"

"Saturday night I got to the Courthouse just as the play let out. I wanted to talk to Jessica. But she'd already left. And then there was, there was Sharon." He wiped his hand across his face. "I was worried about Jessica. I saw her sneaking into Jean's house, so I waited for her outside. But she went off with, with your sergeant there. I knew she was in real trouble then."

"You thought Jessica might have murdered Sharon?" Stephanie asked.

"I don't know what I thought. I've been dithering so badly ever since she moved here—it's stupid, I know. If I were Danish you could just call me Hamlet. To be or not to be, can't make up my mind."

"Can't make up your mind whether to kill yourself or someone else?"

A literary point to Stephanie, thought Jean.

"Whether to try and win Jessica back, or to let her go."

Jean thought, *Ouch.* Even Alasdair shifted uneasily at that one.

"And you were seen," Stephanie said, "outside Mr. Cameron's house this afternoon."

"I wanted to talk to Jean, apologize for causing her and her—friend—any alarm, but I guess she'd gone somewhere else after she left my office, not straight home."

"You could have called me," Jean said.

"I didn't want to get you while you were driving or something," Matt told her. "Besides, if you're going to grovel, face-to-face is the way to do it."

"Did you take her laptop computer?" asked Stephanie.

"How could I? I was never inside the house. I knocked, no one was there, I played with the cats a few minutes, I went for a walk around town and saw some friends at a coffee shop. They can vouch for me, if I need—an alibi." The word came out awkwardly. "I went to the memorial concert—it's not Wes's fault Jessica got to him—but when I saw Rachel sneaking out, I knew, I just knew, she was going to see that boy. Dylan Dingwall." He covered his face with his hands.

Jean looked from his now-concealed profile to Alasdair's, crisp as ice. She just couldn't see Matt killing Sharon. The iron in his soul was too deeply rusted.

"Let's get you down to the station for a formal statement," said Stephanie. "And I want you to talk to Jessica, convince her that holding back information is just making it look worse for her."

Matt looked up. "Oh. Yes. Okay."

Olson stowed his notebook and pen and, taking Matt's elbow, guided him to the door as though Matt was older than his mother. Matt glanced back from the hallway. "Sorry, Jean."

She couldn't say, "That's okay," so she simply sent him a nod.

The door shut. Jean told herself that this wasn't a French farce, with various actors running on and off the stage, this was a Scottish… No, not farce. This Scottish play was, like *Macbeth,* a tragedy of marriage and ambition.

The outside door opened and shut and footsteps walked away. Stephanie asked the air, "So did Matt kill Sharon hoping Jessica would be charged with the murder?"

"Like a black widower," murmured Jean, and, louder, "I

think he does still love her, like he said. He's had flashes of vindictiveness, but..."

"He's not got the grit to murder anyone," Alasdair said. "In my not-inexperienced opinion."

"But it's an opinion all the same." Stephanie paced toward the door. "We know who stole the replica Witch Box. We know who burgled Wesley's apartment. We know who murdered Wesley and we even pretty much know why. But who killed Sharon?"

"And who took my laptop?" added Jean. "Although that's a secondary issue."

"Jessica couldn't have taken it, she was in custody. Maybe Kelly, to see how far up the creek with the replica she is."

"But that's Alasdair's case—why would I have any notes..."

Stephanie's sarcastic eye touched Jean's.

"Because she figures I'm the dominant person in the relationship. Right." Beside her Alasdair laughed so dryly powder swirled around him. "Well, I am usually a few paces behind you, it seems," she told him.

"Jean..."

A uniformed officer appeared in the doorway, holding up Sharon's tote bag. "Yes! Dylan was telling the truth!" Stephanie seized it and dumped its contents onto a chair.

Alasdair jumped up and offered his hand to Jean, who, after all, had been sitting a lot longer. He not only pulled her onto her feet, he almost pulled her off of them again, but she managed to keep her balance, and stumbled beside him to the impromptu display.

There were the photocopies she had glimpsed outside the Cheese Shop, pictures of the Witch Box itself, probably, rather than the replica. The gap for the charm stone was circled in red ink—ink that had run in the dampness, and now matted the paper like bloodstains.

Along with the photocopies were actual photos, tacky but not yet sticking together, and plans of such exceeding neatness it was hard to believe they'd been drawn by human hands, even the delicate ones, like fine instruments, of Wesley Hagedorn.

Stephanie shook out the bag. Down onto the papers clattered several polished agates and discolored patches of metal, as well as two polished silver triangles sheened with tarnish. The one etched with a sinuous knotwork design bristled with prongs ready to clasp a stone. "He was going to make a replica of the charm stone, too?" she asked. "And the Dingwalls thought he had the real one? And they were in the churchyard trying to fit these bits onto a gravestone? They're nuts."

"Aye," said Alasdair, his tone conveying an entire paragraph of response.

There were nuts, and then there were nuts, Jean thought. She picked up one of the agates and rolled it between her fingers. It was smooth and cold. The real charm stone, be it agate or emerald or something else, was probably as cold. But was it as smooth? Maybe it wasn't even polished, not like the quartz of the Ardvorlich charm stone. "A rolling charm stone gathers no moss," she said, and put the pebble back down.

Now it was Stephanie who was looking at her with cautious amusement. Alasdair, though, was almost smiling, albeit mordantly. "Even if they turned up the charm stone, it'd not be opening any vaults or charming the birds from the trees, wishes not being horses and all."

Good heavens, the man was sounding like her. He must be really tired. Jean returned his almost-smile and focused on Stephanie. "Never mind my crack about capstone and everything—that's what the Dingwalls said, I didn't make it up—never mind what they think, anyway—the crux of this whole situation isn't Francis Bacon's papers, it's Edmund Malone's gift to Charlotte Murray."

"The document?" asked Stephanie.

"Yes. It's being authenticated because everything with the Dingwalls' fingerprints on it is suspect. Jessica doesn't want anyone to question the academic points she makes off that document. Same with the Dingwalls themselves. They've taken a lot of flak over the years—justifiably, yes—but they didn't rush ahead with using the document in their move because, like Kelly said, they also need it to be authenticated. They're smart enough to know that you can hang a lot of extrapolation—sorry—pin a lot on one solid source, especially if it's a spectacular solid source."

"Spectacular?" Stephanie asked.

"Charlotte's message and drawing are interesting, cool, whatever. The thing is, they're written on the back of something else. I think it might be a page out of a Shakespeare Folio, one of the first printed editions of his works."

Stephanie's lips pursed but she didn't quite whistle. "That's why Jessica's being vague about it. There is a lot at stake. And there's another motive for her to kill Sharon, over and beyond revenge for Sharon killing Wesley."

"How did she know Sharon killed Wesley, then?" Alasdair asked.

"Yeah. Well." Stephanie looked back down at the plans.

"Oh!" Alasdair hadn't suddenly answered his own question, he'd remembered Jean's phone. Pulling it out of his pocket, he handed it over. "Miranda's left a message, I reckon."

Jean fired up the phone again and checked. Yes, Miranda had left a message. Backed by the glissando of crystal chiming and silver sliding across porcelain, she said, "I've spoken with Gordon Bilsson from the Folger. The document's there, right enough, and looks like being authentic. He's saying nothing more, but he's going about like a cat with Atholl Brose on its whiskers. He'll be in touch with Stephanie soon as may be."

"That's helpful." Jean replayed the message, this time holding the phone in mid-air so Alasdair and Stephanie could hear.

"Atholl Brose?" asked Stephanie.

"Cream, honey, oatmeal, whiskey. Delicious stuff. The implication is…"

"That much I get. She means there is something spectacular about the document."

"Yep." Jean shut the phone and tucked it into her bag. All three of them stood silently, Jean, at least, less mulling over all the evidence than simply watching her brain sprawl in her skull like something the cat dragged in. Like something the cat had regurgitated in the middle of the rug.

Alasdair turned toward her, eyes still hard but no longer cold, bleached with weariness. "Let's be getting ourselves to the house. Tomorrow…"

"…and tomorrow and tomorrow," Jean couldn't resist concluding. Wasn't that the passage where Macbeth reacted to his wife's death by proclaiming that life was no more than a player spending an hour on stage, signifying nothing? She had her moments, but she wasn't that far gone.

Stephanie was scooping the papers and stones back into the bag. "As soon as I hear from the guy at the Folger, I'll let you know. If I hear anything from anybody, I'll let you know."

"Likewise," said Alasdair, and Jean said, "Good night."

They headed outside to discover that even though the room had been dim, the night was dimmer. The stars were veiled by thin cloud, smeared as though seen through teary eyes. A train whistled behind the Palace, and as Jean and Alasdair walked away, side by side, close together but not touching, she thought, how lonely the sound was, the wail of a lost soul.

Right now she was lonely, too, if not lost. Even if not alone.

Alasdair took her hand, and yet his lay cold, heavy, inert in her grasp.

TWENTY-NINE

JEAN CONSIDERED HER toothbrush, angled away from the other one in the glass beside the sink. Flicking the glass with her fingernail produced an anemic ding. The Liberty Bell, she thought again. There was independence of the body politic, and then there was independence of the body personal.

Last night she and Alasdair had staggered into the Dinwiddie Kitchen, finding it unattended by either cats or ghosts, although the Bellarmine bottle had moved yet again, back into the pantry. Jean left it there while she made cocoa for both her and Alasdair, he declining her half-hearted offer to join him in a wee dram at the Lodge.

Too drained to contemplate any more than default detente, they'd slept side by side, if not exactly together. Thomasina's ghost could have driven a team of spectral oxen through the house and Jean, at least, wouldn't have heard it.

Now, in the living room, Alasdair was telling Eric that no, the computer hadn't yet turned up, and no, no one was blaming him, and thank you kindly for bringing the breakfast, here's a bittie something for yourself.

Jean trudged into the living room, noting that the daylight outside was as uncertain as her own feelings. Today was All Souls Day, or *El Dia de los Muertos* back in Texas, a celebration of family, of ancestry, rather than a shrinking away from the certainty of death.

Way to start the morning, she told herself. Exchanging a polite greeting with Alasdair, she hunkered down over a cup of coffee while he paid more attention to the newspaper than his breakfast.

Jessica had said something about men and women living next door to each other. Hugh had said something about Agnes, Jean's other neighbor, moving out. Was there any way she could get Alasdair to move next door?

She smiled at that, and the smile heartened her enough to nibble at a muffin.

She was going to miss Agnes and her flowerpots, quibbles over Dougie's intimate habits aside… Jean stopped, holding the muffin in mid-air, and heard a faint peal of bells high in her brain's belfry. What had Matt said about his mother's apartment?

Dropping the muffin, she leaped for the desk, brushed aside the cell phone and its electronic umbilical—at least she'd remembered to hook it up last night—and dived into her bag. Billfold, hairbrush, protein bar… There. Her notebook.

Alasdair, she realized, was staring at her quizzically.

"Here it is," she said. "Matt said his mother lives in an apartment, that she's so busy she doesn't have any pets or even potted plants. But Miranda said… Damn!"

Alasdair removed his glasses.

"I was standing there at the crime scene. Miranda came up. She'd been waiting for us at the church. We didn't show up. Barbara Finch came in and Miranda remembered her from the reception and chatted with her. And then she, Barbara, went on inside because the concert was starting and Miranda came looking for us."

Alasdair folded the newspaper.

An emphatic mental ding-dong almost rattled Jean's teeth. "Miranda said Barbara was a keen gardener! But she didn't even know what a chrysanthemum was."

"Whyever should Miranda be saying that, then?"

"My point exactly." Jean freed the phone from its tether, switched it on, punched Miranda's number. And, again, got her voice mail. "Dang. We're playing tag."

"It's early for Miranda, not yet half nine."

"Especially after the reception last night." Into the phone Jean said, "Call me. I need to know what it was about Barbara Finch at the church Saturday night that made you think she's a keen gardener." She snapped the phone shut and laid it and the notebook beside her plate while she retrieved her muffin and took a hearty bite.

Alasdair's eyebrows were almost knitting a sweater. "You were saying yesterday, at the pond, that Barbara was at the concert at the time of the murder. But we heard the organ well after we found Sharon's body, didn't we now?"

Jean swallowed the sweet mouthful and raked back through her memories. The chase through the shrubbery, the interviews at Chowning's. Oh. "Yes, we sure did, now that I think about it. Barbara was at the Courthouse helping Rachel dress for the play—she said that last night, right? And that's when…" Back to the notebook she went. "That's when Jessica left the message for Sharon, changing their meeting place from behind the Courthouse to the Lodge. What if…"

"…Barbara overheard. Has Stephanie asked the other cast members if Barbara left early as well? After Jessica, but before…"

"…the play ended. Before we found Sharon in the tree."

They stared at each other across newspaper, plates, cups, eyes lit with wild if dire surmise. "Revenge?" hazarded Alasdair. "Barbara was Wes's pal. And while she's no pal of Jessica's, she's after protecting Jessica's reputation because Jessica's Rachel's mum."

"She was almost too careful to alibi Rachel last night, wasn't she?" Jean gulped her coffee and started forking in her omelet, suddenly hungry. "But then, Jessica's in jail for the murder."

"She'll not be charged, not if the forensics don't match—the hair in the mobile and the skin cells caught beneath Sharon's nails."

"Where Sharon scratched her attacker. On the wrist or arm, probably."

"Like as not. She had the torn fingernail as well, catching up a thread." Alasdair opened a packet of marmalade, turned his nose up at it, dumped it on his toast anyway.

"When I saw Barbara Sunday morning she was wearing long sleeves. Last night at the concert, she was wearing gloves up to her elbows. Not that that's suspicious—Lady Dunmore would have done the same. Barbara took the gloves off when she began to play the harpsichord, but it was dark, and she was leaning over the keyboard with her back turned."

"She was wearing the gloves after the concert."

"Again, nothing suspicious in that, not in itself." Jean bit off another chunk of muffin, then almost choked on it. "The hair. The hair in the phone. Stephanie said it was the same color as Jessica's. But did she mean blond or the same color as Jessica's silver streak? If it's silver, then the hair could be Barbara's."

Throwing down his napkin, Alasdair reached for the phone and punched in a number.

"You know what Barbara said to me, outside the church?" Jean frowned, trying to remember the exact words. "There aren't many insults as bad as 'old woman,' because that implies not just weakness but incompetence, even invisibility."

"She's been invisible, right enough. No more, though. Stephanie, good morning, we've been thinking..."

"But if the motive is revenge," Jean said aloud, if not directly to Alasdair, "we're back to wondering how Sharon's killer knew she killed Wes? And why, if it was Barbara, didn't she just go to the police and say she knew?"

Just as his bright blue gaze acknowledged her caveat and filed it away, the telephones sitting on the desk and beside the bed rang in concert, like alarm bells in a fire station. Jean got to the one on the desk before they rang a second time. "Hello?"

"Hullo, Jean. Ian here, from P and S in Edinburgh. Alasdair asked me to ring him the day, once I'd dug out some answers for him."

Alasdair walked into the bedroom, having a heart-to-heart—or more likely, brain-to-brain—with Stephanie. "Aye, she's fit enough to have got the best of Sharon. A wee bit scraggy, but fit."

"He's on the other, well, not line," Jean told Ian. "He's on the other phone. Can I take a message?"

"Oh aye, that you can."

Jean grabbed the hotel-logo pad and pen. "Shoot."

"First item. Blair Castle's got no clue whether they've ever had a note from Charlotte Murray, Lady Dunmore, with a sketch of the Witch Box."

"That's helpful," Jean said.

"No, I'm afeart it's no helpful at all," said Ian.

Okay, he didn't have the world's best sense of humor, but he was a good steady helpmeet, probably providing serious relief to Alasdair after her comical flights and dips.

"Second item. I've tracked the company shipping the stolen replica. United Parcel Service. That is, they've shipped a sturdy parcel from Kelly Dingwall in Edinburgh to the U.S.A., express. I'm thinking Alasdair will be wanting that checked out in the event it is the replica."

"Yes, he will. Where was it sent?"

"The parcel was addressed to a Robert Mason in Williamsburg, Virginia."

"Robert Mason?" For a moment Jean saw a shipping box sitting on the grave behind Bruton Parish Church. Then she asked, "What's the address?"

"Seven-fifty-six Columbia Road, apartment number two-oh-five."

Jean copied that down, telling herself she knew that address, she'd seen it before… Her memories obligingly fell into place, if with a sound like the clattering of garbage cans down an alley. Dunwich Grove. Wesley Hagedorn's apartment complex. "Ian, I don't have my computer here—could you do a search on that address, see who it belongs to? It's not Robert Mason's, I can tell you that."

"Oh aye. Half a tick. Well, likely a bit longer than that."

Alasdair emerged from the bedroom shutting the phone. "Is that Ian?"

"Yes. Kelly sent the replica here. To Wesley… Wait a minute. You said Wes's apartment was on the ground floor. The package went to apartment two-oh-five. That's the second floor. The first floor, y'all would say, which makes no sense, but we're not discussing semantics."

Alasdair plucked the phone from her hand. "Ian? Alasdair here."

Jean paced to the window and looked out at the misty, moisty morning, translucent wool concealing anything beyond the front gate, as though Williamsburg had been whisked away and stored behind the stage.

She paced back again. She finished her coffee and ate two more bites of her omelet. She needed calories. She had work to do.

"Well, well, well," said Alasdair, with a relish that sounded positively Miranda-like. "That's Barbara Finch's address, is it?"

Whoa, Jean thought, and the forkful of egg and cheese skidded greasily across her stomach lining. It wasn't surprising that Barbara Finch lived in the same apartment complex as Wesley. But Kelly had sent *her* the replica?

"Oh aye, thank you kindly." Alasdair flicked the phone shut and turned to Jean with a humorless smile, every tooth glinting like a panther's when scenting prey. "Look for the woman, I said, by way of making a joke, but I wasn't far wrong, was I?"

"We knew Barbara tried to help Sharon out, just like she helped Jessica, before everything went wrong, but she was helping the Dingbats with their movie? Good God, there really was a conspiracy!"

"And like most conspiracies, it could not be sustained without one conspirator breaking away. A falling out among thieves, oh aye." Again they stared at each other, dire surmise ebbing into dread certainty.

"Maybe," Jean essayed, "Kelly just saw Barbara's place as a convenient mail drop. Sharon and Dylan had already burgled one apartment there, and Kelly couldn't have known Wesley had been murdered when she put the replica Box in the mail, and..." She ran down, not just losing the thread of her thought but realizing it was no more than cobweb to begin with.

"No one saw Wesley walking down to the pond on the Friday afternoon," said Alasdair, trying a thread that had already been tested. "No one saw anyone else. But an old woman, a resident herself, would anyone have noticed?"

"You're not thinking Barbara killed Wes? All the evidence points to..."

"...Sharon. No, I'm thinking Barbara, say, had herself a dauner down to the pond, set on reminding Wesley of the reception that evening, and overheard the stramash between him and Sharon."

"And, being a discreet older lady, she withdrew. Or maybe she thought Wesley was plotting with Sharon and went off in a huff. Either way, she didn't find out about Wesley's death until the reception, Matt said. I saw her sitting there with her fists clenched, pretty upset."

"Still, though, why did she not come forward with her information? If Stephanie had collected Sharon on the Friday night, or on the Saturday, come to that…"

"…she'd be in jail but she'd be alive." Certainty, oh yes. "Barbara thought if she'd intervened in the argument, Wes would still be alive."

"And she's set herself up as judge, jury, and executioner, then." His features now set in a scowl, Alasdair snapped off the last bite of his toast.

The cell phone erupted and Jean grabbed it. *Yes!* "Hi, Miranda. Sorry to be asking questions so early, but we're onto something."

"You're never suspecting Barbara Finch to be Sharon's murderer?" asked Miranda, her voice fully alert and beautifully polished, never mind the hour.

Yeah, Jean thought with a smile, every time she thought she had her ducks in a row, here came Miranda with swans doing water ballet. "Yes, we're suspecting Barbara," she said, and filled her colleague in on last night's apprehension and subsequent interviews. "What did Barbara say when you were chatting with her outside the church—inside the lobby of the bell tower, wherever—to make you think she was a keen gardener?"

"She did not say a thing about gardening. I was generalizing from what I was seeing and…"

"She had scratches on her arms and told you she'd gotten them pruning roses?"

Miranda emitted her usual throaty chuckle. "The night was right cold, Jean. Even if she'd been exposing her arms, I'd not have asked her about a few scratches."

"Oh." Jean saw not ducks, not swans, but wild geese chasing away into the distance. "What was she wearing?"

"A polyester coat, the sort that's knit—" Jean heard the delicate shudder in Miranda's voice "—one that looked to be a size too large. With a whacking great ladder in one sleeve, as though she'd caught it on a nail."

A runner in one sleeve, Jean paraphrased. And yes, maybe she had caught it on a nail. One of Sharon's. Gesturing patience at Alasdair, who was hovering, she went on, "But the gardener..."

"She tucked a pair of gardening gloves into her pocket just outside the door, as she was paying close attention to wiping her shoes. She was still carrying a bit of a manure pong when she came in."

"Gloves! Something they can test! And a smell of manure? Y'all say 'manure' when you mean garden-variety fertilizer—or were you smelling actual horse manure?"

"Horses, I'm thinking. I've got a right sensitive nose, as you're knowing for yourself, the times I've taken a glass of plonk from your hands and offered you a better vintage or a finer distillate, depending."

Alasdair leaned in close enough to hear Miranda's voice issuing from the tiny speaker. "Oh aye," he muttered. "She's got a pernickety palate—if she says she was smelling manure on Barbara's shoes then she was. There was enough of it beneath the tree, some of it mashed into the leaves and loam by the struggle."

"That's what you're on about," said Miranda, her hearing being finely tuned as well. "And such a polite lady. Well, you'd best be getting onto your American detective, then."

"Thanks, Miranda. Stand by." Jean barely punched the "end" button before Alasdair whisked the phone out of her hands and once again called Stephanie.

Jean allowed herself a very brief and somewhat shamefaced vision of Stephanie's forensical boyfriend examining Sharon's shoes, with Barbara's soon to come, a clothespin on his nose.

She poured herself a second cup of coffee, added milk, and then jerked around at a knock on the door. Eric, come to collect the dishes? She opened the door to reveal not the black pawn but the white. "Come on in, Sergeant Olson," she said, and took the opportunity to check out the front walk. No cats, although they could be just outside the gate, where a police car was no more than a darkish patch in the mist.

Olson stepped aside, his fair cheeks encrimsoned by the damp chill, and handed Jean a file folder. "Here you go. It's the fax from the Folger. A fully authenticated and, they say, very valuable transcript of a scene from *Macbeth*."

Never mind caffeine. Every nerve in Jean's body sat up, took notice, and palpitated in anticipation. She opened the folder and pulled out another ordinary piece of copy paper.

Alasdair appeared at her side, saying something to Olson about Monday morning, when all the tradesmen return from their weekends, but she didn't really hear him. There, before her, was a slightly smudged typeface with its trailing s's, in two columns. Quickly she scanned the text—which broke off with a smear in mid-dialog, leaving a quarter of the page empty.

"What else did the cover letter say?" she asked.

"Basically, you wanted to see this, here it is," Olson answered. "And something about, we're studying this further, it might well be unique."

"Unique?" asked Alasdair, and leaned over her shoulder.

"Could be," Jean said. "This looks like a printer's experimental version, rough draft, reject. See how it stops in the middle of the scene?"

Olson retreated. "I need to go. We've got uniforms on

their way to Barbara Finch's apartment. And one heading for the UPS depot, too, to intercept that package."

"Good lad," said Alasdair, beaming, although the moment Olson walked through the doorway, Alasdair's beam collapsed. He wanted to be in on the—not the kill, the capture. Well, surely Stephanie would let him sit in on the interview.

Barbara. Jean felt sure it had been her idea to put Mason's name on the package—it seemed too subtle a joke for Kelly.

Matt's mother, Rachel's grandmother. Accomplice to theft. Murderer.

Slightly sick, but not from the omelet, Jean turned back to the paper and eyed each line, only aware she was thinking aloud when Alasdair reappeared in her peripheral vision. "This is from scene three, I think. The three witches are talking to each other and one of them's mad because a sailor's wife wouldn't share her chestnuts. Second witch: 'I'll give thee a wind.' First witch: 'Thou'rt kind.' Third witch: 'And I another.' First witch: 'I myself have all the other…' They're cursing the sailor. '…He shall live a man forbid, Like ill-famed Francis tried, Banished, set aside. Weary sennights nine times nine, Shall he dwindle, peak, and pine, No pork to break his fast, Nor calm before his mast. Though his barque cannot be lost, Yet it shall be tempest-tossed. Look what I have.'"

That didn't sound quite right. She waited for a bell to chime but none did.

She went on, "Second witch: 'Show me, show me.' First witch: 'Here I have a charming stone, And a bit of flesh and bone, Here I have a pilot's thumb, Wrecked as homeward he did come.' And then there's the stage direction, 'Drum within,' as Macbeth shows up and the witches tempt his ambitions by calling him Thane of Glamis, Thane of Cawdor, and king hereafter. And Banquo questions the witches. 'If you can look into the seeds of time, And say which grain will grow and which will not, Speak then to me.' And that's the end of the page."

"A charming stone?" asked Alasdair. "That's why the scholar-villain…"

"Malone."

"…gave the page to Lady Dunmore?"

"And probably the 'Francis,' too. The whole play was supposedly written to flatter King James, who, also supposedly, was descended from Banquo. So the banished Francis might have been Francis Stewart, James's cousin, Lord Bothwell, the witch. The 'charming stone' may be the one on our, so to speak, Witch Box. The thing is…" She trawled through her hazy memories of *Macbeth* but came up with nothing. The last time she'd read or seen the play, Francis Stewart and his charm stone had been sailing well below her event horizon. She could call Louise and ask if this was a slightly different version—unique, the Folger had said—but she'd already taken advantage of the woman once. This time honor would demand that she reveal all, and all wasn't yet ready to be revealed.

"Eh?" Alasdair prodded.

"If those lines were in the original, would there have been as much fuss over the Charlotte document? It's valuable, yes, but on more than one level."

"Ah, I see your meaning. Sharon and Tim are thinking 'Francis' and 'pork' are code for 'Francis Bacon.' This page is by way of being their cipher."

"Oh yeah. Tim said something about if Bacon wrote Shakespeare then that proved he came up with the plans for world peace and so on *ad nauseam*. I bet they're seeing hidden meanings in this, all right, while the gravestone is important for the names and the charm stone slot."

"Right," Alasdair said, just as the cell phone in his hand trilled again. "Hullo, Stephanie. How… What? Oh aye. We'll be there, soon as may be."

"Where? What?" Jean reluctantly slipped the paper back into the folder along with her copy of Charlotte's note and document, and tucked them into a drawer.

"Barbara's not at home. Matt's saying she's got a breakfast meeting at the Williamsburg Lodge on the Mondays, some sort of psychical society."

"A psychical society? Is that what she meant with her heaven and earth, Horatio?"

Alasdair was already halfway to the bedroom, and his "Eh?" flew back over his shoulder like a pinch of salt.

"And last night, she said that Matt's father was never far from her while she was raising him. What, has she been talking to him at seances? Alasdair, the Dingwalls have made a big deal out of not believing in the paranormal, supernatural whatever, but Barbara does."

"Mmph," Alasdair said, probably around his toothbrush.

The minute he left the bathroom, Jean hustled in, utilizing toothbrush and cosmetics, and noted as she left that their toothbrushes were now nestled cozily together. Maybe that was an omen.

She found Alasdair considering the mantelpiece with its clock and antique cooking implements. "Have you seen the wee bottle?"

"Oh. No." Jean looked around—desk, coffee table, pantry, dresser, it wasn't in any of its usual haunts. "It's gone."

"And just now we'd best be getting on ourselves." Alasdair opened the door and stood poised on the threshold.

With one last, futile glance around the house, Jean threw the phone into her bag and the coat onto her back and joined him.

THIRTY

SIDE BY SIDE, THEY WALKED quickly toward the Lodge, or, rather, where they knew the Lodge to be. Tree branches materialized overhead and faded again, not one leaf stirring. To their left, the white Williamsburg Inn was no more than thickening of the fog, an ideal of elegance. If the mist suddenly lifted, Jean asked herself, would they find themselves in a completely different place? Faerie, perhaps, surrounded by archers, arrows nocked? Or a Scottish moor, a battlefield littered with fallen bodies, torn standards, broken weapons? Was that the music of the pipes she heard?

No, she was hearing a weed-trimmer. A gardener was cutting the verge. "Has Stephanie released Jessica?" Jean asked. "How about Matt?"

"Neither's been exonerated yet," replied Alasdair.

"Well, no." Jean shrugged her bag further onto her shoulder.

The loggia edging the Lodge's facade appeared from the mist, three cars lined up before it. A bellman was negotiating away from the van at the back with a pile of luggage. In the center, big and black as a funeral coach, Barbara's SUV stood with its hatch gaping open.

Jean grabbed Alasdair's arm and yanked him to a stop. "That's hers, that's Barbara's car. There she is."

The tall, thin figure straightened from setting a plastic bin down on the sidewalk and reached back into the car's storage area. She pulled out a couple of flat boxes, the sort a bakery would use for doughnuts, and piled them on top of the bin.

Alasdair jerked forward, Jean beside him. "Good morning, Mrs. Finch."

She looked sharply around. "Already detecting, Mr. Cameron? Miss Fairbairn?"

"Oh aye, that we are."

Jean wrapped her arms around her coat, warding off not only the chill of the mist but the chill radiating from Barbara's honey-brown eyes. Car exhaust added a foul smell and a murk to the mist—knowing she couldn't park beside the loggia, Barbara had left the car running.

"If you'll excuse me," she said, "I'm due at a meeting."

"Let me help you." Alasdair reached into the back of the car and picked up a sturdy cardboard box a little bigger than a toaster oven.

"That's not going inside, thank you just the same."

Alasdair stood transfixed, staring down at the box in his arms, at the UPS stickers, at the British customs forms: Contents, reproduction antique. Value, fifty pounds.

"You get your UPS deliveries early," Jean said, wondering if her voice sounded as artificial to Barbara as it did to her.

It did. "What makes you think I haven't had that in the back of my car for a week?" Barbara demanded.

"It's time we were having us a chat," said Alasdair, matching chill for chill.

Barbara's eyes narrowed into a canny gleam. In one sudden leap she dived between Jean and Alasdair. A hard double-sided shove sent Jean toward the cold metal horizontal of the hatch and Alasdair against the hood of the van behind. Two running steps, three, and Barbara scrambled into the driver's seat.

The car lurched backward. Jean's duck to avoid smashing her head against the hatch became a jackknife roll over the back bumper into the storage space. One brain cell thought, *Wow, that was smooth. You couldn't do that again.*

Another cell saw Alasdair, every tooth clenched, spinning across the front of the van and springing clear just as the bumpers crunched, juggling the box all the while.

The impact threw Jean against the back seat. Her bag slipped off her arm and landed with a thump against the wheel well. She shouted, "Barbara, don't! Stop, wait!"

With a clash of gears and a squeal of tires, Barbara hit the accelerator and the SUV jumped forward. Metal crumpled as her fender skinned the back corner of the car in front.

"Jean! Jean!" Alasdair's bellow, more of pain than of anger and alarm, barely penetrated the squeal of tires and the roar of the engine.

Oh, shit, Jean thought.

Barbara's hard left and harder right out of the parking lot threw Jean backward, toward the open door. Frantically she dug her fingernails into the gritty carpet. Her bag flew out the back and crashed onto the street.

Jean cast one frenzied look behind her to see Alasdair throwing the box toward the bellman and his horrified face. Then Alasdair, the loggia, and the Lodge itself was swallowed by the mist.

Slowly, one movement at a time, Jean locked her hands around the back seat headrest. She looked up, only to catch the glint of amber eyes, hard as Stephanie's jet black, in the rearview mirror. "Nice move," said Barbara. "Now what?"

Jean croaked, "I'd suggest stopping."

"I don't think so," Barbara said.

She turned and turned again, probably on two wheels—Jean was thrown to the side, her heart in her throat, her stomach in her toes—a hazy retaining wall shot past the window and she realized Barbara had turned onto the Colonial Parkway. Heading south.

Jean dredged her mind for a map. The Parkway looped like graceful Jeffersonian script from Yorktown, through and beneath Williamsburg, to Jamestown. Where it ended. Wasn't Jamestown on a peninsula? Stephanie couldn't send any police cars from the other end, then.

Barbara lived here. She knew the lay of the land. She had to know she couldn't escape this way. Maybe she'd been confused by the fog.

The phone was in Jean's bag. It was probably electronic litter now. She visualized Alasdair tearing into the Lodge like a wounded bull, grabbing the first landline he came to—would he remember that here in the U.S. emergency was 911, not 999? Would he remember Stephanie's phone number? Or was Stephanie almost at the Lodge anyway? Jean visualized Alasdair running into the street and throwing himself into a squad car. *They went thataway.*

A sound resolved itself from the mist, a distant banshee-wail. A siren. Barbara sped up.

Okay. Jean gulped her heart back down to her chest. The sludge of her omelet seethed like a tar pit and she told it to stay in her stomach. This wasn't going to end well. All she could do was hope she survived long enough to have that long-overdue conversation with Alasdair. Finish off the investigation. Work a little while longer on earning a gold crown and a white robe, alleluia.

But today was *El Dia de los Muertos.* The Day of the Dead.

With another little gulp and squeak she didn't allow herself to analyze, Jean inched into the passenger side of the back seat and buckled herself up. Sweat oozed down her back and between her breasts, tickling like that slow stroke of the paranormal.

Barbara's profile was an axe cutting through the misty landscape. The car sped along in its own little bubble of space and time, enclosed by uncertainty, every now and then an embankment, a tree, another car materializing and then vanishing again. She said nothing.

Her blood hammering in her ears, Jean tried Alasdair's ploy. "You went down to the pond to remind Wes about the reception, and you heard him arguing with Sharon. For whatever reason, you didn't intervene. You left them alone. And then, later, you found out Wes was dead."

Barbara faced front, but her hands tightened on the steering wheel, so that her knuckles glinted ivory through her skin. Her coat slid up her arms, revealing two angry red scratches on the almost-transparent skin of her right wrist. Jean thought of Lady Macbeth, trying to wash her victim's imagined blood from her hands. But the blood on Barbara's hands was her own.

"You didn't tell the police what you'd heard at the pond," Jean said. "When you overheard Jessica asking Sharon to meet her behind the Courthouse, you went there yourself. After detouring to the cabinetmaker's shop to pick up one of the chair spindles you knew were stacked outside. You were that sure Sharon was the murderer."

Was the siren a bit closer? Hard to tell. The mist distorted the sound. It probably was distorting the speed of the car, too. At least Jean hoped it wasn't going as fast as it seemed.

"Just as Wesley assumed Sharon wasn't a physical threat, Sharon assumed you weren't. You made small talk—something about the Witch Box, probably—long enough to get her to the tree. And then you went for her throat."

The terrible eyes considered Jean in the mirror.

Jean wanted to yell, "Don't look at me, look at the road!" Instead she tried lowering her voice, like Alasdair with his menacing purr, trying to sound like she knew what she was talking about even though she was now edging into terra less cognita. "You took my computer from the Dinwiddie Kitchen. Either you called Matt after you left the church or he called you—you've probably got a cell phone, who doesn't? Either way, you heard that I was going around asking questions, that Alasdair was on the trail. You figured I wouldn't be able to function without my electronic brain, so you took it. To buy yourself some more time. Maybe you'd get lucky, and Jessica would be convicted."

Barbara shook her head. Perhaps she was only stretching the tight muscles in her neck. Perhaps she was imagining the last sensation Sharon might have felt.

"Your life work is in healing traditions. You think witches were actually village healers, and were persecuted by the new medical establishment. You sympathize with Robert Mason's study of witchcraft, an iffy hobby in his day, because you've taken criticism for your own work. You've been marginalized and insulted for being a woman on your own, like the women called witches here and in Salem. All you've wanted is to find your own place."

Barbara chuckled, a sound so dry it made Alasdair's usual desiccated chuckle sound lush as a rose garden.

"You agreed to receive stolen goods, let Kelly send you the replica Witch Box, to get the Dingwalls off Wesley's back. But it was too late to save him. You helped Sharon track the charm stone, but she betrayed you, killing one of your best friends. You were willing to hold your nose and work with them because, well…" It had to be, Jean told herself, and concluded, "You wanted the charm stone for yourself."

From what Jean could see of Barbara's expression, it seemed to have eroded a bit. The car seemed to be slowing down. The siren—more than one siren, now—was closer.

The heat in Jean's face and body was ebbing swiftly in the cold rush of wind from the open hatch. She glimpsed an expanse of dull pewter, the glassy surface of the James River paralleling the road, its rim matted with fog.

Choking down what felt like rubber cement, she went on, "Tim and Sharon don't believe in the paranormal. You do. Or you believe in the supernatural, which isn't quite the same thing. Heck, attending church proves you believe in the supernatural. Me, I see ghosts. Have you ever seen the ghost of your husband?"

To her surprise, Barbara answered. "No. I've felt his presence. I'm not whole without him. But I've been without him for many years now."

Alasdair, Jean thought, her other half. She pitied Stephanie having to deal with him right now, his icy facade breaking, melting, flooding into steaming pools. Shattering and simmering because of Jean herself.

What was I thinking, not throwing myself into his arms when I had the chance?

She said, "Maybe Tim and Sharon had it right, there's nothing supernatural, that nowadays junk news is the opiate of the people. But they themselves were intoxicated by their own vision."

"If some people perceive a world beyond this one, is that so wrong? What's wrong with wanting more?"

"Nothing. There is more." Jean didn't think she'd find Barbara talking sense, but here they were. And the car was definitely slowing. "Why did you kill Sharon?"

"I don't have enough time to wait for justice to work its slow, halting, all-too-imperceptive course. I have a cerebral aneurysm. I could die at any moment."

Jean felt her mouth drop open. Her first thought was *Please don't do it right now.* Her second was *Oh yes, this road was a dead-end in more than one way.* Barbara never intended to escape, just to make an end on her own terms.

Jean's third thought was the one she vocalized, as soon

as she retrieved her jaw from her chest and her heart from the pit of her stomach. "Your motive was revenge for Wesley's murder. And more. Frustration at getting involved with the Dingwalls to begin with."

"I tried to warn Jessica off them. She can be obnoxious, but she was right about Sharon, the woman was a witch. Not a village healer. A witch in the traditional sense. Enchantment, charm, conjuration, slander, scandal, all of the above. She used her erudition and intelligence to beguile me into an alliance. She promised me the charm stone once they'd put it to use."

"But there's nothing to use. It's not a healing stone. It's not even a cursing stone, and yet, well, look at us here, now. Look at this mess we're in."

"I know! I dragged Wesley into this, recommending he make a replica Witch Box, giving Jessica every opportunity to get her claws into him. You can't choose your relatives, but you can choose your friends. He was my friend. It's my fault he was murdered. It's my fault Jessica's in jail, but I don't want her to be convicted—I was going to leave a note."

Right, Jean thought.

"But you'll be my witness, won't you? Yes, I killed Sharon. I decided she deserved to die, and I acted. I take responsibility for it all, lies, thefts, murders, however much this has cost the authorities, everything."

Jean heard once again Barbara's words at the reception, gently rebuking Matt, light, almost joking. *That's the one good thing about getting old, you can damn well say what needs to be said and do what needs to be done.*

The cold wind from the open hatch had sucked the rush of heat from Jean's body. She shriveled into her coat, but she wasn't half as chilled from the wind as from Barbara's permafrost voice. Jean tried, "If you perceive that it's all your fault, then you perceive that it's your place to fix it. It's not either one."

"I never thought the stone would heal me. I just wanted to *know.* To touch something beyond this world. But it won't be long now, and I'll have all my answers."

"What about Matt? What about Rachel?"

"I've already failed them." Barbara's voice was so bitter it acid-etched the windshield. "Matt? Jesus, look what the man's done to himself, marinating in self-pity. And Rachel, wasting herself on that Dingwall boy in spite of all the opportunities women of my generation, of her mother's generation, gained for her. But that's the young generation."

Jean, neither as young as Rachel nor as old as Jessica, said nothing.

The eyes in the mirror saddened, adding rue to bitterness. "Rachel's intelligent, she's talented. The jewelry she was wearing at the reception, she made it from some agates Wes gave her and some pebbles—she's like a magpie, always picking up pretty things to use in her jewelry—he said she had excellent potential in both design and execution."

Jean wasn't sure if one of her bells jangled at that. All their clappers were chattering like her teeth.

Hitting the brakes, Barbara turned the wheel. The car skidded into a parking area on a small spit of land surrounded by reeds and stopped. Jean jerked forward against the seat belt, fell back, then loosed the buckle and seized the door handle. It didn't work.

"Childproof locks." Barbara leaned into the passenger seat, considered something lying there, and then turned to Jean. Her eyes glittered. The gun in her hand did not. The hole in the muzzle looked wide as a church door, deep as a well.

Jean shriveled even further. She wasn't sure she was breathing. Her entire perception was centered on the gun, and the pale, scrawny hand holding it, and beyond it the river. The fog was thinning, revealing mysterious shapes and shadows—the opposite bank, the three ships bringing the original settlers to Jamestown, Tolkien's last ship into the west gliding away, never to return.

That whining noise wasn't coming from her own throat, it was a siren, two, maybe three, shattering the stillness. That thumping wasn't her own heart, it was a helicopter beating through the mist overhead. The same one they'd seen Friday night hovering over Dunwich Pond, or a news helicopter—Jean could see every news station on the East Coast leading with a piece on the desperado grandma and the mild-mannered, well-meaning journalist who was her inadvertent hostage.

Tires screeched and skidded. Doors slammed. Voices shouted. Jean heard one in particular, Alasdair's, calling her name. Then silence fell, broken only by the thrum of the helicopter. And by Barbara's heavy sigh.

Out of the silence came another familiar voice. "Mrs. Finch. It's Detective Venegas. Throw the gun out of the window."

Barbara didn't move.

Jean could feel Alasdair's presence, the intensity of his emotion. If she'd been a ship, she could have navigated to his north star, to his lodestone. *Oh, Alasdair, I'm sorry...*

"Mrs. Finch!" Stephanie called.

A shuffle of footsteps, several clicking, scraping noises. Weapons, probably. There was enough firepower out there to blow the entire car to kingdom come.

Barbara smiled the ghastly smile of the crone, Mother Death—certainty, irony, regret. And then calm. She called, her voice strong, "Yes, I killed Sharon Dingwall. Not murdered, killed."

Jean saw Mary Napier at her trial, saw the Berwick

witches, the accused at Salem, confessing because all eyes were on them.

"You never suspected me, did you? You never even talked to me about Sharon's death, only asked me if Wesley had had any enemies. I told you then, yes, he did, but you did nothing."

What more could Stephanie have done?

"I'm sorry," Barbara said to Jean, "I didn't mean to make a public spectacle of myself, here and now."

Jean tried to say something, anything. The words didn't get past the knot in her throat. The noose around it.

"I didn't mean to involve you. You're not guilty. I am." Turning the gun away from Jean, Barbara fell back into the driver's seat and aimed it at her own head.

A hoarse shout. Racing footsteps. Something large and black—an armored policeman—hit the passenger-side window. Barbara's face jerked toward him. The driver-side door beside her opened. She spun back that way, gun still raised.

The sound of the shot smashed into Jean's skull like a wrecking ball. She felt her features shaping into a scream. She felt the scream welling up in her chest.

Move, move, move, she ordered her leaden limbs. Like an ungainly spider, more whimpering than screaming, she scrambled over the seat and out the back, falling to her hands and knees on cold rough asphalt. She sucked in air, damp air, tinged with fish, mud, swamp, and below those odors the salt-sweet of the open sea.

Alasdair's white face, the scorched blue of his eyes—fixed on her face, oddly startled—the broad shoulders of his jacket, his sweater, sank into her line of sight. He was crouching over her.

No. Even as her eyes reveled in his presence and her heart leaped toward him his crouch collapsed into a huddle, and she saw the crimson stain spreading across the green of his sweater.

Her cry of anguish swelled in her own ears, making the second shot seem a long way away.

THIRTY-ONE

JEAN FIGURED IT was a good sign that the ambulance was speeding back to Williamsburg without the siren blaring. Bracing herself against the side of the gurney, she clasped Alasdair's cold hand between her dirty, trembling ones, hanging on for dear life.

The paramedic peeled off his gloves. "The bullet just creased the skin between your ribs. No internal damage, and I don't think either rib is cracked, but they'll check you over and bandage you up. You're one lucky cuss."

"Aye, I reckon so." Alasdair's voice was threadbare but steady. His whey-colored face turned toward Jean. "I'm sorry. Your sweater's spoilt."

"I'll knit you twenty more," she choked out. "Every color of the rainbow. Wool, cotton, silk, cobwebs. Nettles, like in the fairy tale. Anything."

Jean could still see Barbara's intense face, shifting from guilt to pride to regret and finally settling on contentment, even peace, as she put the gun to her own head.

Jean could see Stephanie's frown as she bent over Alasdair, hear her sharp voice shouting orders. She felt Olson's hands—small, tentative hands—helping her to her feet and into the ambulance. She listened to her own oddly weak voice detailing what Barbara had said, a confession before dying, as though absolution was in Jean's power.

As the ambulance pulled away, Stephanie had been standing beside the old black SUV and the wiry form slumped across its front seats, waiting for the crime scene people, the medical examiner's team, all the official requirements of sudden death, one last expense put down to Barbara Finch's account.

"I'm sorry," Jean told Alasdair. "I'm sorry you took a bullet, any bullet—you tried to get the gun away from her."

"I didn't ken how strong she was. How determined to finish in her own way."

"None of us did." She stared at his features, so familiar and yet so strange, memorizing every finely constructed angle of flesh and bone, each glint of character in the sea-deep of his eyes. "I'm sorry for what I said Saturday night and how I've marinated in doubt and how I could have been gathering rosebuds with you and everything."

His taut mouth softened and he laughed, then gasped. "Jean, Bonny Jean, don't set me to laughing, not just now."

The paramedic, pretending he hadn't heard a thing, adjusted the dressings. The ambulance stopped, and emergency-room people flocked forward.

Jean found herself sitting in a plastic chair in a waiting room, clutching her battered mini-backpack. She had no idea where it had come from. Maybe Alasdair had picked it up, maybe one of the policemen had. Slowly, shakily, with only part of her mind—the rest being in the treatment room—she evaluated each object as though she'd never seen it before.

Even her tiny make-up mirror in its plastic case was unbroken. Her cell phone worked just fine. *Lucky. Oh yeah.*

Three messages waited from the usual suspects. Jean tackled Miranda first. "Yes, we're fine, he's fine, more or less. They really were calling her the desperado grandma? No, she didn't make it."

"Well then," said Miranda, and, after a moment of grim silence, "You've had your answer from the Folger?"

"It looks like a misprinted page from *Macbeth.* I need to

compare it with a copy of the play. And there's the Dingwalls, and the police, and..." She ran down. She was tired, hungry, thirsty. She was dirty. "I need to clean up. I think I was crying. I don't remember crying."

"I'll be back in Williamsburg on the Wednesday. I'll catch you up then. Have a care, Jean."

"Thanks. See you Wednesday." Jean got up, went into the restroom, splashed water on the fish-belly-white face with the crazed eyes that looked back at her from the mirror, then went back to the waiting room and returned Rebecca's call.

Second verse, same as the first. "Yes, we're okay, sort of."

"Michael and I are on our way there. Where's the hospital?"

"I don't know," Jean said, and, spotting Olson in the doorway just as he spotted her, "We'll get the cops to take us back to the house and meet you there, okay?"

"Sure. Anything we can bring? Lunch?"

Lunch. What a thought. Jean's stomach flapped pitifully beneath her own ribs. "Great, thanks. Anything would be fine. Oh, and stop at the college bookstore and get a copy of *Macbeth,* okay? I've got the other side of the Charlotte document and need to do a compare and contrast."

"You've got it," said Rebecca.

What Jean had was Alasdair. Here he came, rolled out of the treatment room in a wheelchair, as a matter of policy, the orderly said, not to imply he couldn't walk. The color in his face was better, Jean saw with relief, roses not exactly blooming in his cheeks but at least promising to bud.

They all met in the middle of the waiting room. Olson, Jean saw, was carrying a computer. Her computer, judging by the coffee stain and the cat-scratch on the lid. "It was in her car, right?"

"Right. No, that's okay, I'll carry it for you. I've got a car outside to take you back to your place." The faintest tinge of green shaded his jaw, but his set and solemn features acknowledged no qualms. He walked along beside the wheelchair, ticking off points. "We've retrieved the box with the replica from the Lodge and Stephanie's going to turn it over to Rodney Lockhart at the Museum this afternoon, about three, if you feel up to being there. You can work out what to do with it with him."

"Very good," said Alasdair. "I'm hoping someone gave that bellman at the Lodge a large tip."

"Not to worry," Olson replied. "Stephanie's considering dropping the charges against Dylan Dingwall, since he cooperated. We're still surveilling all of them, though—they're not going anywhere yet."

Olson led them to the back door of the hospital, well away from the clamor of reporters at the front. Jean was astounded to see the sun shining and hear birds chirping as though all was right with the world. Not that it wasn't all right. The world was ambiguous as always, demanding compromise.

"Jessica's been released," Olson concluded. "So has Matt. Here's the car. Mr. Cameron…"

Rejecting any assistance from either the orderly or Olson, Alasdair eased himself into the police car. Jean allowed Olson to install her on the other side of the back seat, and accepted her computer from his hands. "Thank you. Thank you for everything."

Olson touched his fingertip to his eyebrow. "Yes, ma'am. Y'all take care of yourselves, now."

"Thank you, Sergeant," said Alasdair, and returned the stylized salute.

The noon sun beamed down upon the town. Visitors representing every race of mankind and maybe even a Martian or two were out and about the Historic Area, called together because of one moment in American history. Interpreters expounded, children called, horses clopped. Every building, every leaf, sparkled with cinematic intensity beneath a cobalt-blue sky. A sky the color, Jean thought, of Alasdair's eyes.

Wincing but not groaning, he climbed out of the police car on his own, and made it up the front walk of their little home away from home.

Now that the sunshine had returned, so had Bushrod and Bucktrout. The two cats play-pounced along the sidewalk, chasing pebbles, leaves, invisible fairies, for all Jean could tell. Alasdair kicked a bit of gravel toward them and they chased that, too.

Smiling at the cats and at the sky and the trees, Jean opened the door and stood aside while Alasdair walked into the house, smiling at him, too, as the founding father of all the other smiles.

The dishes had vanished from the table. The living room smelled of potpourri, the bedroom of fresh linens, the bathroom of cleansers. Leaving Alasdair to clean himself up and dispose of the torn, cut, bloodstained sweater and the shirt beneath, Jean returned Hugh's phone call.

Third verse, a blessed refrain. "We're okay."

"That's good to hear. I'd not want to be losing more of my neighbors," Hugh said, but she heard the quaver behind the words. "The lads and I are playing on the patio at the Cheese Shop this afternoon at four. Music, drink, good for what's ailing you."

"That sounds wonderful. We'll try to be there."

Jean quickly booted up her computer—no, it was none the worse for its adventures. She wished she could say the same for Alasdair. When she shut the computer down she wondered if Barbara had ever bothered to turn it on. It had been a matter of depriving Jean of a tool, was all. It wasn't as though she'd known anything Barbara had not.

Or had the old woman known about the Bellarmine bottle moving around the Dinwiddie Kitchen in the hands of a ghost? Jean turned carefully around from the desk, but felt nothing and saw nothing, not even the bottle itself. It hadn't returned as mysteriously as it had gone. Thomasina was trying to tell them something…

The knock on the door had to be friends and lunch. Jean admitted Michael's and Rebecca's sympathetic faces, expressions they turned on Alasdair as soon as he emerged clean and tidy once again. "It was not pretty," he told them. "But Jean's all right, as am I. That's the most important."

He settled down onto one end of the couch and leaned his head against the back. Jean stopped herself from dropping down beside him and instead sat delicately on the next cushion. Rebecca and Michael distributed sandwiches, chips, and bottled drinks. "I reckon they gave Alasdair a pain tablet or two at hospital, but he'll be needing a wee dram as well." Michael laid out four glasses and opened a bottle of Lagavulin.

"They gave me tablets, aye, but they're in my pocket and can stay there."

"Why am I not surprised?" Jean asked.

Rebecca asked Michael, "Is that the glass the toothbrushes were in?"

"I gave it a good rinse. We're needing four, aren't we now?" He poured a generous dollop into each glass, doled them out, and raised his in a salute. "Slainte."

"Slainte," they all chorused, and Jean added, "Live long and prosper." When she clinked her glass against Alasdair's, they rang like bells.

She tipped the essence of golden, sun-warmed, seasprayed, smoke-infused grain into her mouth. The aroma wafted up to her sinuses. The liquid teased her stomach. She remembered Banquo's lines: "If you can look into the seeds of time, And say which grain will grow and which will not..."

The first few bites of her chicken salad caught in her throat, reminding her of Sharon. Then it loosened and she once again enjoyed the pleasures of the flesh. One of them, at least.

Beside her, Alasdair bit into a thick Virginia ham sandwich with good appetite. For a time the friends discussed the events of the past few days, and the coda playing out this afternoon. Then Rebecca asked, "So where's the page from the Folger?"

"Oh, sorry," Jean said. "In the desk drawer, along with Charlotte's note and drawing."

"Ah, I see," said Rebecca, retrieving the folder and its contents. Michael leaned over her shoulder with a paperback copy of *Macbeth* at the ready. "Charlotte didn't know what she had, did she? The couplet about Francis being banished, the one about breakfast and the mast, and the one about the charming stone, flesh and bone, those aren't in the, well, what's come to be called the definitive version."

"Jessica knows what she's got," Michael said. "But you'll not be banging her up for theft, will you now?"

"The document's never been reported stolen," Alasdair told him. "We can try appealing to her better nature, if she's got one."

Rebecca took the book from Michael's hand. "Oh, I like this, just a few lines further down. The witches vanish and Banquo says, 'The earth hath bubbles, as the water has, And these are of them.'"

The room fell so silent that the sound of children playing filtered inside... Jean looked around, the faintest of tremors lifting the hairs on the back of her neck. Was that a handful of pebbles thrown against the window, or footsteps crunching on gravel outside, or what? No more than a membrane of perception divided this world and another, the next, the last, the long gone.

"Right." Alasdair set his glass on the coffee table and picked up the daily schedule. "Michael, Rebecca, I'm seeing here that Benedict Arnold's appearing at the Capitol, likely asserting that he's no traitor, the traitors are Washington and his ilk. But the winners write the history."

Exchanging wise nods, Michael and Rebecca started for the door. "We'll come back in good time to be driving you to the Museum," Michael said.

And Rebecca leaned close to Jean's ear. "Michael's mother told me once that marriage holds you together when everything else falls apart. Think about it. You two deserve each other, and I don't mean that sarcastically."

"Come along, hen, leave them be." Michael opened the door. "Well now, this wasn't here a wee while ago." From the step he picked up the Bellarmine bottle.

Rebecca took it from his hand. "Oh my. This has a real vibe to it, like a bell still resonating after the sound dies away. It's one of Banquo's bubbles, I think. I'll set it down here, shall I?" Placing the bottle on the desk, between Jean's computer and the drawer, Rebecca flexed her fingers, used them to wave encouragingly, and stepped out the door.

Jean looked from the blank face of the door to the somewhat less blank face of the little bottle. The cats had been playing with a pebble on the front walk. What if…

Right now she needed to deal with the ghosts of relationships past, present, future. Sending thanks to Rebecca for breaking the last fragile layer of ice, so that they could take the plunge, Jean lay against Alasdair's unwounded side. He wrapped his arm around her shoulders and laid his cheek on her head. She rested there, safe, comfortable, listening to his breath, his heart, feeling his subtle resonance.

At last he said, "I thought you'd gone off me, given it up as a bad job."

"You went to bed mad at me. I thought you'd changed your mind."

"Your best defense is offense, is it?"

"My best defense is pretending I don't want something anyway so I'm not sorry to lose it."

"That's quite the effective one." With a soft, moist chuckle, his voice restored to velvet richness, he went on, "Jean, I'm mad at you from time to time, aye. But I'm mad for you as well."

She could lie against him and listen to his voice forever, especially when it said things like that. Forcing a deep breath to the very bottom of her lungs—soap, whiskey, an elusive hint of beer brewing and bread baking—she said, "I want to be part of your life. I want you to be part of mine. You have your work, I have mine, they're not mutually exclusive."

"Who's saying they are?"

"You are. I am." For a wordsmith, she was suddenly pitifully inept, not sure what she wanted to say, let alone how to say it. "I just want it, this, us, to work. We've been married, and our marriages failed, and now..."

"Now what?" he asked softly, without shying away at the m-word. "Jean, there's nothing wrong with wanting something more."

No. Especially where there was more. "How does the song go, freedom's a way of saying you don't have anything left to lose? Well, I'm free, you're free. If we, if the premise is that we love each other..."

He clasped her even more closely. "So we're getting married now, are we?"

"Oh." Every thought tumbling through her head settled into place, pieces in a kaleidoscope at last making a pattern. "Is that a proposal?"

"You'll excuse me not kneeling down on the floor."

He had fallen to his knees at the back of the SUV, startled eyes seeking her face, as though her face was what he wanted for his last sight on earth.

She turned to him with something between a laugh and a sob. "Yes, yes, yes. There'll be times I want to throw something at you, break up that great stone face routine of yours…"

"And there'll be times I'm wanting to fill up your mouth with a sock, but we'll not be knowing if we're never trying." He was smiling, every line, every crease turned upward and smoothed, and the glint in his eye was either humor or joy or both. She didn't care.

She said, in the same moment he said, "I love you."

Laughing, they clinked glasses again, and this time the chime was that of wedding bells. But it was the kiss, slow and thorough, that sealed the deal.

They only broke off when the door resounded to a flat, dull knock.

THIRTY-TWO

"THEY'RE BACK," ALASDAIR said against Jean's mouth, fully resuscitated.

"That was quick." With another caress, a promise for the immediate as well as the distant future, Jean hauled herself to her feet and, wobbling a bit, headed for the door. "General Arnold must have had to run for his life, chased by irate citizens… Oh."

Jessica stood on the doorstep, hair lank, face drooping and washed-out, bare of cosmetics and pretension both. "May I come in?"

Jean stepped back.

"Detective Venegas told me about Barbara. I can't believe it, except I can. Are you all right?"

"We'll do," said Alasdair.

"I'm sorry for my role in what happened. Really." Jessica sank down in the same wingback chair she'd occupied Saturday night. "Is that Lagavulin?"

Now it was Jean and Alasdair's turn to exchange a wise mutual nod. She got one of the coffee cups from the pantry, poured a finger of whiskey in it, and handed it to Jessica.

Jessica tossed the drink down in one gulp. Her face puckered like a drawstring bag and she fell back in the chair. "I guess my tax money's been going to the local jail, but I'd just as soon have skipped the weekend vacation there."

"The Charlotte document," Alasdair said, not cold, but not warm, either.

"They had Matt exert his charm—not—on me last night.

Still, I'd made up my mind to tell all when Venegas tells me I don't have to, you've figured it out, and by the way, my mother-in-law's been fingered for Sharon's murder and just killed herself." Jessica sagged, then buoyed herself up and went on, "I've got to hand it to Sharon, she was one well-read woman. A shame she wasted her knowledge on conspiracy guff. We probably could have compromised, except… Well, that's why we were trying to get together Saturday night. Enough of the catfight, we needed to compromise, figure out some way of my using that document academically and her using it for that movie."

"What's going to happen to their operation now that she's gone?" Jean asked.

"Kelly will step in. Tim's a typical male weakling and the boys, well, I don't know about the boys. I just wish they'd go away."

"I thought Tim was by way of being a brute and a savage," said Alasdair.

"Same thing. Compensation for inadequacy, you know."

"Right." Alasdair allowed himself a quick eye-roll, especially since Jessica was now looking at the Bellarmine bottle, not at him. "Was part of your compromise returning the document to Blair?"

Her pallid lips tightened in a sickly smile. "How about if I get credit for finding it and recognizing what it is?"

"That might could be arranged," Alasdair said in his best grating purr.

No bad deed goes unrewarded, Jean thought, and followed Jessica's gaze to the bottle.

The little face looked back. This time she was free to pursue her thought, chasing it up into the belfry—you could throw pebbles at a bell and that would make it ring… "What did you say about bringing Rachel and her friends here to see the archaeological excavation?"

"Eric mentioned the excavation as well," Alasdair said. "That's when they turned up yon bottle."

"I brought Rachel and her friends to a sort of open house here," replied Jessica. "That bottle was the most interesting thing."

"And what was in it?" Jean asked.

"Scrap metal, nails, pebbles."

"You said you don't often find pebbles in a witch bottle."

"No, but, you know, people attribute magical properties to all sorts of things."

"Your mother-in-law believed in, well, not magic exactly." Jean blinked and regained her focus. "That necklace Rachel was wearing at the reception Friday night. Barbara said she made it from some agates Wes gave her and some pretty pebbles she found. That she's a magpie, always picking up things for her jewelry."

"Yeah," said Jessica, "Wes said she has real talent, if she doesn't make it as a silversmith she might make it as a litter-picker."

Every bell rang in unison, spilling melody down Jean's spine. "Rachel pocketed one of the pebbles on display here, didn't she?"

"She was looking at them, especially a sort of moss-colored one. She might have taken one. They were just pebbles."

"Were they now?" Alasdair's face lit with comprehension. "A rolling charm stone gathers no moss."

"Huh?" Jessica asked, half-smiling, probably wondering if they were trying out for re-enactments at the Public Hospital-cum-sanitarium above the Museum.

Jean fixed Jessica with what she suspected was a manic eye. "Thomasina inherited the charm stone from her mother. Feeling responsible for it, she didn't give it back to a member of Francis Stewart's family—no matter how charming and/or enlightened Lady Dunmore was. Thomasina kept the stone in a Bellarmine bottle to negate its evil influence. That's where it's been the last two-hundred-and-fifty years, beneath the hearth of this little house. What do you want to bet that one of those bits of scrap metal is the original silver mounting?"

"One of the stones on Rachel's necklace is the charm stone? *The* charm stone? Holy shit!" Jessica, looking pretty manic herself, dived into her purse, produced her cell phone, and punched at its keys. "Rachel! Are you still at home? Listen, when I took you and Brittany and Madison to the archaeology open house at the Dinwiddie Kitchen, did you pick up a pebble? No, it's all right if you did, just tell me, yes or no."

Nodding a vigorous affirmative at Jean and Alasdair, Jessica went on, "It's that sort of dull greenish one that's on the necklace Wes helped you make, isn't it, the one you were wearing Friday night. Yeah, that one. You've got to bring it..."

"To the Museum," Jean prompted. "Three P.M. this afternoon."

"To the Museum at three. Because that's the charm stone from the Witch Box, that's why. It was hidden in the witch bottle all these years, and—Rachel, who are you talking to? Dylan? What's he doing there, you know I don't want you to have boys over there while I'm gone—I know, I know, you're an adult, you're free—yes, you've just lost your grandmother, I'm sorry. Where's your father? Identifying the bod—Rachel, please, sweetheart, don't cry."

"Oops," Jean said beneath her breath, and Alasdair only now exuded a groan.

"All right, all right. We'll meet you there." Jessica slapped the phone back into her bag. Her smile held no humor, only teeth. "Sorry about that. Dylan's calling his dad and they're all going to meet us at the churchyard. Why the churchyard, I don't know."

"Because Tim thinks the charm stone will open up Francis Bacon's secret vault."

"Oh, for the love of—give me a break, already!" Jessica jumped to her feet. "You're right—that stone is a cursing stone. Rachel and Dylan actually have something in common now, a dead mother, a dead grandmother, and he's going to be around her neck… Well, come on, let's get over to the church. We don't want to miss this."

"No," said Jean, "we don't."

It was the work of only a moment to call Rebecca and rearrange their meeting plans, and the work of only two to head out the door. Alasdair might not have been moving as swiftly and surely as usual, but he only stopped for a moment, to whisper to the cats, "I'm thinking you, the both of you, you've been trying to call our attention to the stone. In league with a ghost, are you?"

Jessica slammed through the gate. Jean and Alasdair started to follow, then stopped when Eric called from the corner of the Inn parking lot, "I'm glad you folks are all right."

"Thanks for everything," Jean called. "You've been a big help."

"Well, ma'am, you're welcome, but I really didn't do anything." He went on his way, his brow puckered with faint puzzlement.

Jessica was halfway across Francis Street. At a more sedate pace, hand in hand, Alasdair and Jean followed. The traffic was light enough they were able to stop and gaze long and hard at the bosky hollow where Thomasina died, her death probably making no waves in the tsunami of the Revolution. "That's why she was attracted to us," Jean said.

"We kept asking questions about the Witch Box and the charm stone. I don't know how these things work, but..."

"She heard us," concluded Alasdair. "I hope she rests in peace now that the stone's going to a museum, neutral ground."

Jessica was waiting for them on Duke of Gloucester, across from the Courthouse. "I don't know why I'm in such a big rush. I'll be dealing with all of this for years to come, Rachel, Matt—I know Barbara left instructions for her funeral, but I figured she'd go on forever."

"You didn't know about the cerebral aneurysm?" Jean asked.

"The what?" Jessica said so loudly that a couple of visitors looked around at her.

"Well," said Jean, and once again narrated what she'd said to Barbara and what Barbara said to her, while they walked slowly between the Greenhow Store and the Geddy House.

By the time they crossed Palace Green, Jessica's face had gone from washed-out to wan to waxen. "I don't believe it. I just don't believe it. But it makes sense, that's exactly the kind she was, organized, controlling. She'd cook an entire Thanksgiving dinner with a broken arm just to prove she could." With a shaky breath, she leaned against the churchyard gate for support.

Discreetly, Alasdair and Jean walked on into the dappled shade of the brightly colored trees and sat down on a bench. "Why is it," he asked, "you're not often hearing of ghosts in cemeteries, not that any of us go whistling past one, mind."

"It's because they're places of peace," Jean told him. "Or should be. Alert, alert..."

Jessica's pallid complexion suffused with red. She jerked back from the gateway as first Kelly and then Tim filled it. Passing by her as though she was no more than a squirrel, and passing by Jean and Alasdair ditto—Jean was tempted to make chattering noises—they walked to Robert Mason's grave. Tim, in full stuffed turkey mode, said smugly, "We should wait for the media, I suppose, but we can re-create the opening when the time comes."

Quentin galloped in the gate. "Oh, hi," he said in non-specific greeting, and he, too, went to stand by the grave.

Jessica ran forward as Rachel, Dylan at her side, appeared from around the bell tower end of the church. In her jeans and sweatshirt, Rachel looked very small and fragile. Her red-rimmed eyes took in Jean and Alasdair and narrowed, probably pegging them as the bad influence.

"Here," she said to her mother, and pulled a cascade of silver from her pocket.

"This is the stone you picked up at the Dinwiddie Kitchen?" Jessica asked.

Quentin's voice muttered, "At the Dinwiddie Kitchen? You mean Mr. Scottish Guy had it all along?"

Rachel held up the necklace. Reflections like sparkling confetti danced across the weathered tombstones and the brick of the church. The stone in the center of the entwined silver strands, no larger than the end of Rachel's thumb, glowed a murky, mossy green, illuminated by the secret, even slightly sinister, glow of forest glades and deep pools.

"It's this one," she said. "I thought it was some kind of onyx, but now, you know, I bet it's an uncut emerald. They got emeralds from Egypt way back when. What kind of mineral did you expect the charm stone to be? Something polished and faceted, like the diamond in an engagement ring?"

Probably, yes. Jean craned forward. Behind her, ponderous steps shifted on the turf. "Bring it here," ordered Kelly.

Sniffing and then wiping his nose on his sleeve, Dylan

tried to take the necklace. Rachel snatched it back. "It's mine. Well, most of it's mine."

With a *so there* look at Dylan, Jessica followed the couple past the low barricade and onto the turf. Jean swung around one way, Alasdair the other, the better to lean on the back of the bench and enjoy the show. Michael and Rebecca scooted in the gate. "Have we missed anything?" she whispered.

"Bang on time," replied Alasdair.

Side by side, Jean could tell Dylan from Quentin only by Dylan's long red ponytail çompared with Quentin's agitated buzz cut. Both red heads bent over the gravestone. Tim grabbed for the necklace, and again Rachel held it back. "Right here? On this little wingedy design? Okay, here goes."

Holding the bulk of the necklace in her left hand, Rachel grasped the stone—the charm stone—between the thumb and forefinger of her right and pressed it against the stylized winged skull, the fight of the soul.

A long, slow creak reverberated across the churchyard. "Yes!" Tim shouted. *No way,* screeched Jean's brain. Beside her Alasdair's eyebrows knotted.

But the sound had come from behind them. Jean spun around to see that the cellar door of the church had opened. From it stepped a woman carrying a choir robe and a hymn book. "Good afternoon," she called across the terrace, and disappeared behind the bell tower.

Alasdair exhaled. Jean quelled a giggle. Beside them, Rebecca and Michael grinned.

Tim swayed back and forth drunkenly in front of the intact tombstone, the grave intact beneath his feet. "No. No. We proved the vault was here."

Kelly grasped his arm with one hand and gave him a good shake. With the other she grabbed the necklace from

Rachel. She tried the green stone against the weathered face of the gravestone, and the other stones on the necklace, and finally kicked at the gravestone petulantly.

Quentin shrugged. Dylan slumped. Jessica seized the necklace from Kelly, picked her way among the other graves, and held it out to Jean. "Here. Take the damn thing to the Museum. When they get the stone pried off the necklace, they can give the rest of it back."

The entwined metal strips and the stones affixed to them jingled softly into Jean's palm, warm and smooth.

Rachel wasn't quelling her giggles at all. Dylan looked at her, shocked and dismayed, while Quentin strolled away shaking his head. Kelly glared Lady Macbeth–style daggers at Tim. He replied, "The document proves Bacon authored Shakespeare's works. Why else would those lines have been censored, except to cover up the truth?"

Because those lines were redundant, Jean answered silently. *Because every writer needs an editor.*

Tim was still gobbling. "The stone didn't work because it's not in its original setting, it's still on the necklace, the fit wasn't close enough—our probe, our probe showed traces of wood…"

"It's a cemetery, you idiot!" Kelly spat. "Of course you're going to find traces of wood!"

"Kelly, I don't think that tone is at all appropriate—oh hell!" Tim mopped at the top of his head, setting the lacquered strands of his comb-over on end, and glowered up at the tree limb above. A burst of birdsong replied, sounding suspiciously like, "So there!"

Jessica sat down on the bench and laughed until tears streamed down her face.

As swiftly as they could, Jean and Alasdair, with Michael and Rebecca at their sides, exited the scene. Once back on Duke of Gloucester, they assumed a more leisurely pace toward the Museum.

"Alas, poor Dylan," said Michael. "The course of true love never does run smooth. Is that *Romeo and Juliet?*"

"Midsummer Night's Dream," Rebecca told him. "All about illusions. Can I hold the stone, please?"

This beautiful afternoon might be a dream, Jean thought, but the morning had been a nightmare. She poured the necklace into Rebecca's outstretched hand and checked her watch. Almost three. With her hand to steady him, Alasdair levered himself over a curb.

Silently, they crossed the western end of Francis Street, where it became France Street—Jean made a mental note to ask about that. The Public Hospital's geometric harmony, cupola and all, rose beyond its green lawn, the grass shimmering more vibrantly than the *Clach Giseag* or *Am Fear Uaine,* the charm stone itself.

"What do you think?" she asked as they started up the path to the front door.

"There's a faint twinge," Rebecca replied, "but I'm not getting much more than that. It's like the vibe of the Witch Box itself, the weight of time and story. They belong together."

"Well then, let's join them up again." Alasdair felt his way up the steps, slow but purposeful, and they rode the elevator in silence to the marble halls of the Museum.

Today the atrium was empty except for a few visitors rambling up and down the stairs. Jean and Alasdair took the elevator to the second floor, and met Michael and Rebecca at the door of the exhibit just as Rodney Lockhart and Stephanie Venegas disappeared into it.

Blithely walking past a sign reading, *Exhibit Temporarily Closed,* Alasdair and Jean, Rebecca and Michael, joined the two arms of officialdom in front of the Witch Box.

Today the ancient artifact looked more dark and dour than ever. The Box that sat on a dolly beside it was almost identical. It lacked the patina of age on the wood and metal and the sinister leer of the little faces. In Wesley's version, the faces hinted of comic exaggeration, as though the threatening spirits of the past had not vanished but evolved.

"We lost a fine craftsman when we lost Wes," said Lockhart somberly. "As for Barbara Finch, I'm, I'm..."

Speechless, Jean finished for him. She tightened her grip on Alasdair's hand, there in front of God and Stephanie and John Murray, Lord Dunmore.

Stephanie seemed less somber than stunned, but her eyes were black holes of determination. Jean knew the feeling. Once your forward momentum stopped, you fell over in a heap. So you'd better keep up the momentum.

Stephanie considered the Witch Box. "So that's what's been causing trouble, for what, four hundred years now?"

"No," Jean replied. "People's perceptions cause the trouble. Always have. Always will."

"Yeah," Stephanie said, and after a moment of reflection, "We're comparing the skin caught beneath Sharon's fingernails to Barbara's. There is some leaf mold and horse fecal matter in Barbara's shoes, and some bits of fuzz, probably from Sharon's cardigan. The strand of hair caught in Sharon's phone is silver-white. We'll do a comparison on that, too, and on the thread caught in Sharon's fingernail. But it's all moot now, more a matter of doing paperwork."

Alasdair nodded. "There's always the paperwork."

"I need a formal statement from you, Jean. Tomorrow's fine. And I need to talk to you, Alasdair, about the theft in the U.K."

"Extraditing Kelly and Quentin might be more trouble than it's worth," he returned, "now that we've recovered the replica. And whilst Barbara confessed her collusion to

Jean—sorry, Jean—but that's not sworn testimony. I'll have a word with Perthshire. There's little hope of the Dingwalls doing porridge, in any event."

"I beg your pardon?" Lockhart asked.

Rebecca paraphrased, "Doing time," just as Jean said, "Going to jail."

"I've released Wesley's and Sharon's bodies to their relatives," Stephanie went on. "In Wes's case, that's a distant cousin. Barbara, well, maybe tomorrow. Her son didn't take it well."

"He was taken by surprise," said Jean.

"When are you going home?" Stephanie asked her.

Home. "Friday. I'm still hoping we can have a bit of a holiday."

"You will." The taut skin of Stephanie's face stretched into a semblance of a smile. "You should have seen Alasdair, Jean. I'm not sure whether I was more scared of him or of the crazy old lady with the gun."

Jean had felt his terror and rage. Now she looked from his bland expression to Stephanie's. "She wasn't crazy."

"No, I guess not. Mr. Lockhart…"

"It's your fault," said a voice palpitating at the far end of grief.

Everyone spun around. Matt stood in the doorway, eyes bloodshot, face blotchy, quivering forefinger pointed at Jean. "You caused the last minutes of her life to be filled with fear. All she wanted was justice."

She wanted revenge, thought Jean. That's where even freedom had its limits.

"She could have had more time, lots more time, but no, you came to town, little Miss Detective and the kilted wonder there."

Michael and Rebecca might have smiled at that, but they didn't. They stepped back.

Matt didn't know about the aneurysm, either. Jean stepped forward. "She was never afraid, Matt. She was, she had…" Alasdair's hand drew her back again.

"I went to the church to see about her funeral. Jessica and the Dingwalls, they said you were here—something about Rachel and the charm stone—damn them all, they caused everything."

Jean didn't point out that he'd contradicted himself. She said, one last time, "I'm sorry, Matt."

Setting both her shoulders and her jaw, Stephanie strolled to where Matt stood weaving like a drunkard. "Let's get you home, Mr. Finch. Do you have a friend who could come and sit with you?" She grasped his arm, one hand above his elbow, the other on his wrist, friendly enough. And ready to twist his arm behind his back if he gave her any trouble. With a piercing glance behind her, she guided him away.

My fault, Jean thought. *Your fault. Everyone's fault. That's why we have to compromise.* Right now her compromise was between dwelling on the immediate past and letting it go.

With a heavy intake of breath, one shared among the others, Lockhart said, "I need to talk to you about the replica, Mr. Cameron."

"I'll speak with Blair Castle, suggest leaving it here for a bit, as a memorial to Wesley."

"Ah, yes. Good idea. Thanks."

"Oh, and we've found—we're thinking we've found—the charm stone that once fit in that empty patch."

From her pocket Rebecca drew the necklace and indicated the green stone at its center.

"Say what?" Lockhart asked.

Jean ran through the story—the material parts of the story—the Dinwiddie Kitchen, Thomasina, the Bellarmine bottle, Rachel, the necklace.

Lockhart took the necklace and held it up. Caught in its mesh of silver, the charm stone glowed mysteriously. "It's possible that this is the original stone. We'll never be able to prove it, though."

"No," agreed Alasdair. "There's no proof at all."

"The original mounting might be one of the metal scraps from the Bellarmine bottle," Jean explained. "It's probably buried in the archaeological labs."

"I'm recommending not telling the Dingwalls," Alasdair concluded.

"Don't worry," Lockhart told him. "Dr. Campbell-Reid and Dr. Campbell-Reid, would you like to come down to the curator's lab with me, remove this stone from the necklace and help work up a new explanatory plaque?"

"The pleasure's ours," Michael told him. "You get on, we'll catch you up."

Still holding the necklace in front of his face, its glints reflecting on his features, Lockhart walked out of the room.

"Well," said Jean with a smile, "we've got something old, the Witch Box, something new, the replica, something borrowed, the necklace. All we need is something blue. Unless you count green, the stone itself."

"Is there anything you two would like to tell us?" Rebecca wheedled.

Alasdair grinned, Atholl Brose dripping from his whiskers. "Not just yet. Jean and I have a wee bit errand first."

"What?" Jean asked him, but he was already pulling her toward the door. "See you for dinner?" she called to Michael and Rebecca.

"Oh aye, Linda's having a day out with the grandparents," Michael called after them.

Jean and Alasdair, on their own once again, took the first elevator down and the second one up. Alasdair made it down the front stairs with more spring in his step than when he went up. Let go of the past, yes.

"An errand?" Jean asked.

"There's a jeweler's shop amongst the others, is there?" Gesturing toward Merchant's Square, he drew her onto the oyster-shell path.

"A jewelry… Oh, Alasdair, no, I don't need an engagement ring."

"If it's worth doing, and it is that, then it's worth doing properly. Do you fancy an emerald, a polished one? Or a pearl, reminding you that I'm the grain of sand beneath your shell, just as you're the grit beneath mine?"

She had to smile. An engagement ring. A public declaration of chances chosen and decisions made. Of vows to come. "No, I want a diamond. You know, the hardest of stones. A small one. I'll pay for half."

"No, you'll not be paying for half."

"Yes, dear," she said, and her smile spread into a laugh.

Not just holding hands but bumping shoulders, they crossed Henry Street. As they rounded the corner into Merchant's Square they were greeted by a burst of music. "Mairi's Wedding," a cliché on the Celtic-music circuit, but then, nothing became a cliché without becoming a favorite first.

Hugh and his band occupied the front corner of the Cheese Shop patio. The music of pipes, keyboard, guitar, and fiddle leaped and swirled across the street like guests dancing at a wedding. Diners and passersby alike clapped and jiggled. As Jean and Alasdair walked by, Hugh caught her eye and winked.

She waggled her naked left hand at him, imagining the band encircling her ring finger, with a stone to catch the sunlight and break it into its component parts, brilliant because the sum of those parts made a greater whole.

Alasdair opened the door of the jewelry store for her.

She looked into his face, the face of her other half. There was the something blue, two blues, his eyes grave, solemn, revealing the subtlest of sparkles.

I'm going to get used to this, she thought, and stepped inside.

* * * * *